ALSO BY DON WINSLOW

The Power of the Dog

California Fire and Life

The Death and Life of Bobby Z

THE WINTER OF FRANKIE MACHINE

THE WINTER OF FRANKIE MACHINE

Don Winslow

WINS
C.1

ALFRED A. KNOPF   NEW YORK   2006

THIS IS A BORZOI BOOK
PUBLISHED BY ALFRED A. KNOPF

Library of Congress Cataloging-in-Publication Data
Winslow, Don, [date]
The winter of Frankie Machine / Don Winslow.—1st ed.
p. cm.
ISBN 1-4000-4498-7 (alk. paper)
1. Assassins—Fiction. 2. San Diego (Calif.)—Fiction. I. Title.
PS3573.I5326w56   2006
813'.54—dc22   2006045263

Manufactured in the United States of America
First Edition

To Bill McEneaney
Teacher, friend, virtuoso in the art of life

THE
WINTER OF
FRANKIE
MACHINE

1

It's a lot of work being me.

Is what Frank Machianno thinks when the alarm goes off at 3:45 in the morning. He rolls right out of the rack and feels the cold wooden floor on his feet.

He's right.

It *is* a lot of work being him.

Frank pads across the wooden floor, which he personally sanded and varnished, and gets into the shower. It only takes him a minute to shower, which is one reason that he keeps his silver hair cut short.

"So it doesn't take long to wash it" is what he tells Donna when she complains about it.

It takes him thirty seconds to dry off; then he wraps the towel around his waist—of which there's a little more these days than he'd like—shaves, and brushes his teeth. His route to the kitchen takes him through his living room, where he picks up a remote, hits a button, and speakers start to blast *La Bohème*. One of the nice things about living alone—maybe the only good thing about living alone, Frank thinks—is that you can play opera at 4:00 a.m. and not bother anyone. And the house is solid, with thick walls like they used to build in the old days, so Frank's early morning arias don't disturb the neighbors, either.

Frank has a pair of season tickets to the San Diego Opera, and Donna is kind enough to pretend that she really enjoys going with him. She even pretended not to notice when he cried at the end of *La Bohème* when Mimi died.

Now, as he walks into the kitchen, he sings along with Victoria de los Angeles:

> *". . . ma quando vien lo sgelo,*
> *il primo sole è mio*
> *il primo bacio dell' aprile è mio!*
> *il primo sole è mio! . . ."*

Frank loves his kitchen.

He laid the classic black-and-white floor tile himself and put in the counters and cabinets with the help of a carpenter buddy. He found the old butcher block in an antique store in Little Italy. It was in tough shape when he bought it—dried out and starting to crack—and it took him months of rubbing oil to get it back into prime condition. But he loves it for its flaws, its old chips and scars—"badges of honor," he calls them, from years and years of faithful service.

"See, people *used* this thing," he told Donna when she asked why he didn't just buy a new one, which he could easily afford. "You get close, you can even smell where they used to chop the garlic."

"Italian men and their mothers," Donna said.

"My mother was a good cook," Frank replied, "but it was my old man who could *really* cook. He taught me."

And taught him good, Donna thought at the time. Whatever else you want to think about Frank Machianno—such as he can be a genuine pain in the ass—the man can cook. The man also knows how to treat a woman. And maybe the two attributes aren't unrelated. Actually, it was Frank who introduced this idea to her.

"Making love is like making a good sauce," he said to her one night in bed during the "afterglow."

"Frank, quit while you're ahead," she told him.

He didn't. "You have to take your time, use *just* the right amount of the right spices, savor each one, then *slowly* turn the heat up until it bubbles."

The unique charm of Frank Machianno, she thought, lying there next to him, is that he just compared your body to a *Bolognese* and you don't kick his ass out of bed. Maybe it's that he really does care so much. She has sat in the car while he's driven back and forth across town, going to five different stores for five different ingredients for a single dish. ("The *salsiccie* is *better* at Cristafaro's, Donna.") He brings the same attention to detail into the bedroom, and the man can make, shall we say, the sauce bubble.

This morning, like every morning, he takes raw Kona coffee beans from a vacuum-sealed jar and spoons them into the little roaster he bought from one of those chef's catalogs he's always getting in the mail.

Donna gives him endless crap about the coffee bean thing.

"Get an automatic maker with one of those timers," she said. "Then it would be ready when you get out of the shower. You could even sleep a few minutes later."

"But it wouldn't be as good."

"It's a lot of work being you," Donna said.

What can I say? Frank thought. It *is*.

"You've heard of the phrase 'quality of life'?" he asked her.

"I have," Donna said. "Usually referring to the terminally ill, whether they pull the plug or not."

"This is a quality-of-life issue," Frank replied.

And it is, he thinks this morning as he enjoys the smell of the roasting coffee beans and puts the water on to boil. Quality of life is about the *little* things—doing them well, doing them *right*. He takes a small pan from the rack that hangs over the butcher block and puts it on the stovetop. He lays a thin slice of butter in it, and when the butter just starts to bubble, he breaks an egg in the pan, and while it's frying, he slices an onion bagel in half. Then he carefully slips the egg out with a plastic spatula (*only* plastic—metal would scratch the nonstick surface, which is something Donna can't seem to remember, which is why she's not allowed to cook in Frank's *cucina*), lays it on one of the slices, puts the other over it, and wraps the egg sandwich in a linen napkin to keep it warm.

Donna, of course, gives him grief about the daily egg.

"It's an *egg*," he tells her, "not a hand grenade."

"You're sixty-two years old, Frank," she tells him. "You have to watch your cholesterol."

"No, they found that wasn't true about the eggs," he says. "They got a bum rap."

His daughter, Jill, harasses him about it, too. She just graduated premed at UCSD, so of course she knows everything. He tells her otherwise. "You're *pre*med," he says. "When you're *med,* then you can give me agita about the eggs."

America, Frank thinks—we're the only country in the world afraid of our food.

By the time the lethal egg sandwich is ready, the coffee beans are roasted. He pours them into the grinder for exactly ten seconds, then pours the ground coffee into the French-press maker, pours the boiling water in, and lets it sit for the suggested four minutes.

The minutes aren't wasted.

Frank uses them to get dressed.

"How a civilized human being can get dressed in four minutes is beyond me," Donna has observed.

It's easy, Frank thinks, especially when you lay your clothes out the night before, and you're going to a bait shop. So this morning, he puts on a clean pair of underwear, thick wool socks, a flannel shirt, an old pair of jeans, then sits on the bed and puts on his work boots.

When he goes back into the kitchen, the coffee is ready. He pours it into a metal go cup and takes his first sip.

Frank loves that first taste of coffee. Especially when it's freshly roasted, freshly ground, and freshly made.

Quality of life.

Little things, he thinks, matter.

He puts the lid on the go cup and sets it on the counter as he takes his old hooded sweatshirt from the hook on the wall and puts it on, jams a black wool beanie on his head, and takes his car keys and wallet from their assigned place.

Then he takes yesterday's *Union-Tribune,* from which he's saved the crossword puzzle. He does it late in the morning, when the bait business is slow.

He picks the coffee back up, grabs the egg sandwich, flicks off the stereo, and he's ready to go.

It's winter in San Diego and cold outside.

Okay, *relatively* cold.

It's not Wisconsin or North Dakota—it's not the painful kind of cold where your engine won't turn over and your face feels like it's going to crack and fall off, but anyplace in the Northern Hemisphere is at least chilly at 4:10 a.m. in January. Especially, Frank thinks as he gets into his Toyota pickup truck, when you're on the wrong side of sixty and it takes a little while for your blood to warm up in the morning.

But Frank loves the early hours. They're his favorite time of the day.

This is his quiet time, the only part of his busy day that's actually tranquil, and he loves to watch the sun come up over the hills east of the city and see the sky over the ocean turn pink as the water changes from black to gray.

But that won't be for a little while.

It's still black out now.

He turns to a local AM station to get the weather report.

Rain and more rain.

A big front moving in from the North Pacific.

He pays half attention as the announcer gives the local news. It's the usual—four more houses in Oceanside have slid down a slope in the mud, the city auditors can't decide if the city is on the verge of bankruptcy or not, and housing prices have risen again.

Then there's the city council scandal—the FBI's Operation G-Sting has resulted in the indictment of four councilmen for taking bribes from strip-club owners to repeal the city ordinance prohibiting "touching" in the clubs. A couple of vice cops have been paid off for looking the other way.

Yeah, it's news and it's not news, Frank thinks. Because San Diego is a port town for the navy, the sex trade has always been a big part of the economy. Bribing a councilman so that a sailor can get a lap dance is practically a civic duty.

But if the FBI wants to waste its time on strippers, it's nothing to Frank.

He hasn't been in a strip club in—what, twenty years?

Frank switches back to the classical station, opens the linen napkin on his lap, and eats his egg sandwich while he drives down to Ocean Beach. He likes that little bite of the onion in the bagel against the taste of the egg and the bitterness of the coffee.

It was Herbie Goldstein, may he rest, who had turned him on to the onion bagel, back in the days when Vegas was still Vegas and not Disney World with crap tables. And back when Herbie, all 375 pounds of him, was an unlikely player and unlikelier ladies' man. They'd been up all night, hitting the shows and clubs with a couple of gorgeous girls, when Herbie had somehow pulled into his orbit. They decided to go out to breakfast, where Herbie talked a reluctant Frank into trying an onion bagel.

"Come on, you guinea," Herbie had said, "stretch your horizons."

That was a good thing Herbie had done for him, because Frank enjoys his onion bagels, but only when he can buy them fresh-made at that little kosher deli up in Hillcrest. Anyway, the onion bagel–egg sandwich is a highlight of his morning routine.

"Normal people sit *down* to eat breakfast," Donna told him.

"I *am* sitting down," Frank replied. "Sitting down driving."

What is it Jill calls it? The kids these days think they invented doing more than one thing at a time (they should have tried raising kids in the old days, before the disposable diapers, the washer-dryers, and the microwaves), so they came up with a fancy name for it. Yeah, "multi-tasking." I'm like the young people, Frank thinks. I'm multi-tasking.

2

Ocean Beach Pier is the biggest pier in California.

A big capital *T* of concrete and steel jutting out into the Pacific Ocean, its central stem running for over sixteen hundred feet before its crosspiece branches out to the north and south an almost equal distance. If you decide to walk the entire pier, you're looking at a jaunt of about a mile and a half.

Frank's bait shop, O.B. Bait and Tackle, sits about two-thirds of the way up the stem on the north side, just far enough from the Ocean Beach Pier Café so that the smell from the bait shop doesn't bother the diners and the dining tourists don't bother Frank's regular fishermen.

Actually, a lot of his customers also hit the OBP Café on a regular basis for its eggs *machaca* and lobster omelette. So does Frank, for that matter, a good lobster omelette (okay, *any* lobster omelette) being a difficult thing to come by. So if there's one right next door, you tend to take advantage of it.

But not at 4:15 in the morning, even though the OBP Café is open 24/7. Frank just polishes off his sandwich, parks his van, and walks out to his shop. He could drive out there—he has a pass—but unless he has some equipment or something to bring in, he likes to walk. The ocean at this time of the day is spectacular, especially in winter. The water is a cold slate gray, heavy this morning with the ominous swell of an approaching storm. It's like a pregnant woman this time of year, Frank thinks—full, temperamental, impatient. The waves are already slapping against the concrete support pillars, making little explosions of white water burst into the air below the pier.

Frank likes to think about the long journey that the waves make, starting near Japan and then rolling all the way across thousands of miles of the North Pacific just to break against the pier.

The surfers will be out in force. Not the spongers, the wannabes, or the kooks—they will and should stay onshore and watch. But the real guys, the gunners, will be out for these swells. Big waves, thunder-crushers, that will crash all along the old spots and breaks, which read like a litany in a surfers' church service: Boil, Rockslide, Lescums, Out Ta Sites, Bird Shit, Osprey, Pesky's. Both sides of the OB Pier—south side, north side—then up along the coast—Gage, Avalanche, and Stubs.

Frank gets a kick just reciting the names in his head.

He knows them all—they're sacred places in his life. And those are just the breaks around OB—go farther up the San Diego coast and the litany continues, from north to south: Big Rock, Windansea, Rockpile, Hospital Point, Boomer Beach, Black's Beach, Seaside Reef, Suckouts, Swami's, D Street, Tamarack, and Carlsbad.

These names have magic for a local surfer. They're more than just names—each place holds memories. Frank grew up at these spots, back in the golden sixties, when the San Diego coast was paradise, uncrowded, undeveloped, when there weren't a lot of surfers and you knew practically every guy who went out.

Those *were* the endless summers.

Each day seemed to last forever, Frank thinks as he watches a wave roll in and smack the pier. You'd get up before dawn, just like now, and work hard all day on the old man's tuna boat. But you'd get back by the middle of the afternoon; then it was off to meet your buddies at the beach. You'd surf until dark, laughing and talking shit out there in the lineup, goofing on one another, showing off for the bunnies watching you from the beach. Those were the longboard days, plenty of time and plenty of space. Days of "hanging ten" and "ho-dadding" and those fat Dick Dale guitar riffs and Beach Boys songs, and they were singing about *you,* they were singing about *your life,* your sweet summer days on the beach.

You'd always stop and watch the sunset together. You and your bud-dies and the girls had that ritual, a common acknowledgment of—what, *wonder*? A few quiet, respectful moments watching the sun sink over the horizon, the water glowing orange, pink, and red, and you'd think to yourself how *lucky* you were. Even as a kid, you knew you were just damn lucky to be in that place at that time, and you were just wise enough to know that you'd better enjoy it.

Then the last sliver of red sun would slide over the edge, and you'd all gather firewood and build a bonfire and cook fish or hot dogs or hamburgers or whatever you could scare up, and you'd eat and sit around the fire and someone would pull out a guitar and sing "Sloop John B" or "Barbara Ann" or some old folk song, and later, if you were lucky, you'd slip away from the firelight with a blanket and one of the girls and you'd make out, and the girl smelled of salt water and suntan lotion, and maybe she'd let you slide your hand under her bikini top, and there was nothing like that feeling. And you might lie with her all night on that blanket, and then wake up and hustle down to the docks just in time to catch the boat and get to work and then do the whole thing all over again.

But you could do that in those days—get a couple hours of sleep, work all day, surf all afternoon, play all night and shake it off. Can't do that anymore—now you put in a short night and you *ache* the next morning.

But those were the golden days, Frank thinks, and suddenly he feels sad. Nostalgia, isn't that what they call it? he thinks as he shakes himself from his reverie and walks toward the bait shack, remembering summer on a cold, wet winter day.

We thought those summers would never end.

Never thought we'd ever feel the cold in our bones.

Two minutes after he opens, the fishermen start coming in.

Frank knows most of them—they're his OBP regulars—especially on a weekday, when the weekend fishermen have to go to work. So on a Tuesday morning, he gets his retired guys, the sixty-five-and-ups, who have nothing better to do with their time than to stand on the dock in the cold and wet and try to catch a fish. Then, more and more over the years, you have your Asians—mostly Vietnamese, along with some Chinese and Malaysians—middle-aged guys for whom this *is* work. This is how they put food on the table, and they always still seem amazed that they can do this pretty much for free, buy a fishing license and some bait and throw a line into the ocean and feed their families from the bounty of the sea.

But hell, Frank thinks, isn't this what immigrants have always done here? He's read articles about how the Chinese had a fleet of fishing junks down here way back in the 1850s, until the immigration laws shut them down. And then my own grandfather and the rest of the Italian immigrants started the tuna fleet, and dived for abalone. And now the Asians are doing it again, feeding their families from the sea.

So you got the retirees, and the Asians, and then you got the young blue-collar white guys, mostly utility workers coming off night shifts, who consider the pier their ancestral turf and resent the Asian "new-comers" for taking "their spots." About half these guys don't fish with poles at all, but with crossbows.

They're not fishermen, Frank thinks; they're hunters, waiting until they see a flash in the water and shooting one of their bolts, which are attached to long cords so they can pull the fish up. And every once in a while they shoot a little too close to a surfer coming in by the pier, and there have been a few fights over this, so there's some tension between the surfers and the crossbow guys.

Frank doesn't like tension on his pier.

Fishing and surfing and the water should be about fun, not tension. It's a big ocean, boys, and there's plenty for everybody.

That's Frank's philosophy, and he shares it freely.

Everyone loves Frank the Bait Guy.

The regulars love him because he always knows what fish are running and what they're hitting on, and he'll never sell you bait that he knows won't work. The casual fishermen love him for the same reason, and because, if you bring your kid on a Saturday, you know that Frank is going to hook him up right, and find him a spot where he's most likely to catch something, even if he has to nudge a regular aside for a little while to get it done. The tourists love Frank because he always has a smile, and a funny saying, and a compliment for the women that's a little flirtatious but never a come-on.

That's Frank the Bait Guy, who decorates his shack every Christmas like it's Rockefeller Center, who dresses up at Halloween and gives out candy to anyone who comes by, who holds an annual Children's Fishing Contest and gives prizes to every kid who enters.

The locals love him because he sponsors a Little League team, pays for uniforms for a local kids' soccer team, even though he hates soccer and never attends a game, buys an ad in the program for every high school drama production, and paid for the basketball hoops at the local park.

This morning, he gets the bait for his early customers, and then there's the usual lull, so he can relax and watch the surfers who are already out on the Dawn Patrol. These are the young, hard chargers, getting in a session before they have to go to work. A few years ago, that would have been me, he thinks with a slight pang of jealousy. Then he laughs at himself. *A few years?* Get real. These kids with their shortboards and their cutback maneuvers. Christ, even if you could do one of those, you'd probably just throw your back out and be in bed for a week. You're twenty years out from being able to compete with those kids—you'd just get in their way, and you know it.

So he sits and does his crossword puzzle, another gift from Herbie, who had turned him on to the puzzles. Herbie Goldstein has been on his mind a lot these days, particularly this morning.

Maybe it's the storm, he thinks. Storms bring up memories like they drop driftwood on the beach. Things you think are lost forever, and then, suddenly, there they are—faded, worn, but back again.

So he sits and works the puzzles, thinks about Herbie, and waits for the Gentlemen's Hour.

The Gentlemen's Hour is an institution on every California surf spot. It starts around 8:30 or 9:00, when the young guns have hustled off to their day jobs, leaving the water to guys with more flexible schedules. So the lineup consists of your doctors, your lawyers, your real estate investors, your federal worker early buyouts, some retired schoolteachers—in short, gentlemen.

It's an older crowd, obviously, mostly with longboards and straightahead riding styles, more leisurely, less competitive, a lot more polite. No one's in a particular hurry, no one drops in on anybody else's wave, and no one worries if he doesn't get a ride. Everyone knows that the waves will be there tomorrow and the next day and the next. Truth be known, a lot of the session consists of sitting out on the lineup, or even standing on the beach, swapping lies about gigantic waves and ferocious wipeouts, and talking stories about the good old days, which get better with each passing rendition.

Let the kids call it "the Geriatric Hour"—what do they know?

Life's like a fat orange, Frank thinks. When you're young, you squeeze it hard and fast, trying to get all the juice in a hurry. When you're older, you squeeze it slowly, savoring every drop. Because, one, you don't know how many drops you have left, and, two, the last drops are the sweetest.

He's thinking this when a fracas breaks out across the pier.

Oh, this is going to make a good story for the Gentlemen's Hour, Frank thinks when he gets over there and sees what's what. This is rich—Crossbow Guy and Vietnamese Guy have caught the same fish and are about to come to blows over who caught it first, whether Crossbow Guy shot it while it was on Vietnamese Guy's hook, or Vietnamese Guy hooked it when it was on Crossbow Guy's arrow.

The poor fish is hanging in the air at the apex of this unlikely triangle, while each guy plays tug-of-war with their lines, and one look at it tells Frank that Vietnamese Guy is in the right because his hook is in the fish's mouth. Frank somehow doubts that the fish got shot clean through the body with an arrow and *then* decided it was hungry for a nice minnow.

But Crossbow Guy gives a hard yank and pulls the fish in.

Vietnamese Guy starts yelling at him, and a crowd gathers, and Crossbow Guy looks like he's going to pound Vietnamese Guy into the pier, which he could easily do because he's big, bigger even than Frank.

Frank steps through the crowd and stands between the two arguing men.

"It's his fish," Frank says to Crossbow Guy.

"Who the hell are *you*?"

It's an amazingly ignorant question. He's Frank the Bait Guy, and anyone who frequents OBP knows it. Any regular would also know that Frank the Bait Guy is one of the pier's sheriffs.

See, every water spot—beach, pier, or wave—has a few "sheriffs," guys who, by virtue of seniority and respect, keep order and settle disputes. On the beach, it's usually a lifeguard—a senior guy who's a life-saving legend. Out on the lineup, it's one or two guys who've been riding that break forever.

On Ocean Beach Pier, it's Frank.

You don't argue with a sheriff. You can present your case, you can express your grievance, but you don't argue with his ruling. And you sure as hell don't ask who he is, because you should know. Not knowing who the sheriff is automatically labels you as an outsider, whose ignorance probably put you in the wrong in the first place.

And Crossbow Guy has East County written all over him, from the down vest, to the KEEP ON TRUCKIN' ball cap, to the mullet underneath it. Frank's guessing he's from El Cajon, and it always amuses him how guys who live forty miles from the ocean can get territorial about it.

So Frank doesn't even bother to answer the question.

"It's obvious he hooked it first and you shot it while he was reeling it in," Frank says.

Which is what Vietnamese Guy is saying fast, loudly, continuously, and in Vietnamese, so Frank turns to him and asks him to chill out. He has to respect the guy for not backing down even though he's giving away a foot of height and a bill and a half in weight. Of course he won't back down, Frank thinks; he's trying to feed his family.

Then Frank turns back to Crossbow Guy. "Just give him his fish. There's a lot more in the ocean."

Crossbow Guy isn't having it. He glares down at Frank, and one look at his eyes tells Frank that the guy is a tweeker. Great, Frank thinks, a head full of crystal meth will make him a *lot* easier to deal with.

"These fucking gooks are taking *all* the fish," Crossbow Guy says, reloading the crossbow.

Now Vietnamese Guy may not speak a lot of English, but from the look in his eye, he knows the word *gook*. Probably heard it a lot, Frank thinks, embarrassed.

"Hey, East County," Frank says. "We don't talk that way here."

Crossbow Guy starts to argue and then he stops.

Just stops.

He might be a moron, but he isn't blind, and he sees something in Frank's eyes that just makes him shut his mouth.

Frank looks square into Crossbow Guy's methed-up eyes and says, "I don't want to see you on my pier again. Find a different place to fish."

Crossbow Guy's in no mood to argue anymore. He takes his fish and starts the long walk back down the pier.

Frank goes back to the bait shack to change into his wet suit.

3

"Hey, if it isn't the dispenser of justice!"

Dave Hansen grins at Frank from his board out in the lineup. Frank paddles up and pulls alongside. "You heard about that already?"

"Small town, Ocean Beach," Dave says. He stares pointedly at Frank's longboard, an old nine-foot-three-inch Baltierra. "Is that a surfboard or an ocean liner? You got stewards on that thing? I'd like to sign up for the second sitting, please."

"Big waves, big board," Frank says.

"They'll be even bigger tomorrow when we talk about them," Dave says.

"Waves are like bellies," Frank says. "They grow with time."

Except Dave's hasn't. He and Dave have been buddies for maybe twenty years, and the tall cop's belly is still washboard flat. When Dave isn't surfing, he's running, and, except for a cinnamon roll after the Gentlemen's Hour, he doesn't eat anything with white sugar in it.

"Cold enough for you?" Dave asks.

"Oh yeah."

Yes, it is, even though Frank's wearing an O'Neill winter suit with a hood and booties. It is damn cold water, and to tell the truth, Frank had considered giving the Gentlemen's Hour a pass this morning for that reason. Except that would be the beginning of the end, he thinks, an admission of aging. Getting out there every morning is what keeps you young. So as soon as the kid Abe got in, Frank forced himself to climb into his wet suit, hood, and booties before he could chicken out.

But it *is* cold.

When he was paddling out and had to duck under a wave, it was like sticking his face into a barrel of ice.

"I'm surprised you're out here this morning," Frank says.

"Why's that?"

"Operation G-Sting," Frank says. "Funny name, Dave."

"And people say we have no sense of humor."

Except G-Sting is no joke, Dave Hansen thinks. It's about the last vestiges of organized crime in San Diego bribing cops, councilmen—there might even be a congressman in the mix. G-Sting isn't about strippers; it's about corruption, and corruption is cancer. It starts small, with lap dances, but then it grows. Then it's construction bids, real estate deals, even defense contracts.

Once a politician is on the hook, he's hooked for good.

The mob guys know it. They know that you bribe a politician only once. After that, you blackmail him.

"Outside!" Frank yells.

A nice set coming in.

Dave takes off. He's a strong guy, with an easy, athletic paddle-in, and Frank watches him catch the wave and get up, then drop down, ride the right-hand break all the way in, then hop off into the ankle-deep water.

Frank goes for the next one.

He lies flat on his board and paddles hard, feels the wave pick him up, then goes into a squat. He straightens up just as the wave drops, points the front of his board straight toward the shore. It's classic, old-school straight-ahead longboard style, but for the thousands of times Frank has done it, it's still the best kick there is.

No offense to Donna, or Patty, or any of the women he's made love to in his life, but there's nothing like this. Never has been, never will be. How does the old song go? "Catch a wave and you're sitting on top of the world." That's it, sitting—well, standing—on top of the world. And the world is going about a thousand miles an hour, cold and crisp and beautiful.

He rides the wave and hops off.

He and Dave paddle back out together.

"We're looking pretty good for old men," Frank says.

"We are," Dave says. When they get back out to the shoulder, he says, "Hey, did I tell you I've decided to pull the pin?"

Frank's not sure he heard him right. Dave Hansen retiring? He's *my* age, for God's sake. No he isn't—he's a couple of years *younger*.

"The Bureau's offering early retirement," Dave says. Kind of gently, because he sees the look on Frank's face. "All these young kids coming up. All the terrorism crap. I talked it over with Barbara and we decided to take it."

"Jesus, Dave. What are you going to *do*?"

"This," Dave says, waving his hand toward the water. "And travel. Spend more time with the grandkids."

Grandkids. Frank's forgotten that Dave's daughter, Melissa, had a baby a couple of years ago and is expecting another one. Where does she live? Seattle? Portland? Some rainy place.

"Wow."

"Hey, I'll still be here for the Gentlemen's Hour," Dave says. "Most of the time. And I won't have to leave so early."

"No, listen, congratulations," Frank says. "*Cent' anni*. Every happiness. Uh, when . . ."

"Nine months," Dave says. "September."

September, Frank thinks. The best month on the beach. The weather is beautiful and the tourists have gone home.

Another set comes in.

They both ride it in and then call it a session. Two solid waves on a day like this are enough. And a cup of hot coffee and a cinnamon roll are sounding pretty good right about now. So they go up and clean up at the outdoor shower on the back of the bait shack, get dressed, then grab a table at the OBP Café.

They sit there, drink coffee, consume fat and sugar, and watch the winter storm now brewing on the edge of the sea.

Dark gray sky, thickening clouds, a wind building from the west.

It's going to be a ripper.

4

After the Gentlemen's Hour, Frank starts on his busy day.

All Frank's days are busy, what with four businesses, an ex-wife, and a girlfriend to manage. The key to pulling it off is to stick to a routine, or at least try to.

He has tried—without conspicuous success—to explain this simple management technique to the kid Abe. "If you have a routine," he has lectured, "you can always deviate from it if something comes up. But if you *don't* have a routine, then *everything* is stuff that comes up. Get it?"

"Got it."

But he doesn't get it, Frank knows, because he doesn't *do* it. Frank does it, religiously. Actually, more than religiously, as Patty reminded him the last time he was at the house, to fix a drip under the kitchen sink. "You never go to church," she told him.

"Why should I go to church," Frank asked, "and listen to some priest who *schtupps* little boys lecture me on morality?"

He got that word from Herbie Goldstein and prefers it to the alternative words. Frank doesn't approve of profanity, and somehow saying it in Yiddish is less vulgar.

"You're terrible," Patty said.

Yeah, I'm terrible, Frank thinks, but from the last few times he's balanced her checkbook, he's noticed she doesn't give as much to the church as she used to. The priests should know what Italian husbands have always known: Italian wives will always find a way to punish you, and it's usually in the wallet. You piss her off, she'll still do the job in the bedroom, but then she goes out and buys a new dinette set. And never says a thing about it, and if you got any brains at all, you won't, either.

And if the priests have any brains at all, they aren't going to get in that pulpit and bitch about the shrinking receipts in the collection plate, because they'll start seeing nickels and dimes in there.

Anyway, church isn't part of Frank's routine.

His linen-supply business is.

The first two hours of his post–bait shop day are spent driving around to the various restaurants he serves, making what he calls "happy calls"—that is, talking to the owners and managers and making sure they're happy with the service, that their orders have come in right, that the tablecloths, napkins, aprons, and kitchen cloths are spotless. If the restaurant is also a fish customer, he goes into the kitchen to say hello to the chef and make sure he's happy with the quality he's getting. They usually go into the walk-in refrigerator, where Frank inspects the product personally, and if the chef has any complaints, Frank writes it down in his little notebook and takes care of it right away.

God bless cell phones, Frank thinks, because now he can call Louis from the car and tell him to get some fresh tuna over to the Ocean Grill inside the next twenty minutes and make it *good* this time.

"Why do you write it down if you make the call right away?" the kid Abe asks him.

"Because the customer *sees* you write it down," Frank tells him, "and he knows you take his business seriously."

By one o'clock, Frank has visited a dozen or so of the best restaurants in San Diego. Today, he works his way from south to north so he'll end up in Encinitas to meet Jill for lunch.

She's a vegetarian, so they meet at the Lemongrass Café off the PCH, even though the restaurant isn't one of Frank's customers and he doesn't get comped there.

She's already seated when he gets there.

He stands in the foyer for a second, looking at her.

For so long, he and Patty thought they couldn't have a baby. They'd resigned themselves to the fact, then boom.

Jill.

My beautiful daughter.

All grown up now.

Tall, pretty, shoulder-length chestnut hair. Dark brown eyes and a Roman nose. Dressed casual but smart in blue jeans and a black sweater. She's reading *The New Yorker* and sipping on a cup of what he knows is herbal tea. She looks up and smiles, and that smile is worth everything in the world to him.

They were estranged for a long time after he and Patty split up, and he doesn't blame her for being bitter. Those were tough times, Frank thinks. I put her and her mother through a lot. Through most of college, she barely spoke to him, even though he paid all the tuition and room and board. Then, at the end of her junior year, something just clicked in her. She called and invited him to lunch, and it was awkward and shy and totally terrific, and from there they slowly built their relationship back up.

Not that it's *Father Knows Best* yet. She still harbors some resentment, and can be a little sharp from time to time, but they have a steady Tuesday lunch date, and he won't break it for anything, no matter how busy a day he's having.

"Daddy."

She sets the magazine down and stands up for her hug and kiss on the cheek.

"Sweetie."

He sits down across from her. The place is your typical Southern California hippie-Buddhist-vegetarian joint, with natural-fiber everything on the tables and walls, and waiters who speak in whispers, as if they're in a temple and not a restaurant.

He looks at the menu.

"Try the tofu burger," she says.

"No offense, sweetie, but I'd rather eat dirt."

He sees something that looks like it might be an eggplant sandwich with seven-grain bread and decides to go with that.

She orders soup with tofu and lemongrass.

"How's the bait business?"

"Steady," he says.

"Have you seen Mom lately?"

"Sure." Like every day, Frank thinks. If it's not her checkbook, it's the car needing maintenance, and there's always something with the house. Plus, he pays the alimony every week, in cash. "You?"

"We did the dinner and shopping thing last night," Jill says. "Part of my continuing, albeit futile, campaign to get her to buy an article of clothing that's not black."

He smiles and doesn't mention her sweater.

"She dresses like a nun since you left her," Jill says.

Well, at least we got the obligatory mention of *that* out of the way early, Frank thinks. And, just for the record, sweetie, I didn't leave her—she kicked me out. Not that she didn't have her reasons, or that I didn't deserve it.

Just for the record.

He doesn't say it, though.

Jill reaches for something on the seat beside her, then hands him an envelope across the table. He looks at her curiously.

"Open it," she says. She's beaming.

He takes his reading glasses out and puts them on. Getting older is a bad idea, he thinks. I should give it up right away. The stationery is from UCLA. He takes out the enclosed letter and starts to read it. Can't finish, though, because his eyes start to mist up. "Is this . . ."

"I got accepted," she says. "UCLA medical school."

"Sweetie," Frank says. "That's fantastic. I'm so proud . . . happy . . ."

"Me, too," she says, and he remembers that at her better moments she is totally without guile.

"Wow," he says. "My little girl is going to be a doctor."

"Oncology," she says.

Of course, he thinks. Jill never does anything by half. When she jumps in, it's always at the deep end of the pool. So Jill isn't just going to be a doctor; she's going to cure cancer. Well, good for her, and I wouldn't be a bit surprised if she does.

UCLA Medical School.

"I don't start until fall," she's saying, "so I thought I'd work a couple of jobs this summer, then get a part-time job during the school year. I think I can swing it."

He shakes his head.

"Work the summer," he said. "But you can't go to med school and work at the same time, sweetie."

"Daddy, I—"

He holds his hand up, palm out. "I'll take care of it."

"You work so hard, and—"

"I'll take care of it."

"Are you *sure*?"

This time, she gets just the hand, no words.

But those are going to be some heavy bills, Frank thinks. That's a lot of bait, linens, and fish. And rental properties—Frank spends his afternoons looking after his property-management business.

I'm going to have to kick it all up a notch, he thinks. That's okay. I can kick it up a notch. I handed you a lot of shit in your life; I can find a way to give you this. And to have a daughter named Dr. Machianno. What would my old man have thought of this?

"This is such a happy thing," he says. He stands up, leans over, and kisses her on the top of her head. "Congratulations."

She squeezes his hand. "Thank you, Daddy."

The food arrives and Frank eats his sandwich with fake enthusiasm. But, he thinks, I wish they would let me go back in the kitchen and show them how to fix eggplant.

They make small talk through the rest of lunch. He asks her about boyfriends.

"Nobody special," she says. "Besides, I'm not going to have time for med school and a love life."

Classic Jill, he thinks. The kid has always had a good head on her shoulders.

"Dessert?" he asks when they finish the entrée.

"I don't want anything," she says, looking fixedly at his belly. "And neither should you."

"It's my age," he tells her.

"It's your diet," she says. "It's all the cannoli."

"I'm in the restaurant business."

"What business *aren't* you in?"

"The tofu business," he says, gesturing for the check. And you should be glad I'm in all those businesses. It's all those businesses that paid for your college and are going to find a way to pay for your med school.

I just have to figure out how.

He walks her out to her little Toyota Camry. He bought it for her when she started college—safe, good mileage, reasonable insurance. It's still in perfect shape because she maintains it. The future oncologist knows to how to check the oil and change spark plugs, and God help the mechanic who tries to pull a fast one on Jill Machianno.

Now she's looking at him real seriously. Those sharp brown eyes can be remarkably warm sometimes. Not often, but when they are . . .

"What?" he asks.

She hesitates, then says, "You've been a good father. And I'm sorry if I—"

"Sorries are for yesterday," Frank says. "All God gives us is today, sweetie. And you're a wonderful daughter and I couldn't be prouder of you."

They hug tightly for a minute.

Then she's in her car and gone.

With her whole life in front of her, Frank thinks. What that kid is going to do. . . .

He's barely back in the van when the cell phone rings. He glances at the screen. "Hello, Patty."

"The garbage disposal," she says.

"What about it?"

"It's not disposing garbage," she says. "And the sink is all filled up with . . . garbage."

"Did you call a plumber?"

"I called *you*."

"I'll stop by this afternoon."

"What time?"

"I don't know, Patty," he says. "I have things to do. I'll get there when I get there."

"You have the key," she says.

I already know that, he thinks. Why does she have to remind me every time? "I have the key," he says. "I just had lunch with Jill."

"It's Tuesday," she says.

"Did she tell you?"

"About medical school?" Patty asks. "She showed me the letter. Isn't it wonderful?"

"Absolutely wonderful."

"But how are we going to pay for it, Frank?"

"I'll figure it out."

"But I don't know—"

"I'll figure it out," Frank says. "Patty, I'm going to lose you here. . . ."

He clicks off.

Terrific, he thinks, now I have a clogged-up garbage disposal to add to my day. Ten to one, Patty was peeling potatoes in the sink and tried to wash them down the disposal. And even though I've got at least four plumbers on the arm that I could send over there, it has to be me, or Patty doesn't believe it's fixed. Unless she's got me under the sink barking my knuckles on a wrench, she's not happy.

He pulls off at a strip mall in Solana Beach, goes into Starbucks and buys a single cappuccino with skimmed milk and a cherry but no whipped cream, puts a cover on it, hops back into the van, and drives over to Donna's little boutique.

She's behind the counter.

"*Skimmed* milk?" she asks.

"Yeah, like every other day I bring you a skimmed milk," Frank says, "but today I bring you a *whole* milk."

"You're a darling." She smiles at him, takes a sip, and says, "Thank you. I didn't have time for lunch today."

Time for what? Frank thinks, because lunch for Donna is a raw carrot slice, a piece of lettuce, and maybe a beet or something. Then again, it's why she's pushing fifty and looks more like mid-thirties, and why she still has the Vegas showgirl body. Long, thin legs, no waist, and a balcony that, while big, isn't in danger of collapsing. Combine all that with her flame red hair, green eyes, a face to die for, and a personality to match, and it's little wonder he brings her a cappuccino every time he's passing through.

And flowers once a week.

And something shiny on Christmas and birthdays.

Donna is a high-maintenance broad, as she will readily admit.

Frank understands this—high quality and high maintenance go together. Donna takes good care of Donna and she expects Frank to do the same. Not that Donna is a kept woman. Far from it. She put away most of her money from her showgirl days, moved to San Diego, and opened her pricey boutique. Not a lot of inventory, but what she has is top quality and very stylish, and attracts a loyal customer base, mostly from San Diego Ladies Who Lunch.

"You should move the shop to La Jolla," he told her.

"You know the rents in La Jolla?" she replied.

"But most of your customers are in La Jolla."

"They can drive ten minutes," she said.

She's right, Frank thinks. And they do drive to her shop. Right now, there are two ladies inspecting the racks and another one in a changing room. And it doesn't hurt that Donna wears her own merchandise and looks stunning.

If the store was empty, Frank thinks, I'd like to take her into one of those fitting rooms and . . .

She reads the glint in his eye.

"You're too busy and so am I," she says.

"I know."

"But what are you doing later?"

He feels a little twinge in his groin. Donna never fails to do that to him, and they've been together—what, eight years?

"Did you have your lunch with Jill?" she asks.

He tells her about Jill's news.

"That's wonderful," Donna says. "I'm so happy for her."

And she means it, Frank thinks, even though she and Jill have never as much as met. Frank has tried to bring the subject of Donna up to his daughter, but she's cut him off every time and changed the subject. She's loyal to her mother, Frank thinks, and he has to respect loyalty. Donna does, too.

"Hey," she said when all this came up, "if she were my kid, and my ex wanted her to meet his new squeeze, I'd want her to act the same way."

Maybe, Frank thought, although Donna is more sophisticated than Patty about matters romantic. But it was nice of her to say it anyway.

"She's a good kid," Donna says now. "She'll do well."

Yeah, she will, Frank thinks.

"Gotta go," he says.

"Me, too," Donna says, eyeing a customer coming out of the dressing room with an outfit that would be a disaster on her. He nods and heads out the door as he hears her say, "Honey, with *your eyes,* let me show you . . ."

5

Rental properties, Frank thinks, is a polite way of saying *hemorrhoids.*

Because they are an itching, burning pain in the butt. The only difference is that rental properties make money and hemorrhoids don't, unless you're a proctologist, in which case they do.

He thinks this as he drives around Ocean Beach checking on the half dozen condos, houses, and small apartment buildings he looks after as a silent partner in OB Property Management, a limited partnership, which is limited basically to Frank and Ozzie Ransom, whose name appears on all the paperwork and who takes care of the money. Except that after Ozzie counts the money, Frank counts it all over again to make sure that Ozzie isn't robbing him like a bartender. It's not that he doesn't trust Ozzie; it's just that he doesn't want to put his "partner" in the way of temptation.

Frank is similarly protective about the moral well-being of his "partners" in the linen business and the fish business. He checks their books on a regular basis and he also checks them on an "irregular" basis, as he calls it. They never know when Frank might drop in to check the accounts, the receipts, the inventory, or the order sheets. And every quarter, Frank has his accountant and attorney, Sherm "the Nickel" Simon

("A nickel here, a nickel there . . ."), go over all the books both to do his taxes and to make sure that even though the government is robbing him blind, his partners aren't.

Frank is a fanatic about paying his taxes.

He calls it "the Capone factor."

"Al Capone," Frank once said to Herbie Goldstein, "ran the biggest bootlegging operation in history, bribed cops, judges, and politicians, kidnapped, tortured, and murdered people in broad daylight on the streets of Chicago, and what did he go to jail for? Income tax evasion."

It's as true now as it was then, Frank thinks—you can do about *anything* in this country as long as you kick up to the feds. Uncle wants his taste, and as long as he gets it, you can pretty much do what you want as long as you don't rub it in Uncle's nose.

Frank is meticulous on both counts.

He pays his taxes and does nothing to draw attention to himself. If The Nickel comes up with a deduction that's even on the edge, Frank nixes it. The last thing in the world he wants is an audit. And Frank doesn't even go near the businesses that attract the feds' attention— garbage, construction, bars, porno. No, he's just Frank the Bait Guy and his side endeavors are all totally legit. He works his linen supply, his fish, his rental properties.

Renters are a pain, especially in a beach community where people tend to be somewhat transient, anyway. People come to the beach thinking it's paradise and that they're going to spend all day beachcombing and all night partying, and they forget that somewhere in all that they still have to make a living.

They always think they can make the rent, and then find that they can't, so what they do is move in a roommate or five, very often people they met at a bar, who may or may not have the rent money on the first of the month.

Not that Frank doesn't counsel them—he does. When he's taking their application, he goes over first month/last month/damage deposit. He gets a credit check, a bank statement, and references, and more than half the time tells them that they just can't afford to live by the beach.

But the young people didn't come to California *not* to live by the beach, so they get some roommates and dive into an obligation they can't handle. The result is that Frank has a lot of turnaround, and turn-around is the bane of rental-property management. It means cleaning costs, repairs, advertising, interviewing, credit checks, and running down references and employment. On the other hand, you do collect the last month's rent and the damage deposit, because the kids always damage the place, usually as a result of a party.

Frank has the whole enchilada on his plate this afternoon. He has to show an apartment and interview a couple of young ladies who will be either waitresses or strippers, or waitresses who will soon decide that there's more money in stripping. Then there's a kitchen upgrade he wants to check in on. Then he has to check on the cleaning of an apartment that's in transition, and make sure that the carpet cleaners have *steamed* the vomit stains left by the previous tenants/party animals out of the carpet.

He shows the two young ladies the apartment. They're strippers all right, and a nice semi-married lesbian couple, so Frank doesn't have to worry about their ability to pay the rent or about them having skanky guys from the strip clubs moving in. They want the place and he takes their deposit on the spot. The credit check will be a formality and he'll give the club a quick call to confirm employment.

Next, he hustles over to the condo to check on the kitchen upgrade, which looks pretty good with the new Sub-Zero refrigerator-freezer and flat-surface stovetop. After that, he takes a walk around the outside to make sure the landscapers and gardeners are keeping the place up, whereupon he notices that the ice plant needs a little trimming.

Then he goes "opportunity shopping," scouting the neighborhood for rental properties that have good locations but look a little shabby or run-down. Maybe they need a coat of paint, or the lawn has been neglected, or a window screen is torn and hasn't been fixed. He makes a note of their addresses and will track down their ownership, because maybe the owners might need a manager or a change of managers. Or maybe they're tired of the work that comes with ownership and might be looking to sell low.

He finds three or four possibilities.

Then he heads over to Ajax Linen Supply, plops down in the old wooden rolling chair behind the Steelcase desk, and reviews the week's orders. The Marine House order on kitchen towels is down 20 percent, and he makes a note to find out if Ozzie has started selling some of his own towels along with the company's. But the orders from the rest of the customers are the same or up, so probably it's something specific to the Marine House, and he makes a note to drop by there and find out what's what. He makes a quick check of the day's receipts, then heads down to the docks to the Sciorelli Fish Company offices, where he reviews and compares the price of yellowfin tuna with that of his competitors, and then decides that they can reduce the price by two cents a pound for their prime customers.

"They're buying at this price," Sciorelli argues. "They're happy."

"I want them to *stay* happy," Frank says. "I don't want them looking around for the better deal. We'll *give* them the better deal, keep their eyes from wandering." He also tells Sciorelli to buy as much of the Mexican shrimp as he can get—the storm is going to keep the shrimp boats in for a week or so and the *camarones* will be getting prime price.

Things change and they don't, he thinks as he gets in the van and heads back toward OB Pier. My daughter is going to be a doctor, but we're still selling tuna. And there are other things that don't change, he thinks as he drives to Little Italy, right up the hill from the airport—I'm still fixing things in the old house.

6

The old house is just that—an old house, something that's getting more and more rare in downtown San Diego, even over here in Little Italy, which used to be a neighborhood of old, well-kept single-family homes but is now giving way to condo buildings, office buildings, trendy little hotels, and parking structures to service the airport.

Frank's old house is a beautiful two-story Victorian, white with yellow trim. He parks in the narrow driveway, hops out of the van, and finds the right key on his big chain. He has the key in the lock when Patty opens it from the inside, as if she heard the van pulling up, which maybe she did.

"Took you long enough," she says as she lets him in.

She can still get to me, Frank thinks as he feels a pang of annoyance. And something else, too. Patty is still an attractive woman. She's gotten a little matronly, maybe, around the hips, but she's kept herself in good shape, and those brown almond-shaped eyes still have a way of, well, getting to him.

"I'm here now," he says, kissing her on the cheek. He walks past her into the kitchen, where one half of the deep double sink looks like high tide in a Third World harbor someplace.

"It's not working," Patty says, coming in behind him.

"I can see that," Frank says. He sniffs the air. "Are you making gnocchi?"

"Uh-huh."

"And did you peel all the potatoes and try to put them down the disposal?" Frank asks as he rolls up his sleeve, plunges his hand into the dirty water, and feels around the drain.

"Potato peels are garbage," Patty says. "I tried to dispose of the garbage. Isn't that what a garbage disposal is supposed to do?"

"It's 'garbage disposal,'" Frank says. "Not 'garbage dispose-*all.*' I mean, you don't put tin cans down there, do you? Or *do* you?"

"You want some coffee?" she asks. "I'll make some fresh."

"Sounds good, thanks."

He goes to a hallway closet to get his tool chest. They go through this routine every time. She'll make some fresh, weak coffee in the Krups maker that he bought her and that she refuses to learn how to run properly, and he'll take a polite sip while he works and then leave the rest in the cup. Frank has discovered that rituals like this are even more important to a peaceful relationship when you're divorced than when you were actually married.

But when he comes back down the hallway, he hears the whir of a coffee grinder, and when he reaches the kitchen, there's a French press sitting on the stove beside a kettle of water on the boil. He raises his eyebrows.

"This is the way you like it now, isn't it?" Patty says. "Jill says this is the way you like it."

"That's how I make it, yeah." He doesn't say a word when she pours in the boiling water and presses the plunger down right away instead of waiting the requisite four minutes. Instead, he keeps his mouth shut and crawls into the cabinet under the sink, stretches out on his back, and starts to work the crescent wrench on the disposal trap, where the potato peels are no doubt trapped. He hears her set the coffee cup on the floor by his knee.

"Thanks."

"You could take a minute and have a cup of coffee," she says.

Actually, I can't, Frank thinks. He still has to get back to the bait shack for the sunset rush, then go home, shower, shave, and dress, and go pick up Donna. But he doesn't say this to her, either. The subject of Donna might cause Patty to kick the coffee over on his leg accidentally, or to try to flush an entire roll of paper towels down the upstairs toilet. Or maybe just to kick me in the balls while I'm vulnerable, Frank thinks.

"I have to get to the bait shop," he says. But he slides out, sits up, and takes a sip of the coffee. It's actually not bad, which surprises him. He didn't marry Patty for her cooking. He married her more because she looked like that movie star Ida Lupino and still does, and he was crazy about her, and, her being a good Italian girl, she wouldn't let him past second base without a ring on her finger. So Frank did the bulk of the cooking at home when they were married, and they were already divorced when the term *control freak* came into vogue. Now he says, "This is good."

"Surprise," she says, sitting on the floor next to him. "That's really something about Jill, isn't it?"

"I'll find a way to pay for it."

"I'm not nagging you about money," she says, looking a little hurt. "I just thought it would be nice to take a moment and share some parental pride."

"You did a good job with that kid, Patty," Frank says.

"We both did."

Her eyes start to tear up, and Frank feels his own eyes get a little moist. He knows what they're both thinking about—that morning in the delivery room, after the long, hard labor, when Jill was finally born. And it was a busy morning, lots of babies, so the doctors and nurses finished up with them, and Frank was so tired that he crawled onto the gurney with his wife and new baby and they all fell asleep together. She gets up suddenly and says, "Fix the damn thing. You've got to get to the bait shop, and I'm going to be late for yoga."

"Yoga?" he says, getting back under the sink.

"At our age," she says, "it's 'use it or lose it.'"

"No, look, I think it's good."

"It's mostly women," she says, so quickly that Frank instantly gets that it's mostly women but there's at least one man there. He feels this little twinge of jealousy. Which is irrational and unfair, he tells himself. You have Donna; Patty should have somebody in her life. But still, he doesn't like the thought. He gets the trap off, then reaches in and pulls out a wad of sodden potato peels. He holds it up to her and says, "Patty, please? *Cooked* food, not raw, and not five pounds at a time, okay?"

"Okay," she says, but can't help adding, "They should make those things better, though."

So he knows she's going to do it again, or something just like it, and he thinks, Next time, let your boyfriend fix it. With all that yoga, he can get under the sink with no problem, right?

He puts the trap back on, tightens it down, and crawls back out from under the sink.

"You want to try the gnocchi?" she asks.

"I thought you had yoga."

"I could skip a class."

He thinks about it for a second, then says, "No, you want to keep up with that. 'Use it or lose it,' like they say."

You jerk, he thinks when he sees her eyes get sharp and cold. What a stupid thing to say. And Patty being Patty, she isn't going to let it slide. "You could use a little yoga yourself," she says, looking at his belly.

"Yeah, maybe I'll join your class."

"That's all I need."

He washes his hands, then gives her another quick kiss on the cheek, which she tries to turn away from.

"See you Friday," he says.

"If I'm not here," she tells him, "just leave the envelope in the drawer."

"Thanks for the coffee. It was really good."

He gets back to the bait shack just in time for the dusk rush. The kid Abe can handle the slow midafternoon business, but he starts to panic when the night fishermen begin to line up and demand their bait. Besides, Frank wants to be there to close out the register. He helps the kid Abe through the rush, closes out, locks the joint up, and heads home to grab a quick shower and wash the fish smell off him.

He showers, shaves, changes into a suit with a dress shirt but open collar, and takes the Mercedes, not the van, out of the garage. He has time to drop by three new restaurants before he goes to pick up Donna. His routine is the same at each place: He has a tonic water at the bar and asks to see the manager or owner. Then he presents his card and says, "If you're happy with your linen service, pardon the intrusion. If you're not, give me a call and I'll tell you what I can do for you."

Nine times out of ten, he gets the call.

He picks Donna up at her condo, which is in a large complex over-looking the beach. He parks in a visitor's slot and rings the bell, even though he has a key to her place in case of emergencies, or if she's traveling and the plants need to be watered, or if he's coming in late at night and doesn't want to get her out of bed.

She looks terrific.

She always does, and not just for a woman in her forties but for a woman of any age. She's wearing a basic black dress, just short enough to show off her legs and cut just low enough to show a little cleavage.

Back in the day, Frank thinks as he opens the car door for her, we would have called her a "classy broad." Course, you don't talk like that anymore, but that's what Donna is. Always was. A Vegas showgirl who didn't hook or hustle, didn't succumb to the booze or the dope, just did her job, saved her money, and knew when it was time to call it a day. Took her savings, moved to Solana Beach, and opened her boutique.

Makes herself a nice life.

They drive up the coast to Freddie's by the Sea.

It's an old San Diego place on the beach in Cardiff, and sometimes, like tonight, the water laps right up against the restaurant. The hostess knows Frank and shows them to a table by a window. With the storm front coming in, the waves are already approaching the glass.

Donna looks out at the weather. "Well, it will give me a chance to catch up on inventory anyway."

"You could take a couple of days off."

"You first."

It's a constant joke between them, and a constant hassle, two business-minded people trying to find time to go off for even a few days' vacation. She doesn't really feel comfortable with anyone else running the boutique, and Frank is, well, Frank. They made it to Kauai for five days three years ago, but since then, they've managed one overnight in Laguna and a weekend at Big Sur.

"We need to stop and smell the roses," he tells her now.

"You could start by having two jobs instead of five," she says. Still, she has a sense that maybe one reason their relationship works so well is that they *don't* have too much time for each other.

The waiter comes back and they order a bottle of red and then, in the interest of time, go ahead and order their appetizers and entrées, too. He goes for the seafood soup and the shrimp scampi; Donna orders a green salad—no dressing—and the baked halibut with tomatoes.

"The scampi is tempting," she says, "but butter shows up on me the next day."

She excuses herself to go to the ladies', and Frank takes the opportunity to scamper into the kitchen for a hello call to the chef, for the usual: How's the fish been? Any complaints? Wasn't that yellowtail terrific last week? Hey, just to let you know, I'm going to have a good supply of shrimp next week, storm or no storm.

When he gets to the kitchen, John Heaney isn't there.

Frank has known him for years. They used to surf a lot together back when John owned his own restaurant in Ocean Beach. But John lost that place on a *Monday Night Football* bet.

Frank was there that Tuesday morning, at the Gentlemen's Hour, when John paddled out, hungover and looking like death.

"What's the matter with you?" Frank asked him.

"Twenty large on the Vikes to cover," John replied. "They blew an extra point. A goddamn fucking extra point."

"You have the money?"

"No."

So bye-bye restaurant.

John went to work out at the Viejas casino, which was kind of like an alcoholic going to work at the Jack Daniel's distillery. Every two weeks, he'd pull a paycheck in the red, and finally the casino canned him. John bounced from job to job until Frank got him the gig at Freddie's.

What are you going to do, Frank thinks. A buddy is a buddy.

John makes good money at Freddie's, but good money is never good enough for a degenerate gambler. Last time Frank heard, John was moonlighting as the late-shift manager at Hunnybear's.

"Where's Johnny?" he asks the sous-chef, who nods his head toward the back door.

Frank understands: The chef is out back by the Dumpster, grabbing a smoke and maybe a quick drink. You go to any Dumpster in back of any restaurant, you're going to find a pile of butts and maybe a few of those little airline bottles of booze that the staff is too lazy to toss into the garbage.

John's sucking at a ciggy and staring at the ground like it has an answer for something, his tall, skinny frame bent over like one of those cheap sculptures made out of clothes-hanger wire.

"How's it going, Johnny?" Frank asks.

John looks up, startled, like he's surprised to see Frank standing there. "Jesus, Frank, you scared me."

Johnny's got to be—what, mid- to late fifties, maybe? He looks older.

"What's wrong?" Frank asks.

John shakes his head. "World of shit right now, Frank."

"This G-Sting business?" Frank asks. "Is Hunnybear's involved in that?"

John holds his hand, palm down, up under his chin. "What if they close the place? I need the fuckin' money, Frank."

"It'll blow over," Frank says. "This stuff always does."

John shakes his head. "I dunno."

"You'll always work, John," Frank says. "You want me to drop a word somewhere . . ."

It would be easy to hook John up with a second job at some good restaurant. He's a good cook, and besides, he's a popular guy. Everybody likes him.

"Thanks, Frank. Not right now."

"You let me know."

"Thanks."

Frank makes it back to the table just before Donna, and blesses the fact that there's always a line at the ladies' and that women take a lot longer to get all that complicated gear off and on again.

"How's the chef?" Donna asks as he gets up and holds the chair out for her. Frank sits back down and shrugs with a look of hurt innocence.

"Incorrigible," Donna says.

The rain really starts coming down while they're having dessert. Well, Frank's having dessert—cheesecake and an espresso—and Donna's having a black coffee. The rain starts with slow, fat plops against the window, then picks up, and it's only a minute or so before the wind starts to drive sheets of rain against the glass.

Most people in the restaurant cease their conversations to watch and listen. It doesn't rain that often in San Diego—less than usual, in fact, the past few years—and it rarely rains hard like this. It's the true beginning of winter, the short monsoon season in this Mediterranean climate, and the people just sit back and gaze at it.

Frank watches the whitecaps picking up.

It's going to be something tomorrow.

Donna's condo doesn't have an ocean view. Her place is on the back side of the complex, away from the beach, so she got it for about 60 percent less. Doesn't matter to Frank—when he goes to Donna's place, all he wants to look at is Donna.

Their lovemaking has a ritual. Donna isn't one of those off-with-the-clothes-and-into-bed women, even though they both know that's where they're headed. So tonight, like most nights he comes over, they go into her living room, and she puts some Sinatra on the stereo. Then she goes and gets two snifters of brandy and they sit on the sofa and neck.

Frank thinks he could live in the crook of Donna's neck and never leave. It's long and elegant, and the perfume she dots there makes his head whirl. He spends a long time kissing her neck and nuzzling her red hair, and then he moves down to her shoulder, and after some time there, he eases the strap of her dress off her shoulder and down her arm. She usually wears a black brassiere, which drives him crazy. He kisses the tops of her breasts while his hand makes the long, slow trip up her leg, then kisses her lips and hears her purr into his mouth. Then she gets up and takes him by the hand and leads him into her bedroom and says, "I'm going to get comfortable," and disappears into her bathroom, leaving him lying, fully dressed, on her bed while he waits to see what she's going to wear.

Donna has great lingerie.

She gets it wholesale from her suppliers. So she indulges herself. Well, she indulges *me*, Frank thinks as he leans over to take off his shoes and then loosens his tie. Once, just once, he took all his clothes off and was in bed naked when she came out, and she asked, "And what are *you* assuming?" and asked him to leave.

The wait is interminable, and he enjoys every second of it. He knows she's dressing carefully to please him, freshening her makeup, putting on perfume, brushing her hair.

The door opens; she shuts off the bathroom light and comes out.

She never fails to knock him out.

Tonight, she's wearing a sheer emerald green peignoir over a black garter belt and hose and has high freaking heels on. She turns around slowly, to let him enjoy every angle of her, and then he gets up and takes her in his arms. He knows that now she wants him to take over.

He knows you don't "have sex" with Donna; you make love to her—slowly, carefully, finding each little pleasure spot on her amazing body and lingering there. And she's a dancer—she wants it to be a dance, so she glides over him with a dancer's grace and eroticism, using her breasts, her hands, her mouth, her hair on him, undressing him and making him hard. Then he lays her down on the bed and moves down her long frame and pushes up the peignoir, and she's dotted perfume on her thighs, but she doesn't need any perfume there, Frank thinks.

He takes his time. There's no hurry and his own need can wait, wants to wait, because it will be all the better for the waiting.

It's like the ocean, he thinks later, like a wave coming in and then receding. Again and again, and then building like an ocean swell, thick and heavy and picking up speed. He likes to look at her face when he's making love to her, likes to see her green eyes brighten and the smile on her elegant lips, and, tonight, hear the sound of the rain pelting the window glass.

They lie there for a long time afterward, listening to the rain.

"That was beautiful," he says.

"Always."

"You okay?"

Frank, the working guy, always checking his work.

"Oh yeah," she says. "You?"

"That was me screaming," he says.

He's lying there politely, considerately, but she knows that he's already restless. It's fine with her; she's not that much of a cuddler, and anyway, morning comes early and she sleeps better alone. So she gives the standard cue: "I'm going to wash up a little."

Which means that he can get dressed while she's in the bathroom, and when she comes out, they can go through the comfortable ritual:

"Oh? Are you heading out?"

"Yeah, I think so. Busy day tomorrow."

"You can stay if you want."

And he'll pretend to consider it, then say, "Nah, I'd better get home."

And then they'll have a warm kiss and he'll say, "I love you."

"I love you, too."

And then he'll be gone. To go home, grab a little sleep, and start the whole thing over again.

It's the routine.

Except tonight turns out different.

7

Tonight, he drives home and there's a car in the alley.

A car he doesn't know.

Frank knows the neighbors, knows all their vehicles. None of them owns a Hummer. And even through the now-driving rain, he can see there are two guys sitting in the front seat.

They aren't pros; he knows that straight off.

Pros would never use a vehicle as conspicuous as a Hummer. And they aren't cops, because even the feds don't have the budget for a vehicle like that. And third, professionals would know that I love life, and because I love life, I haven't, in thirty years, pulled into my house at night without driving around the block first. Especially when my garage entrance is in an alley where I could get cut off.

So if these guys were pros, they wouldn't be sitting in the alley; they'd be at least half a block down, wait for me to pull into the alley, and then come in.

They spotted him, though, as he drove by.

Or they think they did.

"That was him," Travis says.

"Bull fucking shit," J. answers. "How can you tell?"

"No, that was him, Junior," Travis says. "That was Frankie fucking Machine. A motherfucking legend."

Parking isn't easy in Ocean Beach, so it takes Frank about ten minutes to find a spot on the street three blocks away. He pulls in, reaches under the seat and finds his .38 S&W, puts it in the pocket of his raincoat, pulls his hood up, and gets out of the car. Walks another block out of his way so that he'll hit the alley from the east and not from the west, where they might be expecting him. He comes around to the alley and the Hummer is still there. Even over the rain he can hear the bass vibrating, so the dumb mooks are in there listening to rap music.

Which is going to make it easier.

He walks up the alley, his feet sloshing in the puddles, ruining the shine on his shoes, and he's careful to stay dead center with the back of the Hummer so he's less likely to get spotted in either rearview mirror. As he gets closer, he can smell the reefer, so now he knows he's dealing with complete doofs—kids, probably, drug dealers—sitting in their cool sled, getting high and listening to tunes.

He's not even sure they hear him when he opens the back door, slides in, sticks a gun in the back of the driver's head, and pulls the hammer back.

"I told you it was him," Travis says.

"Frankie," J. says. "Don't you recognize me?"

Yeah, Frank maybe recognizes him, although it's been years. The kid—maybe in his mid-twenties—has short black hair gelled into spikes, some sort of stud stuck through his bottom lip, and earrings through the tops of his ears. He's decked out in surfer clothes—a long-sleeve Billabong shirt under a Rusty fleece, and workout pants.

"Mouse Junior?" Frank asks.

The other one chuckles, then quickly shuts up. Mouse Junior doesn't like being called Mouse Junior. He prefers "J.," which is what he tells Frank now.

The other one is also dressed like a clown. He's got the gel thing going, too, and a wispy goatee, and he's wearing one of those surfer's beanies on his head, which Frank resents, because Frank wears one to keep his head warm when he's come out of the cold water after actually *surfing,* and not to look pseudo-hip. And both of them are wearing sunglasses, which is maybe why they couldn't see a full-grown man coming up behind them. He doesn't tell them this, though, and he doesn't put the gun down, even though holding a gun to the son of a boss is a major violation of protocol.

That's okay, Frank thinks. He doesn't want *But he respected protocol* carved on his headstone.

"Who are you?" he asks the other one.

"My name is Travis," the other says. "Travis Renaldi."

This is what it's come to, Frank thinks. Italian parents giving their kids Yuppie names like Travis.

"It's an honor to meet you, Mr. Machianno," Travis says. "'Frankie Machine.'"

"Shut up," Frank says. "I don't know what you're talking about."

"Yeah, shut the fuck up," Mouse Junior says. "Frankie, could you put that gun down now? Could we go inside, maybe you could offer us a beer or a cup of coffee or something?"

"This is a social call?" Frank asks. "You waiting in the alley in the middle of the night?"

"We figured we'd wait until you were done with your booty call, Frankie," Mouse Junior says. Frank's not sure he knows what a "booty call" is, but he can figure it out from the nasty tone of Mouse Junior's voice. He hasn't seen Junior in probably eight years, and the kid was a spoiled teenage punk *then*. He hasn't matured any. Frank would like to give him a hard cuff in the ear for the "booty call" remark but there are limits to what you can do to a boss's kid, even a boss as limp as Mouse Senior.

Mouse Senior—Peter Martini—is boss of what's left of the L.A. family, which also includes what's left of the San Diego crew. Peter got the nickname "Mouse" after L.A. police chief Daryl Gates famously referred to the West Coast mob as "the Mickey Mouse Mafia," and the name stuck. He became Mouse Senior after he had his son and named him Peter.

But the rules are the rules: You can't lay hands on a boss's kid.

And you can't refuse him hospitality.

Frank doesn't like it, though, as he leads them into his place. For one thing, he doesn't like letting them get the lay of the land, in case they come back later to try something. Second, it's not a good idea in case they ever flip and take the witness stand. It will be harder for him to deny that a meeting ever happened if they can accurately describe what the inside of his house looked like.

On the other hand, he knows his house isn't wired.

He pats them both down the second they come in.

"No offense," he says.

"Hey, these days . . . ," Mouse Junior says.

No kidding, these days, Frank thinks. This is probably what this little sit-down is about anyway—Mouse Senior sending Mouse Junior down to get reassurance that Frank is still on the reservation.

Because Mouse Senior hasn't been named on the Goldstein hit, even though he was the one who ordered it done, and Frank knows it.

Like Mouse Senior is so careful, Frank thinks. For three years, *three years,* back in the late eighties, Bobby "the Beast" Zitello was wearing a wire, while Mouse Senior thought the sun shone out of his ass. Bobby's "Greatest Hits" album went platinum and put half the family in the joint for fifteen years. Now Mouse Senior is out, and he doesn't want to go back in.

But the Goldstein thing might put them all in the can for good. Poor Herbie got clipped back in '97 and a couple of low-level mokes confessed to it. But there's no statute of limitations on murder, and the Goldstein killing has come back like a ghost. The feds have been all over it lately, as part of Operation Button Down, their attempt to put the last nail in Mouse Senior's coffin. What probably happened is the two mooks found out they didn't like prison so much and decided to trade up. For all Frank knows, Mouse Senior might be under a sealed indictment and be looking to make some trades of his own.

So Frank pats Mouse Junior down pretty thoroughly.

He doesn't find any wires or mikes.

Or guns.

That would be the other possibility—Mouse Senior wanting to make absolutely *certain* that I don't tell the feds who ordered up the Goldstein thing. But Mouse would have sent one of the few soldiers he has left. Even Mouse wouldn't send his own kid on a mission to try to hit Frankie Machine.

You want your son to bury *you.*

"You want coffee or beer?" Frank asks, taking off his raincoat. He keeps the pistol in his hand.

"Beer, if you got it," Mouse Junior says.

"I have it," Frank says. Good, he thinks, it saves me the trouble of brewing up a pot. He goes into the kitchen, grabs two Dos Equis, then changes his mind and takes two of the cheaper Coronas instead. He comes back out, hands them the beers, says, "Use coasters."

The two kids sit on his sofa like bad students in the principal's office. Frank sits down in his chair, with his pistol on his lap, and kicks off his wet shoes. That's all I need, he thinks, a cold. They go through the preliminaries: "How's your father? How's your uncle? Give them my regards. What brings you boys to San Diego?"

"Dad suggested it," Mouse Junior says. "He said I should come talk to you."

"About what?"

"I got a problem," Mouse Junior says.

You got more than one problem, Frank thinks. You're stupid, you're lazy, you're uneducated, and you're careless. What did the kid do, a year and a half of junior college before he dropped out to "help Dad with the business"?

"We—" Mouse Junior begins.

"Who's 'we'?" Frank asks.

"Me and Travis," Mouse Junior explains. "We have a sweet little porno operation running. Golden Productions. We're getting a piece of half the distribution that comes out of the Valley."

Frank doubts it. You can read the papers and know the San Fernando Valley produces billions in porn every year, and these kids don't look like billionaires. Maybe, maybe, they have the arm on a few operations, but that's about it.

Still, it's lucrative. How many times did Mike Pella try to get me to invest in the porn business? And how many times did I refuse? For one thing, it used to be all mobbed up, back when it was illegal. Two, as I told him, "I have a *daughter,* Mike."

But since porn went mainstream, most of the money in it is strictly legit. You set up shop, or you invest, like you would with any other business. So what . . .

"Bootlegs," Mouse Junior explains. "We invest in the studio so we can get a good master. We distribute a bunch of those on the legit market, but for every one we sell legally, we bootleg three."

So they sell one of the company's videos and three of their own, Frank thinks. Basically, they cheat their own partners.

"It's even easier with DVDs," Travis explains. "You can press them out like pancakes. The Asians can't buy enough of blondes with big tits fucking and sucking."

"Watch your mouth," Frank says. "This is my home."

Travis turns red. He forgot what J. had warned him, that Frankie Machine doesn't like profanity. "Sorry."

Frank talks to Mouse Junior. "So what's your problem?"

"Detroit."

"Can you be a little more specific?" Frank asks.

"Some guys from Detroit," Mouse Junior says, "friends of ours, have done a little porn out here, and okay, maybe they introduced us to some people. Now they think they're owed."

"They are," Frank says. He knows the rules.

Besides, Detroit—aka "the Combination"—has had a piece of San Diego forever, since back in the forties, when Paul Moretti and Sal Tomenelli came out and opened a bunch of bars, restaurants, and strip clubs downtown. Back in the sixties, Paul and Tony ran a lot of heroin through those joints, but after Tomenelli was murdered, they settled into loan-sharking, gambling, strip clubs, porn, and running whores.

Anyway, they carved out their piece.

Because of Moretti's prestige, his son-in-law Joe Migliore got a pass in San Diego, never having to kick up or even answer to L.A. It was like Detroit had its own separate little colony in the Gaslamp District. They still do—Joe's kid, Teddy, still has Callahan's down in the Lamp, and runs his other businesses from the back room.

"If Detroit set you up with these connections," Frank tells Mouse Junior, "you *do* owe them."

"Not sixty percent," Mouse Junior whines. "We do all the work— make the videos, set up the warehouses, do the bootlegs, get to the Asian markets. Now this guy wants a majority share? I don't *think* so."

"Who's the guy?"

"Vince Vena," Mouse Junior tells him.

"You're sideways with Vince Vena?" Frank asks. "You do have a problem, kid."

Vince Vena is a heavy guy.

Word is, he just made it on the ruling council of the Combination. No wonder Mouse Junior is scared. The L.A. family was never that strong—it used to bow to New York, then Chicago, and now there's a power vacuum as the East Coast families are getting hammered by old age, attrition, and the RICO statutes. So now Detroit is positioning itself to move in on what's left of the West Coast, and in one of the few profit centers left. And it makes sense to start with Mouse's kid, because if you pull that off, you're proving a point: Mouse Senior is so weakened by the Goldstein indictments, he doesn't have the strength to protect his own son.

If Vena succeeds in extorting sixty points out of Mouse Junior, the L.A. family might just as well give up the ghost entirely. Which is fine with me, Frank thinks. New York, Chicago, Detroit, it's all the same. It's all going the way of the dinosaur anyway. Doesn't matter who shuts the lights out—it's still dark.

"Why are you coming to me?" Frank asks, even though he knows the answer.

"Because you're Frankie Machine," Mouse Junior says.

"What does *that* mean?"

What it means, Mouse Junior explains, is that they've "calendared" a sit-down with Vena to hammer out a deal.

"Do it," Frank says. "If Vena says sixty, he'll take forty, maybe even thirty-five. You give him a cut of the pie, then you just go out and make a bigger pie, that's all. There's enough for everybody."

Mouse Junior shakes his head. "If we don't stop it here . . ."

"You stop it here," Frank says, "you start a war with Detroit."

And let me tell you what your old man already knows, kid. You don't have the troops. But Mouse Junior's too young to know that. Too much testosterone bouncing around in there.

Mouse Junior says, "I'm not rolling over for this guy."

"So don't," Frank says.

It's not my problem.

I'm retired.

"Fifty K," Mouse Junior says.

That *is* high, Frank thinks. There must be more money in this porn thing than I thought. It shows they have resources, but it also shows how weak they are. You don't normally pay cash to have this kind of thing done—you give it to one of your soldiers in exchange for future business considerations, or maybe getting him straightened out.

But L.A. doesn't have many soldiers left. Not good ones anyway, guys who could do this kind of work.

Fifty K is a lot of money. Invested well, it would pay a lot of tuition.

"I'm going to take a pass on this one," Frank says.

"Dad said you might turn it down," Mouse Junior says.

"Your father is a wise man."

Actually, he's a jackass, but what the hell.

"He said to tell you," Mouse Junior continues, "that he would consider this a personal favor, a matter of loyalty."

"Meaning what?"

Frank's going to make him say it.

"With everything that's happening in Vegas," Mouse Junior says, his voice quivering a little, scared. "The Goldstein stuff . . . Dad would like to know that you're, you know, on the team."

So there it is, Frank thinks. It's two birds with one stone. Mouse Senior gets his Detroit problem taken care of, and he gets an insurance policy on my silence over Goldstein, because I can't go to the feds with a fresh hit on my hands. And if I don't do the Vena job, I make myself suspect as a possible rat. So either I take Vena out or I put myself in the bull's-eye. But if Mouse Senior doesn't have the soldiers to take Vince himself, why does he think he has the resources to make a run at *me*? Nobody in the Mickey Mouse Club has either the skills or the stones.

Who could he send?

He'd go outside the family. New York, maybe Florida, maybe even the Mexicans.

He could get it done.

It's a problem.

"Tell you what," Frank says. "I'll get Vena off your back, one way or the other. Set up a meeting with him. I'll come along. If he sees me there, he'll be more reasonable. If not . . ."

He lets it hang there. The rest is obvious.

Travis likes the idea, anyway. "That'll work, J.," he says. "If Vena sees that we have Frankie freaking *Machine* on our team, he'll shit his pants."

"No, he won't," Frank says. "But he will negotiate more reasonable points." He turns to Mouse Junior. "You don't want a war if you can help it, kid. I've seen war. Peace is better."

Something you'll learn when you get a little older, Frank thinks, if you don't get yourself killed first. Young guys, they always want to prove how tough they are. It's a testosterone thing. Older guys see the beauty in compromise. And save the testosterone for better things.

Mouse Junior thinks it over. Judging by the expression on his face, it's apparently a grueling process. Then he asks, "What about the fifty K?"

"The fifty is for solving your problem," Frank says. "Either way."

"Half now," Mouse Junior says, "half when the job is done."

Frank shakes his head. "All of it up front."

"That's unprecedented."

"*This* is unprecedented."

Them approaching him directly, that is. The protocol is that they should have gone through Mike Pella, capo of what's left of San Diego, who'd collect a referral fee.

It would be good to talk to Mike about this Vena thing, get his take. Mike Pella is an old-school mafioso, among the last of a dying breed. He and Frank have been tight since forever. Mike's been his friend, his confidant, his partner, his captain. Mike would be able to give him the lay of the land, steer him clear of the land mines.

But Mike, with his instinct for survival, has been in the wind since the Goldstein thing came back up.

Good place for you to be, Mike.

Stay there.

"Two-thirds, one-third," Mouse Junior says.

"I'm not *negotiating* with you, kid," Frank says. "I gave you the conditions under which I'll work. If it's worth it to you, fine. If not, it's also fine."

The money's in the Hummer.

Mouse Junior sends Travis out to get it. He brings back a briefcase containing fifty K in used bills, nonsequential.

"Dad *said* you'd want it all up front," Mouse Junior says, smiling.

"Then why were you busting chops?" Frank asks. Because you're a smarmy, wise-ass punk, Frank thinks, trying to prove how smart and tough you are. And you're neither. If you were smart, you wouldn't have gotten yourself into this predicament. If you were tough, you'd take care of it yourself.

"It's just business," Mouse Junior says. "Nothing personal."

Frank wishes he had a dime for every time he's heard that line. The wise guys all heard it in the first *Godfather* and liked it. Now they all use it. Same with the term *godfather,* for that matter—until the movie came out, Frank never heard the word in that context. The boss was just the "boss." Those were good movies and all—well, *two* of them were—but they had nothing to do with the mob, not the mob that Frank knows, anyway.

Maybe it's just a West Coast thing, he thinks. We never went in for all that heavy "Sicilian" stuff.

Or maybe it's just too warm out here for all those hats and overcoats.

"Mr. Machine?" Travis is saying.

Frank shoots him a dirty look.

"Mr. Machianno, I meant," Travis says. "There's one other thing."

"What's that?"

"The sit-down is tonight," Mouse Junior says.

"Tonight?" Frank asks. It's already after midnight. He has to be up in three hours and forty-five minutes.

"Tonight."

Frank sighs.

It's a lot of work being me.

8

Mouse Junior hands him a cell phone.

"It's on speed dial," he says, pressing the button for him.

Vena doesn't answer until the fifth ring.

"Hello?" He sounds like the phone woke him up.

"Vince? Frank Machianno here."

There's a long pause, which is what Frank expected. Vince's mind has to be whirling, he figures, wondering why Frankie Machine is on the phone, how he got this number, and what he wants.

"Frankie! Long time!"

"Too long," Frank says, not meaning it.

If he never talked to Vince Vena again, he'd be very happy. He knows Vince from the old days, back in the eighties in Vegas, when it was open territory and everybody's playground. Vince was a fixture at the Stardust, practically furniture. When he wasn't at the blackjack table, he was out catching the comedians' shows, and then he'd annoy everyone by constantly reciting their routines. Vince liked to think he did a pretty good Dangerfield, which he didn't, although, unfortunately, that never stopped him from doing it.

Poor Rodney, Frank thinks now. That was a truly funny man.

"Hey, Vince," Frank says, "This thing with Mouse Ju—with Pete's kid."

"J.," Mouse Junior prompts.

Vince's voice sounds pissed off. "What is it? Mousedick Junior been whining to you?"

"He reached out."

Frank chooses these words deliberately, because they have a very specific meaning: *I'm involved now. You're dealing with me.*

Vince hears it. "I didn't know you was in the DVD business, Frank. If I did, I'd've come to you in the first place. No disrespect, huh?"

"I'm not in the business, Vince. It's just that, well, the boss's kid reaches out to me, what am I going to do?"

"The boss?" Vince laughs, then sings, "'Who's the leader of the club that's made for you and me? M-I-C-K-E-Y M-O-U-S-E.'"

"Anyway," Frank says. "I'm going to come along for the sit-down, you don't mind."

Or even if you do.

"These kids," Frank continues, "they don't know what's right"—he casts a pointed glance at the two doofs sitting across from him, who look down at the floor—"but you and me, I'm sure we can get it straightened out."

He's sure they can. What he'll do is, he'll take ten K of the fifty along as a gesture, then negotiate Vince down to fifteen points on the rest of the deal. That's a fair offer, one that Vince should accept. If not, Mouse Senior is in a position to bitch to Detroit about Vena, get him in line. If none of that works . . .

Frank doesn't want to even think about that.

It'll work.

"Hey, whatever's right, Frankie," Vince is saying.

Which means he's going to be reasonable, Frank thinks. He says, "See you in a little bit, Vince."

"Give it a half hour," Vince says. "Me and this chick are making some waves, you know what I mean."

"I don't know what you mean," Frank says. And who says "chick" anymore?

"Didn't Mousedick Junior tell you?" Vince says. "I'm on a boat. Here in San Diego."

"A boat?"

"A cabin cruiser," Vince says. "I'm renting it."

"It's *winter,* Vince."

"A friend of ours cut me a deal."

Classic wise guy, Frank thinks. Long as they think they're getting a deal, they'll go for it. So you got a cheap shakedown artist on a boat he can't use, in the rain.

Classic.

He knows what's coming next.

Vince doesn't disappoint him. "So if the boat is rockin'," Vince says, "don't come knockin'."

"Finish your beers," Frank says. "Then let's go get this straightened out."

He goes into the kitchen, opens a drawer, and takes out an envelope. Then he comes back into the living room, counts ten thousand out from the fifty, puts it in the envelope, and slides it into his jacket pocket.

"What are you doing?" Mouse Junior asks.

"Didn't your parents teach you any manners?" Frank asks. "You never go to a person's empty-handed."

In the same spirit, he checks the load on his .38 and slips it in the waistband of his slacks, underneath the back of his coat. He looks at the boys. "Are you carrying?"

"Sure."

"Absolutely."

"Leave the hardware in the car," Frank says.

When they start to object, he says, "Something goes south—which I don't expect, but it might—the last thing I want is one of you blowing my brains out by accident. If the stuff hits the fan, you hit the deck and stay there until it gets real quiet and you hear me telling you to get up. You don't hear me telling you to get up, it's because you're dead, and then it doesn't make any difference anyway. And you let *me* do the talking. *Capisce?*"

"Got it."

"Absolutely."

"And quit saying 'absolutely,'" Frank tells Travis. "It annoys me."

"Abso—"

"We'll take your car," Frank says to Mouse Junior. No sense in burning up *my* gas, he thinks, the prices at the pump these days.

Even in the rain, Frank loves the view of San Diego from the harbor.

The lights from the tall downtown buildings reflect red and green on the water, and on the horizon, the Coronado Bay Bridge's lights shine in the night sky like the diamonds of a necklace on an elegant woman's neck.

The rain just makes everything sparkle all the more.

He loves this city.

Always has.

They have no trouble finding a parking spot, or the slip where Vena's cabin cruiser is docked. Walking down the floating dock, Frank reminds them, "Remember, leave everything to me."

"But we could help," Mouse Junior says.

"If anything goes down," Travis clarifies.

"Don't help me," Frank says.

Where do they learn to talk like this? The movies, I guess, or television. Anyway, the only thing that's going to "go down" is Vena's percentage, which will drop an automatic ten points just by virtue of me being there. He knows what Vena's move will be—try to get Frank alone and tell him that if he makes Mouse Junior give up forty points, he'll cut Frank in for five.

And I'll turn the offer down because it's a boss's kid, which Vince will understand; then we'll get down to the real *hondeling*. Another word Herbie taught me, God rest.

He finds the boat, the *Becky Lynn*. The name tells the story—two guys finally get their wives' permission to buy a boat together and name it after both wives so they don't get jealous. Not of each other, of the boat.

Which never works, Frank thinks.

Women and boats mix like . . .

Women and boats.

He steps down off the dock onto the afterdeck. The cabin is all shut up against the rain, but the lights are on and Frank can hear music inside.

"Ahoy!" he yells, because he can't resist it.

The door opens and Vince Vena's ugly face pops out. He never was a good-looking guy, Vince. Got this thin face with old acne scars and his eyes are a little too close together. Now he grabs his shirt collar, gives it a tug, and says, à la Rodney, "My wife and I were very happy for twenty years. . . ."

"Then we met," Frank thinks.

"Then we met," Vince says, and laughs. "Come in out of the rain, Frank. Prove everyone wrong, what they say about you."

Vince goes back into the cabin and leaves the door open.

Frank steps in, the door shuts, and the garrote is around his neck and cutting into his throat before he can get his hands up. Which is a good thing, because your instinct is to try to get between the wire and your throat, and that's actually the last thing you should do—you only end up getting your fingers sliced along with your windpipe.

The guy is huge. Frank can feel his height and his bulk and he knows he's not going to outmuscle him. So he reaches behind him and jams his fingers into his attacker's eyes, which doesn't make the guy let go but does make him suck his breath in, and Frank uses that second to squat low, grab the man's wrist, pivot, and hip-roll the guy to the deck.

His would-be strangler lands with a crash on the little dining table and Frank continues his roll, getting his body under the table just as Vince pulls a pistol and crouches to shoot him.

Frank's gun slides out in one easy move. All he can see are Vena's legs, so he aims at a point above them and fires twice, then sees Vince's legs stagger back and collapse against the bulkhead, and hears Vince yell, "Oh fuck! Oh fuck!"

Frank closes his eyes and shoots through the bottom of the table three times. Splinters of plywood hit his face, and then everything is quiet. Frank opens his eyes and sees blood dripping down.

He stays under the table in case there's a third guy.

He can hear running on the dock, two pairs of feet beating it out of there, and he figures it's Mouse Junior and Travis.

Absolutely.

Frank makes himself wait for thirty seconds before he crawls out from under the table.

The would-be strangler is dead, two bullet holes and a bunch of plywood splinters in his face. And the guy is enormous—four bills easy. Frank checks out what's left of the guy's face. He recognizes him from someplace but can't quite remember where.

Vince is still breathing, sitting with his back against the bulkhead, his hands trying to hold his guts in.

Frank squats down beside him. "Vince, who sent you?"

Vince's eyes stare out into space. Frank has seen the look before—Vince isn't going to make it. Whether he's looking at the white light, or whatever, he's already checked out of *this* motel, and whatever sound he's hearing now, it isn't Frank's voice.

Frank gives it one more try, though. "Vince, who *sent* you?"

Nothing.

Frank puts the pistol barrel against Vince's heart and pulls the trigger. Then he sits down to catch his breath, surprised and pissed off that his chest is pounding. He makes himself take a few long, deep breaths to slow his heart rate.

It takes a minute.

You're not getting any younger, he thinks. And you almost weren't getting any *older,* either. And don't deserve to, either, being so stupid and careless.

Letting a punk kid like Mouse Junior set you up.

And that's what he did. How do the kids say it these days? He "played" you. Worked on your ego and set you up.

Frank gets up and takes a long look at the dead guy on the table.

The wire garrote is still clutched in his hands. Old-school, Frank thinks, using a wire. But they probably didn't want to risk the noise of a gun unless they had to. Use a silencer, then. Unless the garrote was meant to make it slow and painful, in which case this hit was *personal.*

But who has that kind of beef with me? he wonders.

Get real, he tells himself, it's a long list.

Frank starts the engine. Then he goes back out and unmoors the boat from its slip. One piece of luck is that the two flanking boats are both empty, battened down for the winter. He goes back in, lets the engines warm up, then backs the boat out of the slip.

He steers it into the channel and heads out to sea.

9

Not a good night to be out on the open ocean.

Too much swell and chop, and the roll coming out of the storm keeps working the boat back toward the coast.

Frank hacks it out about ten miles into the ocean anyway. He fished these waters hundreds of times as a kid. He knows every current and channel and he knows just where he wants to dump the bodies so if they ever come to shore, it'll be in Mexico.

The *federales* will figure it's a dope deal gone bad, and put about two minutes' work into solving the case.

Still, it's a bitch out here tonight, with the wind and rain and the roll, and Frank's biggest fear is that he'll run into a Coast Guard vessel that will stop him and want to know what kind of jackass is taking a boat out on a night like this.

I'll just play stupid, Frank thinks.

Which shouldn't be hard, given my track record tonight.

His neck hurts from the wire. But pain is good, he figures, seeing as how by all rights he shouldn't be feeling anything.

It had to be Mouse Senior, he thinks, making sure I don't flip on the Goldstein hit.

Don't think about that now, he tells himself.

Take care of one thing at a time.

He finds the current he's looking for, tosses out an anchor, and shuts the running lights out.

It's a lot of work, dragging two bodies over the side. Hence the expression *dead weight,* he thinks as he gets his arms under Vince's and hefts him to the afterdeck. Fortunately, it's a sportfishing boat with a step-down aft, so he doesn't have to lift him over the rail, just drag him to the aft and kick him off.

The other guy is a bigger problem, literally, and it takes Frank a good ten minutes to drag him out onto the deck, then get down behind him and roll the body into the water.

Now what? Frank thinks.

You have to go off the radar for a while, until you can find out who wants you dead, and why, and what to do about it. You can't just take the blood-soaked boat back to the slip and walk away, because you don't know who might be waiting for you back there. The *best* option would be the cops, and that's no option at all. No one's going to believe that "Frankie Machine" gunned down two mob guys in self-defense.

So . . .

He goes back into the cabin and looks around. He gets lucky in a storage locker, where he finds scuba gear, tanks, and, underneath that, a piece of gold in the form of a wet suit that he can fit into. He undresses, wriggles into the wet suit, which is very tight. But better tight than loose, Frank thinks. Then he shoves his clothes, a towel, the envelope with the ten K, and Vince's gun into a wet bag. He wipes his own gun down, then reluctantly throws it over the side. He'll miss the .38, but it's a murder weapon, at least in the jaundiced eye of the law.

Frank steers toward shore, running the boat in about five hundred yards off the coast, then stops the engine. He cranks the wheel out again toward the open ocean, clamps a wheel lock onto it, starts the engine again, ties the wet bag to his ankle, and goes over the side.

The water is cold, even with the wet suit on, and a definite shock to his uncovered head. Five hundred yards is a long swim in these conditions, and his plan is to start slowly and then taper off. He knows right where he is, though, and gets himself into a current that will pull him to the tip of Ocean Beach down by Rockslide. The trick is going to be getting through the break without getting slammed against the rocks, so he swims slowly and lets the current do the work for him.

Frank's a strong swimmer, more than comfortable in the ocean, even in frigid water at night. He stays in the current, aims himself toward the lights of shore, and only starts swimming hard when he hears the waves breaking.

It's going to be tough, and he can't let himself be pulled south of Rockslide, because the next stop is Mexico. So he pulls himself out of the current, puts his head down, and starts doing a hard Australian crawl straight into the break. He feels a wave lift him and push him toward shore, which is a good thing, but then it starts to pick up speed and take him right toward the rocks, and there's nothing he can do about it except hope his luck holds out.

It does.

The wave breaks a good twenty yards from the rocks, and he manages to get to his feet and wade the rest of the way in. He gets down on all fours and crawls across the slippery rocks onto shore.

The air feels colder than the water, what with the wind and the rain, and he hurriedly wriggles out of the wet suit, dries off, and gets back into his clothes. Then he stuffs the wet suit into the bag and starts walking.

But not home.

Whoever tried to clip him is going to try again, going to *have* to try again, and his only advantage is Mouse Junior and his little friend running back and saying, inevitably, "Frankie Machine sleeps with the fishes."

Good, that will buy me a little time. A few hours, max, because when they don't get the phone call from Vena that "it's done," they're going to start wondering. If they have any brains—and you have to stop underestimating them—they're going to assume the worst.

Still, it gives me a narrow window of time to go off the radar.

Every prudent professional hit man has a spider hole, and Frank is nothing if not prudent. His is a vacant apartment on Narragansett Street, a little efficiency unit on the second floor of a house that's a ten-minute walk away. It has a separate entrance up a back stairway. He bought it twenty years ago, when property was still pretty cheap, put it up for rent, and never rented it. Only went there every few months to check up on it, and then only stayed a few minutes after making sure that he wasn't being followed.

No one else knows about the existence of this place—not Patty, not Donna, not Jill.

Not even Mike Pella.

He walks there and lets himself in.

First thing he does is take a shower.

He stands under the spray for a long time, shivering at first, until the hot water finally warms him up. It takes a while, because he's chilled to the bone. He reluctantly gets out, vigorously rubs himself dry, then puts on a heavy terry-cloth robe and walks back into the bedroom/living room/kitchen, where he opens up the bottom drawer of a dresser and takes out a heavy sweatshirt and sweatpants and puts them on. Then he goes into the closet and opens up a little safe bolted to the floor behind some coats and jackets.

Inside the safe is his "parachute pack"—an Arizona driver's license, an American Express Gold card and a Visa Gold card, all under the name Jerry Sabellico. Every month or so, he makes a phone purchase with cards to keep them current, and pays them with checks from his Sabellico account. There's also ten thousand in cash in used, mixed bills.

And a new, clean .38 Smith & Wesson with extra ammunition.

He reaches up to a trapdoor that opens to an attic crawl space. He feels around and quickly finds what he's looking for, a case that holds a Beretta SL-2 twelve-gauge pump shotgun with the barrel sawed off to fourteen inches.

Now what you need is sleep, he thinks.

A tired body and a fatigue-foggy head will get you killed. You need to think and act sharp, so the next thing is to get in bed and sleep. It's a matter of will, turning off the paranoia, thinking rationally, and knowing that you're safe here. An amateur would lie awake all night, starting at every noise, making up sounds when there aren't any.

He's hunted enough guys to know that their own heads can be their worst enemies. They start seeing things that aren't there, then, worse, not seeing things that are. They worry and worry, and chew on their own insides, until, when you do track them down, they're almost grateful. By this time, they've been killed so many times in their minds that the real thing is a relief.

So he gets into bed, closes his eyes, and is asleep in about ten seconds.

It isn't hard—he's exhausted.

He sleeps for eleven full hours and wakes up feeling rested, although his arms are a little sore from the long swim. He makes himself some coffee—just cheap grind from an automatic maker—and breakfasts on a couple of granola bars he stored away like a Mormon.

The apartment has one small window, facing west, and rain is pounding on the glass. Frank sits at the small, cheap table and starts to work on the problem.

Who wants me dead?

Mike, where are you? You could tell me what's going on.

But Mike isn't around—maybe Mike is dead, too, because he and Frank did a lot of work together. Together, they put a lot of guys in the dirt.

Frank starts at the beginning.

10

His first hit was on a guy who was already dead.

That was the weird thing about it. Well, the whole thing was weird, Frank thinks now, looking at the rain coming down outside.

The whole thing with Momo's wife.

Marie Anselmo was a hot little number.

That's what we would have called her back in 1963, Frank thinks. Nowadays the kids have shortened it to just "hottie," but the idea is the same.

Marie Anselmo was hot and she was little. Petite, but with a nice rack tightly packed in that blouse, and a pair of shapely legs that led Frank's nineteen-year-old eyes up to an ass that would give him an instant woody. Not that *that* was so tough, Frank remembers. When you were nineteen, anything would get you hard.

"I used to get a chubby riding to school in the morning," he once told Donna, "just bouncing in the car. For two years, I had an affair with a '57 Buick."

Yeah, but Marie Anselmo was no Buick. She was pure Thunderbird, with that body, and those dark eyes, and the bee-stung lips. And that voice, that smoky come-do-me voice that would drive Frank up the wall, even if she was just telling him where to turn.

Which was mostly all Marie ever said to Frank, whose job it was in those days to drive her around in Momo's car, Momo being too busy collecting the money he had out on the street or running his gambling wire to take his wife grocery shopping, or to the hairdresser's or the dentist's or wherever.

Marie did not like to stay home.

"I'm not one of your standard guinea wives," she said to Frank one day after he'd been chauffeuring her for a couple of months, "who's going to stay home, crank out babies, and make the pasta. I like to get out."

Frank didn't answer.

For one thing, he had a hard-on that could cut stone, so most of the blood in his body wasn't concentrated in the part responsible for speech. And two, he wanted to *keep* the blood in his body, which could be an issue if he started to discuss anything of a personal nature with a made man's wife.

That was not something that was done, even in the more than casual mob culture of San Diego, where there was barely a mob at all.

Instead, he said, "Are we going to Ralph's, Mrs. A.?"

He knew they were, although Marie wasn't dressed like most women dress when they are going to the supermarket. That day, Marie had on a tight dress with the top three buttons undone, and black stockings, and a string of pearls around her neck that drew your eye right to her cleavage. Like her cleavage couldn't have done that all on its own, Frank thought as he sneaked a glance and wondered if she was wearing a black bra under that dress. When he pulled into a parking spot in Ralph's lot and stopped the car, her skirt rode up as she got out and he got a peek at those white thighs against the black hose.

She pulled her skirt down and smiled at him.

"Watch for me," she ordered.

It's going to be a long struggle with Patty tonight in the Ocean Beach parking lot, that's for sure, he thought. He'd been dating Patty almost a year by then, and the most he could get was a little tit on the outside of her blouse if he pretended it was an accidental brush. Patty had a set on her, too, but her bra was built like a fort, and as for going *down*stairs, forget about it, it wasn't going to happen.

Patty was a good Italian girl, a good Catholic, so she'd steam up the windows French kissing with him because they'd been going steady a year, but that was it, even though she said she'd like to give him the hand job he'd been begging for.

"I got blue balls," he told her. "They hurt."

"When we're engaged," she told him, "I'll jerk you off."

But it's going to be a long night tonight, Frank thought as he watched Mrs. A.'s ass switch across the parking lot. How a guy as ugly as Momo Anselmo had nailed *that* was a question for the ages.

Momo was this skinny, kind of hunched-over guy with a face like a hound. So Marie sure as hell hadn't fallen for his looks. And it couldn't have been the money—Momo did well, but he didn't do *great*. He had a nice little house and all, and the required wise-guy Cadillac, and enough cash to flash around, but Momo wasn't no Johnny Roselli or even Jimmy Forliano. Momo was a big deal in San Diego, but everyone knew that San Diego was really run from L.A., and Momo had to kick up heavy to Jack Drina, even though the word was that the L.A. boss was dying of cancer.

But Frank liked Momo a lot, which is why he felt a little bad lusting after the man's wife. Momo was giving him his shot, letting him break in, even if it was as an errand boy, but that's how most guys broke in. So Frank didn't mind going out for the coffee and doughnuts, or the cigarettes, or washing Momo's Caddy, or even driving his wife to the supermarket. At least he didn't have to go in with her and push the cart around—even an apprentice wise guy wasn't expected to do that—so he got to hang out and wait in the car and listen to the radio. Even though Momo bitched that it ran down the battery, Momo didn't have to know about it.

Which beat the hell out of busting his ass working on the tuna boats, which was what he would have been doing if Momo hadn't given him a shot. That was what Frank's old man did, and what *his* old man had done, and what *his* old man had done. The Italians had come to San Diego and taken over the tuna-fishing business from the Chinese, and that was what most of them still did, and what Frank had done from the time he was big enough to shovel bait.

Out there on a tuna boat before the sun came up, cold and wet, ass-deep in a smelly bait pit, or, worse, cleaning out the scuppers. When he got bigger, he'd graduated to working the net, and then when his old man figured he could wield a knife without cutting his own hand off, he'd gotten to clean the fish, and when he complained about how disgusting and filthy it was, the old man had told him that was why he should finish high school.

So Frank did. He got his diploma, but then what was he supposed to do? His choices seemed to be the Marines or the tuna fleet. He didn't want to stay on the tuna boats or get his head shaved at boot camp. What he really wanted to do was hang out on the beach, surf, drive up and down the PCH, try to lose his cherry, and surf some more.

And why the hell not. That was what you did when you were a young guy in San Diego in those days. You surfed with your buddies, you cruised the strip, and you chased girls.

Just one of the guys trying to find a way to keep up the sweet life.

Which wasn't the tuna boat or the Marines.

It was Momo.

The old man didn't like it.

Of course he didn't. The old man was old-school. You get a job, you work hard, you get married, and you support your family, end of story. And even though there weren't a lot of wise guys in San Diego, the old man didn't especially like the ones who were there, Momo included.

"They give us a bad name," he said.

And that was about all he'd say, because what *could* he say? Frank knew full well why the old man got a fair price from the fish buyers, how his catch got unloaded while it was still fresh, and why the truckers took it straight to the markets. If it weren't for the Momos of the world, then the good, honest, hardworking civilians of the business community would have screwed the Italian fishermen like a two-dollar whore in a Tijuana donkey show. You ask what happened to the longshoremen in this town when they tried to get a decent wage and organize a union and they didn't have the wise guys backing them up. The cops beat them and shot them until blood ran down Twelfth Street like a river to the sea, that's what. And that didn't happen to the Italians, and it wasn't because they worked so hard (which they did) to support their families.

So when Frank started to spend less time on the boat, and didn't go into the Marines, but signed on with Momo instead, the old man griped a little bit but mostly kept his mouth shut. Frank was making money, he was paying room and board, and the old man didn't really want to know the details.

Actually, the details were pretty boring.

Until the thing happened with Momo's wife.

It started out okay.

Frank was hanging out one day when Momo came out and told him to wash the Caddy and wax it, 'cause they were going to the train station to pick up a special visitor.

"Who, the Pope?" Frank asked, because he thought he was a funny guy in those days.

"Better," Momo said. "The boss."

"DeSanto?"

Old Jack Drina had finally died and the new boss, Al DeSanto, had taken over in L.A.

"*Mr.* DeSanto to you," Momo said, "if you open your mouth at all, which you shouldn't unless he directly asks you something. But yeah, the new king is coming down to visit the provinces."

Frank wasn't quite sure what Momo meant by that, but he picked up this tone, and he wasn't sure what that was, either.

"Jesus, I'm gonna drive the boss?"

"You're going to wax the car for *me* to drive the boss," Momo said. "I'm gonna bring him to the restaurant; you're going to go pick up Marie, bring her over after."

After they've discussed business, Frank knew.

"And dress decent," Momo added, "not like a surf bum."

Frank dressed up. First he polished that car until it shined like a black diamond; then he went home, showered, scrubbed his skin until it hurt, shaved again, combed his hair, and changed into his one suit.

"Look at you," Marie said when she answered the door.

Look at me? Look at *you,* Frank thought. Her black cocktail dress was cut low, practically down to the nipple, her full breasts pushed up by what had to be a strapless bra. He couldn't help but stare at them.

"You like the dress, Frank?"

"It's pretty."

She laughed, then went to her dressing table, took a drag on her cigarette and another swallow of the martini that was sweating on the table. Something in her manner told Frank that it wasn't her first drink of the night. She wasn't drunk, but she wasn't exactly sober, either. She turned back to Frank and gave him the whole view, then patted her frosted hair to place it perfectly on her neck, picked up her little black bag, and said, "So you think they're done with their business now?"

"I don't know about that, Mrs. A."

"You can call me Marie."

"No, I can't."

She laughed again. "Do you have a girl, Frank?"

"Yes, Mrs. A."

"That's right," she said. "That little Garafalo girl. She's pretty."

"Thanks."

"*You* had nothing to do with it," she said. "Does she put out?"

Frank didn't know what to say. If a girl put out, you didn't tell, and if she didn't, you didn't tell that, either. Anyway, it wasn't any of Mrs. A.'s business. And why was she asking, anyway?

"We better get to the club, Mrs. A."

"There's no hurry, Frank."

Yes, there is, Frank thought.

"Can't a girl finish her drink?" she asked, setting those bee-stung lips into a pretty pout. She reached back and picked up her drink and sipped on it, never taking her eyes off his, and it was like she was giving him a blow job, which Frank had never had but which he'd heard about. In fact, this was just like a scene from one of those dirty books he'd read, except reading one of those books wouldn't get him killed and this could.

She finished her drink, looked kind of hard at him, then laughed again and said, "Okay. Let's go."

His hand was shaking as he opened the door.

She saw it and it seemed to make her a little happier.

They didn't talk on the drive to the club.

It was the most expensive supper club in town.

Momo wasn't going to take the L.A. boss anyplace but the best; plus, the club was owned by a friend of his. A friend of *theirs*. So they got a big table in the front, right by the stage, and most of the wise guys in San Diego were there with their wives, the girlfriends having been left in their apartments for the night with strict orders to wash their hair or something, but not to go anywhere *near* the club. This was a state visit, Frank knew, to establish that DeSanto was the new boss of Los Angeles, and therefore also the boss of San Diego.

Except DeSanto hadn't brought his wife. Neither had the handful of guys he'd brought down with him. Nick Locicero, DeSanto's underboss, was there, and Jackie Mizzelli and Jimmy Forliano, all very heavy guys sitting at that table, all guys who were going to expect to get laid that night. Frank was glad he didn't have *that* job, but he knew it was all set up, that a few of the cocktail waitresses had already agreed to go with these guys after the party but were supposed to stay away from the table in the meantime.

So was Frank. Not that he'd expected to be at the table. He knew he was about thirty-seven rungs down that ladder and his job was to hang around the edges of the room in case Momo looked up like he needed something.

Momo was sitting at the center of the table, next to DeSanto, of course.

Except DeSanto wasn't talking with Momo.

He was talking with Marie.

And saying something funny, too, because Marie was laughing real hard, and leaning way over and showing him a lot of tit.

DeSanto was looking, too, not even bothering to disguise it. And she was giving him lots of chances, leaning over so he could light her cigarette, so he could smell her perfume, leaning in real close, pretending she couldn't hear him over the music and the conversation.

Frank was watching this; he couldn't believe what he was seeing.

There were rules about wise guys and their women, different sets of rules for sisters, cousins, mistresses, and wives. You wouldn't treat a made guy's *gumar* the way DeSanto was acting toward Momo's *wife*. And if a guy's girlfriend flirted with another guy the way Mrs. A. was flirting with DeSanto, that girlfriend was letting herself in for a good beating when they got back to her place.

There are rules, Frank thought, even for a boss.

He had certain privileges, but this wasn't one of them.

So Frank was pissed off for Momo, and he also had to admit he was a little jealous. Shit, Frank thought, she was making a move on me two hours ago. Then he felt guilty thinking that about Momo's wife.

He watched her laugh again, her tits jiggling, then saw DeSanto lean into her neck and whisper something in her ear. Her eyes widened, and she smiled, then playfully slapped him on the cheek, and he laughed back.

DeSanto's not a *bad*-looking guy, Frank thought. He's no Tony Curtis, but he's no Momo, either. He wore glasses with thick black frames and had his graying hair Brylcreemed straight back, with a little widow's peak in the middle of his receding forehead, but he wasn't ugly. And he must be kind of charming, Frank thought, because he's sure as shit charming Mrs. A.

Momo didn't look so charmed.

He was steaming.

He wasn't stupid enough to show it, but by this time Frank knew Momo well enough; he could tell the man was pissed off. Frank could feel the tension coming from the whole table—all the guys were drinking a lot, laughing a little too loudly, and the wives—the wives were torqued off. It was hard to tell if they were angrier at DeSanto or Mrs. A., but their necks were stiff from not looking even as their eyes couldn't stay off the little scene. And they were leaning down and whispering to one another, the way wives do, and it didn't take any imagination to know what they were talking about.

When Momo got up to go to the men's room, one of the San Diego guys, Chris Panno, went with him. Frank waited until they went in; then he wandered down the corridor and stood outside.

"He's your boss."

"Boss or no boss, there are rules!" Momo said.

"Keep your voice down."

Momo lowered his voice a little, but Frank could still hear him say, "L.A. pisses on us. They piss all over us."

"If Bap was here . . . ," Frank heard someone say.

"Bap ain't here," Momo said. "Bap's inside."

Frank knew they were talking about Frank Baptista, who'd been the San Diego underboss until he got hit with a five-year rap for trying to bribe a judge. Frank had never met Bap, but he'd sure heard about him. Bap had been a legendary button man since the thirties. There was no telling how many guys Bap'd put in the dirt.

"Jack would not have allowed this," Momo was saying.

"Jack's dead and Bap's in the joint," Panno said. "Things are different now."

"Bap'll be out soon," Momo said.

"Not tonight he won't be," Chris Panno said.

"This isn't right," Momo said.

Then Frank saw Nick Locicero coming down the hall.

Shit, what to do?

He decided fast and walked into the men's room. The guys looked at him, like, What the fuck?

"Uhh . . . ," Frank said. He jerked his head toward the hallway. "Locicero."

The guys looked at him for a second, then got their faces on.

Locicero came in.

"What are we, broads?" he asked. "We all gotta go the little girls' room the same time?"

Everyone laughed.

Locicero looked at Frank. "Or is this the little *boys'* room?"

"I'm just going," Frank said.

"D'you come in to take a piss?" Momo asked Frank. "Take a piss."

Frank had a hard time with it. He unzipped, stood at the urinal, but nothing came out. He pretended it did, though, shook his dick off, put it back in. He was relieved to see that the men were all carefully washing their hands and paying no attention to him.

"Nice party," Locicero was saying.

"The boss seems to be having a good time," Momo said.

Locicero looked at him, trying to see if he was just busting balls or if he was serious. Then he said, "Yeah, I think so."

Frank just wanted to get out of there. He headed for the door.

"Frankie," Momo said.

"Yeah?"

"Wash your hands!" Momo said. "What are you, raised by wolves?"

Frank blushed as the men laughed. He stepped in, washed his hands, and managed to get to the door, when Momo said, "Kid, nobody else comes in here, okay?"

Jesus, Frank thought as he stood on guard in the hallway. What's going to happen in there? He half-expected to hear gunshots, but he only heard voices.

Nicky Locicero was saying, "Momo, we came down here to be nice."

"What's going on out there is *nice*?"

"You guys have been going your own way down here," Locicero said, "for too long. It's time you came back under control."

"When Jack—"

"Jack is gone," Locicero said. "The new guy out there wants you to understand that you are not your own family down here; you are just another L.A. crew, a hundred miles down the road, that's all. He wants your respect."

Chris Panno weighed in. "If he *wants* respect, Nick, he should *show* respect. What's going on out there is not right."

"I don't disagree," Locicero said.

A guy came down the hall to use the men's room.

"You can't go in there," Frank said, stepping in his way.

The guy was a civilian. He didn't get it. "What do you mean?"

"It's broken."

"All of it?"

"Yeah, all of it. I'll let you know, okay?"

The guy looked for a second like he might want to argue the point, but Frank was a big kid, with muscles showing beneath his jacket, so the guy turned around. Frank heard Locicero say, "Look, Momo, all respect, but your Mrs. has had a little too much to drink. Have your kid drive her home; then there's no problem."

"There's a *problem,* Nick," said Momo, "when this guy who wants respect treats our wives like whores!"

"What do you want me to say, Momo? He's the boss."

"There are rules," Momo said.

He came out of the men's room, grabbed Frank by the elbow, and said, "Mrs. A. is going home. You drive her."

Holy hell, Frank thought.

"Go tell the valet to get the car," Momo said.

Frank had to go through the main room to get outside. He looked up at the table and saw DeSanto whispering into Mrs. A.'s ear again, except now she wasn't laughing. And the boss's hands weren't on the table. Frank couldn't see them under the long white tablecloth, but he could guess where they were.

They were downstairs.

Five minutes later, Momo was pulling Mrs. A. out of the club. Frank got out and held the door open for her.

"You're such an asshole," she said to Momo.

"Stupid twat, get in the car."

He pushed her in. Frank closed the door.

"Take her home and stay with her till I get back," Momo told him.

Frank just hoped he'd get home *soon.* Marie didn't say a word on the drive home, not a word. She lit a cigarette and sat there puffing on it so the car filled with smoke. When he got to Momo's place, he jumped out and opened the car door for her and she walked pretty fast up to her own door and stood there impatiently while he fumbled with the key to the front door.

When he got it open, she said, "You don't have to come in, Frankie."

"Momo said I did."

She looked at him funny. "Then I guess you'd better."

Inside, she went straight to the bar and started making a Manhattan.

"Do you want one, Frankie?"

"I'm too young to drink." It'd be two more years before he could get a legal drink.

She smiled. "I'll bet you're not too young for *other* things, are you?"

"I don't know what you mean, Mrs. A."

But of course he did, and it scared the hell out of him. He was in a jam here—if he got up and left, which was what he wanted to do, he'd be in big trouble. But if he stayed here and Mrs. A. kept making moves on him, he'd be in bigger trouble.

He was working through this when she said, "Momo can't fuck me, you know."

Frank didn't know what to say. He'd never even heard a woman say *fuck,* never mind what Mrs. A. was telling him.

"He can fuck every cheap whore in San Diego and Tijuana," she continued, "but he can't fuck his wife. What do you think of that?"

Just *hearing* this could get me killed—that's what Frank thought of that. If Momo found out that I know this, he'd clip me so I couldn't tell anyone else. Which Momo really doesn't have to worry about, because I'm never going to say this even to myself. Doesn't matter, though. If Momo knew that *I* knew that he wasn't taking care of business with his wife, he'd kill me just because he couldn't look me in the eye.

"A woman has needs," Marie was saying. "Do you know what I mean, Frankie?"

"I guess so."

Patty didn't seem to have them.

"You guess so." Now she sounded angry.

Frank figured she couldn't be too angry, though, because she started to slide her dress off her left shoulder.

"Mrs. A. . . ."

"'Mrs. A.,'" she mimicked. "I know you've been looking at my tits all night, Frankie. They're nice, aren't they? You should feel them."

"I'm leaving, Mrs. A."

"But Momo told you to stay."

"I'm leaving anyway, Mrs. A.," he said. Now he could see the top of her breast in the black brassiere. It was round and white and beautiful, but what he reached for was the doorknob, thinking, You screw a made man's wife, what they do is they cut your balls off and make you eat them. That's *before* they kill you.

Those were the rules.

"What's the matter, Frankie?" she asked. "Are you a homo?"

"No."

"You have to be," Mrs. A. said. "I think you're a homo."

"I'm not."

"Are you afraid, Frankie, is that it?" she asked. "He won't be home for hours. You know how these things go. He's probably with some whore right now."

"I'm not scared."

Her face got softer now. "Are you a virgin, Frankie? Is that it? Oh, baby, there's nothing to be afraid of. I'll make you feel so good. I'll show you everything. I'll show you how to please me, don't worry."

"It's not that. It's—"

"You don't think I'm pretty?" she asked, her voice getting an edge. "What, you think I'm too old for you?"

"You're very pretty, Mrs. A.," Frank said. "But I gotta go."

He was turning the doorknob as she said, "If you leave, I'll tell him you did it. I'm in for a beating, anyway, so I'll just tell him that you fucked me until I screamed. I'll tell him you screwed me silly."

Frank remembered it, what, forty years later, how he was standing there with his hand on the doorknob and his chin on his chest, thinking, What's this drunken broad saying? That if I don't screw her, she's going to tell her husband that I did?

But if I do screw her . . .

You're dead anyway, he thought.

Frank felt the panic welling up in his chest as he looked at that hot little number Marie Anselmo standing there with her little black dress half off, holding a lipstick-smudged Manhattan glass up to her bee-stung lips, her perfume swirling around him like a sexy, deadly cloud.

What saved him was the door opening.

She turned from him and got her dress back on just as Momo came into the room.

He didn't look so good.

They had beaten the shit out of him.

Nicky Locicero shoved him into the room and told him to sit down on the couch. Momo did it because Locicero had a .38 in his hand. Locicero looked at Frank and said, "Get some ice for your boss."

Frank stepped over to the ice bucket at the bar.

"Ice *cubes,*" Locicero said, "from the *freezer,* dipshit. In the kitchen."

Frank hustled into the kitchen, got a tray out of the freezer, and cracked a few cubes into the sink. Then he found a dish towel in a drawer, put the ice in the towel, and wrapped it up. When he got back into the living room, Al DeSanto was there. He had a real smirk on his goofy-looking face.

Marie wasn't smiling. She just stood there like she was a piece of ice herself. Frozen, stone-cold sober now.

Frank sat next to Momo on the couch and held the ice up to his cut, swollen eye.

"He can do it himself," Locicero said.

Frank heard him but didn't listen. He kept holding the cloth up to Momo's eye. A trickle of blood ran down the towel, and Frank twisted it to keep the blood from getting on the sofa.

"We have some unfinished business," DeSanto said to Marie.

"No, we don't," Marie said.

"I disagree," DeSanto said. "You don't play with a man like that, then leave him high and dry. It isn't nice."

He grabbed her wrist. "Where's the bedroom?"

She didn't answer. He slapped her across the face. Momo started to get up, but Locicero pointed the gun at his face and Momo sat back down.

"I asked you a question," DeSanto said to Marie, his hand cocked again.

She pointed to a door off the living room.

"That's better," DeSanto said. He turned to Momo. "I'm just going to go give your wife what she wants, *paisan.* You don't mind, do you?"

Locicero, leering, stuck the pistol in Momo's temple.

Momo shook his head.

Frank could see him trembling.

"Come on, honey," De Santo said. He walked her to the bedroom door and pushed her in. He went in himself, started to shut the door, then changed his mind and left it ajar.

Frank saw him toss Marie face-first onto the bed. Saw him grab her by the neck with one hand and rip the dress down with the other. Saw her kneeling on the bed in her black lingerie as DeSanto pulled her panties down and unzipped his fly. The guy was already hard and he shoved himself into her.

Frank heard her grunt, saw her body quiver under DeSanto's weight.

"You had it coming, Momo," Locicero said. "You ran your mouth."

Momo didn't say anything, just put his head in his hands. Bubbles of snot and blood ran down from his nose. Locicero put the pistol barrel under Momo's chin and lifted his face so he had to look.

DeSanto had left the door open so that Momo had to see him pulling Marie's hair back and riding her hard. Frank saw it, too. Saw Marie's face, her lipstick smudged, her mouth twisted into an expression Frank hadn't seen before. DeSanto was pulling her hair with one hand and mauling her breasts with the other. He grunted with effort and his glasses were askew on his face as his sweat made them slide down his nose.

"This is what you wanted, isn't it, bitch?" DeSanto asked. "Say it."

He yanked her head up.

She murmured, "Yes."

"What?"

"Yes!"

"Say, 'Fuck me, Al.'"

"Fuck me, Al!" Marie cried.

"Say *please*. 'Please, fuck me, Al.'"

"Please fuck me, Al."

"That's better."

Frank saw him push her face into the mattress and lift her ass up so he could drive into her harder. He was really piling into her, and Frank heard Marie start making noises. He couldn't tell if it was pleasure or pain or both, but Marie started moaning and then yelling, and Frank saw her small fingers grip the bedspread as she screamed.

"Jesus, Momo," Locicero said, "your wife is a hot little number."

DeSanto finished and pulled out. He wiped himself off on her dress, zipped his fly back up, and got off the bed. He looked down at Marie, still lying facedown on the bed, her chest heaving. "Anytime you want more of that, baby," he said, "you have my number."

He walked back into the living room and asked, "Did you hear the bitch come?"

Locicero said, "Hell yes."

"Did *you* hear her, Momo?"

Locicero nudged Momo with the gun.

"I heard," Momo said. Then he asked, "Why don't you just shoot me?"

Frank felt like he was going to throw up.

DeSanto looked down at Momo. "I don't shoot you, Momo, because I want you to keep earning. What I *don't* want is any more of this San Diego bullshit. What's mine is mine and what's *yours* is mine. *Capisce?*"

"*Capisce.*"

"Good."

Frank was just staring at him. DeSanto noticed and asked, "What, kid, you got a problem?"

Frank shook his head.

"I didn't think so." DeSanto looked back toward the bedroom. "You want sloppy seconds, Momo, I don't mind."

He and Locicero laughed and then walked out.

Frank sat there in shock.

Momo got up, opened a dresser drawer, pulled out a wicked-looking little .25 revolver, and started for the door.

Frank heard himself say, "They'll kill you, Momo!"

"I don't give a damn."

Then Marie was standing in the hallway, leaning against the door-jamb, her dress still pulled down, her makeup smeared over her face like a crazy clown, her hair a tangled mess. "You're not a man," she said, "letting him do that to me."

"You liked it, you cunt."

"How could you—"

"He made you come."

He lifted the pistol.

"Momo, no!" Frank yelled.

Momo said, "She *came* for him."

He shot her.

"Christ!" Frank screamed as Marie's body twirled and then corkscrewed to the floor. He wanted to lunge and take the gun away, but he was too scared, and then Momo took a step away from him, put the gun to his own head, and said, "I loved her, Frankie."

Frank looked at those sad hound eyes for a second; then Momo pulled the trigger.

His blood spattered all over Kennedy's smiling face.

Funny thing, Frank thinks now, that's what I remember more than anything—that blood on John Kennedy. Later, when Kennedy was killed, it didn't seem like such a surprise to him. It was like he'd seen it already.

Marie Anselmo survived—it turned out that Momo had hit her in the hip. She rolled around on the floor screaming while Frank frantically called the police. The ambulance took Marie away and the detectives took Frank. He told them most of what he'd seen—that is, that Momo had shot his wife and then himself. He left out any mention of Al DeSanto or Nicky Locicero, and was relieved to hear later that Marie had also kept her mouth shut about the rape. And if the San Diego cops were busted up over Momo's suicide, they kept it hidden pretty well, unless open laughter was what they used to suppress their grief.

Marie spent weeks in the hospital, and had a barely detectable limp after that, but she lived. Out of respect for Momo, Frank used to deliver groceries to the house, and when she recovered enough, he still used to drive her to the supermarket.

But after that, Frank was disillusioned. All the stuff Momo had taught him about "this thing of ours"—the code, the rules, the honor, the "family"—was straight-up bullshit. He'd seen their fucking honor that night at Momo's house.

He went back to working on the tuna boats.

And that probably would have been my life, he thinks now, looking out the window at the gray ocean and the whitecaps, except that, six months later, who should show up but Frank Baptista.

11

Bap came on the dock one night when Frank had just finished squaring the deck away and was headed for a shower and a night of struggling against Patty's virtue. You didn't see a lot of guys in suits and ties on the dock, so Frank lamped Bap right away as something different, but he didn't know who he was.

Except the guy seemed to know Frank.

"Are you Frankie Machianno?" Bap asked.

"Yeah." Frank was afraid now that the guy was a cop and maybe Marie had decided she wanted to press charges against DeSanto after all.

The guy stuck out his hand. "We got the same first name. I'm Frank Baptista."

Frank was shocked. This guy sure didn't look like a famous button man—round, chubby, soft body, meaty jowls, bottle-thick glasses over owl eyes. Balding, with a greasy comb-over. Bap made Momo look like Troy Donohue.

This is the guy, Frank wondered, that killed Lew Brunemann, "Russian Louie" Strauss, and Red Sagunda when the Cleveland mob tried to move on San Diego? This is the guy who was boss here since the forties, until he went into the can for bribery?

"Can I buy you a drink?" Bap asked. "A cup of coffee?"

I should have said no, Frank thinks now. I should have said, No offense, Mr. Baptista, but I'm out of that now. I seen enough. But I didn't. I went for a beer with the Bap.

Frank followed him up to Pacific Beach to one of the joints near Crystal Pier. They got a booth in the back, where Bap ordered a coffee for himself and a beer for Frank. Bap spent a long time stirring milk and sugar into his coffee, and then he asked, "Did you like Momo?"

"Yeah, I did."

"I hear you still bring Marie her groceries," Bap said. "That speaks well of you. It shows you have respect."

"Momo was always good to me."

Bap took this in, then made small talk, but it was clear to Frank that the former boss wasn't really interested in chitchat, so Frank finished his beer and said he had a date. Bap thanked him for his time and said it was nice meeting him. Frank figured that was that, but about a month later, Bap showed up at the dock again and said, "Come on, let's go for a drive."

Frank followed him to a Cadillac parked on Ocean Avenue. Bap tossed him the keys and sat in the front passenger seat. Frank got behind the wheel and started the engine. "Where do you want to go?"

"Don't matter. Just drive."

Frank pulled onto Sunset Drive and headed south, cruising alongside his surfing spots.

"You drive good," Bap said. "You're my driver now."

And that was it. Frank went to work for Bap. He drove the man everywhere—to the grocery store, the barber's, to clubs, to Momo's old house to visit Marie, to the track when the horses were running at Del Mar. He took Bap to see all the bookies, the loan sharks, the hustlers in San Diego.

DeSanto didn't like it.

The L.A. boss knew that Bap was out, that he was going to want his old territory back. He was going to want a piece of the money on the street, the gambling, anything else they had going in San Diego, and DeSanto didn't want to give him any of that. Bap was a big name, a guy with ambitions, and L.A. didn't want a strong guy down in San Diego wanting to go his own way again.

"We just got those Indians back on the reservation," DeSanto told Nicky Locicero. "Last thing we need is a guy who thinks he's a chief running around down there."

So he tried to throw Bap a few crumbs off the table, and Bap wasn't shy about expressing his dissatisfaction.

That was always Bap's problem: He could never swallow a resentment. It always came out his mouth. At the end of the day, it's what killed him. Frank could still remember Bap mouthing off back in '64, right at the Del Mar track, with half the wise guys in Southern California within earshot. "What am I, a dog? He throws me a few *bones?*"

Frank was running Bap's bets to the window, and Bap wasn't doing so good. No wonder he needs money, Frank thought; he has a fondness for slow horses. Bap threw another handful of losing tickets at his feet and said, "I'm in the joint for three years, not earning. This guy has to let me eat, for Chrissakes."

He said this right in front of three L.A. guys down for the race season, so he had to know it was going straight back to DeSanto as soon as they could get to a telephone. And the L.A. boss wasn't going to be happy hearing this shit from Bap.

Especially what Bap said next: "Maybe I should just start my own fucking thing down here."

Which was Bap just *begging* to get clipped.

DeSanto wasn't long in honoring the request. He set up a meet at which Bap would be killed.

And his driver with him, if it fell that way.

They met in a vacant lot up in Orange County.

In those days, Frank remembers, Orange County was mostly just that, orange groves with Disneyland thrown on top. Memory is a funny thing, because he can still smell the oranges from that night.

Anyway, he pulled into this red dirt lot alongside an orange grove on an isolated road. DeSanto and Locicero were already there, Locicero behind the wheel of DeSanto's black Cadillac, the boss sitting behind him in the backseat.

"Don't worry," Bap said when he saw the scared look in Frank's eyes. "Nick has guaranteed my safety."

Bap got out and walked over to the Cadillac. Locicero got out, snubbed his cigarette out in the dirt, and walked over to him. Bap raised his arms and Locicero patted him down, then nodded, and Bap got into the back with DeSanto.

Locicero leaned back against the hood, keeping an eye on Frank. Nodded at Frank and smiled.

As he did, another car pulled into the lot, right in back of Frank, trapping him. Frank started to sweat. He looked in the rearview mirror and saw that there were two guys in the front of the Lincoln. One he recognized as Jimmy Forliano; the other he didn't know.

It was a younger guy, about his own age. But this guy had a confident look that made him seem older.

Then Frank saw what looked like lightning in the back of DeSanto's Caddy, and it took him a second to realize that they were muzzle flashes.

Locicero smiled and lit another cigarette.

You were so scared, Frank remembers now. You tried to start the car, but your hand was shaking on the key and there was no place to go anyway, so you started to open the door and try to make a run for it, but Forliano was already at the window.

"Easy, kid."

"I didn't see anything."

Forliano just smiled.

And then the back door of the Caddy opened up and—

Bap got out. Waved his hand at you to come over.

Forliano opened the door for you and you walked over to Bap, your legs shaking, your knees rattling, and then Bap handed you the gun.

"Momo was your friend, wasn't he?"

"Yeah . . ."

"He was my friend, too," Bap said. "This cocksucker had to go."

Hitting a *boss*? Frank wanted to pay DeSanto back for Momo, too, but hitting a boss was suicide. Even if you did manage to get to him, you'd have every family in the country after you. And maybe Bap used to be the boss in San Diego, but he was demoted to a common soldier when he went into the can.

"You gotta put a couple into him," Bap was saying.

"That's okay," Frank said.

"No, you gotta," Bap said, "so you can't be a witness. This boat, we got to be in together."

He walked Frank over to the other side of the Caddy and opened the door. De Santo's body, with two holes in the head, toppled halfway out. His glasses slid down his nose and dropped in the dirt.

"Put two in his chest," Bap said.

Frank hesitated.

"I like you, kid," Bap said. "I don't want to have to leave you in this field with him."

Bap walked away. Frank knew he was listening for the shots, waiting for the flashes. He tried to lift the gun and shoot, but he just couldn't do it. Then he heard someone come up behind him.

"Your first one?"

It was the young guy from the car parked behind him. Jet-black hair, medium height, wide shoulders on an otherwise-thin frame.

"Yeah," Frank said.

"I'll help you," the guy said. "It's easier than you think."

The guy helped him aim the gun at DeSanto's body.

"Now just pull the trigger."

Frank did. His hand was shaking, but he couldn't miss at that range.

The body jolted with each shot, though. Then it slid down the open door and onto the dirt, raising a little cloud of dust when it hit. The guy beside Frank took his own gun out and put two more into DeSanto's corpse.

"Now," the guy said, "we're in it together. You and me."

Bap walked back over and pissed on the body.

This was years before all the DNA stuff, so nobody cared in those days. Bap just whipped his thing out and pissed into DeSanto's gaping mouth.

"This is for Marie," he said. He finished, zipped up, and then said to Frank, "Drive me home."

Frank sort of shuffled back to the car. Forliano stopped him and took the gun out of his hand. "We'll take care of this."

"Okay."

"You did good, kid," Forliano said. "You're all right."

The younger guy was standing there, too, smiling at Frank like he was in on some kind of funny practical joke. "Don't worry about it," he said. "You did fine."

He had an East Coast accent.

"Thanks," Frank said. "You know, for helping me out there."

"Forget about it." The guy offered his hand. "Mike Pella."

"Frank Machianno."

They shook hands.

Locicero got into the car with Forliano and Pella and they took off. Frank got behind the wheel and this time managed to turn the key in the ignition. The wheels spun in the dirt as he hit the gas.

"Drive slow, not fast," Bap instructed him. "Always drive the speed limit leaving a job. Last thing you want is to get stopped for speeding; you get a cop putting you near the scene. Just get out on the highway, get in the flow of traffic."

Frank did what he was told. They were a good twenty miles south on the 5 before Bap said, "I been in Chicago."

Okay, Frank thought.

"You don't get what I mean," Bap said. "I mean I talked with certain people there."

Which did nothing to enlighten Frank.

"L.A. runs San Diego," Bap explained, "but L.A. don't run L.A. L.A.'s never really been its own thing. Used to be it answered to New York, to the Jews, Siegel and Lansky. Now L.A. can't shake its own dick after it takes a piss, it don't put a call in to Chicago first."

"I didn't know that."

"Because you ain't supposed to," Bap said. "L.A. don't want San Diego guys crying to Chicago, they got a problem with L.A."

But that's what you just did, Frank thought.

"I go back," Bap said, like he read Frank's mind. "I was doing work for Chicago when Al DeSanto was getting Jack Drina his coffees. I talked with certain people there, and they didn't like the cocksucker, either."

"They gave the okay?" Frank was shocked.

"That ain't the way it works, Frankie," Bap said. "They don't say yes. They just don't say no. That means, something happens to the guy in L.A., they ain't gonna do nothing about it. Makes you feel any better, Detroit said the same thing."

Now Frank got it. "And Locicero's the new boss."

"Everyone has his price, Frankie," Bap said. "Never forget that."

Frank didn't.

So that was that, Frank remembers now.

Locicero became the boss, Bap got San Diego, although as a captain in the L.A. family.

Except that wasn't quite it, was it?

There was that afternoon you picked up Marie Anselmo's grocery order and brought it to the house and she answered the door but wouldn't let you bring the bags in like usual, but you could see through the open door.

Bap, in the hallway, pulling his pants on.

He married Marie six months later.

After that, no one ever whispered a word about what happened that night at Momo's with DeSanto.

Frank sure as hell didn't.

He'd decided to go straight. So one day, he drove to Oceanside, saw the recruiter, and was in the Marines about five minutes after that.

Like the Surfaris song that was so popular then:

> *Surfer Joe joined Uncle Sam's Marines today*
> *They stationed him at Pendleton, not far away . . .*

It's funny, Frank thinks now.

I got my training from the federal government.

12

Frank turns from the window, gets on the phone, and calls the bait shop.

The kid Abe answers on the first ring.

"Frank, you okay? I came in and the shop was closed."

"You know what, Abe?" Frank says. "Let's shut it down for a few days."

There's an incredulous silence, then: "Shut it down?"

"Yeah, with the storm, we're not going to do much business anyway," Frank says. "Let's take a few days off. I'll call you when I want to reopen. Why don't you go down to Tijuana, see your mom and dad or something."

Abe doesn't need to be asked twice.

Patty's going to be a tougher nut.

"Patty, it's Frank."

"I recognized the voice."

"Patty, I was thinking, you haven't been to see your sister in a while, have you?" Patty's sister Celia and her husband moved up to Seattle ten years ago, following the aerospace industry. They have a house—where is it? Bellingham, maybe?

"Frank, you *hate* my sister."

"Go up and visit her, Patty," Frank says. "Go today."

She hears the tone in his voice. "Are you all right, Frank?"

"I'm fine," Frank says. "I just need you to go."

"Frank—"

"I'm fine," Frank repeats.

"How long will I be gone?"

"I don't know yet," Frank says. "Not long. Go upstairs and pack."

"I *am* upstairs."

"Then pack."

"Frank?"

"What?" he snaps. He doesn't want to be on the phone too long, in case they have her line tapped.

"Take care of yourself, okay?" she says. "I love you."

"I love you, too."

The next call is to Donna.

"Nonfat latte, two shots of espresso," she says when she hears his voice. "Please?"

"Now listen," Frank says, "and, just for *once,* do exactly what I tell you without argument or discussion. Close the shop, go home and pack, get on a plane to Hawaii. The Big Island, Kauai, doesn't matter, just go. Today. Take your cell phone. Don't tell anyone where you're going, and don't come back until you've heard from me. Not a *message* from me, from me *personally*. Will you do that?"

There's a silence as she takes all this in; then she simply says, "Yes."

"Good. Thank you. I love you."

"I love you, too," she says. "Will I see you again?"

"Absolutely."

Now they've got *me* saying it, he thinks.

He calls Jill and gets her answering machine: *Hi, I'm off skiing in Big Bear. Aren't you jealous? Leave a message and I'll call you back.* He tries her cell and gets pretty much the same message. Oh well, he thinks, she's safe in Big Bear—even if "they," whoever they are, want to try to get her, they can't track her down there.

So the people I love are safe.

Which is a good thing on its own, and also gives me freedom of movement.

And it's time to move.

He packs the shotgun and some clothes into a gym bag, straps on a shoulder holster for the .38, then slips into a raincoat and heads out the door. He takes a taxi downtown, then goes to Hertz and uses his Sabellico identification to rent a nondescript Ford Taurus.

He heads north on the Pacific Coast Highway.

Toward L.A.

13

Dave Hansen walks out onto the beach.

The wet sand looks like dark, shiny marble and the cold rain pelts him in the face. Two thousand miles of coastline, he thinks, and the floater had to wash up on federal land, in weather like this. He's at the edge of America, literally. Point Loma is the last stop in the continental USA, the end of the line.

The floater just made it.

A few feet the other way and the body would have been a Mexican problem.

A bunch of sailors from the Coast Guard station and a few San Diego cops are gathered around the body.

"We didn't touch it," the police sergeant tells Dave. "This is your jurisdiction."

He sounds pleased as punch.

"Thanks," Dave says.

Actually, the San Diego cops like Hansen. He has a light touch, for a fed. The sergeant says, "We haven't had any missing persons report. Usually do in a drowning. I checked with Coast Guard, too. Nada."

"He didn't drown," Dave says. "He's not blue."

The skin of drowning victims, even if they've been in the water for only a few minutes, turns a ghastly blue. No one who's seen it ever forgets it. Dave squats down by the body. He opens up the guy's jacket and sees the large entrance wound right where the guy's heart used to be. He keeps looking and finds the other entrance wound in the stomach.

Whoever killed the John Doe shot him in the gut, then pressed the gun against his chest and finished him off. Even after an unknown number of hours in the water, the powder burns on his clothes are unmistakable.

"Probably a dope run gone wrong," the sergeant said.

"Probably," Dave says. He keeps looking through the guy's clothes. The shooter also removed John Doe's ID. No wallet, no watch, no ring, nothing. Dave looks closely at the victim's face, or what's left of it after the fish pecked at the eyes. He doesn't recognize him, didn't expect to, but there's something vaguely familiar about him.

A faint memory, or an old dream, washed up onshore like a piece of driftwood.

It's weird.

But it's been a weird day, Dave thinks. Must be the weather; these high-pressure fronts seem to make everything and everybody a little crazy. People do odd things that they wouldn't otherwise do.

Frank Machianno, for instance.

Frank's at the bait shop every morning like clockwork for as long as Dave can remember, and then today he doesn't show up. And Frank, who's been a regular at the Gentlemen's Hour for longer than Dave has, is a no-show for the best waves of the year.

Dave figured he was sick, and called the house to bust his chops about the great waves he missed, but no answer. Tried Frank on his cell, same thing. So he went back to the bait shop, only to find the kid Abe closing it up.

"Frank said to," Abe told him. "Said take a few days off."

"*Frank* said take a few days off."

"What *I* thought," Abe said. "Told me to go home for a while."

"Where's home?"

Abe pointed south. "TJ."

Like, where else?

So Dave took a drive over to Frank's house. His van and his Mercedes in the garage, the house all locked up, no Frank.

So it's been a strange day.

A murdered body that by all the rules of normal tide and current should have drifted down the Baja coast manages instead to snag itself up on the last tip of America.

When Dave first heard they had a floater, he was afraid it was Tony Palumbo. The star witness in G-Sting has been undercover for years as a bouncer at Hunnybear's, and he was supposed to meet with Dave earlier that morning.

He didn't show up.

He wasn't anywhere to be seen, and a four-hundred-pound man is hard to miss.

So Tony Palumbo is 441.

And Frank goes off the radar.

14

James "Jimmy the Kid" Giacamone walks into the bar of the Bloom-field Hills Country Club in suburban Detroit and looks for his father. He spots Vito William Giacamone, aka "Billy Jacks," sitting at a banquette by the window, sadly contemplating the snow-covered eighteenth green.

Billy Jacks turns and looks at his son. The kid comes to the country club dressed in baggy pants and an old sweatshirt with the hood up. Like one of them rappers—what's the white one's name, the local kid? . . . Some kind of candy . . . M&M's.

His son thinks he's M&M's.

Then again, Billy thinks, the kid just did a hard stint—five years for extortion. And the boy has done some other work that, thank Saint Anthony, the feds didn't make him for. The boy may look like a clown, but he's a good worker.

And he's back with me, so let him look like what he wants. This life of ours, you never know how much time you have with your kids, so why bust balls?

Jimmy slips into the booth beside him and signals the bartender to bring him his usual.

"It's gonna be months," Billy says, "before we can get out there."

Jimmy doesn't care. Golf is for old guys.

A waiter sets a vodka and tonic in front of Jimmy and walks away.

"You heard from Vince?" Billy asks.

Jimmy shakes his head. "B Company ain't comin' back."

Which is what happens, Jimmy thinks, when you send a guy like Vince against a legend like Frankie Machine.

Billy accepts the verdict. What choice does he have? If Vince was alive, he would have checked in. He hasn't, and the silence can only mean one thing—Vince Vena better hope he was current with his Acts of Contrition.

Fuckin' shame about Vince, though. After a life of service, the guy finally makes it to the ruling council of the Combination and then gets himself whacked just a few weeks later. Then again, it means there's going to be a vacancy on the council.

Jimmy sits there listening to his father's brain grinding away on overtime. He can see the old man working through the stages of grief. First there's acceptance: Vince is dead. Then there's anger: Fuck, Vince is dead! Then there's ambition: Vince is dead and someone's going to get his seat at the table.

They're like hyenas, these old guys, thinks Jimmy, who watched a lot of shows on Animal Planet when he was in the joint. They run together, they hunt in packs, they share the kill, but one of them goes down, the rest will eat his bones and suck the marrow.

And Vince's bones have some juicy marrow in them.

There's only two street bosses, Jimmy thinks, my dad and old Tony Corrado, so one of them is going to move up. And if Dad can rescue this San Diego deal, it's going to be him.

"They should have sent *me*," Jimmy says.

"You asked," Billy says.

Jimmy shrugs. It's true, he made a big play with Jack Tominello, but the head of the council, the real boss, agreed that it should be Vince. After all, San Diego was going to be Vince's territory, so he should take care of his own business.

Except he couldn't.

"Now what?" Billy asks.

He's come to that age when he's asking advice from his own kid. But youth must be served, and Jimmy the Kid is an up-and-comer, at only twenty-seven years of age the Combination's biggest earner, and there's a seat practically reserved for him at the council table.

In his turn, in his time. And the first step would be I move up to the council; then Jimmy gets my street-boss slot.

"Now what?" Jimmy asks. "I kill Frankie Machine, that's what."

Billy Jacks shakes his head.

"Dad," Jimmy says, "we can't let this guy kill a member of the ruling council and walk away. Besides, we promised certain people. . . ."

"I know what we promised," Billy says. He looks off again at the snow and then gets mad again about Vince.

"A bunch of California beach bums," Jimmy says.

"Let me remind you," Billy says, "one of those 'beach bums' killed Vince Vena."

"You think I can't handle the guy?"

Frank Machianno, Frankie fucking Machine, Jimmy thinks. The guy has to be on the wrong side of sixty. He might be a legend and all that, but a bunch of old war stories don't make the man bulletproof.

Jimmy likes the fact that Frankie Machine is a legend.

Killing a legend makes *you* a legend.

You ain't the man until you beat the man who *was* the man.

That's what his uncle taught him.

Tony Jacks was a *man.* Uncle Tony made his bones the old way, chased the old Jewish Navy out of Detroit, then was a freaking warrior in the long war between the east and west sides that finally settled into the Combination. It was Tony Jacks who brought Hoffa into the fold, and Tony Jacks who finally, reluctantly, gave the word to have him clipped.

But now Uncle Tony is retired, ill, living out his last days in God's Waiting Room in West Palm.

That's the problem with this thing of ours these days, not enough *men* like Uncle Tony. Jimmy loves his father, but the old man is like most of the old men these days—worn out, tired, and reluctant to pull the trigger. It took generations to build this thing of ours, and now the old men are just giving it away to the moolies and the Jamaicans and the Russians.

Or beach bums out on the West Coast.

We're just soft these days.

But Jimmy the Kid is a throwback. He's old-school—he ain't afraid to pull the trigger. He figures it's time for the new generation to take over and restore their thing.

And the best way to move up and do that is to *step* up, Jimmy thinks.

Take out a legend like Frankie Machine.

Let them know there's a new kid in town.

15

Dave Hansen walks into Callahan's.

The popular bar is in the heart of the Gaslamp District in downtown San Diego. Once a rough neighborhood of SRO hotels, strip clubs, and porno shops, the area has become a tourist attraction of faux seediness.

Callahan's has made a lot of money in the transition.

Dave Hansen is about as welcome at Callahan's as a cold sore on a lip.

Two wise guys make him the second he walks in, and they shuffle quickly to the back room, where Teddy Migliore keeps his office. Young Teddy's mob genealogy couldn't be more solid—he's old Joe Migliore's son and Paul Moretti's grandson. Teddy did a pop for loan-sharking a few years ago, but has kept his nose clean until recently.

Until Operation G-Sting started to bring up some troublesome connections. Like the fact that Teddy is the silent owner of Hunnybear's and several other strip clubs in the area. Like the fact that John Heaney is a night manager at Hunnybear's.

Teddy comes out of the office.

"My lawyer will be here in five minutes," he says.

"I'll be gone by then," Dave tells him.

"Can you make it four?"

"Trust me," Dave says. "I won't spend a second longer in this rat hole than I have to."

"Good," Teddy says. "What do you want? I'm sick to death of this FBI harassment just because I have an Italian surname and I'm a Migliore."

"Tony Palumbo is missing," Dave says.

He watches for Teddy's reaction.

Teddy smiles. "Follow a trail of Twinkie wrappers, you should find him."

"Did you kill him?"

"You're kind of jumping to conclusions there, aren't you?" Teddy asks. "One, that he's dead; two, that I'd *want* him dead; three, that even if I *did* want him dead, I would take matters into my own hands."

Dave steps up to him.

Teddy's two boys start to move in, until Dave says, "Yeah, why don't you? I'm in an ugly mood and I haven't gotten my exercise today."

The FBI agent is six four and *cut*.

They back off.

Dave gets right in Teddy's face.

"If I find out you did him," Dave says, "I'll be back. And I'll make Ruby Ridge and Waco look like SpongeBob SquarePants."

"Are you threatening me?" Teddy asks.

"Goddamn right."

"I'll sue your ass off."

"Your *estate* will sue my ass off," Dave says. He turns to walk out.

"You're looking at the wrong people," Teddy says to his back. "You might want to be looking for Frank Machianno."

Dave turns around.

"Your surfing buddy," Teddy adds.

Frankie Machine.

16

Jimmy the Kid rents a car at the airport and drives out to his uncle's place in West Palm.

It's nice to be in Florida. Nice to be cruising in a convertible, getting some sun. Jimmy runs a hand through his dyed-blond hair. He likes his new look—bright blond, almost a buzz cut.

Nice, too, to show off the tatts in short-sleeve weather.

Got him some of those Chinese symbols—"Strength," "Courage," "Loyalty." Got him a big wrecking ball on his right forearm, about to swing down on some geek in an old Caddy.

"The Wrecking Crew."

Nice.

Tony's bungalow is sweltering. It's a hot day anyway, and Jimmy swears the old man has the freaking heat turned on in the house. He glances at the thermostat and it reads 85.

And Uncle Tony has a sweater on.

It's his circulation, Jimmy thinks. The blood just isn't moving. And old men get cold.

Jimmy hugs his uncle and kisses him on both cheeks. The skin feels like parchment paper on his lips.

Tony Jacks is glad to see his nephew.

"Come, sit."

They go into the living room. Jimmy sits down on the sofa and his legs stick to the plastic covering in the heat.

"You want something to drink?" Uncle Tony asks. "I'll call the girl."

"I'm good."

They make the requisite small talk for a few minutes; then Tony Jacks gets to the point. "What brings you here, Jimmy?"

"This mess in San Diego."

Tony Jacks shakes his head. "They'd asked me, I'd've told them Vince couldn't handle that job."

"What I said."

"I've known this Frankie since he was a kid," Tony Jacks says. "He did some work for me, back in the day. A tough nut to crack."

"I want the shot, Uncle Tony."

Tony Jacks looks at him for a few seconds, then says, "That's up to Jack Tominello, nephew. He's the boss."

"*You* should be boss," Jimmy says. "Or my father. It should be the Giacamones, not the Tominellos. I figure I do this thing, I take over whatever Vince had going in San Diego."

"What do you know about that?"

"Something about strip clubs."

"It's a lot more than a few strippers."

"Why such a hard-on for Frankie Machine?" Jimmy asks. "Why did we even want him gone?"

Tony Jacks leans forward. It looks like it takes some effort. His voice drops into a hoarse whisper. "What I'm about to tell you, Jimmy, your father doesn't know. Even Jack doesn't know. And if I tell you, you can never tell another soul as long as you live."

"I won't."

"Swear."

"I swear to God," Jimmy says.

Tony Jacks tells him a story. It goes way back and it takes a long time.

When Jimmy the Kid finally leaves his uncle's house, he is blown freaking away.

Freaking *away.*

17

Tracking down Mouse Junior is a cinch.

Frank simply calls 411, gets the number for Golden Productions, and dials it.

"Hey," he says to the receptionist, "I'm the caterer for the shoot today, and I can't locate it. Can you tell me . . ."

It's in the Valley, of course.

The San Fernando Valley is the porn capital of the world. You can't bounce a tennis ball in the Valley without hitting a bare ass waiting to go on the set. An incorporated part of Los Angeles, it tried to secede a few years back, ostensibly, Frank thinks as he turns on the 101 and heads toward the Valley, to re-create itself as the Republic of Porn.

So you have Hollywood, and then, to the north, you have Holly-*woody.* Gay guys with Viagra-fueled erections banging drug-addicted girls on bare mattresses tossed on lawns in Encino.

About as erotic, Frank thinks, as an intestinal bug.

But the truth is that the "adult-entertainment industry" outgrosses (no pun intended) Hollywood, Major League Baseball, the NFL, and the NBA combined. It's a major money maker, and where you find money being made, you'll find the guys.

He finds the shoot with no problem. It's a big house in Chatsworth, with a walled-in backyard and the inevitable pool. He knows he has the right place because Mouse Junior's Hummer is parked on the street, which just goes to show you how careless this thing has gotten lately, when you take a whack at a guy, miss, then keep using your own car like you don't have a worry in the world.

Unless it's an ambush, Frank thinks.

He drives around, looking for a work car, but he doesn't see one. Nor does he see any guys on the corner. If Mouse Junior has security with him, they're all in there watching the action. Which is really dumb, Frank thinks as he drives up the switchback where he can look down at the backyard. He parks, gets his binos out, and checks the scene.

If I wanted to take Mouse Junior out, I could do it right from the car with a single rifle shot, and then all his security could do for him would be pick his dead body up off the wet grass.

Because there is the dumb little punk, with his dumber wingman, Travis, standing around with the director and the crew, trying to figure out where to shoot now that it's raining. The cast and crew are miserably gathered in a knot inside the covered patio, and the director seems to be trying to figure out how to shoot in there, and, sure enough, a couple of gaffers go out and roll a chaise lounge onto the patio. A production assistant finds a towel and wipes it off.

Which is considerate, Frank thinks—at least the actors get to work on a *dry* lawn chair.

Frank focuses the glasses on Mouse Junior. It would be easy to take him out, but Frank doesn't want Mouse Junior's blood; he wants information. So he has to sit there and wait for a chance.

There are five things that make guys give you an opening:

Carelessness.

Fatigue.

Habits.

Money.

Sex.

That's it. That's the list.

Mouse Junior's already committed carelessness, and it would be enough to kill him, except that Frank doesn't want him dead. So now he has to wait for Mouse Junior to commit one of the other five deadly sins.

Frank's money is on sex.

Which is not a huge long shot, seeing as how Mouse Junior is standing there watching a young lady having sex with herself right now. She's a petite blonde with an enormous chest, a rack off the rack, as it were. And she has the requisite tattoo on the small of her back, the "tramp stamp," as Mike Pella refers to it.

A dolphin, frolicking in a wave.

Frank's offended on behalf of dolphins.

He's *surfed* with dolphins, for heaven's sake. Sometimes they do that, ride along with the surfers, just for fun. And some of the best memories of his life come from watching dolphins play in the break at sunset. He doesn't need to see them depicted on some porn actress's back.

Frank doesn't get the whole tattoo thing anyway, doesn't see the attraction at all. He doesn't think they look good on young bodies, and what happens when gravity takes its inevitable toll and the drawings start to go south?

Not a pretty picture.

Mouse Junior has his eye on Dolphin Girl.

She has her eye on him.

It's porno puppy love.

Kind of sweet, if it weren't so disgusting.

She's playing with herself and moaning and making eyes off-camera at Mouse Junior, who's standing there shifting his weight from one leg to the other and grinning like the congenital idiot he is.

In the meantime, Male Porn Star is getting a smoker from another young man, and now he breaks off and walks onto the set, and Dolphin

Girl takes over the oral chore. Then Male Porn Star returns the favor, and then they go through a tedious rotation of positions—like sexual gymnasts performing their mandatory techniques—which culminates in the requisite money shot on her face, which she receives with apparent enthusiasm, if not downright gratitude.

Then it's lunchtime.

Frank doesn't know if "adult entertainers" have a union, but they seem pretty prompt on the lunch break, and everybody lines up on the patio to work their way down the long table.

Mouse Junior waits as a production assistant hands Dolphin Girl a moist towelette to wipe her face off with, then steps forward and drapes a terry-cloth robe around her shoulders, proving, Frank supposes, that chivalry is not, indeed, dead. He watches as they separate themselves from the group and eat their lunch by the covered barbecue grill.

And talk about what? Frank wonders.

The scene she just did? Or the one she's about to? About her performance, her technique? Some pointers from the "producer"? Career notes? What?

Doesn't matter.

Frank waits until the lunch break is over, then drives closer to the house and finds a parking spot down the street.

Dolphin Girl comes out about two hours later and gets into a Ford Taurus. Frank follows her as she drives down the street to the on-ramp of the 101. He stays a few cars behind her as she drives south, then exits at Encino. She lives in one of those two-story blocks of apartment buildings like thousands of others in the L.A. area. Frank follows her into the parking lot, where she pulls into her assigned slot. He finds an empty space and parks, then watches as she walks up to the second floor and lets herself into her apartment.

Then he drives out, finds a Subway, gets himself a turkey sub and a bottled iced tea, goes to the convenience store in the same strip mall and buys *Surfer,* then drives back across the street from her apartment building and waits.

The sandwich is good—not great, not like he'd build for himself at home, but good. He chose the turkey with whole-grain bread because both Donna and Jill have been after him about his carb intake, what with all the pasta.

Diet fads, Frank thinks—a while back everyone was "carb packing" and you couldn't sell enough pasta at the restaurants, and now carbs are the devil and protein is the thing.

Mouse Junior doesn't get there until almost eight.

Must have been problems on the set, Frank thinks. Script troubles, camera breakdowns, erectile dysfunctions, Astroglide shortage . . .

Anyway, Mouse Junior comes in his Hummer and he comes alone. Carelessness *and* sex, Frank thinks, a deadly daily double. The only question is whether to take him now or wait until *after* he's gotten his rocks off.

It would be better to do it in the apartment than on the street, Frank thinks, but Dolphin Girl has nothing to do with this. So he decides to leave her out of it, hoping that Mouse Junior doesn't spend the night.

In short, Frank thinks, you hope he's *you.*

He sets the alarm on his watch and takes a half-hour nap, knowing that Mouse Junior isn't going to be that fast. He leans back in the seat and sleeps soundly until the little ringer wakes him up; then he gets out, opens the trunk, takes out a slim jim, and walks over to the Hummer.

In the old days, if a boss's son was paying court, as it were, there would've been guys out on the street waiting, taking his back.

Not now.

Frank walks up to the Hummer and opens the door. The alarm goes off, but no one pays attention to these things anymore, and it only takes him a couple of seconds to reach under and disarm the stupid thing.

He climbs into the backseat and lies down on the floor to wait, hoping that Mouse Junior is a bad lover.

Mediocre, as it turns out.

It's nearly 10:30 when Mouse Junior emerges from the apartment building.

Whistling.

Unreal, Frank thinks as he hears Mouse Junior warbling. The kid is a walking cliché. He waits as the door opens and Mouse Junior gets behind the wheel. Then he presses the pistol barrel into the back of the driver's seat so Mouse Junior can feel it poking into his back.

"Press your hands onto the ceiling," Frank says. "Hard."

Mouse Junior does it.

Frank reaches over and finds the pistol in Mouse Junior's shoulder holster, empties the chamber, and tucks the gun into his own waistband.

"Now put your hands on the wheel," Frank says.

Mouse Junior does that, too. "Please don't kill me, Mr. Machianno."

"If I wanted you dead," Frank says, "you'd already be dead. Just understand that if you make me shoot you through this seat, it will be the bullet *and* the hand-tooled leather and God knows what else that will be blowing through your vital parts. *Capisce?*"

"I understand," Mouse Junior says, his voice quivering.

"Good," Frank says. "Now let's go see Daddy."

It's a long drive to Westlake Village, mostly because Mouse Junior develops a case of verbal diarrhea and can't stop the foolishness flowing out of his mouth. About how happy he is that Frank's alive, how shocked he was about what happened on the boat, how he and Travis ran and called his dad right away to see if he could help, how the whole L.A. family has been—

"Junior? Shut up," Frank says. "You're giving me a headache."

"Sorry."

"Just drive," Franks says. He tells him to go to the one place in the world that no one would expect Frank Machianno to go: Mouse Senior's place of business. The coffeehouse will be closed to the public by now, but Frank knows that Mouse Senior and half the L.A. family will be there.

Which is just what he wants.

Get this thing settled so he can get his life back.

When they get there, Frank tells Mouse Junior to pull into the back parking lot, keep the engine running, and use his cell phone to call his dad. Mouse Junior's hand is shaking like an old drunk's as he punches the number on speed dial.

When Frank hears Mouse Senior answer, he grabs the phone.

"Come outside," he says.

Mouse Senior recognizes the voice. "Frank? What the fuck?"

"I have a gun pressed to your kid's back and I'll pull the trigger unless you're out here in ten seconds."

"What are you, drunk?" Mouse Senior asks. "Is this some kind of sick joke?"

"One . . ."

"Frank, what the fuck's wrong with you?"

"Two . . ."

"Frank, I'm looking out the window, I see Junior sitting in his car by himself."

"Tell him," Frank says to Mouse Junior.

"Dad?" Mouse Junior says. "He's here. He's in the backseat. He has a gun."

"That was three, four, and five," Frank says.

"Is this a kidnap thing?" Mouse Senior asks. "Are you crazy, Machianno? *Are you out of your fucking mind?*"

Is it possible, Frank thinks, that Mouse Senior didn't know about the setup?

"Six," Frank says.

"I'm coming out! I'm coming out!" Frank keeps the gun on Mouse Junior's back but rises up just enough to see out the window. Mouse Senior steps out the back door. His brother Carmen is with him, and so are Rocco Meli and Joey Fiella. The Martini brothers won't be carrying guns, Frank knows, but Rocco and Joey will definitely be strapped.

It doesn't matter. Nobody's going to take a shot at him while he's this close to the boss's son. *I* could, Frank thinks. I could make the shot and never splash a drop of blood on the kid, but that's me, that's not them.

And they know it.

They also know that I could have killed the kid already, if that's what I was about. And I would have been within my rights to do it, for setting me up. The fact that I brought him here, where it would be tantamount to suicide to pull the trigger, let's them know I want to make peace.

He says, "Pete, you know your son could be dead already."

"Take it easy, Frank."

Frank hasn't seen Mouse Senior in years. The boss still has that broad, flat, frying-pan face, but the lines in it are a lot deeper and his hair has gone completely white.

"I'm taking it easy," Frank says. "You do the same and you just listen. We've apparently had some sort of bad misunderstanding, Pete, to lead you to think you had to have me clipped. If you think I'm going to flip on you for Herbie Goldstein, you're wrong. I haven't been arrested, indicted, or even questioned about it. And even if I had, I'm not a rat."

"I never thought you were," Mouse Senior says. "What the *fuck* are you talking about?"

"The little sit-down with Vince Vena on the boat?" Frank sees some movement from the corner of his eye. "Tell Joey to stop working his way around the other side of the car."

"Joey, stand still," Mouse Senior orders. "Frank, what the fuck *are* you talking about?"

"He doesn't know?" Frank asks Junior.

Mouse Junior shakes his head.

"You'd better tell him."

"Tell me what?" Mouse Senior glares at his son. "Tell me *what*, Junior? What did you fuck up now?"

"Dad . . ."

"Goddamn it, tell me!"

"Me and Travis were shooting some porn down in San Diego," Mouse Junior says. "Internet porn, Webcam shit . . . streaming video . . ."

"You fucking little asshole," Mouse Senior says. "You know that's—"

"I was trying to make some money, Dad!" Mouse Junior says. "I was trying to earn!"

"Keep talking."

"I was making so much fucking money, Dad," Mouse Junior says. "Then the Detroit guys found out. They jammed me up, said they were going to take it to you unless—"

"What did you *do*, Junior?"

"They just wanted me to set up a meeting," Mouse Junior cries. "Get

Frank to come, sit down with Vena. That's all. I didn't know they were going to kill him; I swear, I didn't know. They just said tell him this story, get him to the meeting, I could keep my business down there."

"Frank, I'm sorry," Mouse Senior says. "I didn't know."

"Baloney," Frank says. "Detroit would never come on your turf and clip one of your guys without you signing off on it. You're the boss."

"The boss?" Mouse Senior asks, his mouth twisting into a rueful sneer. "Boss of *what*? I'm the boss of *shit*."

It's the stone-cold truth.

Most of Mouse's guys are in the joint, what he's got left are garbage, and he's looking down the barrel of another indictment. He *is* the boss of shit—Frank just didn't realize that he knew it.

"So where are we now, Frankie?" Mouse Senior asks. He turns to his son. "You know the man is within his rights to kill you."

"Dad—"

"Shut up, idiot," Mouse Senior says. He turns to Frank. "You have a daughter, Frank. You know how it feels. You want me to give him a good beating, I will. But let him go, please. Father to father, I'm begging you. I'm humbling myself."

"Who?" Frank asks Mouse Junior. "One chance to tell me the truth—who came to you?"

"John Heaney," Mouse Junior says.

John Heaney, Frank thinks. No wonder he looked so edgy when I saw him—could it have been just last night?—outside Freddie's. John, my old surfing buddy, my friend, the guy I helped get half a dozen jobs . . .

That's this world we live in.

"Get out of the car," Frank says.

Mouse Junior practically falls tumbling out of the Hummer. Frank climbs into the driver's seat, slams the door shut, puts the vehicle into reverse, and roars out of the parking lot onto the street. From the rearview mirror, he can already see Joey winging shots at him, Rocco scrambling to a car, and Mouse Senior slapping Mouse Junior upside the head.

But taking a break long enough to yell—

"Kill that cocksucker!"

18

Yeah, well, *wanting* to kill that cocksucker and actually *killing* that cock-sucker are two very different things, Frank thinks.

Hopefully.

The more serious issue is who would send John Heaney to set me up, and why?

Frank makes himself concentrate on more immediate concerns.

Like the fact that Joey Fiella and Rocco Meli are trying to chase him down.

Or not, as the case may be. Joey and Rocco are definitely chasing him, but the last thing they probably want is actually to *catch* him. If they catch him, they'll have to do something about it, which is probably get themselves killed, and they know it.

Still and all, Frank thinks, I can't just let them follow me forever. A bright yellow Hummer stands out like a bright yellow Hummer, and if these bozos have any brains—and he concedes them a certain feral cunning—they'll know he'd have left a work car somewhere near Mouse Junior's girlfriend's place.

So what he needs is a little space.

He puts his foot down on the pedal and guns it, racing toward the 101. It's a lot faster than he usually likes to go, especially in an awkward car he's not used to driving.

But he needs to create a little space.

He stomps on the gas.

19

Joey Fiella cranks the car onto the on-ramp of the 101 South and hopes his Mustang can handle the curve.

It does.

Junior's Hummer didn't.

Its left front fender is crumpled against a light pole and smoke is coming up from the engine.

"Junior's going to be pissed," Rocco says.

"Fuck him," Joey says.

He pulls the car off on the shoulder behind the Hummer.

"This is a piece of luck," Rocco says.

Yeah, but which kind? Joey thinks as he grabs his pistol and opens the door. Rocco does the same, and they approach the Hummer from both sides, guns pointed, like cops on a sketchy traffic stop.

Fuck Junior and his tinted windows, Joey thinks as he gets to the driver's door, because he can't see inside and can only hope that Frankie Machine is slumped against the steering wheel with his melon cracked in half.

He decides not to take any chances. Frankie could be playing possum in there, and besides, another car could be coming up the ramp any second. So Joey Fiella just starts shooting. Rocco catches the panic bug and does the same thing, and the two of them empty their guns into the front windows.

The window glass shatters.

Joey blinks.

Frankie ain't in there.

And his own Mustang is pulling onto the highway, with Frankie behind the wheel.

This isn't good, Joey thinks.

It isn't going to be any fun explaining to Pete how he shot Junior's Hummer to shit and got his own car stolen.

And let Frankie Machine get away.

20

Idiots, Frank thinks.

These are what pass for soldiers these days.

Mouse Senior was right: He *is* the boss of shit, if these clowns are the best he can send out now. Back in the day, it would have been guys like Bap, Jimmy Forliano, Chris Panno, Mike Pella, and, well, *me*.

Now it's Rocco and Joey.

Frank could have gunned them down where they stood, easily, but what would have been the point? You're younger, maybe you kill them because your blood is up and you have this macho thing, but at his age, you know that the less killing, the better.

Besides, he didn't want to create any more vendettas than he already had.

And apparently, he thinks, I have one I don't even know about.

John Heaney? Frank thinks as he drives the Mustang back toward Dolphin Girl's condo to pick up his own car. What did I ever do to John?

21

John Heaney goes out for a cigarette break. Out by the Dumpster in back of Hunnybear's.

It's been a bitch of a night; the place is jammed with both the usual pack of locals and a swarm of tourists—some convention in from Omaha. Anyway, the girls are making money and the bar register's ringing like a twenty-alarm fire.

John takes the pack of Marlboros from his shirt pocket and his lighter from his pants pocket, lights up, and leans back against the Dumpster. Suddenly, he's choking as an arm comes across his throat and he feels himself being lifted off his feet.

Just an inch or so, but it's enough. He can't breathe and he can't get traction to move.

"I thought we were friends, John," he hears Frank Machianno say.

Frankie Machine is standing in the Dumpster, calf-deep in garbage, his strong left forearm locked across Heaney's neck.

"Oh shit," John says.

"Mouse Junior gave you up," Frank says. "What was it, John? Did I give you a delivery of bad tuna, or what?"

"Oh shit," John repeats.

"You'll have to do better than that," Frank says.

The club's back door opens and a wedge of yellow light spills out into the back. John feels himself being jerked up like a fish into a boat, and then he's lying in garbage, Frank's heavy body on top of him.

And a gun barrel pressed against his left temple.

"Go ahead and yell," Frank whispers.

John shakes his head.

"Good decision," Frank says. "Now make it two in a row—tell me who sent you to Mouse Junior."

"Nobody," John whispers.

"John, you're a mediocre cook and a night manager at a titty joint," Frank says. "You don't have the swag to order a hit. And the next lie you tell me, I swear, I'll pop you and leave your body here in the garbage, where it belongs."

"I didn't want to, Frank," John whines. "They said they could help me."

"Who, Johnny? Who came to you?"

"Teddy Migliore."

Teddy Migliore, Frank thinks. Owner of Callahan's and scion of the Combination. It's not good news.

"Help you with what?"

"I've been indicted, Frank."

"Indicted?"

"On this G-Sting shit," John says. "I was the bagman. I brought cash to a cop. He was undercover."

John blurts out the rest of the story. He was being squeezed from both sides, the feds offering him a deal to flip, the wise guys threatening to whack him to keep him from talking.

"I was totally fucked, Frank."

Then Teddy Migliore offered him a way out: If John went to Mouse Junior and made him a deal, he could walk. The mob wouldn't clip him and they'd get him off the indictment, or at least get him a pardon.

"And you *believed* this crap?" Frank asks him, knowing it's a useless question. A condemned man will believe anything that will give him even a little hope.

He cocks the hammer of the pistol and feels John flinch underneath him.

"Don't, Frank, please," John says. "I'm sorry."

Frank eases the hammer back down; then John's body lurches into sobs.

"I'm going to leave now, Johnny," Frank whispers. "You lie here for five minutes before you get out. If you feel bad about what you did to me, you'll wait an hour before you call Teddy. If you don't, well, there's nothing I can do about it."

Frank climbs out of the Dumpster and brushes the garbage off. It'll be good to get someplace where he can take a shower and get a change of clothes, but right now he has something else to do.

He walks to his car and opens the trunk.

22

Frank stands across the street from Callahan's, waiting for it to close.

It's a long, cold wait at two in the morning.

Finally, the trendy young crowd starts to pour out and, a few minutes later, the bouncer goes to lock the door.

That's when Frank steps in.

The bouncer takes a swing at him.

Frank ducks underneath the punch, pulls the softball bat from under his coat and Tony Gwynns the bouncer's shin bones. The resulting *crack,* and the bouncer toppling to the sidewalk, gets some attention from the after-hours crowd inside the bar.

One of the boys rushes Frank.

Frank butts him in the solar plexus with the blunt end of the bat, then swings the handle up in an arc and catches the man under the chin. He takes a step back to let the guy fall, then sees the next man reach in his jacket into shoulder-holster territory. Frank swings the bat and breaks the guy's wrist against the gun butt.

The bartender vaults the bar with a nightstick in his hand and swings it down toward the back of Frank's head. Frank turns, raises the bat horizontally to block the nightstick, pulls his arms back in, and then thrusts the bat back into the bartender's nose, which breaks with a splatter of blood. Then Frank crosses his right foot over his left, whirls, and delivers a home-run swing into the bartender's floating ribs.

Three guys down.

Teddy Migliore stands there like his feet are rooted to the spot.

Then he turns and runs.

Frank lofts the bat low across the floor. It bounces and catches Teddy in the back of the knees, sending him sprawling to the floor. Frank's on top of him before he can *start* to get up. He puts his right knee into the small of Teddy's back, grabs him by the back of the collar, and smashes his face into the expensive tile until he can see blood trickle into the grouting.

"What," Frank yells, "did I ever do to you? Huh? *What did I ever do to you?*"

Frank leans down, slips one hand under Teddy's chin, and lifts as his other arm forms a bar across the top of Teddy's neck. He can either snap Teddy's spinal cord or choke him out, or both.

"Nothing," Teddy gasps. "I just got the word is all."

"Who *gave* the word?" Frank asked.

Frank hears police sirens start to wail. Some citizen must have spotted the bartender writhing on the sidewalk and called the cops. Frank puts more pressure on Teddy's neck.

"Vince," Teddy says.

"Why? Why did Vince want me clipped?"

"I don't know," Teddy groans. "I swear, Frankie, I don't know. He just told me to deliver you."

Deliver me, Frank thinks. Like a pizza. And Teddy's lying. He knows exactly why Vince wanted to kill me, or else he's just laying it all on a dead man.

"Police! Come out with your hands where we can see them!"

Frank lets go of Teddy, steps over him into the office, and lets himself out the back door. As he's leaving, he hears a voice on the answering machine. *"Teddy? It's me, John. . . ."*

Frank steps out in the alley and runs.

Teddy Migliore sits in his office and rubs his throat. He looks up at the uniformed cops and says, "You sure took your time . . . the fucking money we pay . . ."

The cops don't look too eaten up with sympathy. They've stopped taking the money anyway. You'd have to be a fucking idiot to take an envelope from Teddy Migliore these days, what with everything going on.

Operation G-Sting.

"Do you know who did this?" one of the cops asks.

"Do you want to file a report?" asks the other.

"Get the fuck out of here," Teddy tells them.

He's going to file a report all right, but not with these two losers. He waits until they've left, though, to pick up the phone.

Frank jogs out of the alley and back onto the street.

You had it exactly backward, dummy, he tells himself. It wasn't L.A. who contracted with Vince to take you out; it was Vince who used L.A., or at least Mouse Junior, to set you up.

But why?

He can't think of a thing he ever did to Vince Vena or the Migliores. He can only think of something he did *for* them.

23

It was the summer of '68.

The summer Frank came back from Vietnam.

The truth of the matter is, Frank thinks now as he watches the rain splatter against the window of his safe house, the truth is that I killed more men for the feds than I ever did for the mob.

And they gave me a medal and an honorable discharge.

Frank punched out a lot of VC and NVA during his stint in-country.

That was his job—sniper—and he was damned good at it. Sometimes he felt bad about it, but he never felt guilt over it. They were soldiers, he was a soldier, and in a war, soldiers kill soldiers.

Frank never bought into any of that *Apocalypse Now* crap. He never shot any women or children, or massacred any villages, or even saw anyone who did. He just killed enemy soldiers.

The Tet Offensive was made for guys like Frank, because the enemy came out to be shot. Before that, it had been frustrating patrols in the jungle that usually turned up nothing, except when you walked into a VC ambush and lost a couple of guys and still never saw the enemy.

But in Tet, they came out en masse and got gunned down en masse. Frank was a one-man wrecking machine in the city of Hue. The urban house-to-house fighting was a perfect match for his skills, and Frank found himself in mano-a-mano duels with NVA snipers that sometimes went on for days.

Those were battles of wit and skill.

Frank always won.

He came back from Nam to find that the country he'd left didn't exist anymore. Race riots, "peace riots," hippies, LSD. The surf scene was just about dead because a lot of the guys were in Nam, or were screwed up because of it, or they went the hippie route and were living in communes in Oregon.

Frank put his uniform away and went to the beach. Spent long weeks surfing mostly by himself, holding his own small bonfires and cookouts, trying to reclaim the past.

But it wasn't the same.

Patty was.

She'd written him every day he was in-country. Long, chatty letters about what was going on at home, who was dating who, who had broken up, about her secretary work, her parents, *his* parents, whatever. And love stuff—passionate passages about how she felt about him, how she couldn't wait for him to come home.

And she couldn't. The former "good Catholic girl" walked him up to her room the second her parents left the house and pulled him down on the bed. Not that I took much pulling, Frank remembers.

God, the first time with Patty . . .

They got to the brink, like they had so many times in the backseat of his car, except this time she didn't clamp her legs tight or push him off. Instead, she guided him inside her. He was surprised, but he certainly didn't object, and when it came time to pull out—all too quickly, he remembers ruefully—she whispered, "Don't. I'm on the Pill."

Which was a shock.

She had gone to the doctor and then went on the Pill in anticipation of his homecoming, she told him as they lay on her bed afterward, her head snuggled into the crook of his arm.

"I wanted to be ready for you," she said. Then, shyly, added, "Was I okay?"

"You were terrific."

And then he was hard again—God, to be young, Frank thinks—and they did it again, and this time she climaxed and said that if she'd known what she was missing, she would have done it a lot sooner.

Patty was good in bed—warm, willing, passionate. Sex was never their problem.

So Frank got back with Patty and they began the long, inevitable march toward matrimony.

What wasn't inevitable was Frank's future.

What was he going to do now, with his Marine tour winding down? He thought about re-upping, maybe making the Corps a career, but Patty didn't want him going back to Vietnam, and he didn't like being away from San Diego that much. His father wanted him to go into the fishing business, but that didn't sound all that appealing, either. He could have gone to college on the GI bill, but there was nothing he was that interested in studying.

So it was a gimme putt he'd end up back with the guys.

It was nothing dramatic, nothing sudden.

Frank just ran into Mike Pella one day, and they had a beer, and then they started hanging out. Mike told him about his past, how he grew up in New York with the Profaci family and had a little hassle there and then was sent out west to work for Bap until things straightened out.

But he liked California, he liked Bap, and so he'd decided to stay.

"Who needs the fucking snow, right?" Mike asked.

Not me, Frank thought.

He started to go with Mike to the clubs where the guys spent their days, and *this* hadn't changed. *This* had stayed the same, like it was in a time warp. It was comforting, familiar. Famili*al,* I guess, Frank thinks now.

It was all the same guys—Bap, Chris Panno, and Mike, of course. Jimmy Forliano had a trucking business out in East County, and he'd come around sometimes, but that was really about it.

They were a small, tight little group in what was, back then, still a small town. That was the thing about San Diego in those days, Frank thinks now. We weren't really even a "mob," or an obvious family like they had in the big East Coast cities.

And there wasn't a hell of a lot going on.

The normally free and easy San Diego had a new federal prosecutor who was busting everyone's balls. He'd worked up a twenty-eight-count indictment against Jimmy and Bap for some bullshit about the truckers' union and was generally making life difficult for whatever organized crime there was in the city.

Bap also had a silent piece of a local taxi company, and he set Frank up with a job driving cabs.

Washing machines on wheels is what they really were, the guys laundered so much money through those taxis. Gambling money, loan shark money, prostitution money—it all went on cab rides.

And political money.

To city councilmen, congressmen, judges, cops, you name it. The chief of police got a new car every year, courtesy of the cab company.

Then there was Richard Nixon.

He was running for president and needed a war chest, and it just wouldn't have looked good—mobbed-up guys in San Diego writing checks to the Nixon campaign. So the money went through the cab company in chunks "donated" by the owners and the drivers. Frank never would have found out about it except that he saw one of the checks on the office desk one night.

"I'm giving money to Nixon?" he asked Mike.

"We all are."

"I'm a Democrat," Frank said.

"Not *this* year, you ain't," Mike said. "What, you want Bobby fucking Kennedy in the White House? Guy's got a hard-on for us you could cut glass with. Besides, it ain't really your money, is it? So relax."

Frank was sitting in the office of the cab company with Mike, drinking coffee and talking shit, when the call came.

"Are you boys ready to take a step up?" Bap asked.

He was calling from a phone booth.

Bap never called from home, because Bap wasn't stupid. What he'd do is, he'd put rolls of quarters in his pocket and he'd walk four blocks to this phone booth on Mission Boulevard at night and conduct his business from there, like it was his office.

Usually, they'd meet Bap on the boardwalk in Pacific Beach, just a few blocks from the boss's house.

You wouldn't have figured a guy like Bap to have loved the ocean so much.

Something he and Frank had in common, although, of course, Bap never got out on a board, or even went for a swim, as far as Frank ever knew. No, Bap just liked looking at the ocean; he and Marie used to go for sunset walks together on the boardwalk or stroll on Crystal Pier. Their condo had a nice oceanfront view, too, and Bap used to stand at the window and do watercolors.

Bad watercolors.

He had dozens of them, scores of them, probably, and he used to give them out as presents all the time; otherwise, Marie would bitch about him clogging up their whole place with the paintings.

Bap would give them for Christmas, birthdays, anniversaries, Groundhog Day, anything. All the guys had them—what were you going to say, no? Frank had one on the wall of his little apartment on India Street—it was a sailboat heading out into the sunset, because Bap knew that Frank liked boats.

Which was true, Frank did like boats, which made this watercolor all the more painful, because no vessel should have to suffer what Bap did to this boat. But Frank kept it on his wall, because you never knew when Bap might drop by, and Frank didn't want to hurt his feelings.

This worked because he wasn't married yet. The married guys' wives usually made them put Bap's paintings in a closet or something, because the married guys were usually made men and protocol, even in casual San Diego, dictated that even a boss didn't just drop by without a phone call. But there had been some frantic replacements of paintings on walls when the phone call came, with guys scrambling to get one of Bap's hideous watercolors up in the living room before the doorbell rang.

So if it was just normal business, they met at the beach. This day, however, Bap told them to meet him at the zoo, outside the reptile house.

The subject was a guy named Jeffrey Roth.

"Who?" Mike asked.

"You heard of Tony Star?" Bap asked, his face pressed up against the glass, staring at a spitting cobra.

"Sure," Mike said.

They all had heard of Tony Star. He was a rat from Detroit, whose testimony had put half that city's family away. Rocco Zerilli, Jackie Tominello, Angie Vena, they were all doing time because of Tony Star. The papers had a field day with the irresistible headline TONY STAR WITNESS.

"He's 'Jeffrey Roth' now, in the Witness Protection Program," Bap said. He started tapping on the glass, trying to provoke the cobra into attacking. "You think you could get one of these guys to spit at you?"

"I don't think they want you doing that," Frank said. He felt bad for the snake, which was just minding its own business.

Bap looked at him like he was nuts, and Frank got it. "They" probably didn't want Bap killing people, hijacking trucks, shylocking money, and running gambling operations, either, so he probably wasn't going to stop tapping on the glass at the zoo. Indeed, Bap tapped on the glass some more, then asked, "Guess where Star is living now? Mission Beach."

"No shit!" Mike said.

It was a personal affront, a rat living right in their own backyard.

Frank and Mike had had many discussions on the subjects of rats. It was the worst-possible thing in the world to be, the lowest of the low.

"You gotta be a stand-up guy," Mike had said. "We're all grown men; we know the risks. If you get popped, you keep your mouth shut and do your time."

Frank had agreed, absolutely.

"I'd die before I'd go into the program," he'd said.

Now they had a guy who had put half the Detroit family in the joint, and here he was, hanging out and enjoying himself on Mission Beach.

"How'd they find him?" Mike asked.

The spitting cobra had curled itself into a ball and looked like it was asleep. Bap gave up and moved on to the puff adder in the next cage. It was wrapped around a tree limb, coiled and looking dangerous.

"Some secretary in the Justice Department that Tony Jack's got on the arm," Bap said, tapping on the adder's cage. He took a slip of paper out of his pocket and handed it to Frank. The note had an address in Mission Beach written on it. "Detroit wanted to send their own guys, but I said no, it's a matter of honor."

"Fuckin' right it is," Mike said. "Our turf, our responsibility."

"And it's worth twenty grand," Bap said.

The puff adder struck at the glass and Bap jumped back about five feet, losing his glasses in the process. Frank suppressed a laugh as he picked them up, wiped them off on his sleeve, and handed them to Bap.

"Sneaky fuckers," Bap said, taking the glasses.

"They're camouflaged," Mike said.

Frank and Mike went out and bought some geeky clothes that made them look like tourists and checked into a motel on Kennebec Court on Mission Beach. They spent most of their time looking out through venetian blinds at Tony Star's condo across Mission Boulevard.

"We're kind of like cops," Mike said the first night in.

"How do you figure?"

"I mean, this is what they do, right?" Mike asked. "Stakeouts?"

"I guess," Frank said. First time he ever felt sorry for cops, because being on a stakeout was boring. It gave whole new meaning to the word *tedium*. Sitting there drinking bad coffee, taking turns going to Kentucky Fried Chicken, McDonald's, or a local taco joint, eating off your lap on sheets of greasy paper. What this garbage was doing to his insides, Frank could only guess. He *knew* what it was doing to Mike's insides, because it was a small room, and when Mike opened the door as he came out of the bathroom . . . Anyway, Frank started feeling bad for cops.

He and Mike would take shifts, one of them keeping watch out the window while the other grabbed some sleep or watched some bad television show. They only got a break when Star went out, which he did at 7:30 every morning to go jogging.

They discovered this the first morning when Star came out the front door of the building in a purple jumpsuit and running shoes and started doing stretches against the rail of the building steps.

"What the fuck?" Mike asked.

"He's going running," Frank said.

"He *should* go fucking running," said Mike.

"He looks good, though," Frank observed.

Star did look good. He had a nice tan, his black razor-cut hair was neatly brushed back, and he was thin. They decided only one guy should tail him, and Mike took the job. He came back an hour later, sweaty and incensed.

"Fucking guy," Mike huffed, "goes jogging around the marina like he don't have a worry in the world. Scoping the chicks, looking at the boats, soaking in the sunshine, working on his fucking tan. Cocksucker is leading the good life while friends of his are in the hole. I'm telling you, we should *hurt* this motherfucker before we take him out."

Frank agreed—Star *should* suffer for what he'd done—but those weren't the orders. Bap had been very clear about that—"quick and clean" was how he wanted it. Get in, do the job, get out.

The sooner the better, as far as Frank was concerned. Patty hadn't been too thrilled about him going away like this.

"Where are you going?" she'd asked.

"Come on, Patty."

"What for? Why?"

"Business."

"What kind of business?" she'd pressed. "Why can't you tell me? You're just going out to party with your buddies, aren't you?"

Some party, Frank thought. Sharing a cheap motel room with Mike

Pella, listening to his constant toilet mouth, sucking in his cigarette smoke, smelling his gas, spending hour after tedious hour looking out the window, trying to establish the pattern of some rat's pathetic life.

Because that was the key, a pattern.

Bap had coached him on that. "Guys lapse into habits," he had told Frank. "Everyone does. People are predictable. Once you can predict what a guy's going to do and when he's going to do it, then you can find your opening. Quick and clean, in and out."

So they knew he went jogging around the marina every morning. Mike wanted to do it then. "We get ourselves some fag tracksuits, we run up behind him, and we pop him in the head. Done."

Frank vetoed it. Too many things could go wrong. One, him and Mike jogging—they'd stick out like polar bears in a sauna. Two, they'd be out of breath, and it was hard to shoot accurately when you were out of breath, even from short range. Three, there'd just be too many poten-tial witnesses.

So they had to figure something else out.

Problem was, Star wasn't giving them many openings. He lived a very boring life, predictable as death and taxes, but very tight. He'd go jogging in the morning, then come home, shower (presumably) and change clothes, then go to his job at an insurance agency, where he'd work from ten to six. Then he'd walk back to his condo and stay there until he went jogging again in the morning.

"This is one dull motherfucker," Mike said. "He don't go out to no clubs, no bars, don't pick up no broads. What, the guy just sits in there jacking himself off every night? Biggest excitement in this guy's life is 'Pizza Night.'"

Every Thursday night, 8:30, Star had a pizza delivered to his door.

"I love you, Mike."

"You going fag on me?"

"Pizza night," Frank said. "Star buzzes the guy in."

This was on a Tuesday, so they pretty much relaxed for a couple of days, laid low, and waited for Pizza Night. Wednesday night, they ordered a pizza from the same joint, ate it, and saved the box.

At exactly 8:25 Frank was at the front door of Star's building with the pizza box in his hand. Mike was in the work car on the street, ready to drive them out of there and to intercept the pizza guy with some sort of bullshit if he had to.

Frank rang the bell and shouted into the intercom, "Pizza, Mr. Roth."

A second later, the buzzer sounded and Frank heard the metallic click of the lock opening. He went into the building, walked down the hallway to Star's unit, and rang the bell.

Star opened it a crack, keeping the chain on the door. Frank could hear the drone of a television. So this was the rat's big life, Frank thought, treating himself to a pizza while he watches the boob tube.

"Pizza," Frank repeated.

"Where's the usual kid?" Star asked.

"Sick," Frank said, hoping this thing wasn't going south. He got ready to kick the door in, but Star opened it first. He had his money in his hand—a five and two ones.

"Six-fifty, right?" Star asked, holding out the bills.

Frank reached into his pocket like he was digging for a couple of quarters.

"Keep the change," Star said.

"Thanks." A fifty-cent tip, Frank thought. No self-respecting wise guy in the world would give a fifty-cent tip. No wonder he turned rat. Frank handed Star the pizza box, and when the guy's hands were full, Frank pushed him inside, kicked the door shut behind him, and pulled the silenced .22 pistol.

Star tried to run. Frank put the bead on the back of his head and fired. Star fell forward and crashed into the wall. Frank stepped up over Star's prone body and aimed at the back of his head.

"Rat," Frank said.

He pulled the trigger three more times and walked out.

The whole thing had taken maybe a minute. Frank got in the car; Mike put it in gear and drove away.

"How'd it go?" Mike asked.

"Fine," Frank said.

Mike grinned. "You're a machine," he said. " 'Frankie Machine.' "

"Wasn't that the name of a guy that Sinatra played in the movies?" Frank asked.

The Man with the Golden Arm," Mike said. "He was a junkie."

"Great."

"But you," Mike said, "you're the man with the golden *hand*. Frankie Machine."

The name stuck.

They took Ingraham Street down to the floodway. Frank got out, smashed the pistol on some rocks, and threw the pieces into the water. Then they dumped the work car in a strip mall parking lot in Point Loma, where they found two other cars waiting. Frank got into his and drove downtown, dumped the car, took a taxi to the airport, then another taxi back home.

Nothing ever came of it.

The San Diego cops pretty much took a pass on the case, sending a message of their own to the feds: If you're going to put a snitch in our yard and not tell us about it, what the hell do you want us to do?

The truth is, nobody really likes snitches, not even the cops who make their bread and butter from them.

Frank got up the next morning, made coffee, and turned on the television. It was showing the kitchen of some hotel in Los Angeles.

"What, you're surprised?" Mike asked him later that morning.

"Kind of."

"I'm only surprised it didn't happen sooner," Mike said.

And that's the way it is, Frank thought. Bobby gets two in the head, Nixon gets checks.

There was a lot of celebration down at the cab office when Nixon got elected. One of the first things the new president did was to transfer the San Diego federal prosecutor who was putting so much pressure on the guys.

The indictments against Bap were dropped, although Forliano went into the can.

Other than that, it was back to business as usual.

Frank and Mike split two thousand dollars for the Tony Star job.

Frank bought an engagement ring with his cut.

24

So he was a married man when he met President Nixon.

It was 1972.

Partially as a reward for the Tony Star thing, Frank and Mike had been bumped up from driving cabs to driving limousines and Town Cars.

When they weren't driving, they were on the hustle. Frank probably put more hours in than your average working stiff, but it was different. It wasn't like you were working for that hourly wage, with Uncle taking his piece out of it. Even though they were working hard, it didn't feel like working; it was more like playing a game.

Which is why they called it "scoring," Frank guessed.

That's what they did in those days: They scored; they went out on scores. They scored merchandise off the backs of trucks, street tax from bookies, vig from shylock money, no-show jobs on construction projects.

They ran card and dice games, sports books, and lotteries. They made round-trip runs across the Mexican border—alcohol down and cigarettes back. They practically had a license from the San Diego cops to rip off drug dealers.

They were scoring, making money, although not much of it stuck to their hands. Most of it they had to kick up to Chris, who kicked up to Bap, who kicked up to Nicky Locicero. Even with all their scoring and hustling, they really weren't getting ahead. Frank resented it, but Mike, being from the East Coast, was more old-school.

"It's the way it is, Frankie," he'd lecture when Frank would complain. "It's the rules. We're not even made guys yet. We gotta show we can *earn*."

Frank wasn't into the whole "made guy" thing. He really didn't give a damn about all that old Sicilian stuff. He was just trying to make a living, stash away enough money for a down payment on a house.

Three-plus years of busting his hump and he and Patty were still renting a walk-up apartment in the old neighborhood. And he was working all the time—when he wasn't on a score, he was driving the limo, mostly back and forth from the airport to La Sur Mer Spa up in Carlsbad.

Mike about shit when he heard Frank had driven Moe Dalitz from the airport to La Sur Mer, or just "the Sur," as it was known to the locals and cognoscenti. Dalitz went way back—he had been an admiral in Detroit's "Little Jewish Navy" before the Venas moved in and chased him to Cleveland. He eventually became Chicago's eyes and ears in Vegas, where he was considered "the Jewish Godfather."

"Dalitz fucking *built* the Sur," Mike said. "He got the Teamsters to put up the money."

The Teamsters' Central States Pension fund was jointly controlled by the Chicago and Detroit families, Mike explained. The go-between was a insurance executive named Allen Dorner, the son of "Red" Dorner, who was buddies with Chicago boss Tony Accardo.

"Dorner?" Frank asked. "Yeah, he was in my car."

"Dalitz *and* Dorner!"

"Yeah, they were going to play golf," Frank said.

The Teamsters played a lot of golf at La Sur. They kept Frank and Mike very busy running them back and forth from the airport, or around town, or out at night. Frank figured that's why he'd been bumped up to Town Cars—the bosses wanted a connected guy driving the car so that the Teamsters and the wise guys could talk without worrying about it.

"Just drive," Bap had told him. "Keep your ears open and your mouth shut."

It wasn't just Dalitz and Dorner, either. It was also Frank Fitzsimmons, who had taken over as president of the Teamsters while Hoffa was serving his sentence. Fitzsimmons loved the Sur so much, he bought a condo there and started holding the union's annual board meeting at the hotel.

Then there were the out-and-out wise guys, mostly East Coast higher-ups getting out of the snow for a while. There was Tony Provenzano, "Tony Pro," who ran the New Jersey Teamsters, and Joey "the Clown" Lombardo, who was the liaison between Chicago and Allen Dorner.

And Detroit guys—Paul Moretti and Tony Jacks Giacamone, who ran Hoffa.

One day, Bap called Frank and Mike, told them to get their limos "spit and polished," to look sharp themselves, and be over at the airport exactly at nine the following morning.

"What's up?" Frank asked. He figured something big was going on, because the night before he'd made two trips to the airport to pick up Joey the Clown and Tony Pro, and they'd checked into suites at the Sur.

What was up was that Frank Fitzsimmons, president of the Teamsters, was going to hold a press conference at the Sur to announce that the union was going to endorse Nixon for reelection.

There's a surprise, Frank thought. The whispers around the Sur were that the Teamsters had funneled millions of dollars of illegal funds into Nixon's campaign fund. In fact, the spa had become the virtual West Coast headquarters for the Teamsters since Dorner had bought himself a condo overlooking the fourth green.

Frank smirked. "So this is why Nixon pardoned Hoffa?"

Bap smiled and said, "Hoffa is nothing but a cheap leg breaker, out of his league with the big money. Fitzsimmons and Dorner are raking in so much cash, most people don't want Hoffa back in office. Hoffa wants them clipped, but the fact is they're making everybody too much money. Listen and learn, Frankie. Making money for other people is what keeps you breathing. Never forget that."

Frank didn't.

"Anyway," Bap said, "after the press conference, you're driving the union guys to the Western White House. You might meet the president, Frankie."

"Aren't you coming?"

Bap smiled, but Frank could see there was hurt behind it.

"I'm not on the list," Bap said. "None of the guys are."

"That's not right, Bap."

"It's all bullshit," Bap said. "The fuck do I care?"

But Frank could see that he cared.

In the morning, with his car gleaming, and himself in a freshly pressed black suit, Frank drove to the private airstrip in Carlsbad to pick up Allen Dorner from his private jet. Word was that Dorner had laid out three million dollars to Frank Sinatra for the Gulfstream, and that the money had come from the Teamsters' fund.

"Good morning, Frank," Dorner said as he stepped off the plane onto the tarmac.

"Good morning, Mr. Dorner."

"It's going to be a beautiful day."

"Always is in San Diego," Frank replied, holding the back door of the car open for him.

It was a quick drive to the Sur.

Frank waited in the parking lot with the other drivers as Fitzsimmons made his endorsement speech and the sixteen other board members stood by, beaming. All the board members are here, Frank thought, but the wise guys are nowhere to be seen.

"Do you believe," Mike said, looking very spiffy and a little nervous as he stood beside his immaculate car, "that we're going to the fucking *president's* house?"

After his speech, Fitzsimmons and three other board members got into Frank's car. The other cars followed them as Frank led them out onto the 5 and drove up to San Clemente, to the Western White House.

Frank had been there before.

Well, not exactly to the house, but right below it, under the red bluff. He and some surfing buddies had hiked up from Trestles and found this great right-hand break under the Western White House. For some reason or other, this spot had the name Cottons.

Maybe I should tell Nixon about it, Frank thought as he pulled up to the gate, where Secret Service agents in their dark suits, sunglasses, and earpieces stopped him and checked the car out. Then again, he thought, it's a little hard to picture Richard Nixon on a board.

Waving that *V* for victory thing he did while hanging ten in the soup. *Cowabunga, dude.*

The Secret Service guys let the caravan through. Why not, Frank thought. Nixon couldn't be safer in his mother's arms than he was with this delegation, although none of them was strapped, having received strict orders to leave the hardware at home. After all, we're his people. We're all making money together.

Another Secret Service agent directed him where to park. He did, then got out to open the doors for Fitzsimmons and his boys and saw the president of the United States walking down to meet them.

Frank, even with the twenty-something cynicism that was part and parcel of the seventies, had to admit he felt a little awed, maybe even intimidated. This was the *president of the United States,* the commander in chief, and the former Marine in Frank made him straighten his posture a little bit, and he had to fight the impulse to salute.

He felt something else—this little stirring of pride at being in on this, even as a chauffeur. It was this feeling of being part of something . . . so powerful . . . it could bring them to the home of the president of the United States, and the man would personally walk down from his house to greet them.

Nixon opened his arms wide as he walked toward Fitzsimmons and said, "I hear you have good news for me, Frank!"

"*Very* good news, Mr. President!"

It must have been, because Nixon was in a very good mood. He embraced Fitzsimmons and then went around and shook everybody's hand, working the crowd like the career politician he was. He shook all the board members' hands, then came around and even shook the drivers' hands.

"Nice to meet you," Nixon said to Frank. "Thanks for coming."

Frank didn't know what to say. He was afraid of saying something stupid, like what was in his head, which was, You have a great break here, Mr. President, but Nixon had already moved on well before Frank formed the words.

That's the last Frank saw of him that day.

The Teamsters' board went up to the house and the drivers waited by their cars. The house staff brought them barbecued chicken and ribs— the same meal the big shots were getting up on the lawn. Later on, some staffer came and gave them each a golf ball with the president's signature on it.

"I'm going to keep this for fucking ever," Mike said. Frank could swear he saw tears in his eyes. Frank wandered down to the edge of the bluff. He had lots of time because the Teamsters were scheduled to play a round on the president's three-hole golf course, and that was going to take a while.

So Frank sat by the ocean and watched Cottons break below him. There were no surfers out there, never were when Nixon was in residence. I guess the Secret Service is afraid of some surfing assassin or something, Frank thought, although it would be one hell of a shot from the beach up to the lawn.

He looked south and, sure enough, could see the westernmost buildings of the Sur glistening white in the sun, and he wondered what Joey the Clown and Tony Pro were doing while everybody else was visiting the president's house, wondered if they felt bad being left out.

That was the summer of '72, the summer of Richard Nixon.

By the winter of '75, it had all gone to shit.

25

Nicky Locicero died in the fall of '74. His funeral was pathetic, just immediate family—none of the guys showed up because they didn't want to give the feds any ammo.

The feds were *pounding* the L.A. family. It was like the FBI was living inside the guys' heads, the prosecutors seemed to know everything, and the feds' Xerox machines were breaking down, they were cranking out so many indictments.

And the indictments were rock-solid. Even Sherm Simon advised the guys to plead out, which they did. Peter Martini got popped for four years, Jimmy Regace, who had just taken over as boss, for two. He named old Paul Drina as acting boss.

Bap thought it should have been him. He was very pissed off.

"Tom is a lawyer who's never got his hands wet," Bap said to Frank. "What's he ever done other than be Jack's brother? And they jump him over me? After all I've done for them?"

This was Bap's constant refrain back in the seventies, the "after all I've done for them" mantra. The fact that it was justified didn't make it any less tedious or futile, though. Fact was, Frank was sick of hearing it.

There comes a time in a man's life, he figured, the infamous midlife crisis, when a guy has to face the reality that what he has is all he's going to get, and he needs to find his peace and his happiness in his life as it is. Most guys managed to get that done, but not Bap—he was always griping about how he'd been screwed, how this guy or that guy had done him dirt in a deal, how there were guys who were "dead wood" and he was sick of carrying them, how L.A. never cut him in for his fair piece of the pie.

What pie? Frank thought as he heard this litany for maybe the thousandth time. There's practically no pie to cut up, what with half the guys in the can and New York and Chicago picking the bones like vultures.

Which was why Frank had taken his meager savings and gone into the fish business. Mike could laugh at him all he wanted, and make jokes about how Frank smelled like a mackerel (which wasn't true—(a) Frank showered meticulously after work, and (b) there were no mackerel in the Pacific Ocean), but the money was clean and safe. And while he wasn't raking it in like you could with the rackets when everything was good, everything *wasn't* good.

And they couldn't expect any help from on high, either, because the guy in the White House had his own problems, and he wasn't about to reach a hand out to a bunch of mobsters.

So it was a bad time for things to go haywire at the Sur.

But they did.

June, the summer of '75, Frank got a call from Bap's phone booth office. "You and Mike, get your asses here quick."

Frank heard the urgency in his voice and told him they could be in Pacific Beach in half an hour.

"Not Pacific Beach," Bap said. "The Sur. And come heavy."

It was Fort Sur Mer.

Driving up to the main building, Frank spotted half a dozen wise guys, all dressed casually, like guests, but posted to control the avenues of access. And Frank knew that under the polo shirts and the gabardine trousers, or tucked in golf bags or tennis frames, the guys were carrying serious hardware.

Frank parked in a slot across from Dorner's condo. Bap must have seen them pull up, because he was walking toward them before Frank even turned the motor off.

"Come on, come on," Bap said, opening Frank's door.

"What's up?"

"Hoffa's making his play," Bap said. "He might be putting a hit out on Dorner."

Frank had never seen Bap this worked up. When they got into Dorner's condo, Frank could see why.

The heavy drapes were pulled closed against the big glass slider that normally looked out on the golf course. Jimmy Forliano stood at the edge of the curtain, peeking out, a holster with a .45 strapped on his shoulder. Joey Lombardo was in the kitchen, getting a beer out of the fridge.

Carmine Antonucci sat on the sofa, sipping coffee. Dorner sat next to him, a gin and tonic sweating on the glass-top coffee table at his knees. In a big chair across from them sat Tony Jacks, looking cool and collected in a white linen suit and a royal blue tie.

Dorner looked up at them as if he'd never seen them before, even though they had hauled him back and forth from his private jet at least a few dozen times. He didn't look good. He looked pale and tired.

"Hi, guys," he said.

His voice was weak.

"You stay tighter on Dorner than his own asshole," Tony Jacks said. "He don't shit, shave, or shower, he don't look over his shoulder and not see one of you there. Anything happens to him, it happens to you next."

The siege went on for three weeks.

"Hey," Mike said about a week in. "If you're going to go to the mattresses, there are worse places to do it than the Sur."

More *Godfather* jive, Frank thought. If anybody had ever "gone to the mattresses" in San Diego before this, they were air mattresses in swimming pools.

Dorner started to get cabin fever.

"I want to get out," he said. "Play a little golf, just take a fucking walk. Get a little sun."

Frank shook his head. "No can do, Mr. Dorner."

He had strict orders.

"I feel like a prisoner in my own home," Dorner said.

It's not far from the truth, Frank thought, beginning to wonder if they were protecting Dorner *from* Hoffa or *for* him. He expressed this to Bap one day as he was walking him out of the condo.

Bap looked at him for a long moment.

"You're a smart boy, Frankie," Bap said. "You're going to go places."

It could go either way, Bap explained. Chicago and Detroit were working it out; all they could do was wait.

Basically, Tony Jacks was fighting for his boy Hoffa, while the Chicago boys were taking up for Fitzsimmons and Dorner. Bap was betting on Fitzsimmons and Dorner, because they were the better earners, but then again, Hoffa's Detroit connections were long and strong.

And Tony Jacks was lobbying hard for both Dorner and Fitzsimmons to get the chop.

"Don't let yourself get too close to the guy," Bap said, meaning Dorner. "You don't know what you might have to do, huh?"

So that was it.

They were guarding Dorner and they were *guarding* him. They weren't letting anybody in and they weren't letting him out. It was weird, sitting there playing rummy with the guy night after night, knowing you might be called on to whack him.

So it was tense.

It got a lot more tense when Mike came back from a little walk, took Frank aside and whispered to him, "We gotta talk."

He was *shook*.

Mike Pella, who was usually *ice,* looked shaken.

"It's Bap," Mike said.

"*What's* Bap?" Frank asked with this edge to his voice, but he already knew the answer. He felt like he could throw up.

"*Bap's* been talking to the feds," Mike said. "He's been wearing a wire."

"No," Frank said, shaking his head. Except he already knew it was true. It made sense—Bap had finally found his way to take out the L.A. leadership—cooperate with the feds and put them in jail. Then, when they'd made Paul Drina boss instead, he decided he needed to finish the job.

"How do you *know* this?" Frank whispered. Dorner was asleep in his bedroom, but Frank wasn't taking any chances he'd overhear.

"The guys set him up," Mike said. "They tossed him some bullshit about a porn shakedown and the feds showed up at it."

And now, Mike said, L.A. was wondering if *all* Bap's guys were in on this coup by cop.

"Frank," Mike said, "you gotta figure they're thinking about clipping *all* of us."

He was freaking out now, paranoia pumping adrenaline. "What if Bap gave *us* up, too?"

"He didn't," Frank said, still hoping.

"We don't know that," Mike said. "What if he takes the stand? He could put us up for DeSanto, Star. . . ."

"If he had," Frank said, "we'd have been arrested by now. The feds don't sit on murder indictments."

No, if this was true, Bap's strategy was to get rid of L.A. by giving them up to the feds, then basically replace the L.A. guys with his own San Diego crew. Which was why not a single San Diego guy had been named in the sweeping indictments the previous summer. It had always been Bap's dream to run California from San Diego.

"We'd be his two captains," Frank said.

"The fuck you talking about?"

Frank laid out his analysis of Bap's plan and repeated, "Bap is planning to make us the captains in his new family. He kept us out of the indictments; he kept us off the tape."

"So, what, we owe him?"

"Yeah."

"Do we owe him our fucking *lives,* Frankie?" Mike asked. "Because that's what we're talking about here."

Mike was right. Frank hated to admit it, but Mike was absolutely right. It was either/or. Either they took Bap out or they jumped in the boat with him.

And that boat was going down.

So there it was. The afternoons in Dorner's luxurious jail cell got real long. Now there were three guys sitting around wondering if they were going to get whacked, trying to keep their minds off it by watching other guys rat on their boss.

The end of July, they got the word.

Jimmy Hoffa had disappeared.

So, Frank thought, I guess Chicago and Detroit worked it out. And, he learned, if it's a contest between old connections and money, put your money on money.

Dorner took a big sigh of relief and kicked the two men out of his house.

They weren't so glad to go. Nobody was going to clip them in Dorner's condo. Outside, it might be a different story. Frank went home and got an uneasy night's sleep.

Bap called at ten in the morning from his phone booth, telling Frank to come right over, that he had some news. Frank met him on the boardwalk at Pacific Beach. Bap had his easel set up. He was out there painting, and the man was *beaming.*

"They made me *consigliore,*" Bap said.

The pride in his voice was palpable.

"*Cent' anni,*" Frank said. "It's overdue."

"It's not boss," Bap said. "It's not all I wanted, but it's a significant honor. It's an *acknowledgment,* you know what I mean?"

Frank wanted to cry. Maybe that was all the man had ever wanted: an *attaboy,* a pat on the back. Not a lot to ask. But Frank knew what it really was. It was poison wrapped in candy, a sleeping pill to lull Bap into a feeling of security.

It was a death sentence.

Frank almost told him.

But he choked the words back.

"I'm going to take care of you," Bap said, tranquilly painting his crappy watercolor of the ocean. "Don't you worry, you and Mike. I'm going to see that you get straightened out."

"Thanks, Bap."

"Don't thank me," Bap said. "You've earned it."

Marie came out of the house with two tall glasses of iced tea for them. She wasn't a hot little number anymore, but she still looked good, and it was clear from the way she looked at her husband that she adored him.

"You're almost done with this painting, huh?" she said, looking over her husband's shoulder. "It's good."

It isn't, Frank thought. Only a loving wife would say it was.

The next call came from Mike.

They met down at Dog Beach, watched golden retrievers fetch Frisbees.

"It's a done deal," Mike said. "L.A., Chicago, and Detroit have all signed off. Chris Panno gets San Diego; we report to Chicago until L.A. gets its act together."

"Yeah? When will *that* be?" Frank asked, avoiding the real topic.

"We gotta do it," Mike said.

"He's our *boss*, Mike!"

"He's a fucking rat!" Mike said. "He has to go. You want to go with him, that's your choice, but I'm telling you right now, it ain't mine."

Frank stared out at the ocean, thinking he'd like to get out on a board and just paddle. Maybe get his ass kicked in a big wave and get . . . *cleansed.*

"Look, *I'll* do it, that makes you feel better," Mike said. "*You* drive this time."

"No," Frank said. "I'll do it."

He went home that afternoon, turned on the television, and watched Nixon walk to a helicopter, then stand there and wave.

Jimmy Forliano made an appointment for Bap to call him that night. It was raining that night along the coast. Bap was wearing a Windbreaker and one of those old wise-guy fedoras like they used to wear in the movies. He took it off when he got inside the phone booth.

Frank sat in the car and watched him take the roll of quarters out of his pocket and knock it against the little metal shelf to break the paper open. Then he started feeding quarters into the phone.

Forliano was up in Murietta.

A long-distance call.

Frank couldn't hear him say "It's me," but even through the rain and the glass, he could see his lips move. He waited until Bap was in the middle of the conversation, not worried about it ending early. Forliano was a bullshit artist; if there was anything he could do, it was talk.

Frank had a .25 pistol for this job, not his usual .22. ("Don't sign your work," Bap had told him.) He flipped the hood of his Windbreaker up over his head and stepped outside. The street was empty—people in San Diego don't come out at night in the rain. Only Bap did that, to come to his office.

Bap dropped the roll of quarters when he saw Frank. They clattered to the floor, some of them rolling around like they were trying to escape. Bap tried to hold the door shut.

He knew, Frank thought.

He knows.

There was a little hurt look in his eyes as he tried to hold the door, but Frank was too strong and just ripped it open.

"I'm sorry," Frank said.

He put four shots into Bap's face.

The blood followed him back into the street.

Frank went to the funeral. Marie seemed inconsolable. Later on, she sued the FBI for negligence. The suit didn't get very far.

Neither did the murder investigation.

The feds liked Jimmy for it, and charged him, and threw the hit into the indictment salad against L.A. with everything else, but they had no evidence and couldn't prove anything.

And Frank got his button for that night, him and Mike.

They had a cheesy "ceremony" in the back of a car pulled off the I-15 near Riverside, with Chris Panno and Jimmy Forliano. That was it: Chris just pulled off the side of the road and Jimmy turned around to the backseat, pricked Frank's thumb with a pin, kissed him on the cheeks, and said, "Congratulations, you're in."

They didn't hold burning paper, or a stiletto or a gun, or anything like that. It was nothing like it was supposed to have been in the old days, nothing like it was in the movies.

Mike was disappointed.

Frank went straight after the hit on Bap.

Mike went to San Quentin.

He had gotten popped for extorting local gamblers—the feds had a wire tap of him and Jimmy Regace discussing it, so they were both jacked up good. The feds tried to put him behind the wheel for the Baptista hit, with Forliano as the triggerman, and tried to get him to trade up, but Mike didn't buy the bluff, and he wouldn't have taken the deal anyway.

Whatever else Mike was or wasn't, he wasn't a rat.

And he never breathed Frank's name.

Nobody did, and Frank sweated it out (literally) down in Rosarito. That same spring, the California Crime Commission listed ninety-three names on its "Organized Crime" list, and Frank wasn't on it. He figured that he had dodged a big bullet, so it was time to lay low.

Frank saw Richard Nixon one more time.

It was the autumn of '75, and the president wasn't the president anymore, but the *ex*-president, in exile and disgrace in San Clemente.

He came down to the Sur in October to play in Fitzsimmons's golf tournament, his first public appearance since being hounded out of office. Frank was in the parking lot when Nixon's limo pulled in and he saw him get out of the car. Nixon didn't look jaunty anymore; he looked beaten and old, but he played a full eighteen holes, and this time he didn't seem to mind being seen with the likes of Allen Dorner and Joey the Clown and Tony Jacks, who were playing, too.

They didn't mind being seen with Richard Nixon.

26

Is it possible? Frank wonders.

Could Marie Baptista, Bap's widow, have learned something in her suit against the FBI? Bided her time, saved her money, maybe? Put out a contract on me that Vince picked up?

It's unlikely, but I have to find out.

He gets in the rental car and heads for Pacific Beach.

Marie Baptista still lives in the same house.

Frank hasn't seen her since Bap's funeral, thirty years ago. He remembers the way to the house, though. Now he walks up the narrow little path between the well-tended flower gardens and rings the bell, like he used to do in the old days when he was coming to pay his respects.

Marie still looks great.

Tiny, diminished in the way of old people, but still great. She still has that pretty face, and the bright eyes, and one look at those eyes tells Frank that this old lady could commission a hit to revenge her husband.

"Mrs. Baptista," Frank says, "do you remember me? Frankie Machianno?"

She looks puzzled. She's trying hard, but it's not coming to her. Or she's a terrific actress.

"I used to work with your husband," Frank prompts.

As a matter of fact, I worked for *both* of them, he thinks.

"I used to drive you to get your groceries?" Frank says.

Her face brightens. "Frankie . . . Won't you come in?"

He steps inside. The place has that musty, flowery-perfume smell that comes with old ladies. But it's as neat as a pin and clean. She must have help come in. Bap must have left her comfortable.

Good for Bap.

"Would you care for some tea?" Marie asks. "I don't drink coffee anymore. My bowels."

"Tea would be nice," Frank says. "Can I help you?"

"I just put water on," Marie says. "Sit. I'll only be a minute."

Frank sits on the sofa.

Bap's crappy paintings hang all over the walls. Watercolor after watercolor of ocean scenes—and a bad portrait of her, Bap at his worst, but she must love it. To her, she looks beautiful.

Photos of Bap sit on every flat surface. The bad comb-over, the big bug eyes, the thick glasses, the awkward smile. Frank has a different picture of Bap burned in his head. Bap in the phone booth, blood running . . .

Marie comes in with two cups on saucers. Frank stands and takes one of the cups from her, then steadies her as she sits in her chair.

"It's so nice to see you, Frankie," she says.

"Nice to see you," Frank says. "I'm sorry I haven't come more often."

She smiles and nods. If it was her, Frank thinks, you'd know it by now. She'd look scared, or guilty; you would see it in her eyes.

"Did you bring my groceries?" she asks.

"No, ma'am," Frank says. "I don't do that now."

"Oh." She looks confused. "I thought . . ."

"Do you *need* groceries, Mrs. Baptista?" Frank asks.

"Well, yes." She looks around the room. "My list . . . I thought I . . . Where is it?"

"Is it in the kitchen?" Frank asks. "May I go look?"

She's frowning, looking around the room. Frank gets up, sets his teacup on a doily on the side table, and walks into the kitchen. He finds the list taped near the telephone. She either forgot to call the delivery service, or forgot that she called. Either way . . .

"Mrs. Baptista," he says as he steps back into the living room, "may I go get these for you?"

"That's your job, isn't it?" she snaps.

"Yes, ma'am, it is."

He finds an Albertsons in a strip mall three blocks away. It doesn't take him long, as the list is short—a few cans of tuna fish, some bread, some milk, some orange juice. He goes to the frozen section, carefully chooses a few of the better-quality meals for one, and tosses them into the basket.

He rings the bell again when he gets back. She lets him in and he sets the bags down on the kitchen counter and starts putting things away. He shows her the microwave dinners before he puts them in the freezer. "You can make these in five or six minutes," he tells her.

"I know that," she says impatiently.

Looking into the eyes of this old woman, he has so many memories. Her in her black dress, "the hot little number," Al DeSanto, and Momo. She was a tough lady, surviving all that, then marrying Bap to boot.

She reaches out, touches his arm, and gives him her best charming smile. Oddly enough, it *is* charming. She's still beautiful.

"I'll tell Momo," she says, "you did a good job."

"Thank you, ma'am."

"You can call me Marie."

"I can't do that, Mrs. Baptista."

He puts the dinners in the freezer, says good-bye, and leaves.

Yeah, you're a great guy, he thinks. You kill the woman's husband, so you buy her a couple of frozen dinners.

That should make it okay.

But it wasn't Marie who ordered the hit.

So I'm still stuck with the question, Why did Vince Vena want me dead? And if he wasn't acting on his own, then why did Detroit want me dead?

Doesn't matter, he decides. If Detroit didn't have a beef against me before I killed Vince, they sure do now. They can't just let someone kill a member of the ruling council of the Combination and walk away, even if it was in self-defense.

So this isn't going to be any short mix-up that can be quickly fixed. They'll be coming, in force and for the long haul, and they won't quit until they've put me in the dirt.

This is going to be a war, and I'll need the resources for a war.

He heads up to La Jolla to see The Nickel.

27

"We have an ID on your floater," the rookie agent tells Dave.

He's back in the FBI office downtown. The young agent came in like an acolyte bringing the chalice to a bishop. "How did you know, Mr. Hansen?"

"*Dave,*" Dave says. "I feel old enough already today."

And I can't remember this kid's name, he thinks. The new crop all look alike, just like this one. Slim but muscular, clean-cut, short hair. Tailored black or blue suits, white shirts, understated monotone ties.

This one is particularly meticulous about his clothes. He's wearing the standard white shirt, Dave notices, but it has French cuffs with expensive cuff links.

Cuff links, Dave thinks. What's it coming to? And Troy—that's the kid's name. Troy . . . Vaughan.

"But how did you know, Dave?" asks Troy.

To check the fingerprints against the OC files, he means. Still, that was a lot of files, and Dave's a little surprised they already have a hit. Supercomputers, I guess, he thinks. In the old days, it was a matter of— who cares, these aren't the old days.

"I *didn't* know," Dave says. "It was a hunch."

"Awesome."

"You going to give me the ID?" Dave asks.

Troy blushes and shows him the file.

Vincent Paul Vena looks a lot better in his mug shot than he did on the rocks at Point Loma. He's giving the camera that classic wise-guy "I don't give a shit" smile, the one they must teach in Goombah 101.

Vena has quite a sheet—simple assault, aggravated assault, shylocking, gambling, extortion, arson. . . . He did a five spot in Leavenworth for the fire. The Michigan cops liked him for several murders in the nineties but couldn't hang any on him. And the word is that he'd just risen to the ruling council of the Combination.

None of that means much to Dave. What does mean something— means a lot—is that Vena was the guy in Detroit whom Teddy Migliore kicked up to. It was Vena who looked after the San Diego strip club and prostitution business for the Combination.

"What's a Detroit guy doing in California?" Troy asks.

"Vacationing?" says Dave.

Maybe, Dave thinks, but probably not. More likely he was out here doing damage control from the G-Sting indictments.

Maybe hit somebody.

But it looks like someone hit back.

Dave finishes reading the Vena file, then gets in his car and drives over to what used to be Little Italy. Frank Machianno didn't show up again for the Gentlemen's Hour or at the bait shop, which was still locked up. No one has reported him missing, but he is missing, goddamn it.

Dave walks over to the downtown branch of the library, where Patty Machianno works part-time. Just to have a chat with her, not as an FBI agent, but as a concerned friend.

She's not there.

He walks all over the building and doesn't see her, so he asks a woman her age behind the front desk.

"Is Patty here today?"

The woman looks at him, then glances at his wedding ring.

"I'm a friend of Frank's," he says. Because everyone loves Frank the Bait Guy. "I was in the library, thought I'd say hi."

"Patty called in sick yesterday," the woman tells him. "Said she wasn't sure how long she'd be out."

"Thanks."

Dave goes back to the office, checks out a car, and drives over to Patty's house. He rings the bell half a dozen times, then snoops around the house, peeking in windows. The place is all locked up. He looks in the mailbox, and it's empty. No mail, no newspaper. He knows that Patty takes the *Union-Trib,* because Frank is always bitching about it.

"She could read it at the library," Frank told him.

"Maybe she likes to read it over breakfast, Frank." Patty is a devoted Padres and Chargers fan and reads the sports section every morning. She's *addicted* to Nick Canepa's columns.

Dave calls the newspaper's customer-service line.

"Hey, Frank Machianno here," he says. "I didn't get my paper this morning."

He gives the lady on the phone Patty's address. A few seconds later the girl gets back on the line and says, "Sir, you stopped delivery for two weeks."

Dave ends the call, dials the office, and gets Troy on the line. "Troy, get a license plate number and registration for a Machianno, Patricia, and start looking for the vehicle."

He spells out the name.

"Try the airport," he tells Troy. "Not the main lot, but one of the bargain lots."

A woman married to Frank Machianno for all those years wouldn't pay prime parking fees at the main airport lot. She'd go to one of the cheaper commercial lots off PCH and take the complimentary van to the airport.

Troy asks, "What file should I—"

"You *don't*," Dave snaps. "You don't open a file; you just do what I ask."

"Yes, sir."

"And don't call me 'sir.'"

"No."

Dave feels badly about snapping at the kid. He says, "Troy, you're doing a great job, okay?"

Dave leaves Patty's house and drives up to Solana Beach. He feels a little guilty about doing it, because Frank doesn't know that Dave knows about Donna. Frank has a thing about keeping his private life, well, *private,* and he probably wouldn't like Dave intruding into his personal life. Except that there's a Bureau intelligence file on Frankie, and Dave's studied every word of it.

I'm worried about you, Frank, Dave thinks as he drives north.

Donna Bryant's shop is closed.

Dave gets out of the car, walks up to the door, and reads the hand-lettered sign.

ON VACATION.

Donna Bryant doesn't take vacations.

Dave has checked in on the shop from time to time, and it's always open—seven days a week. If Donna Bryant were really taking a vacation, she would have planned it well in advance and would have arranged for someone to work the shop. At the very least, she would have had a printed sign made up—with a date announcing when she would reopen.

But she doesn't know when she'll be back, Dave thinks.

She didn't know she was leaving, either.

So Frank's in the wind, his ex-wife is gone, and his girlfriend, who is as big or bigger a workaholic than even Frank is, goes on a sudden vacation.

All after a Detroit strong-arm man washes up on the rocks.

No. It doesn't work that way.

Frank Machianno's in trouble.

But Frank would *never* go in the wind without making sure his loved ones were safe first. Patty and Donna being gone is a good sign that Frank is still alive, that he told them to get scarce and then went off the grid himself.

And where is Jill?

He debates whether to call her. On the one hand, he wants to make sure she's safe; on the other hand, he doesn't want to scare the hell out of her. And there's something else: Jill Machianno doesn't know that her father is . . .

And Frank just got back on good terms with her, and that means the world to him, and the last thing Dave wants to do is screw that up.

So find her, he tells himself, put a loose surveillance on her, but let it go at that. In the meantime, it might be a good idea to put a little pressure on Sherm Simon.

See what The Nickel has to say.

28

"Run."

That's what The Nickel has to say when he gets Frank's call. Just the single word, *Run,* before he sets the receiver down. Do not pass Go. Do not collect two hundred dollars. Do *not* come by the office or anywhere near it. Just run.

"Run?" Dave Hansen asks.

He's sitting across the desk from Sherm Simon.

"Japanese movie," Simon answers. "Kurosawa. If you haven't seen it, you should."

"That was *Ran.*"

"*Ran, Run,* what's the difference?"

"A big difference," Dave says, "if that was Frank Machianno on the phone."

"Frank who?"

"Don't play games with me."

"I don't play games," Sherm says. "Do you have a warrant, Agent Hansen? Because if you don't . . ." He gestures to the door.

"Frank may be in trouble," Dave says.

No shit, Frank may be in trouble, Sherm thinks. *I* may be in trouble. We *all* may be in trouble. There's trouble that you've had, trouble that you presently have, and trouble you're going to have—that's the world.

"You hold Frank's mad money," Dave says. It's a statement, not a question.

"I don't know what you're talking about."

"I'm trying to help him," Dave says.

"I seriously doubt that."

Dave gets up and leans over the desk. "Well, don't seriously doubt *this:* The Patriot Act gives me carte blanche when it comes to money laundering, Mr. Simon. I can open you up like a kid's juice carton and spill you out all over the place."

"You know goddamn well," Sherm says, "that Frank Machianno— and I'm not implying any relationship here—has nothing to do with terrorism. The notion is ridiculous."

"That's not what I'll tell the judge."

"No, I'll bet it isn't."

"If you see him," Dave says, "if he contacts you, you let me know right away."

Sherm doesn't make any promises.

29

Troy Vaughan leaves the Federal Building to go grab some lunch. They have a good cafeteria in the building, but Troy feels like getting some air. He tucks the *Union-Tribune* under his arm and leaves his office.

"It's raining," the receptionist tells him.

Troy holds up his umbrella.

There are maybe three people in San Diego who own an umbrella.

Anyway, it's not raining hard, and the umbrella stands up to the wind. Troy walks three blocks down to a little lunch place on Broadway, at the edge of the Gaslamp District. He finds a stool at the counter and sits down.

"What's the soup of the day?" he asks the guy behind the counter.

"Vegetable bean."

Troy orders the soup and half-sandwich special and unfolds his newspaper. He removes the sports section, sets it down on the stool beside him, and starts to read the main section.

A minute later, the guy two stools over gets up, slides his check off the counter, picks up the sports section, and goes up to the register. The man pays his check and walks out into the rain.

Troy cautions himself to ignore the man walking out. He makes himself sit and finish his sandwich and his cup of vegetable bean soup.

Which, he thinks, is not exactly haute cuisine, but good on a cold, rainy day.

30

The fishermen were trying to bag a four-hundred-pound marlin, but they hooked a four-hundred-pound bouncer instead.

Grisly catch.

Dave Hansen gets the call that morning and goes down to the docks to meet the boat. He isn't very worried about the forensics getting screwed up on a body that's been in the water for two days.

Still and all, it isn't hard to ID Tony Palumbo.

A few hours later, Dave gets confirmation that Palumbo was shot with the same gun that killed Vince Vena.

Hypothesis: Vena had come out from Detroit to get rid of Tony Palumbo, and someone had killed them both.

So someone was trying to clean up G-Sting from the top down. And to do it, they contracted with the most efficient hit man in California.

Dave puts a warrant out for Frank Machianno.

31

Frank takes a left on Nautilus Street and pulls off the road at Windansea.

Sherm's single word, *Run,* let him know that The Nickel is hot.

On a normal day, he'd relish the chance to come to Windansea, the legendary surf spot. Especially on a day when the break is going off and some of the world's best surfers will be out. But this isn't a normal day. This is a day when somebody is waiting to kill him.

Let them wait, Frank thinks.

He flirts briefly with the idea of driving into La Jolla anyway and just letting the chips fall.

They don't know what car you're driving, and, better, they don't know that you know that they're there. On the downside, you don't know who they are, or how many, or where they are. All you know is that they—whoever "they" are—will be hanging close to Sherm's office. And besides, what do you gain even if you "win" a shoot-out in the crowded shopping district on La Jolla Boulevard?

Life without parole.

So don't be stupid, he tells himself.

He pulls out of the parking lot and heads east on Nautilus, then south on La Jolla Scenic Drive, then east on Soledad Mountain Road out to the 5. Then he drives north to the 78 and heads east.

32

Jimmy the Kid Giacamone sits in a car and thinks about balls.

Balls is what Frankie Machine's got. Big, clanging brass clappers.

First he snatches Mouse Junior and rides him right into his daddy's place of business, next he pulls John Heaney into a Dumpster, and then he strolls into Migliore's bar, beats half the guys senseless, and roughs up Teddy himself.

The guy's got balls.

Good, Jimmy thinks, because that's the kind of trophy you want hanging on your wall. Not his balls, of course, not literally—but any hunter worth his salt wants the big old bull elephant, the one that, you fuck up, is going to kill you.

Otherwise, what's the point?

Jimmy's in California with his whole crew.

"The Wrecking Crew," they're glossed, because they work out of a car-salvage place out in Deerborn. Jimmy likes the tag—the Wrecking Crew—it says it all.

They didn't come in together, of course. That would've been stupid. They came in on separate flights, and none of them into San Diego, either. Jimmy came into Orange County, Paulie and Joey into L.A., Carlo into Burbank, Tony into Palm Springs, Jackie into Long Beach.

Mouse's guys met them and hooked them up with hardware.

That's all Jimmy asked from those West Coast mooks. "Get us some hardware, clean, untraceable. You guys think you can handle that?"

Maybe yes, maybe no. Frankie M. had come right into their driveway, for Chrissakes, and they let him skate. Way he heard it, Frankie had shot up the kid's Hummer and stolen Joey Fiella's car in the process.

Too fucking funny.

But the Mouseketeers had come through with the arsenal he'd

requested, so his crew was strapped and ready to rock and roll, Motor City–style.

Eight Mile–style.

Jimmy starts to sing:

> *"You only get one shot, do not miss your chance to blow*
> *This opportunity comes once in a lifetime, yo . . ."*

No shit, you ain't gonna blow this opportunity. Take care of business here, go back and jump the old man for the spot on the council. Like, *king* me, Dad. First step in taking the family back from the Tominellos and getting it home where it belongs, to the Giacamones.

Something Dad never had the stones to do.

But I do, Jimmy thinks.

Me and Frankie M., we got balls.

I just gotta blow Frankie's off.

So he sits in the car and waits.

Frankie Machine is going to show up sooner or later.

33

Two hours later, Frank's in the desert.

It's raining there.

Raining in the damn desert, Frank thinks. It just figures. It goes with all the other weird stuff that's going down.

Borrego Springs is an oasis in Anza-Borrego Desert State Park, 770,000 acres of some of the wildest terrain in the country. The town's founders thought it was going to be the next Palm Springs, but that never happened, mostly because there are only two roads into town, both of them bad, both of them winding through miles and miles of tough, inhospitable desert. A dozen or so *mojados* die every year trying to cross the desert from the Mexican side, and the Border Patrol has taken to burying water beneath thirty foot red-flagged poles to try to save lives.

So the town never really flourished, and now it's mostly a small retirement community for snowbirds, along with a couple of thousand hardy souls who live there year-round, even in the summer, when the temps can reach 130.

Frank drives in from Route 22, which snakes in seemingly endless switchbacks down from the mountains onto the vast desert floor and becomes Borrego's main street, which sports a couple of motels, a few restaurants and shops, and a bank.

The bank is what has brought Frank here.

It's a "tame" bank, one of the many places that Sherm launders money, and the prearranged pickup spot for Frank to get cash in case of an emergency. He drives past it, though, looking for cars or people who look out of place.

He doesn't see anything.

He parks the car outside Albierto's, a little Mexican joint where he's eaten before. The food is good, and cheap, and you get a lot of it, because Albierto's caters to the local Mexicans, who work damn hard and want a good meal for their money.

Frank stops outside, gets a *Borrego Sun* from the newspaper machine, walks up to the counter and orders two chicken enchiladas with black beans and rice and an iced tea, then sits down in a booth and waits for them to call his name.

Not a lot happens in Borrego Springs. There's an article about a new archaeological dig, another one about renovations to the high school gym, but the lead story is about the San Diego city council scandal and the grand jury indicting another councilman.

Frank skips over the article and finds Tom Gorton's column. Gorton is the editor and an old-time newspaper guy, and a hell of a good writer. Frank reads his column every time he sees a *Sun* somewhere. This time, Gorton's writing about all the rain they've had this winter, and how it will bring a wonderful spring bloom.

I'd like to see that, Frank thinks.

It's been years since there's been a big desert bloom, the valley floor carpeted with a panoply (puzzle word) of wildflowers. Frank's always found it moving, a miracle, when the sere desert becomes a sea of color and blooms with life. It's an *affirmation* of life, Frank thinks. It's proof that redemption is possible, when flowers blossom from the desert.

I hope I get to see it.

I'll bring Donna out here, maybe Jill, too. Maybe it's a trip that the three of us can do together.

Yeah, right, he thinks. *That's* going to happen, those two in the same car together.

"Bob."

Frank lifts a finger, then walks over to the counter and gets his tray. The food smells great. He goes to another counter, picks two different salsas—a *verde* and a *fresca*—and some spiced carrots.

The food is as good as it smells, the enchiladas smothered in a rich mole sauce, and the rice and beans done perfectly. Frank notices that they have fish tacos on the menu and wonders who supplies their seafood. He thinks briefly about making a pitch, then does the math and decides that the drive out here and then having to deadhead back would more than eat up any profit.

He finishes his meal, tosses the plastic plate into the trash can, and walks outside. The rain is gentle, more of a mist, but the streets are quiet, as if the residents are hiding in their houses, waiting for the sun to come out again.

Frank goes into the bank, walks up to the nice lady teller, and asks for the manager, Mr. Osborne.

"May I say who's calling?" the teller asks.

"Scott Davis," Frank says with a smile.

"One moment, Mr. Davis."

Osborne looks nervous when he comes out from the office. He has a big Adam's apple, anyway, on a skinny neck, but it's bobbing up and down a little more than Frank would like.

Don't get hinky, Frank tells himself. This is just an otherwise-law-abiding citizen a little stressed about committing an illegal act.

Osborne sticks his hand out. His palm is moist, sweaty.

"Mr. Davis," he says, loudly enough for the teller to hear. "Come into my office; let's see if we can do some business about your loan."

Frank follows him back into the office. Osborne opens a safe closet, then the safe, then takes out a canvas bank bag and hands it to Frank.

"Twenty thousand," he says.

"Minus your three points," Frank says. He puts the bag in his jacket.

"Aren't you going to count it?" Osborne asks.

"Should I?"

"It's all there."

"I just assumed it would be," Frank says.

Osborne is looking over Frank's shoulder, out the window that faces onto the street. Frank pulls the .38 and sticks it in the banker's face. "Tell me."

"These men," Osborne says, his voice shaking, "they came to my house this morning. They said to give you the money. Please don't kill me. I have a wife and two children. Becky is eight, and Maureen is—"

"Shut up," Frank says. "Nobody's killing anybody."

Maybe.

Osborne starts to cry. "My career . . . my family . . . prison . . ."

"You're not going to prison," Frank says. "All you need to do is keep your mouth shut, *capisce?*"

"Keep my mouth shut," Osborne repeats, like he's trying to remember directions somebody's giving him over the phone: Turn left on Jackson, second right on La Playa, keep my mouth shut.

"Is there a back door?" Frank asks.

Osborne looks at him. Frank repeats the question.

"You told me to keep my mouth shut," Osborne says.

"Not *now,*" Frank says. "Is there a back way out?"

"I'll have to unlock it."

"What are you waiting for?"

The door is triple-locked and has a security bar across it. It takes a good minute for Osborne to get the door unlocked.

"Don't open it," Frank says.

What are you thinking? he asks himself. Any decent crew will have a guy or two out back. And they'll have heard the door unlatching. You step out that door, you walk into a hail of bullets.

Then again, you walk out the *front* door, you step into the same. You're trapped.

34

That's certainly what Jimmy the Kid thinks.

Frankie M. is totally fucked.

Jimmy's sitting in the car across the street. He's in the passenger seat, rifle in his lap, waiting for the kill shot.

"You're sure he went in?" Jimmy asks.

"I watched him," Carlo says.

Carlo placed himself in the ice cream store across the road. He watched Frankie Machine drive by, then have lunch, then go into the bank. He could have taken the man out himself, except he had strict orders from Jimmy, who'd said, "You see him, you call me." So Carlo called him, then got himself another ice cream—butter brickle this time.

Now Jimmy sits in the car, his foot tapping like a bass drummer in a heavy-metal band.

"Paulie, Jackie, and Joey are in back?"

"Yeah."

"You sure?"

"You can call them, you want."

Jimmy thinks about it, then decides against it. It would be just like Paulie to shout into the phone and tip off Frankie M. No, we want Frankie nice and confident. Let him come strolling through that door with his money in hand and happy thoughts in his head.

Then *blam*.

You only get one shot, do not miss your chance to blow . . .

"What's taking so fucking long?" Jimmy asks.

Carlo doesn't have time to answer, because, just then, sirens start wailing.

Police sirens.

Coming this way.

Carlo doesn't wait for Jimmy to tell him to get in gear and get the fuck out of there.

It's the obvious call.

35

Frank goes out the back as soon as he hears the sirens.

Osborne had hit the silent alarm, just like he'd told him to. Hopefully, the banker will follow the rest of his instructions.

"Tell the state troopers a man came in and tried to rob you, then got nervous and ran out. Give the cops the description of one of the guys who approached you this morning," he'd told Osborne.

"Why don't I tell them the robber got twenty grand?" Osborne asked.

"Are you *supposed* to have an extra twenty K in the bank?" Frank said.

"No."

"Well?"

"Oh, right."

"Just hit the alarm, okay?"

Frank doesn't run out the back alley, though. He finds the ladder that leads to the roof and climbs up. By the time he reaches the top, his heart is hammering and he's gasping for breath.

Jill was right about the red meat and the desserts, he thinks. I have to cut down. He crawls along the rooftop on his stomach, then climbs down the ladder on the other side just as the troopers' cars screech to the front of the bank. Frank walks back to his car, calmly backs out, drives across the street to a gas station, and starts to fill his tank.

"What's going on?" he asks the attendant, who's come out to see what all the excitement's about.

"I don't know," the kid says. "Something with the bank."

"Jeez, no kidding?" Frank says. "That's wild."

He watches as Osborne comes out of the bank with one of the troopers and a citizen runs across from the ice cream parlor and starts pointing west, with one of those emphatic "They went thataway" gesticulations.

One of the troopers rushes back to his car and races west.

Frank fills up his tank.

"I hope they get the guys," he says, and then pulls out and drives east, doing the speed limit.

You're an idiot, he tells himself. Or else you're just getting tired, worn down.

It was the guy in the ice cream shop, across the street. You know him, just can't place him.

Damn getting old.

Come on, think, think, think.

It's flirting with him, skirting the edge of his memory.

Carlo Moretti.

A Detroit guy, a hitter for Vince Vena.

36

It was 1981.

Frank and Patty were already having a tough time in their marriage. They'd been trying and trying to have a baby, to no avail. They'd been to doctor after doctor, but the word was always the same: Frank had a low sperm count, nothing they could do. They talked adoption, but Patty just wasn't into it.

She said she didn't blame him—that would be irrational and unfair, she said—but he knew that part of her, deep down, harbored a resentment. She blamed his schedule, the pressure he put on himself with not just the fish business but the linen business now, too, and he would answer that if they ever did have a baby, he wanted to be able to provide for the kid, offer his child a future.

So it was tough times, their love life had turned into an anxiety-ridden chore, and it was just on one of those days when she was most likely to get pregnant that he got the call from Chicago to go to Vegas and take care of this little problem.

Truth was, Frank was *glad* to get away for a few days.

You need the money, he told himself, and he did, but the truth was that home was turning into a painful place and he was looking for excuses to get away. That was part of the reason for the long hours at work, part of the reason for taking the job in Las Vegas.

He and Patty argued over it.

"You're going off to Vegas with your buddies?" she said. *"Now?"*

Now, Frank thought, when I'm supposed to be dutifully, joylessly performing an act of love. "It's work."

"Work," she scoffed. "Gambling away our money, screwing hookers, some kind of work."

"I don't gamble, I don't screw hookers."

"So what do you do in Vegas?" she asked. "Go to shows?"

He blew up. "It's *work*! It's how I make money! How I put food on the table! How I pay for doctors! How I—"

"What kind of work?" she asked. "What exactly is it you do, anyway?"

"You don't want to know!" he yelled. "Just take the money, keep your mouth shut, don't ask questions about things that are none of your business!"

"None of my *business*? I'm your *wife*!"

"You don't need to remind me!"

That hurt her. He knew it before the words were even out of his mouth and wished he could call them back out of the air. She dissolved into tears. "I want a baby."

"So do I."

His parting words, going out the door. Still, he had to admit that the long drive to Vegas was a relief, a few hours of solitude and *quiet*. No arguments or recriminations, no daunting sense of failure. And time to think about the job, because it was a tricky one.

Donnie Garth was the golden boy, the wunderkind, of the Chicago real estate tycoons. Nobody knew how well he'd done, though, until he up and bought the Paladin Hotel in Vegas. Nobody knew he had *that* kind of money.

It worked out well for a while; then Garth got delusions of grandeur and actually objected to the skimming that the Chicago mob was conducting in his casino.

Frank was the one who drove Carmine Antonucci up to Garth's place in La Jolla to "explain it to him." Garth's home was something else—a Norman-style mansion with a circular gravel driveway and a six-car garage that housed, among other cars, a Ferrari and an Austin-Healey.

There was no denying that Garth had style.

He stepped out the front door that day, a diminutive man with a yellow cashmere sweater tied around his neck, a blue silk shirt open at the collar, and white slacks over loafers.

Frank remembers that he was dwarfed by the huge wooden door behind him. He was all smiles and handshakes, but you could tell that he was embarrassed that actual hoods had showed up at his door, and nervous that the neighbors might see the kind of visitors he was getting.

Visitors like Carmine Antonucci and Frankie Machine.

Carmine was Chicago's man in Las Vegas, supervising the very profitable skim that Garth wanted to mess with. So Carmine politely accepted the iced tea that Garth offered, waited while the butler went and got it, drank a few social sips, then pointed to Frank and said, "Take a good luck at this man. Do you know why they call him 'The Machine'?"

"No."

"Because he's automatic," Carmine said. "He never misses. And if you continue to be an obstacle to the smooth running of my hotel, I'm going to send The Machine to see you. You'll never see him, because you'll be dead. Do we have an understanding?"

"We do."

Garth's hand was shaking like there was an earthquake. You could hear the ice and the long silver teaspoon rattling in the glass.

"Thank you for the iced tea," Carmine said, getting up. "It was delicious and refreshing. We'd love to stay for dinner, thank you, but I have to catch a flight."

And that was that.

Frank never said a word.

He drove Carmine back to the airport, where a private plane flew him back to Vegas.

And Donnie Garth started behaving himself.

Except he soon had a problem.

What had happened was that Donnie Garth was going to take the kink out of his sore neck by taking a steam in the hotel spa, and he was doing this when a piece of Chicago muscle named Marty Biancofiore walked in.

Marty had done some serious work for Garth, intimidating a few other prospective buyers who had also wanted the Paladin, so he got it in his head that he was *owed*. What he said to Garth while they were both wrapped in towels was that Donnie was going to give him a piece of the hotel or he was going to *take* a piece of Garth, and a very essential piece at that.

Which sort of put the kink back in Garth's neck.

His hair was still damp when he called Carmine.

Now, Donnie Garth was a first-rate pain in the ass, but the Paladin was bringing in a lot of money, a lot more money than Marty could ever kick up.

And Garth was scared, skulking around the hotel, half afraid to come out of his office, wanting extra security all the time, so Carmine finally put a call in to Frank.

Because Garth had personally requested "that guy, The Machine."

A lot of people had seen or at least heard about the beef between Garth and Biancofiore, and Chicago wanted to send a message: You do not mess with one of our people. They wanted Biancofiore done right on the Strip, they wanted his body found, and they wanted it ugly.

Marty Biancofiore was no civilian. He had done some work for Chicago himself. He'd be armed and on the lookout. Marty Biancofiore wasn't going to open his door to no pizza guy.

He was the first man you actually had to hunt, Frank remembers. You spent five whole days tracking him, watching his patterns, waiting for an opportunity, thinking it through.

It would have to be at night, he decided. Even Frankie Machine wouldn't try to take someone out on the Strip in broad daylight. No, that would come later, Frank thinks now, when Chicago duked it out old-style with Joe Bonnano and they did just that. Luckily, Marty Biancofiore worked the eight-to-two shift at Caesar's, where he'd been put on the prime-time crew just to bust Garth's balls.

Marty would work his shift, stop at the bar for two comped vodkas to unwind, then walk out to his car in the employees' parking lot. He always looked carefully around and unlocked the car with a remote key, for fear of a bomb, Frank guessed. He always looked into the car before he got in, locked the doors quickly, and drove straight home. One night, he called a hooker; the other three he took a shower, watched some television, and went to bed.

It would be relatively easy to hit him at home, Frank thought. Break in when he's in the shower and pop him there. But that's not how Chicago wants it. Or that little punk, Garth, who's demanding that "a lesson be taught."

It would have to be the parking lot.

But how?

You can't just gun him down when he walks out of the casino—too many potential witnesses, and the risk of a gunfight breaking out is too heavy. Some civilian catching a stray bullet right on the Strip would be unacceptable.

It was one of Frank's absolute rules: You don't put civilians at risk. Guys in the game, they know the risks, and they take their chances, but some Joe Lunchbucket who saves up his money for a Vegas blowout doesn't deserve to die because someone gets sloppy.

So it has to be inside the car.

But if you shim the door, the alarm will go off and that will be that. You could steal the keys and have them copied, get in and wait for Marty, but he checks the car out pretty good before he gets in, and he'd either run away or gun you down while you're lying on the backseat.

So how are you going to get in the car?

Only one way.

Marty has to invite you in.

And how are you going to get him to do that?

Every man has a fatal flaw. Bap had taught Frank that. Not in those words exactly, but the point was that every man had a chink in his armor, and it was just a matter of finding it.

Bap had even listed them for him. "You got your lust, your greed," Bap had said, "you got your ego, your pride, and then you got your wishful thinking."

"What do you mean?"

"Some people believe what they want to believe," Bap had said, "they want it bad enough."

Marty was bragging to anyone who would listen how he had that little shit Donnie Garth shaking in his Guccis, how Garth had better stay out of his way, how he might just put him in the dirt anyway. Frank actually heard him mouthing this crap, sitting at the bar after his shift.

And Marty needed money.

Frank did his homework. Marty had been hitting the sports book hard and it had been hitting him back harder. He had lost a bundle on college football, tried to get well on the Monday-night game, but had only got sicker. He owed a bundle to a nasty shy named Herbie Goldstein and was having trouble just coming up with the vig.

So when the call came from Donnie Garth, Marty *wanted* to believe it. And Garth was a hell of an actor, a natural-born hustler who knew how to put up, well, a *front*. He also knew by then how to follow instructions, and he followed these to the letter.

Frank sat with him when he made the call.

"Marty? It's Donnie."

"You better have good news for me."

"Marty, we're friends," Donnie said. "I've been thinking. I want to do the right thing. How about you take a hundred K, we put this to bed?"

"A hundred? Fuck you."

Frank listened while they negotiated a settlement of $250,000. Bap was right, Frank thought. Biancofiore believed it because he wanted to believe it. It fed his ego and solved his financial problems. What was it Bap had said? "When you want to catch a fish, you gotta give it the bait it's *hungry* for."

"*Cash,* Donnie," Marty said.

Frank nodded and Donnie said, "But look, Marty, this has to stay between you and me. If word gets out that I can be . . . *pressured,* I'll be shit in this town."

"It's nobody business but ours," Marty said.

"That's great, Marty, thanks," Garth said. "Look, I'll get the cash, then swing by your house."

This was the critical moment. Frank held his breath for a second before he heard Marty say, "I think maybe someplace more public."

"You don't trust me, Marty?"

Biancofiore just laughed.

Garth said, "Marty, I can't hand you a briefcase full of cash on the floor of Caesar's Palace."

Marty thought about it for a second. "The parking lot," he said. "My car."

"I'll meet you after your shift."

"Fuck that," Marty said. "Noon."

Because Marty knew what they all knew. No one, *no one,* was going to try to take him out in broad daylight right on the Strip.

Marty looked to Frank.

Frank thought about it for a second, then nodded.

"Okay," Donnie said. "Noon it is. What are you driving these days? What's your slot number?"

"Get out of town for a few days," Frank told Garth. "Go back to your Norman mansion, throw a dinner party, create an alibi." Sip some vintage wine with the beautiful people while I clean up your mess for you, he thought.

So it was Frank, not Donnie Garth, waiting in the parking lot when Marty drove in that day.

Marty didn't like it at all.

He rolled down the window and asked, "Who the fuck are you? Where's Garth?"

"He's not coming."

"What the fuck!"

But Frank saw him eyeball the attaché case in his hand.

"I have the money," Frank said. "Do you want it?"

"People don't walk away from money," Bap had lectured him. "They should, sometimes, but they don't." Marty didn't. He thought about it—Frank could see him thinking—but he didn't walk away. Instead, he got out of the car and carefully patted Frank down from his armpits to his ankles, front and back.

"I'm not wearing a wire," Frank said.

"Fuck the wire," Marty said. "I'm looking for a piece."

He didn't find one. He got back behind the driver's seat, flipped the door locks open, and ordered, "Get in."

Frank slid into the passenger seat.

Marty was holding a .45 on his lap.

"Hey," Frank said.

"I ain't lived this long being careless," Marty said. "You said you got the money?"

"It's in the briefcase."

That was the moment, Frank remembers now. You figured if Marty simply took the case, kicked you out, and drove away, you'd never get near him again. If he opened the briefcase right there, you were a dead man.

You were counting on his character, his caution. This was a man who checked his cars for bombs every night. He wasn't going to take a brief-case away with him.

Anyway, you hoped he wouldn't.

"Show me," Marty said.

"You want me to open it right here?"

"The fuck did I say?"

Frank lifted the briefcase onto his own lap, slid the locks, and the lid flipped open with a metallic click. Frank grabbed the silenced .25 inside and fired five times through the briefcase lid. Then he put the gun back in the case, got out of the car, and walked away.

Right down the Strip.

Frank went back to his hotel room, wiped the gun down with iso-propyl alcohol, did the same with the briefcase. Chicago had offered a cleanup crew to dispose of the weapon, but Frank didn't trust anyone else to clean up after him. He'd chosen a .25 for a reason, knowing that the bullets, after piercing the cheap briefcase, would have the juice to enter Marty's skull, but not enough to exit. A parking lot attendant found Marty about an hour later. He thought the guy slumped on the wheel had had a heart attack until he saw the five holes in his head.

Frank got into his car and drove the back route through the Mojave, found a decrepit mine, smashed the gun into pieces, and tossed it and the briefcase down the shaft.

Yeah, easy to get rid of the gun, harder to get rid of the memories.

They don't stay down the mine shaft.

Actually, there had been instant fallout from the Biancofiore job. Fat Herbie Goldstein started screaming all over town that he was out the $75,000 that Marty was even *less* likely to pay him now that he was dead, and that *someone* owed him this money.

"Tell Garth to pay him," Frank told Mike Pella.

"Are you fucking kidding?"

"Tell him to sell one of his cars and pay the man," Frank said. "Tell him The Machine said so."

Donnie Garth paid Herbie Goldstein his $75K.

Which is how Frank became friends with Herbie Goldstein.

Fat Herbie sought Frank out after he got his money from Donnie Garth. Goldstein actually got on a plane, flew out to San Diego, and requested a sit-down with Frankie Machine. They had it over lunch, of course—if you were with Herbie, you were *eating*.

Now, a lot of mobbed-up guys had the sobriquet "Fat." Frank knew five of them personally. But none of them could play seesaw with Herbie Goldstein—they'd just be up in the air, looking down at almost four hundred pounds of Herbie, who'd probably be sucking on a Fudgsicle.

Anyway, Herbie took Frank out to lunch and said, "That was a decent thing, what you did for me. I just wanted to tell you in person I appreciated it."

"It was the right thing," Frank said.

"Not everybody *does* the right thing," Herbie said. "Not these days."

Herbie picked up the lunch check, which was no small thing, then extended an invitation: "If you're ever in Las Vegas, I'll show you a good time."

Frank didn't plan on going to Vegas, he really didn't. But the invitation lingered in his head. The harder he worked, the longer hours, the dutiful, futile sex with Patty, the fights, the silences all made the offer from the 375-pound gangster seem like a siren song.

So one day, after a chef gave him agita over a perfectly fine unit of yellowtail, Frank threw a few clothes in the car and headed to Las Vegas.

He pulled into town and gave Herbie a ring. Ten minutes later, he was unpacking his clothes in a comped suite at the Paladin. He took a nice long bath in the in-room Jacuzzi, then a nap, then got up and got dressed to go meet Herbie in the lobby.

Herbie had two Playboy models with him, Susan and Mandy.

Susan, a petite blonde with an unpetite chest, was Herbie's date. Mandy was for Frank. She had shiny shoulder-length brown hair, full lips, warm brown eyes and was wearing a dress that showed a body that deserved showing. Frank told himself that she was a platonic date, that's all. A companion for drinks, dinner, and maybe a show, so he wouldn't feel like the third wheel.

They did the town.

God, did they do the town.

The food, the wine, the shows—Frank was never allowed to reach for his wallet. Not that a bill came anyway, it never did. Herbie left a big tip, and that was it. They got the best tables, bottles of the best wine came over with compliments of the management, and they got invited to parties in the greenroom after the shows.

And then there were the women.

Fat Herbie Goldstein was not an attractive man, although he did bear an uncanny resemblance to Pavarotti—if the tenor had gone on an all-pudding diet for a couple months, that is.

And he wasn't charming—if anything, Herbie had a kind of *anti-charm*, where the word *repulsive* came from, Frank guessed. Herbie repulsed most people—with his voracious consumption, nonexistent table manners, and the rivers of sweat that always seemed to be running down his fat cheeks or pooling in his armpits. His clothes were rumpled and usually had food stains on them, he had a mouth like a sewer, and most people in Vegas would cross the street to avoid running into him.

But Herbie pulled women.

There was just no question about it. Frank never saw Herbie after dark without an absolutely drop-dead-gorgeous woman on his arm. And they weren't hookers—they were dancers and models and good-time girls. They accepted presents from him, for sure, sometimes fairly big presents, like condos or cars, but it wasn't just the money.

They really seemed to like being with Herbie, and the more time Frank spent with the guy, the more he did, too.

But that first night . . .

They rolled back into the Paladin around 3:00 a.m. When Frank went to say good night to Mandy, his Playmate, she looked at him funny.

"You don't like me?" she asked.

"I like you fine."

"What is it, I don't turn you on?"

He'd had a hard-on all night. "You turn me on a lot."

"Then let's go make each other feel good," she said.

"Mandy, I'm married."

She smiled. "It's just sex, Frank."

No, it wasn't.

After nine faithful years of marriage, the last few of them fairly unhappy, nothing was "just sex." Mandy did things that Patty would never have thought of and wouldn't have done if she had. Frank was starting in on his usual sexual routine when Mandy stopped him and said gently, "Frank, let me show you how to please me."

She did.

For the first time in his life, Frank felt this sense of freedom about sex, because it wasn't a struggle or negotiation or an obligation. It was just pure pleasure, and when he woke up in the morning, he wanted to feel guilty, but the fact was, he didn't. He just felt good.

It didn't hurt that Mandy had already gotten up and left, leaving only a little note telling him that she felt "well and truly fucked," with one of those little smiley faces above her signature.

Herbie came by to take him to breakfast.

"You should try some Jew food," Herbie said when Frank went for the bacon and eggs.

He ordered Frank an onion bagel with lox, cream cheese, and a slice of red onion.

It was delicious, and the contrasts of tastes and textures—sharp, creamy, soft, and crispy—was a revelation to him. Herbie knew what he was talking about. When you really got talking with him, it turned out that Herbie knew a lot about a lot. He knew about food, wine, jewelry, and art. He had Frank over to his house to see his collection of Erté and his wine cellar. You would never call Herbie a cultured man by any means, but he had some surprises in him.

Take the crossword puzzles, for instance.

It was Herbie who turned Frank on to the puzzles, and Herbie could do the Sunday *New York Times* puzzle in ink. Sometimes, Frank wasn't so sure Herbie needed to write anything down at all—he might have all the words in his head. And he was a walking dictionary, although the funny thing was, he didn't use any of those words in his conversation, ever.

"I guess I'm what you would call an idiot savant," he said one day when Frank asked him about it. Although, when Frank looked up the term *idiot savant,* he realized that no idiot savant would know the expression.

"You and Mandy got along, huh?" Herbie asked as they were walking out of his wine cellar the day after Frank had shattered his marriage vows with multiple, and creative, acts of adultery.

"I guess you could say that."

"We have two different girls tonight," Herbie said. "Very nice girls. Very nice."

Frank left Vegas five days later in need of a vitamin E injection but otherwise feeling rested and satisfied. He went back a lot after that, mostly getting comped at the Paladin, sometimes staying somewhere else and paying his own way because he didn't want to abuse the situation.

37

The wise guys were banging Vegas for everything it was worth.

And why not?

The skim was flowing.

The only problem was, the bosses wanted more and more of it, and other families were looking to get in on it, so the skimmers got to the point that they weren't just skimming; they were tapping deeper and deeper into the well.

But there's only so much water in a desert.

Sooner or later, it would have to end, but none of them saw then that it was going to be sooner. It was just one continuous party then, and Frank, after years of working his ass off, was partying with the best of them. What he'd do was, he'd put in sixteen-hour days in San Diego at his businesses all week, then leave Friday after lunch and drive to Vegas and spend the weekend. Most times, he'd make it back on Monday, but sometimes he wouldn't.

Patty didn't seem to care.

They'd pretty much given up on having a kid, pretty much given up on the marriage itself, so she seemed almost relieved to have him gone on weekends. He made a couple of halfhearted invitations for her to come with him, but she recognized them for what they were and turned them down.

"We'd be the same people in Vegas as we are here," she said once.

"I don't know," Frank said. "Maybe we wouldn't."

He really tried one time.

"We'll go for drinks, dinner, some nice shows," he said. Maybe back to bed afterward—for more than turning over and going to sleep.

"Is this the routine you've got down with your bimbos?" she replied.

There weren't any bimbos, not yet, but he didn't bother to deny it. Let her think what she was going to think. What difference did it make, anyway?

So he went to Vegas by himself.

He was never alone for long.

While Frank enjoyed the solitude of the long drive, listening to his opera tapes on the car stereo, singing along without bothering anyone, he was ready for some companionship by the time he got there.

If you couldn't find company in Las Vegas in those days, it was because you wanted to be alone.

So he'd check into his room, shower, change clothes, then go over to Herbie's place.

Herbie had taken some of his shark money and bought a nondescript little club tucked away in a strip mall among a bunch of auto-body shops. It was far away from the Strip, the casinos, and the usual spots the feds had under surveillance, and that was the point. You didn't know about Herbie's unless you were supposed to, and if a tourist or a citizen waiting for his car to be fixed happened to wander in, he left in a hurry with a polite but firm "This place ain't for you, friend."

Herbie's was for wise guys, period.

For some reason or another, Herbie's became the hangout of choice for the California guys. They were all back from the joint now, and all in Vegas, living large off the skim.

Mike was back—he'd actually moved to Vegas, thinking it was going to be his big chance, and he was usually sitting at a table with Peter Martini, aka Mouse Senior, who had just been made boss. And Peter's brother Carmen was usually there, and so was their nephew, Bobby, a nightclub singer.

And, of course, you had Herbie, sitting doing his crossword puzzles with Sherm Simon in the corner that became known as "Little Israel."

So there were plenty of guys to hang out with, and sometimes Frank sat at one of the tables and listened to the bullshit sessions, but mostly he'd go back into the kitchen and cook.

Those were good times, standing at the stove, listening to the guys while whipping up the *linguine con vongole* and *spaghetti all' amatriciana*, the *baccalà alla Bolognese* and *polpo con limone e aglio*. It was almost like the old days when he was a kid, back when San Diego's Little Italy was still intact and people still made real meals.

Frank had really missed cooking as he spent more time at work and less time at home, and he and Patty had slipped into the routine of having their dinners separately. Herbie had a beautifully equipped kitchen and imported the best ingredients, so the cooking was a pleasure and a joy.

And listening to the guys—the conversations, the jokes, the ball busting.

Hanging out with mob guys, Frank thought, was like being frozen in some perpetual junior high school time warp. The conversations were always about sex, food, farts, smells, girls, small dicks, and homos.

And crime, of course.

The only thing at Herbie's being cooked up more than pasta was crime. Most of the scores never came off, of course—they were just bullshit—but some of them did. There were plots to get in on the legal brothels north of the city, a plan to sell machine guns to motorcycle gangs, a very serious discussion on how to make counterfeit credit cards, and Frank's personal favorite—Mike's theft of three thousand T-shirts and two hundred twenty-inch TV sets from the convention center.

"What are you going to do with two hundred TV sets?" Frank asked Mike after the score had actually come off.

"What am I going to do with three thousand T-shirts?" Mike asked.

Frank was going to ask him why he'd stolen the T-shirts in the first place, but then he realized that it was a stupid question, akin to the "Why climb Mount Everest?" query—the answer was, of course, "Because it's there." The truth was that wise guys would steal anything, even stuff they didn't want and couldn't use, just because they could steal it.

Anyway, these things kept Frank amused.

And it wasn't just the guys; it was also the women.

It had been tough that first time, cheating on Patty, but then Frank started seeing all kinds of women, at first in the gravitational orbit of babe magnet Herbie Goldstein, then on his own.

He saw models, showgirls, croupiers, dealers, and tourists who were in town for a good, uncomplicated time, which Frank gave them. He took them to nice dinners, to shows, always treated them like ladies, and was a generous, caring lover. Frank found out that he really liked women and that they returned the compliment.

Except Patty.

He treated her badly and she returned *that* compliment.

He talked about it with Sherm one night during a quiet moment at Herbie's. "Why can't you be with your wife the way you are with your girlfriends?"

"Different breed, my friend," Sherm said. "Different species entirely."

"Maybe we should marry the girlfriends."

"I tried it," Sherm says. "Twice."

"And?"

"And they turn into wives," Sherm said. "It starts to happen when they're planning the wedding, this metamorphosis from sex kitten to house cat. It doesn't work. You don't believe me, ask my lawyer."

"You *are* a lawyer."

"Ask my *divorce* lawyer," Sherm said. "Tell him I sent you—he has a boat named after me."

"I don't think it's them," Frank said. "I think it's us. Once we stop trying to get them into bed—because now they're *always there*—we stop making the effort. We turn them into wives."

"I think it's just the way of the world, my friend," Sherm said. "The way of the world."

I don't think so, Frank thought.

He resolved to go home and give it a real try with Patty again. Treat her like a mistress instead of a wife and see what happened. But he didn't—it was easier to go to bed with showgirls.

Or just hang out with Herbie.

It was always good spending time with Herbie, working the *New York Times* Sunday crossword over bagels and lox with an opera broadcast as a background, or drinking a wine that Herbie had discovered, or chuckling over the plots and plans of Mike Pella, the Martini Brothers, and the rest of the crew.

They were good times.

They all ended when he had to go kill Jay Voorhees.

38

Jay Voorhees was the security chief at the Paladin, in charge of making sure that the casino wasn't being skimmed, so in the interest of efficiency, he was also in charge of the skim. He was good at it, the Harry Houdini of the counting room, the way he could make coins and bills escape from lockboxes.

Then the FBI got to him, started to put pressure on him, and he caved.

Ran to Mexico, where the feds couldn't get to him. Fine as far as it went, but Chicago wasn't looking to extradite him; they were looking to make Houdini disappear for good. Because Voorhees knew everything—he could give up Carmine, Donnie Garth, everybody. Then the whole house of cards, as it were, would come tumbling down. They had to find Voorhees and put him out.

People think it's easy to disappear.

It isn't.

It's hard and it's tiring and it's expensive as hell. Money *hemorrhages* when you're traveling, anyway, and when you're on the move and trying not to leave any footprints, it bleeds all the faster. You're trying to use cash everywhere, but you see it just flying out of your pocket, and you go to the plastic.

Unless you're prepared to go off the radar, it's a difficult trick to pull off, and Jay Voorhees wasn't prepared. He had just panicked and run. And it was only a matter of time before he figured out that the feds would offer him a pretty good deal to trade up, and he'd get tired of running and come in from the cold.

Frank had to find him first.

"We can put a crew down there," Carmine Antonucci said. "Anything you need."

"I don't want a crew," Frank said.

Bunch of doofs tripping over one another's feet. A pool of potential witnesses when the feds flipped them five years down the line. No, he didn't want a crew, just operating expenses, in cash, because he didn't want to leave any footprints, either.

And there were a lot of footsteps. Frank followed Voorhees from Mexico City to Guadalajara, then across to Mazatlán and Cozumel, then to Puerto Vallarta and all the way down the tip of Baja to Cabo.

A *connection* develops between hunter and prey. Guys deny it as airy-fairy bullshit, Frank thought, but they all know it happens. You track a guy long enough, you get to know him, you're living his life, one step removed, and he becomes *real* to you. You try to get inside his head, think the way he thinks, and if you succeed at that, in a strange way you become him.

And he becomes you, for the same reason. If he has any instinct at all, he begins to feel you. As he runs, as he tries to outthink you, to anticipate your moves and counter them, he gets to know you, too.

You're on the same road—by necessity, you go to the same places, eat the same food, see the same things, share the same experiences. You develop things in common. You *connect*.

Frank missed him by three days in Mexico City, talked to a cabbie who drove him to the airport, bribed a baggage agent who put him on a flight to Guadalajara. He wasn't sure, but he might have glimpsed him on the Cross of Squares there, outside the cathedral. Going to pray? Frank wondered. Maybe he bought a little clay model—a *milagro*—from one of the street vendors and left it at the altar with a contribution and a request for a miracle. He missed him by one night at his hotel, found out he went to the train station. He might have lost the trail there, except that Voorhees used his AmEx to check into a hotel in Mazatlán. Frank went to the resort town and just walked the beach, asking everybody if they'd seen him, throwing around money. He didn't expect to get an answer and he didn't hide the fact that he was there—he *wanted* Voorhees to know.

"Flushing the bird," is what Bap had called it. "The bird might be safe hiding in the bush, but it sees the hunter and flies, and that's what kills it."

Voorhees fled to Cozumel, Frank right after him. Voorhees checked in and out of second-rate hotels. One time, Frank missed him by an hour. He actually *saw* him in Cabo, at a cheap hotel on the Pacific side, drinking a beer and picking at a plate of *camarones*. He was gaunt and thin; his slacks were bunched up awkwardly around his waist.

Voorhees saw *him,* too; he definitely did. He made you, Frank thinks now. He looked at you with those scared, haunted eyes and *knew.* Voorhees paid his check and left the place, and Frank followed him. But there was no place to do it, so Frank let him get on a bus and go.

He knew Voorhees's string was running out.

In every town he'd gone to, the hotels had gotten a little cheaper, the meals a little skimpier. He had started on jets, then had rented cars and taken trains, but now he was on a run-down rural bus, and a bad one at that. Frank checked the route—the bus was headed on the single road up the east coast of Baja.

Now his options weren't radial; they were linear. He had trapped himself along this spine of coastline, with the ocean on one side and impenetrable desert on the other, and all he could do was make his way from one little fishing village to the next.

Frank enjoyed that trip, if enjoyment is a concept that can be hooked to hunting a man down in order to kill him. But he savored the leisure of the bus trip, with nothing to do but marvel at the stark countryside, or read, or watch the startlingly blue water of the Sea of Cortez. He liked playing with the kids on the bus, holding a baby that one time so the mother could get a break, and he reveled in the relentless sun and the baking, soothing heat.

Those were good days, those days following Jay Voorhees up Baja. Frank was almost sorry that it was about to end.

Voorhees went to ground in the little village of Santa Rosalía. He'd found himself a little fisherman's shack on the rocky beach. It's what he should have done in the first place, Frank thought, gone to a little town where he could have bought protection from the local *comandante*. We would have outbid him, of course, but it would have taken me longer to find him, and maybe I never would have.

But that wasn't what happened.

What happened was Frank spent the afternoon at a cantina in the village, sipping a couple of beers and doing crossword puzzles in a little English-language magazine that some tourist must have left behind. It was a long, slow crawl to sunset, the dusk muted and subtle on an eastern-facing coast. But when the blue went out of the water, he headed down to the beach, to the thatched shack that Voorhees had managed to procure with his dwindling bankroll.

The man was sitting on a rough-hewn chair outside, smoking a cigarette and staring out at the water.

"I've been waiting for you," he said when he saw Frank.

Frank nodded.

"I mean, you're the guy, aren't you?" Voorhees said, only a slight quiver in his voice. "The guy they sent?"

"Yeah."

Voorhees nodded.

He looked more worn out than scared. There was this look of resignation on his face, almost relief, not the hard edge of fear that Frank had expected. Yeah, Frank thought, or maybe it's just the soft glow coming off the ocean at dusk that takes the edge off. Maybe it's the fading light that makes Voorhees look tranquil.

Voorhees finished his cigarette, took the pack from the pocket of his faded denim shirt, and lit another one.

His hands were shaking.

Frank leaned over and helped him hold the match steady.

Voorhees nodded his thanks. After he'd gotten a couple of drags down, he said, "It's the *bullet* I'm afraid of. The thought of it smashing in my head."

"You won't feel anything."

"It's just the thought—you know, my head blown away."

"That doesn't happen," Frank said, lying. Do it now, he told himself. Do it before he knows it's happening.

Voorhees started to cry. Frank watched the water well up in his eyes, saw the man bite his lip and try to hold it back, but the tears overflowed and rolled down his cheeks, and then Voorhees just lost it. His head slumped and his shoulders bobbed up and down as he sobbed.

Frank stood there and watched, aware that he was violating one of Bap's key precepts. "You don't need to give them last words or last rites," Bap had lectured. "You ain't a warden or a priest. Get in, do the job, get out."

No, Bap wouldn't have approved of this scene.

Voorhees finished crying, looked up at Frank, and said, "I'm sorry."

Frank shook his head.

Then Voorhees said, "A doctor in Guadalajara wrote some scrip for me. Tranquilizers."

Frank already knew this. The doctor had given it up to him for a couple of hundred in cash. So much for the Hippocratic oath.

"I still have most of them," Voorhees said. "I mean, I think I have *enough*."

Frank thought it over for a few seconds.

"I'll have to stay with you," he said.

"That would be okay."

Voorhees got out of the chair and Frank followed him into the little shack. Frank went into a canvas bag that had once been Voorhees's carry-on and now contained all his earthly goods. He took out a vial of pills—Valium, ten-milligram dosage—and a bottle of vodka, about two-thirds full.

They went back outside.

Frank sat down on the sand.

Voorhees sat back down in the chair, shook a handful of pills into his hand, and swallowed them with a swig of vodka. He waited a few minutes, then did it again, then a minute later took the last of the pills and sat sipping on the vodka bottle as he looked out at the ocean.

"Beautiful, isn't it?" he mumbled to Frank.

"Beautiful."

A second later, he lurched back in the chair, then forward, and he slumped over onto the rocks.

Frank picked him up and put him back in the chair.

He went back to the village, found a working telephone, and made a call to let Donnie Garth know that he was safe.

Frank went home from that job to find that Patty had changed the locks on the doors. Tired, angry, and sad, he kicked the front door in. Called a locksmith buddy at two in the morning to put new locks in, then went upstairs, got into the shower, sat down under the steaming water, and cried.

The next night, he drove to Garth's house—to do what exactly, he didn't know. He parked across the street and sat in the car for a long time. Garth was having a party. He watched the expensive cars and the chauffeured limousines pull into the circular driveway and he looked at the beautiful people in their beautiful clothes get out and go to the door. It looked like a benefit, a fund-raiser for some charity—the men were in black tie, the women in evening dresses, their hair up, exposing long, graceful necks adorned with glittering jewels.

How many people, Frank asked himself, have to die so the beautiful people can stay beautiful?

Question for the ages.

The picture window was open and there was a golden glow inside. Frank could see Garth flitting around, playing the social butterfly, making jokes and glittering conversation, and Frank figured it had to be his imagination, but he thought he could hear the laughter of elegant women and the clinking of priceless crystal.

It would have been an easy shot, he knew, even through the glass. Use something fast and heavy like a .50 sniper rifle steadied against the car window, squeeze the trigger, and blow Donnie's boy-wonder brains all over his lovely guests.

Now *that* would have been a benefit. To a lot of people, Frank thought.

If he had known then . . . but he didn't.

Then he thought it might be fun just to walk in there. Stroll up to Garth in the middle of the glittering crowd and say, "Donnie, your tit's out of the wringer. Again. I killed Jay Voorhees for you, same way I killed Marty Biancofiore." See what your high-class friends would have to say to that.

But he thought, Probably nothing. They'd probably get off on it.

So he sat in the car and watched San Diego's finest come and go. It was in the *Union-Tribune* the next morning, on the society page, how Donnie Garth had raised almost a million dollars for the new art museum.

Frank used the page to wrap fish.

When the news got out that the former chief of security of the Paladin had died of an overdose in Mexico, guys in the know just naturally assumed that Frankie Machine had forced him to take the pills. Frank never did anything to disabuse them of the notion.

It was just a technicality anyway, he thought.

You can't slide on this one just because you didn't hold the gun to his head, just because you gave him a choice, cut the guy a break. I don't know—maybe it *will* mean a couple of centuries less in purgatory. More likely, a slightly nicer niche in hell.

Me and Donnie Garth, at the same party at last.

Garth flipped later, of course. The feds got him in a room and he gave up the whole thing.

Frank waited for the call to come, but it never did.

It took him years to figure out why Donnie Garth got a pass.

39

"He is one smart son of a bitch," Carlo says.

They're sitting in the parking lot of a Burger King in El Centro, sixty miles east of Borrego and hard by the Mexican border. Jimmy has the rest of his crew spread around the town. He took the Burger King, sent Jackie and Tony to Mickey D's, Joey and Paulie to Jack in the Box.

"How come *we* get Jack in the Box?" Paulie had complained.

"What, you want Burger King?" Jimmy had asked.

"Yeah, okay."

"Well, fuck you, *I* get Burger King," Jimmy had said. Burger King's got better french fries and the sodas aren't so gassy. You're cooped up in a car with another guy hours at a time, you don't want gassy sodas. Now he looks at Carlo and says, "He didn't get to be Frankie Machine by being stupid."

"He got away," Carlo says. "Now he's got money, he's got an open road. We don't know where the fuck he is; he could be anywhere."

"Chill," Jimmy says. "One fucking phone call, I'll know right where he is."

Carlo looks at him, impressed and skeptical at the same time. "Who you gonna call?"

"Ghostbusters."

40

Dave watches the little red light blink on the electronic map. The GPS device placed in the bank bag with the money is working perfectly.

"I thought he would have gone down to Mexico," Troy says.

"Mexico is a dead end," Dave answers. "Machianno knows that." Hell yes, he does, Dave thinks; he sure made it a dead end for Jay Voorhees. The Bureau had always liked Frank for that piece of work but could never come close to pinning it on him.

Classic Frankie Machine.

Troy studies the map.

"It looks like he's headed for Brawley," he says.

They keep an eye on the screen into the evening.

The light stops in Brawley and beeps steadily in the same location. They run a cross-check and it comes up positive.

Frank's gone to ground in the EZ Rest Motel two blocks off the 78.

41

"The EZ Rest Motel," Jimmy says, punching off the phone. "Lock and load, rock and roll."

Carlo starts the car.

Lock and load, rock and roll.

He loves Jimmy, but he's kind of an asshole.

"The EZ Rest Motel where?" Carlo asks.

"Brawley, California."

They look at the road atlas. Brawley is only about an hour away.

" 'Ladies and gentlemen,' " Jimmy intones in his best Michael Buffer imitation, " 'for the thousands in attendance and the millions watching around the world . . . let's get ready to rumble!' The Brawl in Brawley!"

The Brawl in Brawley. Carlo chuckles.

Asshole.

42

The town of Brawley is an oasis in the desert.

Back during the Depression, the WPA put thousands of guys to work digging a canal from the Colorado River west into the desert. The result is that the area around Brawley produces some of the best alfalfa in the world. It's startling to fly over it—you've seen nothing but miles and miles of stark, bleached brown, and then suddenly there are these rectangles of emerald green.

Driving into it is less dramatic, but the town does come as a welcome relief to the desert. And it has everything a small agricultural town has to offer—a strip of fast-food places, a couple of banks, a big Agricorp grain elevator, and some motels.

Frank finds the place he's looking for pretty quickly and settles in.

Lies down, stretches out, and closes his eyes.

43

Jimmy walks up the stairs to the second floor of the motel.

He isn't doing any comedy bits now; he's mainlining adrenaline, his asshole gripped tighter than a white-collar con at his first day in the showers.

What's waiting up in that room, after all, is *Frankie Machine*. He might be an old dude, but there's a reason he *got* to be an old dude. Jimmy knows all the stories, and if even half of them are true . . . Jimmy's heard the story about how The Machine walked into that bar in San Diego and gunned down those Brits before they could even get their hands off their teacups. Nevertheless, if you want to be the Man, you got to be the man who *beat* the Man, so Jimmy is psyched for the opportunity.

And Jimmy has a plan.

The Machine probably has the chain lock hooked, so Carlo has one of those DEA warrant-service battering rams to smash the door in with. Then Jimmy will step in and put a few into Frankie M.'s head.

Hopefully, the old fuck is asleep anyway.

Jimmy the Kid nods and Carlo swings the battering ram.

The door isn't exactly Fort Knox material anyway and caves like the Yankees against the Red Sox.

Jimmy goes in.

Frankie M. isn't in bed.

He ain't anywhere in the room.

Jimmy the Kid suppresses his adrenaline rush and swings his gun in a controlled arc, sweeping the room in precise vectors, left to right.

No Machine.

Then he hears water running.

The old bastard is in the shower, didn't even hear the door cave in.

Now Jimmy can see the steam from under the bathroom door.

He grins.

This is going to be easy.

And *clean.*

Jimmy nudges the bathroom door open with his foot.

His hands are on the .38, out in front of him in the approved FBI shooting stance.

Except he don't see nothing in the shower. No shape of a man through the thin shower curtain.

He yanks the curtain open with his left hand.

And sees a note—duct-taped on the shower wall with the little GPS monitor.

Jimmy grabs the note and reads: "Did you think you were playing with children?"

Jimmy hits the deck.

He belly-crawls out of the bathroom and back toward the front door.

Carlo is already down, sitting propped against the wall with his hand pressed against a wound in his shoulder, blood seeping between his fingers, his other hand limply holding his gun.

Paulie lies on the balcony floor, mewling and clutching his right lower leg, looking at Jimmy like a wounded soldier looks at a bad officer, like, What have you gotten us into, and how are you going to get us out?

It's a good fuckin' question, Jimmy thinks as he curls up as tight as he can against the door frame and tries to peer through the balcony rails. He can't see where the shots have come from. He searches for a motion, a reflection, *anything,* but he can't lamp a single thing that might help him. He only knows the next shot could smash into his head. On the other hand, if Frankie M. was shooting to kill, both Carlo and Paulie would already be dead.

Are Jackie and Tony hit, too? Jimmy looks down in the parking lot for their car and can just make them out, slumped down in the front seat, their hands on their guns, looking up at him. Jimmy makes a small gesture with his hand: Stay down, stay put.

"I need a doctor," Paulie whines.

"Shut up," Jimmy hisses.

"I'm bleeding out!" Paulie cries.

No you ain't, Jimmy thinks, looking at his leg. The bullet didn't hit an artery—it was precisely placed to stop but not to kill.

Frankie freaking Machine.

44

Frank lies on the roof of the grain warehouse across the road, his rifle barrel resting on the lower curve of the *g* in the big Agricorp sign.

He places the infrared sight squarely on the kid's forehead. He doesn't recognize this kid, the one who's squeezed against the door, making himself as small as possible.

Not small enough, Frank thinks.

He doesn't know Leg Wound, either, which makes sense. He's too young for me to have ever worked with him, Frank thinks. Or maybe that's just a process of getting older, that everyone looks young to you.

The kid crouching in my sights is no joke. He made a mistake, but he isn't a clown. A clown would have come running out of that room. This guy had the sense to get low and crawl out of there. Even the way he's holding himself now—looking around, not panicking, not overreacting about his wounded crew, controlling his men—says that the kid has something.

Frank can see it in the kid's eyes.

He's *thinking*.

Thinking men are dangerous.

So take him out, Frank thinks.

You can't afford to have this guy on your tail.

He resettles his aim and squeezes the trigger.

45

The bullet smacks the wood a half inch above Jimmy the Kid's head.

His whole body quivers and then he fights for control of himself and wins.

A dumber guy would have thought that Frankie Machine had missed, but Jimmy is smarter than that.

Frankie Machine doesn't miss.

Frankie was sending a peace message: I could have killed you if I wanted, but I didn't.

Jimmy the Kid waits five minutes, then starts cleaning up the wreck of the Wrecking Crew. Carlo's gotten over the shock and can walk, so he and Jimmy haul Paulie down the stairs and into a car. Then they drive out on the highway a little ways, because even the cops have woken up in this sleepy town to the fact that something out of the ordinary has gone down at the EZ Rest.

Then Jimmy puts in the call he really doesn't want to make.

Wakes Mouse Senior out of a sound sleep.

"I got two down," Jimmy says.

"And?"

"And nothin'," Jimmy says. "He slipped us."

"Sounds like he did more than *slip* you," Mouse Senior says, and Jimmy hears a trace of satisfaction in his voice.

"Listen," he says, "what am I gonna do about my two guys?"

"Are you hot?"

"Fuck *yes*."

"Okay," Mouse Senior says, taking on this calming, fatherly-type voice, like he's Jim fucking Backus in *Rebel Without a Cause,* which sends Jimmy up the freaking wall. "You're about twenty-eight minutes from Mexico. Drive across the border to Mexicali. Hold on."

Mouse Senior comes back on the phone about three minutes later and gives him an address. "Go there. The doctor will fix your guys up. You have health insurance?"

"*What?*"

"Just joking, kid."

Yeah, you're Open-Mike Night at the Comedy Store, Jimmy thinks, punching off. I hope you're still yukking it up when I perform your colonoscopy with a Glock and hold the trigger down.

Then Jimmy makes the call he really doesn't want to make.

This guy he doesn't wake up.

This guy answers before the first ring stops; *this* guy has been obviously sitting by the phone waiting for the call.

But not *this* call.

This guy was waiting for the call that said Frankie Machine was at a family reunion with his ancestors. He definitely does not want to hear that Frankie M. is still in this world.

"This is a quid pro quo," the guy says. "Tell your people they cannot expect the quid unless they deliver the quo."

Whatever the fuck *that* means, Jimmy thinks. Not only does he not know what the guy is talking about; he doesn't even know who he's talking *to*. He just has a phone number, and he's supposed to talk to whoever's on the other end.

This very unhappy guy with his quids and quos.

"We'll deliver," Jimmy says, settling for that. He doesn't want to get into it, and besides, Paulie is starting to bleed all over the place.

Jimmy has such a headache when he hangs up, he almost wishes Frankie M. *had* blown his brains out.

Well, you should have, Jimmy thinks.

You fucked up, Frankie M.

Let's hope it's the first of many.

Because I ain't stoppin' and I don't think I "owe you one" either. Nobody fucking asked you for quarter, and nobody's going to give it, either.

Not with what *you* know, old man.

46

Dave Hansen walks into the room at the EZ Rest Motel.

The local cops are all over the place, going nuts, because this is a *thrill*. The run-of-the-mill shootings in this part of the country usually involve drunk *mojados* on a Saturday night or white-trash tweekers any old time of the week, so a shoot-out in a motel is a big deal.

Dave examines the bullet mark on the door frame.

Unlike Frank to miss a shot.

He turns around and looks at the Agricorp sign. That's pure Frank. Good shooting angle down, no shooting angle back up. Dave walks into the bathroom and sees the "Did you think you were playing with children?" note.

No, Frank, I didn't. I should have known you'd suss out the GPS. I should have known you were smarter than that. Tired, worn down, on the run, you'd still keep your head.

Young Troy asks, "What happened?"

"What happened," Dave says irritably, "is that he's Frankie Machine."

But, to be honest, it's a good goddamn question.

What the hell did happen here?

Who came to hit Frank before we got here?

And how did they know where he was?

47

Frank drives across the desert.

He's always liked the desert at night. Even in winter, it has a soft feel to it.

Speaking of soft, Frank thinks, that's what *you're* getting. You should have killed them *all,* left a bloodbath back there that would make any guy in the business reluctant to take the contract on you.

Especially the crew chief, the one who was the spitting image of old Tony Jacks.

No, not *Tony* Jacks, his younger brother.

What's his name?

Billy.

Was that *Billy's* kid?

Frank vaguely remembers something about Billy's kid doing a stint for something. What was it? Extortion, maybe? The kid was precocious, had his own crew . . . with some stupid tag . . .

"The Wrecking Crew," that was it. Worked out of an auto-salvage place and were chopping cars. The kid had a rep, even in the joint.

And now it's making more sense.

The Combination sent Vince out to clip me. Vince was cautious and used cutouts, getting Teddy Migliore to send John Heaney to Mouse Junior to set me up.

Makes sense, makes sense.

The Migliores answer to the Combination.

They kick up from their sex businesses.

Porn, prostitution, strip clubs.

Okay, fine, but I've never had anything to do with any of those.

Be honest, he tells himself.

What about that night at Solana Beach?

And the Strip Club Wars.

48

The damn thing was, the strip club business had started as a limo business.

It was back in '85.

Vegas had collapsed, and Mike and Frank were pretty much alone down in San Diego, unless you counted the Detroit guys, which Frank didn't. The Migliores always did their own business, and they always seemed to do it without getting busted.

Frank didn't care anyway. He was out of it by then.

Three-plus years of relative peace and quiet, and life was good. He had his home, his wife, his little fish business, and the limo service was booming in the easy-money eighties.

And then Patty got pregnant.

It was the most amazing thing. Back in the seventies, they had tried and tried, with no luck. Then, as their relationship deteriorated, they had stopped trying, then stopped making love altogether.

Then one night they went out to dinner. They had a little wine, had a little time together, and then they went home, fell into bed, and *boom*.

When Patty told him the news, he was over the moon.

So, coming into the summer of '85, they were about to have a baby.

"You want to pick up a little easy money?" Mike asked him one day.

Frank did—the baby was due in a couple of weeks and a little extra cash sounded good.

"What's the job?" he asked.

The job was that this banker was having a weekend-long party for a bunch of business associates. All they had to do, Mike told him, was drive a couple of cars, provide security at the party.

"Sounds good," Frank said.

"There's one little thing," Mike said.

Of course, Frank thought. There's always one little thing. "What?"

"The guy putting this party together?"

"Yeah?"

"Donnie Garth."

"I'm out," Frank said.

"Come on," Mike said.

"Is this *you* talking?" Frank asked. "Mr. 'There's Nothing I Hate More Than a Rat' Pella? Garth's the biggest rat there ever was. I'm amazed he's still on top of the dirt."

"He's connected, Frankie," Mike said. "Bigger than you and I can conceive of."

"I've done enough work for Donnie Garth," Frank said. "Pass."

"They asked for you personally, Frank."

"Who did?"

"Old man Migliore," Mike said. "And the guy from New Orleans."

"Marcello?" Frank asked. "I don't have anything to do with Marcello."

"Yeah, but Garth does," Mike told him. "He's president of an S and L, and the guy from New Orleans has an interest. So do the Migliores."

So that's how Donnie Garth has kept breathing, Frank thought. He bought his way out. He paid for his pass.

"What do I have to do?" Frank sighed.

"Just drive," Mike said. "Hang around the party, make sure everything stays copacetic. I'm telling you, it's a straight job."

Yeah, Frank thought, a straight job.

The "straight job" started with him driving one of the S&L officers to a bank in Rancho Santa Fe, where the guy took out fifty thousand in cash and then told Frank to drive him to Price Club.

Price Club? Frank wondered. What are you going to buy with fifty K at Price Club?

Women.

They met the madam in the parking lot. What was her name? Frank wonders now. Karen, that was it. She drove up in a Mercedes 500 convertible, and the bank officer leaned out the window of the limo to give her the cash. When they were driving away, the guy said, "I have an

M.B.A. in finance from Wharton, and this is what I've become—
a pimp."

What was that guy's name? Frank asks himself now.

Sanders—no, *Saunders*—John Saunders, another WASP who was
shocked and appalled that his hands got dirty. Frank didn't bother to tell
him that pimps didn't pay money; they *took* it. And that Saunders wasn't
a pimp, but a procurer. Anyway, he took the guy down to the harbor,
where Garth owned a 120-foot yacht, and dropped him off.

"Pick up the girls at eight," Saunders said as he got out of the car. He
gave Frank an address in Del Mar.

Patty would have had a fit, Frank thinks now, if she had seen the next
part of the "straight job" you were working, swinging by a brothel to
pick up a carful of the most gorgeous working girls you've ever seen.

Summer Lorensen was the prettiest, though.

She didn't have that worn hooker look. Instead, she looked like
your stereotypical corn-fed midwestern farm girl—blond, blue-eyed,
peaches-and-cream complexion, the girl-next-door type that *Playboy*
liked to use for the centerfold. She *spoke* that way, too, with that sweet
"oh shucks" manner, and she even called him "Mr. Machianno." It was
her first time in a limo and she was all excited about that. First time on a
yacht, and she was all excited about *that,* too.

The girls were all dressed to the nines and had clearly been chosen so
that there was someone to suit every taste, although any man would have
been more than happy to have any one of them.

Summer Lorensen, though, she was something else.

So Frank picked up one carload of girls, Mike picked up another, and
they drove to the harbor. Saunders was there to meet them on the dock.
He and Frank and Mike helped the girls in their high heels negotiate the
step down onto the yacht; then Saunders said, "Now, look, what you see
on the boat, *who* you see on the boat, *stays* on the boat. I'm counting on
your absolute discretion."

"Discretion is us," Mike assured him, smiling at Frank. Like, We've
seen things that would make this Yuppie fuck piss his pants, and we've
kept them to ourselves. What do you have to show us?

Well, a lot.

It was almost comical at first, when the girls stepped down onto the deck and these bankers stopped talking and just *gawked,* almost drooled, like fat men at an all-you-can-eat buffet.

Well, they were *mostly* bankers. You also had a couple of federal judges, three or four U.S. congressmen, one senator, and a few just general political types. Frank didn't know who they were, but Mike did, and he stood there pointing them out by name.

"How do you know all this?" Frank asked.

"My business to know," Mike said. "It could come in handy, a congressman in your pocket."

"Tell me you're not thinking of blackmailing one of these guys."

Frank's philosophy was, If the feds aren't messing with you, don't mess with them. Let sleeping dogs lie.

Mike didn't answer because Garth himself got up to make a "welcome aboard" speech to his guests. The guy was actually wearing a captain's uniform, with the blue jacket, white trousers, and the billed hat. He looked like a total doofus, but then again, he was a total doofus who owned his own bank.

Well, a savings and loan, anyway.

So Garth welcomed his guests, greeted the ladies, even used the "What you see on the boat *stays* on the boat" line. Got a good laugh when he said that, as a ship's captain, he could even marry people, the unions being legal as long as they were at sea.

Which would be all night.

With that, they shoved off and headed out into the harbor.

Frank stood along the fore rail and watched as the men picked out their partners. It was remarkable, but even with the knowledge that these were working girls, the partiers seemed to feel the need to chat them up first, have a drink, and flirt. And the girls were pros—they laughed at the jokes, posed prettily, flirted back. It wasn't long before they paired off and started to drift down into the cabins belowdecks.

Discretion, Frank thought.

But inhibitions went south when the coke came out.

Piles of it, served up by John Saunders, like he was a waiter. Pimp and waiter, Frank thinks now, that's the career an M.B.A. got you in the coked-up, easy-money eighties. The straight businessmen and the pols and the hookers were snorting it up with one-hundred-dollar bills, more than one of which Frank saw fly off unnoticed into the night breeze.

The coke turned the party into a floating orgy, a maritime bac-chanalia.

Caligula meets *Captains Courageous.*

It was an incredible scene. With the lights of San Diego as a back-drop, a real-life porn extravaganza was played out on the deck of Garth's yacht. It seemed like the whole party was in on it.

Except Mike Pella.

And Frank.

And Summer Lorensen.

Because it was Frank's job to keep her out of it. Saunders had come up to him earlier and said, "She's not part of the pass-around pack. She's for the *after*-party party. The VIP A list, at Donald's beach house. Keep the riffraff away from her."

"What do you mean?"

"She's bait," Saunders said. "We have her slotted for a particular individual, and not yet."

So Summer sat with Frank and Mike most of the evening, talking, laughing, pretending not to notice the scene that was evolving around them. She told them about her high school days, about going to college for a year but not really liking it and dropping out. Eventually, she told them about getting pregnant and having her daughter and how the boyfriend she'd thought loved her just took off.

And sure, guys came up to hit on her, but Frank or Mike would qui-etly say, "She's not for you," and there weren't a lot of guys on this earth who would take on either Mike or Frank, never mind both of them, so it just wasn't a problem.

There was one guy who ogled her from a distance. He was young, maybe in his late twenties, early thirties, with the boyish face of a per-petual frat rat. He never came close, but from time to time Frank would see him checking her out from ten, fifteen feet away. And he had this smarmy smile on his face—not bold enough to be a leer, but confident, like he had a secret and it was a good one.

Mike noticed Frank checking him out.

"You know who that is?" Mike asked.

"No."

Mike smiled and whispered the answer.

"No kidding?" Frank said, taking another look at the senator's son.

Sure, they already had one senator on the boat, but just like there were bosses and there were *bosses,* there were senators and there were *senators.* Same as you had, say, bosses of Kansas City or Jersey or, for that matter, L.A., and you treated them with respect, even though they weren't in the same league as bosses in Chicago, Philly, and New York.

So this guy's daddy was a *senator* who chaired a key banking committee. Daddy might even be president someday, not of some bank, but of the *United States,* and even the one senator on the boat and a bunch of congressmen were treating junior with some deference, even letting him cut in on the line to blow some coke.

Frank and Mike were watching this action when Mike started to sing:

> *"Some folks are born to wave the flag,*
> *Ooh, they're red, white and blue.*
> *And when the band plays 'Hail to the Chief,'*
> *Ooh, they point the cannon at you, Lord . . ."*

And Frank joined in with him on the chorus:

> *"It ain't me, it ain't me, I ain't no senator's son, son."*

So that was it—they dubbed the frat boy "Fortunate Son," and Fortunate Son was checking Summer Lorensen out like something he thought he should own.

She's bait. We have her slotted for a particular individual, and not yet.

And she was amazing, Frank remembers. Her colleagues were giving blow jobs and doing threesomes and foursomes just feet away from her, and she just kept chattering on about the girls' basketball team at her high school, and how nice the yacht was, and how pretty the city lights were shining on the water.

Caligula meets *Pollyanna*.

She eventually fell asleep, sitting in that deck chair, breathing gently, her mouth just open, a thin sheen of perspiration glistening on the just-visible hairs above her upper lip.

The yacht came back toward the dock that morning like a plague ship, bodies strewn about the deck in various states of undress, moans emerging from unconscious mouths as the smell of stale sweat and sex cut through the salt air.

Forty minutes out, Frank and Mike helped Saunders rouse the partiers, get them dressed, and pour some coffee and orange juice down their throats. The guests left the boat happily exhausted and slunk into waiting cars and limousines.

The lucky few were invited back to Garth's house—not the one in La Jolla, but his "weekend home" ten minutes away in Solana Beach. Frank drove Summer there. She slept most of the way and only woke up as they were pulling into Garth's driveway.

"Wow," she said.

Honest to God, Frank thinks, she actually said "Wow."

Not that Garth's beach house wasn't worth a "Wow." At $1.5 million back in 1985, it should have been pretty impressive, and it didn't disappoint. It was long, sleek, white, and modern, its floor-to-ceiling windows practically inviting the ocean in.

Frank can't imagine what the place would go for now.

Six, seven mil easy.

Mike pulled in and opened the door for a second girl, a stunning redhead with green eyes, sophisticated where Summer was naïve, exuding an aggressive, experienced sexuality in contrast to Summer's innocence.

What *was* her name? Frank tries to think.

Alison. Alison . . . something. She was from someplace in the South, or at least she had the accent.

Garth came out of the house, followed by Fortunate Son, who was dressed in nothing but a smile and the towel wrapped around his waist.

Turned out that he was the entire A list.

You served her up, Frank thinks now. Served her like a special dish.

Get a grip, he tells himself now. She was a *hooker*—the fresh, innocent virgin persona was part of her act. It *was* her hook, her appeal; it drove up her price. The gorgeous girl next door you always wanted but couldn't have.

Unless you were Fortunate Son.

Then there was *nothing* you wanted and couldn't have.

Fortunate Son wanted them both.

Of course he did, Frank thinks. Who wouldn't? Be honest with yourself—if you could have everything you wanted, wouldn't you take it? And if you knew you were going to get what you wanted, you wouldn't have been in any hurry, either. Nobody was going to take it away from you, so why not wait? If you were used to getting anything you wanted, maybe the waiting was better than the getting.

The girls said they really wanted to take showers. They went inside for a while and came out in bikinis; then everyone went for a long walk on the beach, with Frank and Mike trailing behind, out of earshot but within sight.

Nobody went in the water, Frank remembers.

Well, Summer ran in up to her knees and ran back yelling that it was cold, and Fortunate Son wrapped his arms around her and rubbed her back to warm her up. Then they all went back to the house, where lunch was served outside on the deck.

You and Mike sat in the kitchen, Frank remembers, and ate with the cook. You kept the door open so you could see what was going on outside. Funny the things you remember—the men drank beer and the girls had mimosas.

After lunch, the girls said they were sleepy and the men said they could use a siesta, too, and everyone repaired to separate bedrooms. Frank and Mike agreed to split a watch and Frank took the first one. When Mike relieved him, Frank went back to his car, stretched out on the front seat, and fell sound asleep.

When he woke up, he walked back to the house to see what was up. He looked down at the living room through the blue-tinted glass.

Summer, dressed in an open white robe over her bikini, was on her knees on the lush white carpet. Alison was kneeling beside her, gently kissing her neck. Donnie Garth and Fortunate Son sat in two big black leather easy chairs, watching. A bowl of cocaine was set on the chrome and glass coffee table; the remnants of lines looked like white dust.

Alison nuzzled Summer's neck and Summer said, "If you do that, I can't stop you."

Alison said, "I know," and reached around and unclasped the top of the bathing suit. Alison dipped her head down and kissed one breast and then the other and gently pushed Summer down on her back and then slid down herself, kissing her along her stomach and then across the top of her panties as Summer moaned and said, "I've never done this before."

Alison sat up and pulled the panties off, then opened Summer's legs and laid down between them, and soon Summer's hips started to roll; then her back arched and her fingers dug into the lush white carpet.

It was straight from a bad porn movie, Frank thought. A parody, an act—"The Corruption of Innocence"—but a good one, simultaneously stupid, obscene, and compelling. Summer was a good actress—she alternately resisted and succumbed—and, toward the end, she lay with her head in Alison's lap as Fortunate Son, his dick coated with numbing cocaine, moved in for the final act.

That's when the radio squawked in Mike's car. Mike wasn't paying any attention, so Frank got in and answered it. It was the office dispatcher.

"Christ, I'm glad I reached you," she said. "Patty went into labor. She's at Scripps."

Frank hustled out of the car.

"I gotta go," he told Mike.

Mike was transfixed on the scene inside the house.

"Now?"

"Patty went into labor."

Mike didn't take his eyes off the window. "Go. *Go.*"

Frank jumped back into his car and sped out. He made it to the hospital in time and was in the room when Jill was born. He held his daughter in his arms and his life changed.

Like that.

Frank learned later—with the rest of the suckers—that the savings and loan industry was the biggest bust-out scheme in history, dwarfing anything any wise guy ever managed to put together.

Here's how the scam worked:

Garth and the other S&L guys would get themselves savings and loan operations, make unsecured loans to themselves and their partners through shell corporations, then default on the loans and drain their S&Ls of all their assets.

Garth took his own Hammond Savings and Loan down for a billion and a half bones.

Identical in shape to your classic Mafia bust-out, Frank thinks now, except we only managed to do it with restaurants and bars, maybe the occasional hotel. These guys busted out the whole country to the tune of $37 billion and Congress hit up the working guy to pay for it.

The whole S&L house of cards eventually came tumbling down, and Garth and a few of the others did some time polishing their short games at various Club Feds, and the senators and congressmen who had been on the boat, literally and figuratively, got on CNN to proclaim what a disgrace it all was.

Karen Wilkenson did a couple of years for pandering. John Saunders went away for a year for misuse of bank funds.

Fortunate Son went on to become a U.S. senator.

Summer Lorensen had a sadder ending, Frank remembers. They found her body a few days later in a ditch off the road on Mount Laguna. She ended up a victim of the Green River Killer, who picked up prostitutes, raped and killed them, then stuffed their mouths with rocks.

The police didn't catch him for years.

Not surprising. Back then, the cops had a phrase for the murders of prostitutes and junkies: "No humans involved."

But Frank felt bad, thinking about that sweet girl lying off a road with rocks in her mouth.

But then he forgot about it.

He was busy.

The Strip Club Wars were about to break out.

49

Eddie Monaco looked like Huckleberry Finn.

That is, if Huck were fifty years old and had just gotten laid. Blond-haired, blue-eyed, Eddie had this boyish, innocent look about him, and he could always make people laugh.

Nothing seemed to bother Eddie, ever. Life was a party, full of booze, broads, and buddies. And he was no Donnie Garth: Eddie was a legitimate tough guy who had done stints for extortion and counterfeiting. With a sheet, Eddie couldn't get a liquor license, of course, so he had a front guy who technically owned the Pinto Club. But everyone knew that the club didn't belong to Patrick Walsh. The Pinto was Eddie Monaco's.

The strip club sat on Kettner Boulevard, in what had been Little Italy, just a few blocks away from Lindbergh Field. Frank and Mike were running limos out of the airport, and Mike made sure that every business-man who came into San Diego got the word about the Pinto Club.

"We'll pick you up at your hotel," went the pitch, "deliver you to the club, deliver you safely home. You can drink all you want, you don't have to worry about a DUI, and if you happen to want some company on the way back—say, one of the girls, we can arrange for that, too, no extra charge. And if you want to write it off, no problem—we'll give you a clean receipt. We can even give you a restaurant check, if you want it, to prove you were going to a business dinner."

So seeing as how Frank was taking customers there all the time, and seeing as how he'd usually end up driving them home as well, he ended up hanging out there a lot.

The girls were pretty, he had to admit that.

Eddie Monaco knew how to find talent.

And he was generous with it.

"You want anything," he'd tell Frank, "you don't even have to ask. A sandwich, a drink, a blow job, it's yours."

Eddie liked having mobbed-up guys around. It kept things copacetic and gave the place a whiff of notoriety and danger, which brought customers through the door. What did he call it—"gangster chic"? And anyway, Mike and Frank were driving a lot of business up to those doors, so a meal, a little booze, a hummer in the back room, what was that?

Peanuts to Eddie Monaco.

Frank would accept the free food and the comped drinks, but he never took Eddie up on the BJs. There was something sad enough about the girls already, without them having feign enthusiasm on their knees in the office, and besides, with a toddler at home, he was trying to be faithful to his wife.

It wasn't that hard to do. The strippers looked sexy at first—it was because of the lights, the pounding music, the atmosphere of undiluted eroticism—but the appeal wore off in a hurry. Especially when you hung out at the bar and got to know them, talked with them on their breaks. Then, sooner or later—usually sooner—the same tired, depressing stories came out of their mouths. The childhood sexual abuse, the cold, distant fathers, the alcoholic mothers, the teenage abortions, the drug addictions.

Especially the drugs.

These girls were so coked up, it was a wonder they could ever *stop* dancing. Unless they hooked up with some sugar daddy, they were just caught in the spin cycle, until they were used-up coke freaks with more lines on their face than up their nose, and then they were out the door.

And a fresh crop came in.

There was never a shortage of girls.

There was never a shortage of anything, not in the world of Eddie Monaco.

Eddie had five vintage cars, including the Rolls he usually drove around in. He had women—lots of women, and not just the dancers, either—and the women had lots of jewelry that came from Eddie's fingers. Eddie had a big house in Rancho Santa Fe and a condo in La Jolla.

Eddie had nice threads, Rolex watches, and wads of cash.

The other thing Eddie had a lot of was debts.

They went with his ambitions. Nothing was too good for Eddie, and nothing was too good for the Pinto Club. He spent millions remodeling the place—millions he didn't have—but he wanted the Pinto to be the premier topless club in California, the base for a whole string of clubs. Eddie wanted to be king of the strip club world, and he didn't mind spending money to get there.

Problem was, he was spending other people's money.

Eddie *was* the king of OPM. Hundreds of thousands of dollars of it, but it didn't seem to bother him at all. He'd pay off his old debts in fresh OPM, and that way he just kept kiting the debt around. Somehow, people were always willing to give him money.

One of them was a loan shark named Billy Brooks.

Billy used to hang out at the Pinto, ogling the tits and ass and cruising for customers. His two goons were usually with him—Georgie Yoznezensky, known, for obvious reasons, simply as "Georgie Y," and Angie Basso, who was actually Eddie Monaco's favorite dry cleaner when he wasn't breaking legs for Billy.

Angie was your typical goombah, but Georgie Y, Georgie Y was a *case*. A tall, gangly immigrant from Kiev with thick wrists and a thicker head, a guy so stupid and violent even the Russian mob up in the Fairfax district didn't want him hanging around. Somehow he hooked up with Billy, and Billy gave him occasional work, even getting him a job as a bouncer at the Pinto.

Eddie gave him the job as a favor to Billy, and why not—Billy had loaned Eddie $100,000.

And Billy wanted to get paid back.

Eddie blew him off.

Billy would keep coming by the club, asking Eddie for his money. At first, Eddie would tell him, "Tomorrow, I promise," or "Next week, Billy, sure thing." He'd put him off with free girls, who would take Billy back into the office for a blow job, or down the street to a motel for a quickie.

But Billy wasn't satisfied with pussy, Billy wanted his *money*.

And he wasn't getting it.

And he had to sit there and watch while Eddie rented entire clubs for a night and threw himself a party, or drove around in his Rolls with Playboy models cuddled up to him, or gave C-note tips to doormen and coat-check girls and just generally threw money around like paper airplanes and didn't pay Billy penny one.

It didn't help that Eddie was handsome, Eddie was cool, and that Billy was neither. He had a mutt of a face, and this hangdog expression. Bad hair and bad skin. It must have been, Frank thought years later, like Richard Nixon watching Bill Clinton pull chicks.

If Eddie had just been nice to the guy, things might have gone down different, but Eddie got tired of Billy nagging him all the time and started blowing the guy off, ignoring him, not returning calls, brushing right past him in the club like he wasn't there.

"What am I?" Billy said to Mike Pella one night. "An asshole?"

This was New Year's Eve, and they were sitting at the bar of the Pinto Club, where Billy had arranged to meet Eddie to talk about the situation.

The fact that it was New Year's Eve had not sat well with Patty.

"New Year's Eve," she'd complained. "I thought we could go out."

"I have to work."

"Work," she said. "Hanging around with a bunch of whores."

"They're not whores," Frank said. Well, some of them aren't, he thought. "They're dancers."

"What they do isn't dancing."

"It's the busiest night of the year. Do you know the tips I'll make?" Frank asked. Besides, he thought, going out on New Year's Eve to a restaurant or a hotel? Paying double for the same meal, which was usually subpar, with slow service and a mandatory 18 percent service charge thrown into the deal? When I could be out making good money? "Look, we'll go out *tomorrow* night. I'll take you anywhere you want to go."

"No one goes out on New Year's night," Patty said.

"So we can get a table," Frank said.

"Big fun," Patty said. "Two cheap people in an empty restaurant."

"I'll call you at midnight," Frank said. "We'll smooch over the phone."

For some reason, that didn't seem to mollify her. She didn't even speak to him when he left.

When Frank got to the club, he sat at the bar, listening to Billy Brooks bitch to Mike. Mike and Billy had done time together in Chino, so they were old friends. As Frank sat there that night, listening to Billy whine about his Eddie Monaco problem, he knew what Mike would say about that, and Mike did.

"No offense, Billy," Mike said, "but you should know people are talking, the way you're letting Eddie laugh at you. It can't be good for business."

No, it can't, Frank thought.

A loan shark has two assets—cash and respect. You let one guy not pay you—and throw it in your face in public, to boot—and pretty soon, the rest of your customers get the idea they don't need to pay you, either. Word gets out that you're a sucker, a pussy, a wimp, and then you can kiss your money good-bye. It ain't ever coming back, principal or interest.

Then you'd better give up the shylock business and go into something you're more suited to—like nursing or library science.

This was what Billy Brooks was facing, and it was a problem, because Eddie Monaco was a tough guy and he had his own mob connections. If Billy just took Eddie out—like he ought to—he could have serious problems with the Migliores. It was an interesting dilemma.

Truth was, everyone was watching to see how Billy Brooks would handle the situation.

"I'm in a hell of a situation here, Mike," Billy said.

That's all he had to say, *all he had to say,* and Frank knew that Eddie Monaco was a dead man.

Mike Pella was never a guy to let any grass grow under his feet.

"There's money in tits and ass," Mike had told Frank all those years ago. "Big."

Frank wasn't so sure if Mike had meant big tits, big asses, or big money, but whatever he'd meant, he'd been dying to get into the topless club business, and this was his chance. The very next day, New Year's Day, 1987, Mike went to Eddie's condo in La Jolla. Mike waited until noon, because Eddie probably hadn't gone to bed until eight or nine in the morning.

Eddie opened the door, blurry-eyed.

Smiled when he saw it was Mike.

"Hey, guy, what—"

Mike shot him in the face three times.

Billy Brooks got instant respect, and a piece of the Pinto Club.

Mike figured that if Billy had a piece of the club, that meant that he did, too. Now Mike wasn't just dropping customers off at the door, or coming in for an occasional drink; he started hanging around the club all the time, like he was one of the owners, which in his view, he was.

All of Mike's crew started hanging there—Bobby Bats, Johnny Brizzi, Rocky Corazzo—and Mike would comp their drinks, their meals, their back-room blow jobs. Mike was running up a tab at the Pinto as long as his arm, and Pat Walsh didn't have the stones to ask him to pay, and neither did Billy, and Mike never thought anything of it.

He figured Billy owed him.

Which he did.

And Mike being Mike, he wasn't content to take the freebies, sit back, and watch the money roll in. No, he had to squeeze the club for everything it was worth. What he did was, he started selling the girls their coke.

It was a lucrative sideline—sell blow to the girls, let them build up an expensive habit, then put them out to the business trade to let them pay for their jones. Then take 50 percent of their hooker money.

Mike even bought an apartment building near the club and *gave* the girls the first and last month's rent, knowing that the coke habit would take the rest of the rent money. Angie Basso and Georgie Y were always there to shy the girls the rent money, and then they really had them hooked.

The girls could never catch up, and that was the point.

Pretty soon, Mike was getting *all* their money—their tips, their hooker money, their porn money. That was Mike's next entrepreneurial maneuver—take a girl who was hopelessly behind on the vig and the rent and give her the chance to make some money doing a porn video.

A year down this road, Billy came to Frank about it.

"He's going to ruin the business," Billy said. "The cops are all over the place. I've had five girls—count them, five—busted on drug and prostitution charges. He has a six-figure bar tab. . . ."

"What do you want *me* to do?" Frank asked. "I just drive a limo." Thinking, *you* brought him in on this, Billy. "You didn't want Mike, you should have handled your problems yourself."

"Yeah, but *shit,* Frank."

"Shit *nothing,* Billy."

Anyway, Frank thought, I have problems of my own.

Like a divorce.

Patty was threatening one.

I can't really blame her, Frank thought. I'm always working, I'm never home, and when I am home, I'm asleep. Other than that, she spends most of her time wondering where I am, what I'm doing, *who* I'm doing—even though I've told her fifty thousand times I'm not sleeping with the girls.

Still, they had argued about it, and the last fight had been a doozy.

"You knew the deal," Frank had said. "You knew who I was when you married me."

"I thought you were a fisherman."

"Yeah, right," Frank said. "Frank Baptista, Chris Panno, Mike Pella, Jimmy Forliano come to a fisherman's wedding with envelopes of cash. You grew up in the neighborhood, Patty. You're a smart woman. Don't go Diane Keaton on me now."

"You're fucking other women!"

"Watch your language."

Patty laughed. "What, you can *do* it, but I can't *say* it?"

"If you did more *doing* it than *saying* it," Frank heard himself say, "I might not be so tempted to do it!"

"*When* am I supposed to do it!" Patty asked. "You're never here!"

"I'm out putting food on the table!"

"A lot of men put food on the table and still come home at night!"

"Well, I guess they're smarter than I am!"

She told him if things didn't change, she was going to file.

Frank had all this on his mind when Billy was bitching about Mike running the Pinto Club into the ground.

"It's none of my business," he told Billy. "You have a problem with Mike, take it up with Mike."

Yeah, good advice.

Three nights later, Mike grabbed Frank at the bar and told him they needed to have a little talk with Billy. "This guy is giving me shit. Can you believe it?" Mike said. "This fucking ungrate."

"That's *in*grate."

Mike blinked. "You sure?"

"Yeah."

"Because it's *un*grateful, not *in*grateful," Mike said.

"I just did it on a puzzle," Frank said. He was spending a lot of his waiting time these days doing crossword puzzles. "I looked it up."

"Anyway," Mike said. "We gotta straighten this fucking Billy out."

"Mike, I don't have to straighten anyone out," Frank said. Then he thought better of it—Mike had a quick temper. Who the hell knows what could happen, Frank told himself. He decided he'd better go along as a moderating influence.

They went for a cruise in Frank's limo, east on Kettner into the warehouse district. Billy brought Georgie Y along for protection. Frank drove, Georgie Y rode in the front with him, and Mike and Billy sat in the back, arguing.

Mike sounded hurt.

He *is* hurt, Frank thought. That was the funny thing—Mike really loved the club, thought he had a stake in it, and here Billy was, intimating (puzzle word) that he *hadn't* actually hurt Mike's feelings.

"Why are you hassling me, Billy?" Mike asked. "Why are you busting balls? I'm just trying to make a living here."

"So am I!"

"So make! Who's stopping you?"

"You are!" Billy said. "You got half my girls hooked on coke. You got them out turning tricks, doing porn—"

"You want a piece of their shy, Billy? Is that it?" Mike said. "Why didn't you say? I'll cut you in. Just come to me like a man and say—"

But Billy's on a bitching roll, Frank thought, like a woman. Once they get started, they're not happy just solving the problem. No, they have to vent. So Billy just can't take the offer of good money. No, he has to—

"The cops are all over the place," Billy continued. "We could lose our fucking liquor license, and speaking of liquor, Mike—"

"What?"

"Jesus, the *bar* tab you and your crew have run up—"

"What, you counting our drinks, you fucking mutt?"

"C'mon," Frank said. "You guys are friends."

"You're counting our *drinks*?" Mike said. "You cheap-ass, nickel-and-dime piece of shit—"

"Hey!" Billy said.

"'Hey' nothing, you ingrate," Mike said. "You wouldn't *have* the fucking club, it wasn't for me."

"Whoa," said Billy. "I didn't *ask* you to clip Eddie."

That was a mistake, Frank thought. That was the wrong thing to say. Mike just went off.

"You didn't ask? You didn't *ask*?" Mike said. "You didn't *have* to *ask,* because you were my *friend,* Billy, and if you had a problem, which you did, it was *my* problem, too. You didn't *ask*?"

"I didn't ask you to—"

"No," Mike said. "You *didn't* ask. You sat there and *whined* like a little girl. 'I'm in trouble, Mike. I don't know what to do, I don't know what to do.' I took *care* of it for you, motherfucker. I stepped up."

"I thought you were going to *talk* to him, Mike!" Billy said. "I didn't think you were going to—"

"Jesus, maybe I shot the wrong fucking guy," Mike said.

Frank looked back and Mike had a pistol in his hand now. "Mike, no!"

"I think I *did,*" Mike said. "I think I shot the wrong fucking guy! Maybe I should give you what I gave him!"

Georgie Y reached into his pocket for his gun.

Frank cranked the wheel, steered the limo to the curb, and, with his other hand, trapped Georgie's wrist against his waist. It wasn't easy—Georgie Y was a strong boy.

Billy was trying to bail out. He was fumbling with the door handle when Mike started shooting. Three blasts made Frank's ears ring. He couldn't hear a thing; he just saw Georgie Y's lips mouthing the word *Jesus.* Then he turned and saw Billy slumped against the car door, his right shoulder a mass of blood and a bullet hole in his face.

But he was breathing.

Frank jerked Georgie's pistol away from him, put it in his own pocket, then said, "Come on, I have some towels in the trunk."

Frank looked around.

No other cars.

No cop cars with sirens screaming.

He got out, opened the trunk, grabbed the towels, then went around to the backseat. "Get the fuck out of my way, Mike."

Mike got out of the car and Frank slid in. He wrapped towels around Billy's shoulder and then pressed another hard against the head wound. "Georgie, get in here!" He felt the big man flop onto the seat. "Hold this tight against his head. Don't let go."

Georgie Y was crying.

"Georgie, you don't have time for that," Frank said. "Do what I tell you."

Frank got out, grabbed Mike, and pushed him into the front passenger seat. Then he went around, got behind the wheel, and tromped on the gas pedal.

"Where the fuck you think you're going?" Mike asked.

"The E room."

"He ain't gonna make it, Frankie."

"That's between him and God," Frank said. "I think you already did your part, Mike."

"He'll talk, Frank."

"He won't talk."

He didn't.

Billy knew the rules. He knew that if he had been fortunate enough to survive one gunshot to the head, he wouldn't luck out the second time. So he stuck with the story: He'd been coming out of the club and some junkie tried to rob him. He never saw the guy.

He never saw anything else, either. The bullet hit a nerve and left him permanently blind.

"You're going to pay him," Frank told Mike. "Billy keeps his share of the club *and* you're going to cut him in on the shy, like you said."

Mike didn't argue.

He knew Frank was right, and besides, Frank always thought that

Mike felt bad about shooting Billy, even though he'd never admit it. So Billy still owned the Pinto Club, but he didn't come around much after he got out of the hospital. Watching strippers couldn't have been that much fun for a blind guy.

But Billy Brooks kept his mouth shut.

It was Georgie Y they had to worry about.

Mike did, anyway.

"The cops are all over this fucking thing," Mike said to Frank one night. "They know Billy's story is bullshit; they're going to press. You and me, Frank, we can stand up, but I don't know about Georgie. I mean, can you see him in an interrogation room?"

No, Frank thought, I can't.

"And thanks, by the way," he said, "for putting me in the way of an accessory-to-attempted-murder beef."

"This temper of mine," Mike said. "So what are we going to do about Georgie?"

"Have the cops contacted him yet?"

Mike shook his head. "It's the 'yet' I'm worried about."

"We can't clip a guy on a 'yet,' " Frank said.

"We can't?"

"Mike, you do it, I'm done with you," Frank told him. "My hand to God, I'll turn my face away from you."

So Georgie Y kept his life and his job as a bouncer at the club. The only difference was, now he went out and busted legs for Mike instead of for Billy. He even started dating one of the dancers, a skinny little thing named Myrna, and they seemed to get along pretty well.

So that should have been the end of it.

It wasn't.

The Strip Club Wars were just beginning.

Frank will never forget the first time he saw Big Mac McManus.

Hell, nobody ever forgets the first time they saw Mac. A six-foot-six, 250-pound black man with a shaved head and a cut body comes walking into the place, wearing a tailored leopard-skin dashiki and carrying a diamond-studded walking stick, you tend to remember the moment.

Frank was sitting in a booth with Mike and Pat Walsh when Big Mac strolled in. Big Mac paused on the landing just inside the front door, taking in the scene. More to the point, he let the scene take *him* in, which it did. About everyone in the place looked up and stared.

Even Georgie Y was looking up. Big Mac McManus had a couple of inches on Georgie, who seemed to have the sense that he should be doing something, even though he didn't know what that was. He looked over to Frank for direction, and Frank gave him a subtle shake of the head.

Like, Leave it alone, Georgie. This is out of your league.

Georgie let Big Mac through.

Big Mac descended the stairs into the club.

He had three guys with him. Three white guys.

Frank got the sly joke right away. The black man had an entourage, and they were white.

Mac walked right over to the booth and said, "Billy Brooks?"

"That's me," Walsh said.

"Mac McManus," Mac said. He didn't offer to shake hands. "I want to buy your club."

"It's not for sale."

"I have controlling interests in the Cheetah, the Sly Fox, and Bare Elegance, to name a few," Mac said, "I want to add the Pinto to my portfolio. I'll pay you a fair price, with a generous profit figured in."

"Did you hear the man?" Mike asked. "He said it's not for sale."

"Excuse me," Mac said, "but I wasn't talking to you."

"Do you know who I am?" Mike asked.

"I know who you are, Mike Pella," Mac said, smiling. "You're a wise guy who's done stints for assault, extortion, and insurance fraud. The word is that you're with the Martini family, but the word is wrong. You're more of an independent operator with Mr. Machianno here. It's a pleasure to meet you, Frank. I've heard good things."

Frank nodded.

"Meet my associates," Mac said. "This is Mr. Stone, Mr. Sherrell, and, last but not least, Mr. Porter."

Stone was a tall, muscled, blond California dude. Sherrell was shorter, but thicker, with black permed hair that had just gone out of style. Both men were dressed casually, jeans and polo shirts.

Porter was medium height, medium build, his hair cut short. He wore a dark suit, white shirt, and a tie and had a cigarette between lips that otherwise held nothing but a continual smirk. His black hair was greased straight back, and it took Frank a second to figure it out before he realized that the guy was going for the Bogart look. And almost made it, too, except that Bogie had a soft side, and there was nothing about this guy that was soft.

They all nodded and smiled.

Mac took a card from his pocket and laid it on the table. "I'm having a little get-together Sunday afternoon at my place," he said. "I'm really hoping that you gentlemen can attend. Very casual, very mellow. Bring dates if you'd like, but there will be an abundance of ladies there. Say two o'clock or thereabouts?"

He smiled, turned, and left, with Stone and Sherrell at his heels.

Porter paused, made a special effort to get Frank's eye, then said, "Nice meeting you blokes."

"'Blokes'?" Mike said when Porter had walked away.

"British," Frank said.

"Check them out," Mike said.

It didn't take long to get the rundown.

Horace "Big Mac" McManus, was a former California Highway Patrol officer who had done a four-year stretch in the federal pen for counterfeiting. Now forty-six, he was a major player in the California sex trade. It was true that he was a silent partner in the clubs that he had mentioned. He was also a big-time porn producer and distributor and probably ran hookers out of both the clubs and the movie sets.

"He lives," Frank said, "get this, on an estate in Rancho Santa Fe he calls 'Tara.'"

"The fuck is that?"

"*Gone With the Wind,*" Frank said.

John Stone was a cop.

"Jesus shit," Mike said.

"He was McManus's partner before Mac got busted, and he's still on the CHP. He has a piece of all Mac's clubs, and he spends most of his time helping Mac run his business."

"Right-hand man sort of thing?" Mike asked.

"More like a partner."

Danny Sherrell was the manager of the Cheetah. His nickname was "Chokemaster."

"Was he a wrestler or something?" Mike asked.

Frank shook his head. "Porn actor."

"Oh," Mike said. Then *"Ohhhh.* What about the Brit?"

"His name is Pat Porter," Frank answered. "Beyond that, we don't know much about him. He came over here about two years ago. Sherrell hired him as a bouncer at the Cheetah. He must have worked his way up in the world."

"Jesus . . . cops," Mike said. "What are we going to do, Frankie?"

"Go to a party, I guess."

Tara was amazing.

The house had been built to match the antebellum mansion in the movie. The only difference was that all the servants were white, not black. A white teenager in a red vest ran up to Frank's limo, opened the passenger door, and was surprised to find that there was nobody in the back.

"Just me," Frank said, flipping him the keys. "Be careful with it."

Frank walked onto the huge expanse of soft green lawn, where tents and tables had been set up. He was wearing a suit, but he still felt shabby compared to the other guests, who were all arrayed in various forms of expensive, casual California cool. Lots of white linen and cotton, khaki and cream.

Mike had gone the black-on-black route.

He looked just like a goombah, and Frank felt a little ashamed that he was embarrassed.

"You seen this spread?" Mike asked. "They got shrimps, they got caviar, tritip beef, champagne. 'Little party' my ass."

"He does this every other Sunday," Frank said.

"You're kidding me."

Beautiful place, beautiful grounds, beautiful food, beautiful wine, beautiful *people.* That was the thing—all the people were drop-dead gorgeous. Handsome men, incredibly lovely women. We're like mutts here, Frank thought.

I guess that's the point.

Mac made an entrance onto the lawn.

Dressed in an all-white linen suit and Gucci loafers with no socks, he had a woman on his arm who was wearing a slinky summer dress that revealed more than it hid.

"I know that chick," Mike said.

"Yeah, right."

"No, I *know* that chick," Mike said. Then a few seconds later, he blurted, "That's Miss May. That's Miss fucking May. McManus's grooving a *Penthouse* centerfold."

Mac and Miss May worked through the guests, pausing and smiling and hugging, but it was clear that Mac was working his way over to Frank and Mike. When he did, he said, "Gentlemen, I'm so glad you could find the time. Mike, Frank, this is Amber Collins."

Frank was praying that Mike wouldn't bring up his revelation.

He didn't. He just gawped a "Pleasure to meet you."

"Nice to meet you," Frank said.

"Do you have everything you need?" Mac asked. "Something to eat, something to drink?"

"We're good," Frank said.

"How about a tour of the house?" Mac asked.

"Sounds good," said Frank.

"Amber," Mac said. "I'll miss you, but could I ask you to play hostess to the other guests?"

The house was unreal.

Frank, who appreciated quality, recognized that Mac did, too. He knew good stuff and he had the money to pay for it. All the fixtures, the plumbing, the kitchen appliances were top-of-the-line. Mac led them through the enormous living room, the kitchen, the six bedrooms, the screening room, and the dojo.

"I'm into hung gar kung fu," Mac said.

Six six, Frank thought, two and a half bills, cut like stone, and a martial-arts black belt. God help us if we have to take Big Mac McManus down.

In back of the mansion, Mac had his own private zoo—exotic birds, reptiles, and cats. Frank didn't know his zoology all that well, but he thought he recognized an ocelot, a cougar, and, inevitably, a black panther.

"I love animals," Mac said. "And of course, all the movements of kung fu are patterned after animals—the tiger, the snake, the leopard, the crane, and the dragon. I learn just by watching these beautiful specimens."

"You got a dragon here?"

"In a manner of speaking," Mac said. "I have a Komodo dragon. But the dragon is a mythical beast, of course. You keep its spirit in your heart."

They walked back into the house.

"This is like the Playboy Mansion," Mike said as they walked back through the main room.

"Hef's been here," Mac said.

"You know Hefner?" Mike asked.

Mac smiled. "Would you like to meet him? I can arrange it. Let's go to the study, sit down, have a dialogue."

The study was a quiet room in the back of the mansion. All the furniture was dark teak. African masks adorned the walls; the carpet and sofa were zebra skin. The large chairs were some kind of exotic leather that Frank didn't recognize. Large built-in bookcases held a collection of volumes on African art, history, and culture, and the floor-to-ceiling CD racks contained an archival collection of jazz.

"Do you like jazz?" Mac asked, seeing Frank eye the collection.

"I'm more of an opera guy."

"Puccini?"

"You got it."

"*You* got it," Mac said. He pushed a few buttons behind his desk and the opening strains of *Tosca* filled the room. It was the best-quality sound that Frank had ever heard and he asked Mac about it.

"Bose," Mac said. "I'll set you up with my man."

Mac pushed another button, and a butler came in with a tray with two amber-filled glasses, which he set on side tables next to the chairs.

"Single-malt scotch," Mac said. "I thought you might enjoy it."

"What about you?" Frank asked.

"I don't drink. Or smoke or do drugs." He sat down in a chair oppo-site them. "Shall we do some business?"

"We're not selling the club," Mike said.

"You haven't heard my offer."

Frank took a sip of the scotch. It was smoky and smooth, and a sec-ond later he felt its warmth permeate his stomach.

"Congratulations on the Pinto Club," Mac said. "You've done very well with it. But I think that I could take it to the next level in ways that you can't."

"How's that?" Mike asked.

"Horizontal integration," Mac said. "I take my adult-video actresses and book them into the clubs, take my star dancers and put them in the videos."

"We do that now," Mike said.

"In a cheap way," Mac said. "I'm talking about headliners. Names in the industry, people you can't afford. Similarly, you pimp your girls to traveling salesman for a couple of hundred bucks. Our girls go with millionaires."

"You've told us why you want to buy the club," Mike said, "not why we should sell it."

"You can sell it now and make a profit," Mac said. "Or you can wait until I drive you out of business, and lose money. I control six clubs in California, another three in Vegas. Pretty soon I'll be in New York. The headliners, the names, will work my clubs and no others. Another six months to a year, you won't be able to compete. At best, you'll be a bottom-feeding operation selling draft beer to Joe Lunchbucket."

"I might consider selling you forty-nine percent," Mike said.

"But I wouldn't consider buying it," Mac replied. "I *would* consider an eighty percent share. Believe me, you'll make more with that twenty points than with your current one hundred."

He waved his hand as if to encompass his estate, and Frank got what he was trying to say: Boys, look at my home and then look at yours. He's right, Frank thought. It was the move to make—take a profit from the sale of the eighty points, then let Big Mac make money for them.

"What would we have to do with the club if we sold you this inter-est?" Mike asked.

"Nothing," Mac said. "Go to the mailbox, pick up your checks."

And that was the problem, Frank saw. Mike loved the club. He loved playing owner, being the man. This was the flaw in the plan that Mac couldn't see. He hadn't correctly gauged Mike Pella's real interest.

"I'd want to maintain some kind of managerial voice in the operation," Mike said.

"You mean sell coke to the girls and shylock them the money?" Mac asked, smiling. "No, that has to stop. The business is growing up, Mike Pella. You'd better grow up with it."

"Or what?"

"Or I'll drive you out of business."

"Not if you're dead, you won't."

"Is that really the road we want to walk down?" Mac asked.

"You tell *me*."

Mac nodded. He took a deep breath and closed his eyes, as if he was meditating. Then he exhaled, opened his eyes, smiled, and said, "I've made you a business offer, Mike Pella. I encourage you to consider it in a businesslike fashion, and get back to me in a timely manner. In the meantime, I sincerely hope that you enjoy the rest of your afternoon. If you'd like, Amber can introduce you to some friends of hers who are unattached."

Mike liked.

He hooked up with one of Amber's friends and they found their way to a bedroom in the guest house.

Frank went back outside and enjoyed the food, the wine, and the beautiful people. Mac's "associates" were there, of course. John Stone was in the full swing of the party, frolicking in the pool with a couple of young ladies while Danny "Chokemaster" Sherrell played his faithful wingman.

Porter wasn't in the pool.

He was in his same dark suit, sucking on a cigarette, and every time that Frank glanced his way, Porter was checking him out from behind a whirl of smoke. Either the guy is queer for me, Frank thought, which is very doubtful, or he has an agenda. Either way, Frank wasn't going to let it ruin his enjoyment of the party food, which was excellent.

He was munching on a shrimp satay when Mac approached him.

"You're too smart for those people," Mac said. "You're wasting yourself. Come work with me—make some real money in a classy environment."

"I'm flattered," Frank said. "But Mike and I have been together a long time."

"Every additional day is a waste."

"Thanks for the offer," Frank said. "But no thanks. Mike's my guy. I'll stick with him."

"I respect that," Mac said. "No offense."

"None taken."

"But try to get him to do the smart thing, will you?" Mac said. "The smart thing is always good for everybody."

But Mike didn't see it that way.

Later that night, even as he was relating the marvels of sex with a future *Penthouse* model, he was saying, "You know, we're going to have to kill that moolie."

"No, I don't know that," Frank said. "As a matter of fact, I think you should sell him the eighty points."

"You're fucking kidding me, right?"

"I'm serious as a heart attack."

"No fucking way, Frankie," Mike said. "No fucking way."

"He's a *cop,* Mike."

"He's an *ex*-cop," Mike said, "and an ex-con."

"Once a cop, always a cop," Frank said. "They stick tighter than we do. And he's got a cop partner, so it's the same thing."

"I ain't selling the Pinto," Mike said.

He called Mac to tell him so.

The next week, inspectors started coming around the place—fire inspectors, health inspectors, water inspectors. They all found something wrong, and none of them took the usual C note. Instead, they wrote the place up.

The following week, CHP cars started parking across the street. Customers would pull out of the lot and get stopped for DUI. Jerked out of the car, made to walk the line, blow into the tube, the whole nine yards. Even if they weren't legally drunk, it was a hassle.

Undercover cops started coming into the place—sniffing around the men's room for dope, pretending they were johns looking for working girls, trying to buy coke from the bartenders.

Customers started to be afraid to come in.

It hurt business.

"Something's gotta be done," Mike said to Frank, and Frank knew what that something was.

"You want to start a shooting war with the CHP?" he asked Mike.

Mac called and upped his offer by ten grand, as a peace gesture.

Mike told him to go fuck himself.

The next week, two girls were busted for prostitution, and another for possession. The following morning, Pat got a call from the liquor commissioner, who was threatening to yank the club's license.

Mac upped his offer again.

Mike told him to fuck himself in the ass.

Privately, he wasn't so confident.

"What the fuck are we going to do?" he asked Frank. "What the fuck are we going to do?"

"Sell him the club."

Mike had a different answer—more of a traditional wise-guy response.

He firebombed the Cheetah Lounge.

He was very careful to do it after closing, even making sure that the janitor was out; then he and Angie Basso launched two very well-built Molotov cocktails through the window.

The joint didn't burn to the ground, but it was going to be a long time before it opened again. Just to make sure Mac got the point, Mike phoned him with condolences. "Gee," he said, "it's too bad the fire inspectors weren't out there."

Mac got the point.

He got it so well that Angie Basso got jumped coming out of his dry-cleaning business late at night. Pat Porter and Chokemaster Sherrell dragged him to the edge of the sidewalk, held his hands over the edge, and jumped on his forearms, snapping both his wrists.

"You shouldn't play with fire," Porter told him.

"What am I going to do?" Angie asked Mike the next night. "I can't even take a piss by myself."

"Don't look at me," Mike said.

But he responded. He had to, or give it all up.

So, three nights later, Frank waited in the backseat of a car parked across the street from Bare Elegance, waiting for the Chokemaster to lock up. Mike was in the driver's seat, because Frank didn't trust him to make a good shot.

"I'm just going to shoot him in the leg," Mike had said.

"You'd screw up and hit the femoral artery," Frank had told him. "Then Sherrell would bleed out and we'd be in a full-scale war."

"I'd aim for his dick," Mike'd said. "Couldn't miss *that* target."

Mike had rented a couple of Sherrell's old porn videos and shown them in the back room of the club. Frank was half-convinced that Mike had picked the Chokemaster for a target out of phallic jealousy.

Anyway, now he sat low in the backseat of a work car and watched while Sherrell came out, said good night to the bartender, pulled the metal screen down, and started to set the padlock.

Frank stuck the .22 rifle through the car's open window, sighted in on the fleshy part of Sherrell's right calf, and fired. Sherrell went down, Mike hit the gas, and that was it. Frank knew that the bartender would come back and get Sherrell to the hospital. The Chokemaster would be on crutches for a couple of weeks, if that.

All in all, it was a very tempered response to the assault on Angie Basso, whose wrists would take months to heal. If anything it was a *de*escalation of the war, but instead, the other side kicked it up a notch.

Frank saw it happening—literally.

He was at the airport waiting for a pickup when he saw Pat Porter walk into the terminal. Frank gave him a little space and then followed him in, where Porter met a direct flight from Heathrow and warmly greeted two men as they got off the plane.

They were what the Brits would call "hard men." Frank could see that by the way they walked and carried themselves. Heavily muscled, but graceful, like athletes. One was barrel thick and wore a rugby shirt over jeans and tennis shoes. The other was thin and a little taller, sporting an Arsenal football club jersey.

Porter had brought in a crew.

They showed up at the Pinto Club two days later.

It was late afternoon on a Tuesday, just when the after-work construction crowd would start to come in. Pretty quiet, not dead. Frank was sitting in his regular booth, grabbing a quick cheeseburger and a Coke before the evening rush started and he'd have to leave to make pickups.

He spotted the British crew as they came through the door. So did Georgie Y, who left the bar, where he was sitting with Myrna, and started toward the Englishmen. They smiled like he was a meal walking their way.

Frank waved Georgie over to the booth instead.

"Frank," Georgie said. "I don't like them coming in here."

"Did I ask what you like?" Frank said. "Myrna's up. Go watch her dance, think about what she'll be doing later tonight with you."

"Frank—"

"What did I say, Georgie? I have to repeat myself now?"

Georgie gave Porter a bad look, then took a seat ringside and watched Myrna gyrate her little body in a bad imitation of eroticism.

Porter walked over to Frank's booth, his two boys, still decked out in their sporting gear, on either shoulder.

Frank didn't ask them to sit.

Porter was in his uniform—dark suit, buttoned collar, skinny black tie. He looked at Frank and said, "You know, in the end it's going to come down to me and you."

"What is this, *Shane*?" Frank asked, laughing. Looking at Porter's face, he knew one thing for sure about him: Pat Porter didn't like being laughed at.

"Me and you," Porter repeated.

Frank looked over Porter's shoulder. "Then what are they here for?"

"To make sure no one else steps in," Porter said. "I know how you guineas are."

Frank went back to eating his cheeseburger. "I'm on a clock, Sam Spade," he said, chewing. "If you have a point, make it. Otherwise . . ."

Frank jutted his chin toward the door.

"I'm going to kill you, Frankie Machine," Porter said. "Or make you kill me."

"I'll take door number two," Frank said.

Porter didn't get the joke. He just stood there, like he was waiting for something. What, Frank thought, am I supposed to jump up and "draw"? We're going to do B Westerns, 1988 on Kettner Boulevard?

Frank finished the last bite of his burger, took a swallow of the Coke, then stood up and slammed the heavy glass into the side of Porter's face. Rugby Shirt started in, but suddenly Frank had a pistol out. He cocked it, pointed it at the two sidekicks, and said, "Really?"

Apparently not.

Rugby Shirt and Arsenal stood there, frozen.

Keeping the gun on them, he reached down to where Porter was now kneeling with blood pouring down the side of his face, grabbed the man's tie, wrapped it around his neck, and, with his gun on the other two Brits, dragged Porter across the floor, up the stairs to the landing, and out the door.

He waved the pistol at Rugby Shirt and Arsenal and said, "Out."

"You're dead, mate," Arsenal said.

"Yeah. Out."

They walked out the door. Frank came back into the room, stepped carefully over the broken glass and blood, and sat back down in the booth.

He signaled to the waitress for the check.

Everyone was staring at him—the waitress, the bartender, the three construction workers sitting at a table, Myrna and Georgie Y. They were all wide-eyed.

"What?" Frank asked. *"What?"*

I'm in a bad mood, all right? he thought. I haven't seen my kid awake in three weeks, my wife is threatening to call a lawyer, I'm trying to eat a burger before I work all night, and some Brit has to come in and hassle me with bad movie dialogue? I shouldn't have to *explain* myself to you people.

"Get me some club soda and a few bar towels," he said.

"I'll clean it up, Frank," the waitress said.

"Thank you, Angela," Frank said, "but I made the mess. I'll clean it up."

"We have cheesecake today, Frank."

"That's okay, honey. I'm watching my figure."

He cleaned up the blood and broken glass, and was more than normally alert when he went out in the parking lot to start making his pick-ups. When he got back with his first customer, Mike was waiting for him, laughing. "Don't you *ever* fucking lecture me about my temper again."

"The blood came out of the carpet okay."

Mike looked at Frank, then grabbed him by the cheeks and said, "I love you. I just fucking *love* you, all right?"

He turned to the whole bar. "I just love this fucking guy!"

Two weeks later, it happened.

It shouldn't have, *wouldn't* have, except that Mike suddenly had a group of Japanese businessmen who wanted to party, and he needed both limos to take care of them. So Frank would be driving instead of doing what he had planned to do, which was make a pickup of some shy money. It was supposed to have been a very simple, no-sweat errand— this junkie boyfriend of one of the dancers had borrowed some money and was going to make his first payment on the vig.

"Have Georgie do it," Mike said. "He can swing by the guy's place on his way in."

So Frank called Georgie, and he was happy to do it. Frank and Mike went out and drove the Japanese around, and when they got back to the club, it was one in the morning and Myrna was sitting at the bar, two other strippers holding her shoulders as she sobbed hysterically.

It took Frank thirty minutes to get the story out of her.

She had gone with Georgie to make the pickup. The junkie lived in an apartment building in the Lamp. They were going to pick up the money on the way in to work, so that's why she was with him. They pulled into the parking lot and Georgie told her to wait in the car. She said that was fine, because she needed to get her makeup on.

When Georgie got out of his car, three guys got out of another.

"Did you recognize them?" Frank asked.

Myrna nodded, then broke into another fresh bout of sobs. When she recovered, she said, "Frankie, one of them was that guy you beat up the other day. He had bandages on his face, but I recognized him. The other two were the guys who were with him."

Frank felt sick as Myrna told the rest of the story. Georgie tried to fight them, but there were three of them. One of them kicked Georgie in the head and his legs buckled under him. She got out of the car and tried to help him, but one of the guys wrapped his arms around her and held her.

Then the guy with the bandages took something out of his pocket and hit Georgie in the face with it. The other guys grabbed Georgie and held him and this guy just kept hitting him and hitting him, mostly in the stomach, but sometimes in the head, too, and when they let Georgie loose, he just fell to the ground. Then the guy with the bandages on his face kicked him over and over and over again, in the ribs and in the crotch and in the head.

"He kicked Georgie one last time in the head," Myrna said, "and Georgie's neck kind of snapped back and then the guy with the bandages came over and said—"

She broke down again.

"What did he say, Myrna?" Frank asked.

"He said . . . tell you . . ." She took a deep breath and looked him in the eyes. "It was supposed to be *you,* Frank."

It *was* supposed to be me, Frank thought. Porter got this junkie to set me up, but poor dumb Georgie walked into it instead. If it had been me, there'd be three dead Brits lying in that parking lot now, instead of Georgie. . . .

"Where's Georgie now?" Frank asked.

"In the hospital," Myrna sobbed. "He's unconscious. They said he isn't going to wake up. He has a sister. . . . I've been trying to get her number."

Frank and Mike were bedside fifteen minutes later. Georgie Y was all tubes and needles; a respirator was doing his breathing for him. They sat there for three hours, until the sister arrived from L.A.

She gave the okay to pull the plug.

Frank and Mike went to the junkie's apartment. He'd split, of course, but the dancer was home at her place.

"Where's your fucking boyfriend?" Mike asked her after he kicked the door in.

"I don't know. I haven't—"

Mike punched her in the mouth, then stuck the gun barrel through her broken teeth. "Where's your fucking junkie boyfriend, bitch? You lie to me again—"

The little shit was hiding in the bedroom closet.

Junkies aren't smart.

Mike ripped the door off its runners, yanked him out, and punched him in the gut. Frank took a pair of the girl's panty hose out of her chest of drawers and shoved them into his mouth. Then he ripped the phone out of the wall and tied the guy's hands behind his back with the cord.

They walked him out to the car. Frank drove while Mike held the junkie down on the floor in the back.

They drove out to the river floodway and pushed him over the edge. The floodway was dry and the junkie was pretty beat-up by the time he landed on the bottom. Mike and Frank slid down and pulled him up to his knees. The junkie was puking and starting to choke because the vomit was going back down his throat.

Frank pulled the panty hose out of his mouth and the junkie puked. Then he gasped, "I swear I didn't—"

"Don't lie to me," Frank said. He squatted down and spoke quietly in the junkie's ear. "I know what you did. You have one chance to save yourself now. Tell me where they are."

"They hang out down in Carlsbad," the junkie said. "Some English place."

"The White Hart," Mike said.

Frank nodded, pulled his gun, and fired into the junkie until the chambers were empty.

Mike did the same.

They got back in the car and drove to the White Hart.

They both knew the place.

The bar had warm beer, bangers and mash, and satellite feeds of soccer games, so a lot of the SoCal British expats hung out there. A pub-style sign with old-fashioned lettering and a painting of a white deer was hung over the door, and a Union Jack was stretched across the one window.

"Wait here," Frank said when they pulled into the parking lot. He reloaded the .38.

"Fuck that," Mike said. "I'm coming with you."

"This is *my* thing," Frank said. "Just have the motor running and the car in gear, okay?"

Mike nodded. He handed Frank his own pistol.

Frank checked its load, then asked, "You got a kit in the trunk?"

"Sure."

Mike popped the trunk open.

"Clean?" Frank asked.

"The fuck am I?" Mike asked. "Some beaner robbing a 7-Eleven?"

Frank got out of the car, walked back to the trunk, and found what he expected—a twelve-gauge sawed-off shotgun, a bulletproof vest, a pair of gloves, and a black stocking. He took off his jacket, slipped on the gloves, then buttoned up the vest and put his jacket back on over it. Then he stuck both pistols into his belt, tucked the shotgun into the crook of his arm, and pulled the black stocking over his head.

"See you in a minute," Mike said. "Frankie Machine."

Frank stepped through the door.

The place was nearly empty, just a couple of guys at the bar. The bartender and Rugby Shirt and Arsenal were all sitting at a table, drinking pints and looking up at a soccer match on a television set bolted high on the wall, near the ceiling.

Arsenal turned when the door opened.

The shotgun blast blew him out of his chair.

Rugby Shirt tried to stand to pull his pistol from his waistband, but Frank unloaded the second barrel into his stomach and he crumpled onto the table.

Where is Porter? Frank asked himself.

The men's room was at the back of the bar. Frank let the shotgun drop to the floor, took both pistols from his belt, and kicked the door in.

Porter was braced against the sink, his pistol raised. He was wearing his usual black suit, but his fly was unzipped and his hands were dripping water. He fired and Frank felt the three shots *thunk* into the vest, right over his heart, knocking the air out of him, and then he saw the look of alarmed surprise in Porter's eyes when he didn't go down.

Frank fired twice with the gun in his right hand.

Porter's head smashed back against the mirror, cracking it; then he slid down the sink and onto the floor.

Blood pooled onto the yellowed tiles.

They'll never get that out of the grouting, Frank thought as he dropped the gun, turned, and walked out of the bar.

Mike had the car in gear.

Frank got in, and Mike drove slowly out of the parking lot, onto the street, and then pulled on the 5.

Bap would have been proud.

"Where to?" Mike asked.

"Tara," Frank said.

Sometimes you just have to go in.

Usually, you try to be careful. You set everything up. You're patient and you wait until the moment is exactly right.

But sometimes you just have to go in.

They stopped off at Mike's condo in Del Mar first. Mike had an arsenal tucked away in the guest bedroom closet. Frank picked out two .38 snubbies, a Wellington over and under .303 ten-gauge, an AR-15, and two hand grenades.

When they got to Tara, there was no guard at the gate and it was open.

"What do you think?" Mike asked.

"I think they're waiting for us inside," Frank said. "I think we drive in and they ventilate the car."

"Sonny."

"What?"

"Sonny Corleone," Mike said.

"You guys ever watch anything else?"

"*You* guys?"

They drove the car around the back, got out, and climbed over the wall. Frank knew they must have tripped off motion sensors, but nothing happened—no lights, no alarms. Still, he thought, Mac must have night-vision cameras linked to the sensors, and he's probably watching us now, on the monitor. That's okay, you knew when you came in that you were going to fight the battle on his terms.

It was like being back in Vietnam.

Charlie never fought except on his own terms.

If you found him, it was because he *wanted* you to find him.

Frank carried the AR-15 and had the shotgun slung over his back. He liked the automatic rifle for range—the shotgun wouldn't be that useful until they got inside. *If* they got inside.

They had to walk through the zoo to get to the house. It was weird, because the animals were awake at night. The birds started to squawk, and he could hear the cats pacing in their cages, see their eyes flash red.

And, like Vietnam, Frank expected to see other flashes break up the night—the muzzle flashes of an ambush—then he realized that he and Mike were between the shooters and the animals, and Mac wouldn't take a chance on one of his pets getting shot accidentally.

The pool glittered a cool blue. It was lit up, but there was nobody out there, not anyone they could see anyway. They're inside the house, Frank thought, or, better, on the roof, waiting for us to get in so close that they can't miss.

Any second, the night sky is going to light up like the Fourth of July.

Frank edged around the pool, then flattened himself on the patio at the edge of the house and signaled Mike to do the same. Then he trained the rifle's night scope on the roof and scanned it left to right. He didn't see anything, but that didn't mean they weren't up there, lying flat against the dormers or behind the chimneys.

It was about fifty feet of open lawn to the back of the house.

"Cover me," he whispered to Mike.

Then, ducking as low as he could while still being able to run, he dashed toward the house and threw himself flat against the wall. He took one of the grenades out of his pocket, hooked his finger inside the pin, got ready to flip it up onto the roof, and then waved his hand to Mike.

Mike lunged off the ground and raced to the house, and they stayed there for a few seconds, pressed flat against the wall, catching their breath.

The sliding glass door was locked. Frank smashed the glass with the rifle butt, then reached in and pushed the door open. Mike pushed past him and went in with his shotgun at his cheek and swept the room.

Nothing.

Frank leapfrogged past him to the next wall and they made their way through the house like that.

They found Mac in the dojo.

Shirtless and barefoot, wearing only the pants of a black *gi,* he was slowly and rhythmically slamming roundhouse kicks into a heavy bag. The bag doubled up and popped toward the ceiling with every kick, the solid wham of the impact echoing through the empty room.

A jazz flute played quietly on the sound system.

A stick of incense burned in a holder on the floor.

Frank stayed twenty feet back and kept the rifle trained on him. A man of Mac's size and athletic ability could cover that distance in a stride and a half, and the kick would be lethal.

Mac turned his head to glance at them but didn't stop kicking.

"I left the front door open for you," he said. "You went to a lot of needless trouble, upset my animals, *and* you broke my slider."

"They beat the kid to death," Frank said.

Mac nodded and kicked the bag again. The motion looked both smooth and effortless, but the bag flew up toward the ceiling and then dropped again with a shudder. "I heard," Mac said. "I didn't authorize it. I don't approve of it."

"Let's just fucking shoot him, Frank!"

"I've left myself vulnerable to you as a gesture of my sincerity," Mac said, "and of my contrition. If you want to kill me, kill me. I'm at perfect peace."

He stopped kicking the bag.

Frank backed off two more steps and kept the rifle trained, but Mac knelt on the floor, rested his haunches on his heels, took a deep breath of the incense, closed his eyes, and opened his arms with his palms held flat up.

"The fuck is this?" Mike asked.

Frank shook his head.

But neither of them shot.

A long minute went by; then Mac opened his eyes, looked around as if he was a little surprised, and said, "Then let's discuss business. You should know that you are behind the information curve: Mr. Porter has decided to pursue his own agenda. His exact words were, 'I'm tired of working for some jumped-up monkey,' the monkey in question being myself. That being the case, I am willing to accept a fifty percent purchase of the Pinto Club. And if you want me to kill Pat Porter, I'll kill him."

"That's already been taken care of," Frank said.

Mac got to his feet and smiled. "That's what I thought you'd say."

Life was really good for a while.

They'd had to lay low in Mexico for a few weeks, with the cops and the media all over the Strip Club Wars like vultures. It had everything that the eleven o'clock news guys could want and more—sex, violence, gangsters, and more sex. Stripper after stripper gave on-air interviews, and one even held a press conference.

Then some new horror took the pride of place and the media moved on.

The cops had a longer attention span.

Four murders in one night, apparently related, put a lot of heat on the homicide guys, and the FBI came in on the OC angle and started a turf battle. Everyone liked Mike Pella for the Georgie Yoznezensky murder, but for a change, Mike was actually innocent of that, so it never got any traction.

Myrna kept her mouth shut and Mike got her a job at a club in Tampa. The stripper with the junkie boyfriend just split town, and Frank heard years later that she'd overdosed in East St. Louis.

As for the three Brits gunned down in ninety seconds at the White Hart, nobody at the bar could identify the shooter and the guns had no prints and were untraceable. Eventually, the San Diego cops and the feds decided that it had been a London turf battle fought out in Mission Viejo and they put it in the cold file.

So Mike and Frank took a vacation in Ensenada and then came back to the sweet life, because being partners with Big Mac McManus was *cake*.

Mac had the golden touch.

He was like this king, this magnificent emperor of an enchanted land where milk, honey, women, and money flowed in streams.

But Frank didn't get in on any of that. He turned down Mike's offer of a piece of the Pinto, because the feds were all over it. He kept working the limo thing, plowing the money into his fish business or socking it away against the proverbial rainy day. He would go to the Sunday afternoon parties sometimes, though, to get in on the buffet.

"You're going to pick up whores," Patty would say.

"No, I'm not."

It was a tired old argument.

"Sundays should be for your family," Patty argued.

"You're right," Frank said. "Let's all go."

"Nice," Patty said. "Now you want to bring your wife and daughter to an *orgy*."

She had a point there, Frank had to admit. Although he never took part in the sexual escapades. Mostly, he and Mac would repair to the dojo and work out. Mac taught him martial arts, taught him, in fact, the move that would save his life on the boat almost twenty years later.

They'd work out hard—hitting and kicking the bag, then doing some sparring, then hitting the weight bench, where they'd spot for each other. Then they'd go and sip fruit juice and talk about life, business, music, philosophy. Mac taught Frank about jazz, and Frank got him into opera.

They were good times.

They couldn't last.

It was the coke.

Frank never knew when Mac started doing it, but it seemed like all of a sudden that's all he was doing. Mountains of coke would go up Mac's nose, and he would take what seemed like a harem into his bedroom and disappear for days. After a while, he stopped taking the harem and just disappeared by himself, to emerge late in the afternoon, if at all, and demand more coke.

It changed him.

Mac started to be angry all the time. He'd fly into sudden, unpredictable rages, and launch into long, barely coherent rants about how he did all the work and all the thinking and how nobody appreciated him.

Then came the paranoia.

They were all out to get him, all plotting against him. He doubled the amount of security around the place, bought Dobermans that he let prowl the grounds at night, installed more alarm systems, and spent more and more time huddled alone in his room.

He stopped going into his dojo altogether. The heavy bag hung still and unused, a lonely symbol of Mac's decline.

Frank tried to talk to him. It didn't do any good, but Mac loved him for the attempt.

"All these people," he said to Frank one night when they were sitting alone together at the pool. "All these people are hangers-on. They're all parasites. Not you, Frank Machianno, you're a *man*. You love me man to man."

It was the truth.

Frank did love him.

Loved the memory of the distinguished, generous genius that Mac had been, and could be again. Instead of the paranoid, mean, incoherent shell he had become. Mac looked awful—the once-tight body was sagging and thin. The man rarely ate, his eyes were dilated, and his skin looked like dark brown parchment paper.

"These people," Mac continued, "will kill me."

"No, Mac," Frank said.

But they did.

John Stone came to Frank one day at the Sunday party that autumn and said, "He's cheating us."

"Who is?"

"Our 'partner,'" Stone said. He gestured toward Mac's bedroom, where Mac was holed up, as he usually was those days. And the Sunday party wasn't what it used to be, either. Fewer and fewer people came, and those who did were mostly the hard-core sex and coke freaks.

"No way," Frank said.

"Don't tell me no way," Stone said. "Half our money is going up that nigger's nose."

Frank didn't want to believe it, but the "cheating" talk only got worse. Stone and Sherrell met with Mike to show him the figures. Frank refused to be there. He had it rationalized six ways to Sunday: (a) Mac wasn't stealing; (b) even if he was, he was making them so much money, they were better off with him stealing than without him; (c) Mac wasn't stealing.

But Mac was.

He knew Mac was.

Stone confronted Mac with the evidence and Mac threatened to kill him, kill him and his whole family, kill them all.

"He's gotta go," Mike said to Frank.

Frank shook his head.

"No one's asking you for your *vote,* Frankie," Mike said. "The decision's been made. I just came as, you know, a *courtesy,* because I know the guy is your friend."

You just came, Frank thought, because you wanted to make sure that Frankie Machine wouldn't take it personally. See it as a grudge, respond the way I did over Georgie Y's killing. Well, you have a legitimate concern there.

"The guys down in the Lamp," Mike added, "they've signed off on it."

Letting Frank know that if he decided to do something about this, he'd be taking on Detroit, too.

"What do the Migliores have to do with it?"

"They own strip clubs," Mike said. "This moolie getting toxic affects them, too. They don't like it. Headlines are bad for business. He's gotta go, Frank."

"Let me do it."

"What?"

"Let me do it," Frank said.

You guys are scared shitless of him. You'll panic and just blast away until there's nothing left of the man. If it has to be done, let me do it quick and clean.

I owe the man that much.

He's my friend.

Frank found him in the dojo. The sound system was blasting out Miles Davis's "Bitches Brew." Frank walked in and saw Mac standing on one shaky leg, kicking the heavy bag with the other.

The bag barely moved.

And Mac didn't even notice him.

Frank walked up and put two .45 slugs into the back of his head.

Then he went home, got his old longboard out of the garage, and gave it a good waxing. Then he took it out into the water and let the waves pound him.

He never went back to the limo business or the Pinto Club.

Patty filed for divorce later that year.

Frank didn't contest it.

He gave her the house and custody of Jill.

50

Four more bodies, Frank thinks as he drives through the desert.

English Pat Porter and his two boys.

And Mac.

Four more candidates, but not exactly strong ones. Hell, all that was almost twenty years ago. Even back then, the word was that people in London were relieved that Porter and his crew hadn't cashed in on their round-trip tickets.

And Mac?

He'd had no family, no people. And the SDPD hadn't exactly rushed to investigate the murder of a crooked ex-cop.

Of course, Mike lost the Pinto Club. Without Mac to restrain him, he ran it into the ground and ended up burning it down before the IRS, the bank, or the other creditors could take it away from him.

Then he got popped for the arson and went in for a ten spot.

The Migliores eventually took over the whole San Diego strip club business, and the prostitution and porn that went with it, with the Combination as their grand protectors.

But what does it have to do with me? Frank wonders.

Is it possible that the feds have reopened one of the Strip Club War cases and are going after the Migliores? So they're eliminating potential witnesses, including yours truly?

If that's the case, maybe Mike is in the dirt instead of the wind.

Frank pulls off the road.

Tired.

It hits him like a cold, hard wave.

This fatigue, this . . . *despair.* This acknowledgment of reality—that he can run and fight, run and fight, and *win every one,* but that eventually, inevitably, he's going to lose.

Hell, Frank thinks, I've *already* lost.

My life.

The life I love, anyway. Frank the Bait Guy is already dead, even if Frankie Machine ekes out survival. That life is gone—my home, the early mornings on the pier, the bait shack, seeing my customers, sponsoring the kids.

The Gentlemen's Hour.

All gone now, even if I "live."

And Patty.

And Donna.

And Jill.

What's left of them now for me? Brief, tense meetings in hotels somewhere? Hurried embraces in the thick air of fear? Maybe a quick kiss, a fast hug. "How are you?" "What's new?" Maybe there'll be grandkids someday. Jill will send pictures to some post office box. Or maybe I can check in on one of those Internet sites, watch my grandchildren grow up on a little laptop screen.

If life is just running now, why bother?

Why not just swallow the gun right here?

Jesus, he thinks, you've become Jay Voorhees.

This is what kills you, surer than a bullet.

He makes a phone call.

51

The Nickel's been expecting it.

A call from Frank on the backup phone.

Four in the morning, he's in that surreal half sleep when the phone rings.

"Frank, thank God."

"Sherm."

"Look, there's a clean passport and airline tickets waiting for you in Tijuana," Sherm says. "You can be in France tomorrow morning. The EU won't extradite on a capital crime. Everything's taken care of for Patty and Jill. Godspeed, my friend."

"Am I going to walk into another ambush, *friend*?"

"What the hell are you talking about?"

Sherm listens to Frank tell him about the ambush at the bank and the GPS monitor that led to the motel in Brawley.

"Frank, you don't think—"

"What am I supposed to think, Sherm?" Frank asks. "Who knew about that bank? You and me."

"They came, Frankie," Sherm says. "I gave them nothing, I swear."

"Who came?"

"Some wise guys," Sherm says. "And the feds."

"The feds?"

"That buddy of yours," Sherm says. "Hansen. They have warrants out for you, Frank. For Vince Vena and Tony Palumbo."

Tony Palumbo? Frank thinks. That must have been the guy with the garrote on the boat. "You know anything about this Palumbo, Sherm?"

"Word on the street," Sherm says, "is that he was an FBI undercover, an informant, the guy behind the G-Sting indictments."

G-Sting, Frank thinks.

Strip clubs.

Teddy Migliore.

And Detroit.

"Who were the wise guys?" Frank asked.

"I don't know," Sherm says. "All I know is I gave them nothing. Frank, where *are* you?"

"Yeah, right."

Sherm sounds legitimately hurt. "After all these years, Frank."

"What *I'm* thinking, Sherm."

"You have to trust *somebody*, Frank."

Is that right? Frank thinks. Who? There were three people who knew about the existence of that bank—me, Sherm, and Mike Pella. The only one I absolutely *know* didn't flip on me is me.

So I'd better find Mike, and I don't know where he is. There's somebody who might, though.

Can I trust Dave?

Because we've been friends for twenty years?

And because he owes me one?

52

It was in 2002.

Dave hadn't made it to the Gentlemen's Hour in two weeks.

Frank knew why.

Everyone in San Diego knew what was keeping the FBI busy—the disappearance of a seven-year-old girl from her upstairs bedroom in the suburbs. Carly Mack's parents had put her to bed the night before, and when they went to wake her in the morning, she was gone.

Just gone.

Terrifying, Frank thought when he read about it in the paper. A parent's worst nightmare. He couldn't imagine how the Macks felt. He knew that moment of sheer panic when he lost sight of Jill at the mall for ten seconds. To wake up and find her gone? Right from your own house, her own bedroom?

Unimaginable.

So Frank didn't expect to see Dave for a while. The FBI always drew kidnap cases, and he heard Dave on the radio, saying they were doing everything they could to find little Carly Mack and asking anyone with information to step forward. The media were all over this thing like gulls around a fishing trawler, demanding that the cops find little Carly. As if Dave needed the prodding—Frank knew he'd be working this one 24/7.

That's why he was a little surprised that morning to see Dave paddling out. The tall agent was making a beeline for the break, saw Frank, then jutted his chin toward the shoulder. Frank paddled over and met him there, in the spot away from the break where a lot of the older guys went to wait for a wave or just take a breather and talk story.

Dave looked bad.

Normally serene no matter what was going on or how much pressure he was under, that morning Dave had black circles under his eyes and a look on his face that Frank had never seen.

Rage—that's what it was, Frank decided.

Dave's face showed rage.

"Talk to you?" Dave asked.

"Sure."

Dave had quite a story to talk.

Carly's parents, Tim and Jenna Mack, were swingers. Jenna had been in a local bar with a girlfriend named Annette the night before, cruising for people to take home. She'd gotten hit on by a middle-aged guy named Harold Henkel, and shot him down.

About ten o'clock, Jenna and Annette gave up on finding any fresh meat. Annette phoned her husband and he came over to the Macks' for the same old foursome. A little disappointing, perhaps, but better than nothing.

Jenna went upstairs to check on both kids—five-year-old Matthew and little Carly—and found they were both sleeping. She kissed them both on the cheek, shut their doors, then went to the "recreation room" they'd built in the garage and got on with the party.

All four of them admitted to drinking some wine and smoking a little weed. Annette and her husband went home around 1:30 a.m.

Neither Annette nor her husband had left the rec room before heading home. Tim and Jenna didn't look in on the kids again before they went to bed.

About nine o'clock the next morning, the brother, Matthew, went into Carly's room to play with her. She wasn't there. Matthew didn't think anything of it and went downstairs to have a bowl of cereal. Tim asked him if Carly was awake and Matthew answered that he thought she was downstairs.

Jenna was still asleep.

Tim searched the house and didn't find Carly. Getting scared, he went and looked around the neighborhood, then called the neighbors. By this time, Jenna was up, and she was starting to panic. Matthew was crying.

They called the police within fifteen minutes.

"Guess who lives a block and a half away?" Dave asked.

"Harold Henkel," Frank said.

Dave nodded. "We brought him in. He owns an RV that he keeps parked out in the street. Said he was gone all that weekend, out in the desert near Glamis. The RV was spick-and-span, Frank. You could still smell the Pine-Sol."

"Jesus God."

"Monday morning, he took his jacket and some blankets to the dry cleaner's," Dave said. "I got a warrant, searched his house and his computer. The hard drive was full of kiddie porn. The son of a bitch did it, Frank. He took that little girl. But he's shutting down on me and he's about to lawyer up. If I charge him, he'll never tell where Carly is. What if she's still alive, Frank? What if he stuck her out in the desert some-place and the clock is running down?"

Dave's eyes were brimming with tears. The man was about to lose it. Frank had never seen him like this before, nothing even close.

"How can I help you?" Frank asked.

"We have to find out where she is, Frank," Dave said. "And fast. If she's alive, we have to find her before it's too late. If she's dead . . . then the evidence is deteriorating every second. If *we* ask him, Frank, we lose her. But if someone else could make Henkel talk . . ."

"Why are you asking me, Dave?" Frank asked, already knowing the answer.

"Because," Dave answered, "you're Frankie Machine."

Dave booked Henkel that night, without charging him. Warned him not to leave town, then drove him in a darkened van out the back exit of the federal building to protect him from the press, took him downtown, where he could get a cab to wherever he wanted.

"You might not want to go home," Dave warned him. "The media have your house under siege."

Henkel got into the first cab he saw.

A block later, Frank stopped the cab, and Mike Pella came off the sidewalk, got into the backseat, and jammed a needle into Henkel's arm before the man could react.

When Henkel woke up, he was back out in the desert, naked and tied to a chair. A man about his own age, and just a little smaller, sat on a stool in front of him, whistling an aria as he meticulously ran the blade of a fish-skinning knife down two sharpening rods that were set at forty-five-degree angles from a board.

First the right side, then the left.

The right side, then the left.

This was an expensive sharpening tool that Frank had bought to keep his even more expensive Global kitchen knives in top shape. There were few things in the world Frank despised more than a dull knife.

One of them, however, was someone who would harm a child.

That was the top of the list.

He noticed that Henkel had come to.

Small wonder that Jenna Mack hadn't been interested. Henkel was a big man with a roll of fat around his middle. Balding on the top of his head, with a salt-and-pepper mustache and goatee around a full mouth. Pale blue eyes that were just now widening in confusion and fear.

His RV was parked twenty feet away.

In a ravine, in the desert.

"Where am I?" he asked. "Who are you?"

Frank didn't say anything. He just kept running the blade down the two rods, enjoying the sound of steel on stone.

"What the fuck is this?!" Henkel yelled. He strained against the ropes that held his arms tightly bound against the chair. Looked down and saw his ankles securely duct-taped to the legs of the chair.

Frank just kept whistling an aria from *Gianni Schicchi*.

"Are you a cop?!" Henkel demanded. A fine tone of panic had seeped into his voice. "Fucking *answer* me!"

Frank slid the blade down one rod, then the other.

One, then the other.

Slowly, carefully.

"My lawyers will crucify you!" Henkel yelled, stupidly.

Frank looked at him now, then tested the blade against his thumb and winced as it cut him. He set the blade on his lap, removed the two stone rods, put them back in the case, and carefully replaced them with two titanium bars, then started the whole process all over again.

The sun was just starting to come up, faint and pink.

It was still cold out there, so Henkel was shivering anyway, but now he started to shake with fear. He started to scream, "Help! Help!" even though he must have known it was hopeless. A desert rat like Henkel would have known that they were out in the middle of the Anza-Borrego Desert State Park, and that no one was going to hear him.

He must know this, Frank thought, just the way he knew that no one was going to hear Carly Mack's screams.

Frank ran the bar down one rod, then the other.

One, then the other.

Henkel started to sob, then his bladder let go and urine ran down his leg onto the duct tape at his ankles. His chin dropped to his chest and his head bobbed up and down as he cried.

Frank finished the *Gianni Schicchi* aria and switched to *"Nessun dorma.''* Ran the blade down one bar, then the other. One bar, then the other. He tested the blade again, nodded his satisfaction, and carefully stored the bars back in their case. He got up from his stool, laid the blade against the skin on Henkel's chest, and said, "Harold, you have a decision to make—prison for life, maybe a lethal injection, or I skin you."

Henkel moaned.

"I'm going to ask you *once,*" Frank said. "Harold, where's the girl?"

Henkel gave it up.

He'd left Carly in an old mine shaft just eight miles from this spot.

"Is she alive?" Frank asked, trying to keep the quiver out of his voice.

"She was when I left her," Henkel said.

He didn't have the guts to kill her after he'd raped her, so he'd just left her for dead. Frank set the knife down, took a cell phone from his pocket, called Dave, and gave him the location. Then he said to Henkel, "We're going to sit here until it checks out. And if you've lied to me, you piece of crap, I'll take five hours to kill you and God Himself will turn a deaf ear."

Henkel started to mutter an Act of Contrition.

"While you're praying?" Frank said. "Pray that that little girl is still alive."

She was.

Barely—she was close to hypothermia and severely dehydrated, but she was alive. A weeping Dave Hansen called Frank as they were loading her on the chopper. "And Frank," he said. "Thank you."

"Keep it out of the papers," Frank said.

Dave did, of course. So did Henkel. Frank untied him and left him out there with a warning that none of this had ever happened, that Henkel had confessed to the FBI, and that if any other story emerged, he wouldn't last a day in prison.

Mike drove in, whisked Frank away, and the feds arrived ten minutes later. That night, Frank sat in front of the television, watching the reunion of Carly with her mom and dad.

He cried like a baby.

Henkel never opened his mouth.

He pled out, got 299 years, and survived two of them as the cell-

block piñata, until some biker on a crank rush got carried away and rup-
tured his spleen.

Henkel died before the EMTs ambled to the scene.

Charges were dropped against the biker for lack of evidence, mostly
because twenty other guys came forward to claim the honor and would
have testified to it in court, and anyway, the prosecutors had better things
to do.

The Macks moved out of the city and quit "the lifestyle."

Frank and Dave never spoke about it, except for one time, during the
first Gentlemen's Hour after Carly Mack had been found alive.

"I owe you one" was all Dave had said.

Nothing about Frankie Machine, or what he knew about Frank's
other life, nothing about how Frank had gotten Henkel to give it up.

Just, "I owe you one."

53

Dave's pushing his longboard into the back of his van when Frank
comes up behind him.

"Very sketchy, surfing in a rainstorm," Frank says. "God only knows
what toxic crap is pouring out of the storm drains. You're just begging
for hepatitis."

"You have the right to remain—"

"You're not arresting me, Dave."

"Why not?"

"Because you owe me one."

It's the truth, and Dave knows it. "Let's prove everyone wrong," he
says, "and get in out of the rain."

Frank gets into the passenger side of the van. The two men sit there looking at the ocean as raindrops splatter against the windshield.

"You catch anything good?" Frank asks.

"Mostly slop," Dave says. "Where the hell have you been?"

"Running."

"Did you run into a guy named Vince Vena, by any chance?"

Frank stares at him.

"He washed up in my jurisdiction," Dave says. "Thanks a heap."

"Weird tides in weather like this," Frank says.

"Missed it by *that* much."

"If I *were* to say I killed him," Frank says, "which I'm not, I'd say it was self-defense."

"How about Tony Palumbo?" Dave asks. "Was that self-defense, too?"

"As a matter of fact."

"Bullshit, Frank," Dave says, getting angry. "You're taking out the G-Sting witnesses."

"What are you talking about?"

"Palumbo was one of my guys," Dave says, "an undercover. Had been for years. Who paid you? Teddy Migliore? Detroit?"

"Here's how they paid me, Dave."

Frank pulls the neck of his sweatshirt down to show Dave the scar, which is still angry and red. "Your boy tried to take me out, Dave. He had a garrote around my neck."

"That doesn't make any sense," Dave says.

"Palumbo wouldn't be the first UC to work both sides of the fence," Frank says. "Besides, was Vena one of your witnesses?"

"I was hoping he would be after I indicted him," Dave says. "But you took care of that."

"You have this backward, Dave. *They* tried to kill *me*. They didn't get it done."

He tells Dave what Mouse Junior had to say, about his discussion with John Heaney and his confrontation with Teddy Migliore. About a crew from Detroit trying to take him out.

Dave looks at his old friend. Two decades of Gentlemen's Hours, you get to know a man. And then there was the Carly Mack case. . . .

"What's G-Sting have to do with me?" Frank asks.

"Nothing that I know of," Dave says.

"Tell me the truth!" Frank yells. "I'm trying to save my life here!"

"I can help you, Frank."

"Yeah, like you helped me in Borrego?" Frank asks. "Like you helped me in Brawley? You had Sherm Simon wired, Dave. You had the GPS put in with the money. You tracked me and you gave me up to Detroit."

"I tracked you," Dave admits. "But I didn't give you up to anybody."

"You're a dirty cop," Frank says, looking into Dave's eyes for confirmation.

He doesn't see it.

What he sees is that his old friend is angry. He hasn't seen him like this since the Carly Mack case.

"Come in," Dave says.

"I won't go into the program," Frank says. "Whatever else I am, I'm not a rat."

"Then you'd be about the only guy who isn't."

"I can't answer for other guys," Frank says. "I can only answer for myself."

"These guys are trying to kill you!" Dave yells. "And you're going to stand up for them? What has Pete Martini ever done for you? Or *any* of these guys? Ever? You have a daughter, Frank, on her way to med school. What's Jill going to do with you six feet under?"

"Jill is taken care of," Frank says. "So is Patty."

"You stubborn bastard."

"Can you give me my life back?"

"No," Dave says. "But I can give you *a* life back."

Even if it's true, Frank thinks, it's not good enough.

"I have an ask, Dave." Payback for Carly Mack.

"Anything," Dave says.

I owe you one.

"All I can figure is that this has something to do with something Mike Pella and I might have done back in the day," Frank says. "I've been out of the loop for a long time now. I don't know what's what. I have to know if Mike's dead. Or, if he's alive, where the hell he is. I thought you might know something about that."

"I can't do that, Frank."

Frank looks at him for a second, then opens the door to get out.

"Shut the door, Frank."

Frank shuts it.

Dave says, "I need your word you won't kill him."

So Mike's alive, and the FBI has him under surveillance. It's all hooking together.

"I just want to talk with him," Frank says.

The sky is a pearl gray, and, like a pearl, shiny in the rain, almost translucent. It's pretty, Frank thinks. He watches a wave swell on the outside, start to build, a thick wall of water rolling in, a whitecap dancing on the edge like a tightrope walker.

"Pella has no involvement with G-Sting," Dave says.

So . . .

"We like him for the Goldstein murder."

Ka-boom. The wave explodes with a dull bass roar.

In Frank's head.

He feels like he's drowning. Held under in the impact zone.

"That's not possible," Frank says.

Dave shrugs. "He's in Palm Desert. Under the name Paul Otto."

"You guys have him under surveillance?"

Dave shakes his head. "He's in the program, Frank."

Mike's a rat.

54

Frank had been retired for a while back in '97.

Retired from the *life* anyway. No more limo business, no more strip clubs, no more OC. He was working his bait shop, his fish business, his linen service, and his rental managements when Mike Pella came to him to talk about taking back Vegas.

"Take it *back*?" Frank asked. "When did we ever *have* it?"

They were on OB Pier, walking off a heavy lunch at the OBP Café. Mike had aged. There was a lot of silver in that black hair, and the wide shoulders, though still wide, were a little stooped.

"Las Vegas should be *our* thing," Mike told him. "Not New York's, not Chicago's—L.A.'s."

Deck chairs on the *Titanic*, Frank thought. A bunch of hyenas squabbling over a dried-up skeleton. There's nothing to *have* in Vegas, not since Donnie Garth turned state's evidence and RICO shut the whole thing down. Anyway, Las Vegas is Family Town, USA now, Disney World with blackjack. It's all corporations now.

Lawyers and guys with M.B.A.'s.

"Peter is ready to make a move," Mike said. "Take back what's ours. Make our family a real family again."

"How many times have we heard this 'real family' chorus?" Frank asked. "We heard it from Bap, we heard it from Locicero, then Regace, then Mouse before he went away the first time, Mouse before he went away the *second* time. . . ."

"It's for real this time."

"What makes this time different?"

Herbie Goldstein, Mike told him.

Fat Herbie? Frank thought. Pavarotti look-alike Herbie, the Will Rogers of the pastry counter? The man who never met a doughnut he didn't like? This guy is Mouse's ticket to the show?

Time had not been kind to Herbie. He'd done an eight-year stretch for using funny plastic and stealing stamps. *Stealing stamps,* that's what it had come to, Frank thought. In prison, Herbie'd had not one but two bypass operations and a couple of toes amputated because of diabetes. Now he was out, running an auto-body shop so he could launder shylock money through it and dick insurance companies on car repairs at the same time.

"Herbie doesn't have any juice," Frank said.

"He does now," Mike said.

Turned out that Herbie had the arm on a billionaire casino owner named Teddy Binion, who gave Herbie $100,000 to put on the street. Then Herbie did a very smart thing: He turned it all over to an Indian.

"An Indian?" Frank asked.

"Indian *gambling*?" Mike prompted. "This guy goes to reservations, gets them to build a casino, gets the management contract *and* the shy business on the chronic losers. He's getting from both ends—he gets the skim, and he gets the vig from the money he puts out on the street, or the dirt roads, or whatever the fuck they have on these places. Chief Running Deer, or whatever the fuck his name is, kicks to Herbie, who kicks to Binion, who has a wicked coke and showgirl habit, which Herbie provides him both."

"So?"

"So," Mike explained, "Binion is in hot water with the Nevada Gambling Commission over his drug use and his friendship with known mobster Herbie Goldstein. He's a half hour from seeing his name in the Black Book, which means he'll be forced to sell the casino. So he's going to let Herbie come and bust it out, skim the fucking shit out of it.

"And get this," Mike said. "Binion trusts Herbie so much, he gave him all his jewelry—hundreds of thousands of dollars' worth—for 'safekeeping.' Herbie's got them in a safe in his house."

He held up his wrist and showed Frank his new Patek Philippe watch. "Herbie let me have it for a grand."

So much for "safekeeping," Frank thought.

"Herbie," Mike says, "is going to bust out Binion's casino. He's getting a taste of the Indian skim, a slice of the shy. Plus, he's using that auto shop of his to scam insurance companies and fence half the stolen shit in Nevada."

"Good for Herbie."

"Good for *us*," Mike said. "We're going to partner with him."

"Herbie *agreed* to that?"

"Not yet," Mike said. "That's where you come in."

Frank leaned over the railing and looked down at the blue water. "No, that's where I *don't* come in. I like Herbie. We're old friends. He turned me on to onion bagels. Not a small thing, Mike."

"I like Herbie, too," Mike said. "We're not going to clip him, just explain to him that it's not right he should eat alone when his friends are hungry. We'll have a little sit-down, and I figure if he sees *you* there . . . Besides, I want you to have this shot. It's your chance to be a *player.* You want to sell bait the rest of your life?"

As a matter of fact, Frank thought, I do.

That would be just fine.

"Mouse Senior asked me to ask you," Mike said. "He would consider it a favor."

Which, translated, meant it was a command performance.

They met at Denny's.

Denny's, Frank remembers thinking at the time. This is what it's come to—lunch meetings at Denny's. Shiny menus and greasy chins. The Martini brothers were studying the menu like it was the *Daily Racing Form,* arguing over the "Fresh Catch of the Day" item.

"You see a ocean out there?" Carmen asked, pointing out the window at the desert.

"No," Mouse Senior answered.

"Then how the fuck can it be fresh?"

"I think it means it was fresh when they froze it," Mouse Senior replied. "Here's Frank. Ask him. He *sells* fish."

"What about it, Frankie?"

"They catch it, flash-freeze it, then overnight it," Frank told him, taking a seat next to Mike.

"Is this *your* fish?" Mouse Senior asked him.

"I don't sell to chains."

"So, should he get the fish?" Carmen asked.

"No."

Frank felt like his head was about to come off. The sheer tedium . . .

Mouse Senior set his menu down. "Thanks for coming, Frank."

"No problem, Peter."

Carmen nodded his thanks and Frank nodded back.

It took about a year and a half to order, all on separate checks.

Frank asked for an iced tea.

"That's it?" Mouse Senior asked. "That's what you're having for lunch? An iced tea?"

"That's all I want," Frank said.

"That's, like, antisocial," Mike said.

"No offense intended," Frank replied.

The truth was that Frank liked food too much to eat any of this stuff, and, more important, he had a lunch date following this summit meeting. He had met this stunning dancer named Donna the night before at the Tropicana. She had said she'd go to lunch with him but not dinner, and he was going to take her out to someplace really nice.

"Let's get down to business," Carmen said when the food arrived. "Herbie Goldstein."

"He's a greedy, selfish miser," Mouse Senior said, a little dab of tuna salad on the corner of his lip. "That fat Jew boy is making money hand over fist and not paying anybody."

"'Fat Jew boy'?" Frank said. "What's that?"

"What, you're Herbie's big friend all of a sudden?" Mouse Senior asked.

"No, I've been his friend for *years,*" Frank said. "So have all of you."

"Do you know the money he's fucking making?" Mike asked. "Just the fenced shit he has in his fucking house is probably worth a fortune, and he hoards money in there, too."

"Frank," Carmen said. "He has to share."

"I know," Frank said.

"So?" Mouse asked.

"I'll talk to him," Frank said. "Give me a chance to talk to him."

"Not you alone," Carmen said.

"Me and Mike."

"Mike, you good with that?" Mouse asked.

Mike nodded.

"Today," Carmen insisted.

"To*night,*" Frank said.

Everybody looked at him.

"I have a date today," Frank said.

It was agreed—Frank and Mike would have a talk with Herbie that night, and get him on board.

"But Frank," Mouse said, "if Herbie doesn't do the right thing, then . . ."

"Then I'll take care of it," Frank said.

Then it will go the other way, he thought.

And that was it. The guys finished their meals, happy with the knowledge that they were about to use Fat Herbie Goldstein to bankroll their takeover of Las Vegas, then went up to the counter to pay their separate checks. Frank said his good-byes, visited the men's room, and waited there until they had all left. Then he walked past the table and saw just what he'd expected.

Three bucks and change in tips.

The cheap bastards had sat there for two hours, and left three bucks and change. Frank took two twenties out of his wallet and laid them on the table.

Lunch with Donna was great.

He took her to a little French place off the Strip, and the lady knew her away around a menu. They were at the table for two and a half hours, talking, drinking wine, eating good food, enjoying each other's company.

She was from Detroit originally, her father had spent his life on the Ford line, and she knew she didn't want that life. She was good at dancing—she had the body and the legs—so she studied dance: ballet, until she got too tall, then tap and jazz. She went to Vegas with a boy she thought she was in love with, got married, but it didn't work out.

"He liked hitting on cocktail waitresses even more than he liked wailing on me," Donna said.

The boy went home; she stayed.

She met an entertainment director in the buffet at the Mirage and he got her an audition for the line at the Tropicana. She went to bed with him out of gratitude and because he was a nice guy, but nothing came of it except that she got the job.

"I saw other girls," she said, "sleeping around, getting into the coke thing, trying to party their way into something better. I realized that there *was* nothing better and the party scene was a dead-end street, so I pretty much just did my job and went home and washed my hair."

She did get married again, to the chief of security at Circus Circus. The marriage lasted three years—"No kids, thank God"—and then she discovered he was sleeping around with chip girls and was blowing their money hitting on eighteen.

"Why am I telling you all this?" she asked Frank. "I'm usually a very reserved person."

"It's my eyes," Frank said. "I have kind eyes—people tell me things."

"You do have kind eyes."

"You have fantastic eyes."

She told him all about her "business plan."

"I'm going to stay 'on the line' for two more years," she said. "Then I'm going to open a little shop."

"What kind of shop?"

"Women's clothing," she said. "A boutique, upscale but not out of reach."

"Where?" he asked. "Here in Vegas?"

"I think so."

He leaned across the table a little. "Have you ever thought about San Diego?"

She didn't go back to his room with him that afternoon, but she did agree to go out to San Diego when she got a couple of free days. He offered to buy her airline ticket and get her a hotel room, but she said she preferred to pay her own way.

"I decided a long time ago," she said, "that a woman in this world needs to take care of herself. I prefer it that way. I like it."

"I didn't mean to insult you," Frank said.

"You didn't," she said. "I can see your heart."

He and Mike met up that night and went over to Herbie's house. They rang the bell and there was no answer, but they could hear the television and there were lights on. The door was unlocked, so they let themselves in.

"Herbie?" Frank called.

They found him in front of the TV, slumped in his big easy chair.

Three bullet holes in the back of his head.

His mouth gaping open.

"Jesus," Mike said.

"This wasn't supposed to happen," Frank said, surprised that he felt an angry heat coming up on his face.

The place was a mess. It had been tossed—burglarized.

"We better get out of here," Mike said.

"One second," Frank said. He pulled his shirtsleeve down over his fingers, picked up the phone, and dialed 911. Gave them Herbie's address and said that the resident there had suffered a heart attack.

"What the fuck, Frank?" Mike asked.

"I didn't want him decomposing," Frank said as they walked out. "He doesn't deserve that. He didn't deserve *this*."

"Look," Mike said as they were driving away, "half the hustlers in town knew what a pack rat Herbie was."

"What are you saying?" Frank asked. "This was a coincidence?"

"Could have been anybody."

"You know better than that."

Frank checked out of the Mirage, got into his car, and drove all the way to L.A. It was morning when he got to Westlake Village and found Mouse Senior at his coffeehouse, drinking an espresso, munching on a *pain au chocolat,* and reading the *Los Angeles Times.* He looked surprised to see Frank, who ordered a cappuccino and an apricot Danish and sat down next to him.

"It's probably better you don't come to see me *here,*" Mouse said, "at my place of business."

"You want to go someplace else . . ."

"No, it's okay this once," Mouse said. "So, did you get Herbie straightened out?"

"No," Frank said, looking into his face. "*You* did."

It was there. Just a flicker, but it was there, before Mouse composed his face, looked irritated, and asked, "What are you talking about?"

"You gave the nod," Frank said. "Half wasn't good enough for you. You wanted a bigger pie to cut up, so you gave the nod."

Mouse put that *boss* tone in his voice. "The nod for fucking *what,* exactly?"

"To have Herbie done."

Mouse set his newspaper down. "Herbie's gone?"

"Yeah."

"How do you—"

"I saw the body."

"There's a million junkies in Vegas," Mouse said. "They all knew what a pack rat Herbie was. Any one of them—"

Interesting, Frank thought, he used the exact same phrase as Mike— "what a pack rat Herbie was." He shook his head, "Three twenty-twos, to the back of the head. Professionals."

"Herbie made a lot of enemies in his—"

"Cut the crap."

"What are you, drunk?" Mouse asked. "Talking to your boss like that?"

Frank leaned across the table. "What are you going to do about it, *Mouse*? What are you going to do about it?"

Mouse didn't say anything.

"That's right," Frank said.

He was walking away when the young waiter came over with the coffee and Danish. "You don't want your—"

"Nothing personal," Frank said to him, "but your coffee is garbage and your pastry is crap. You serve cheap shit to suckers who don't know any better. I know better."

He walked out and waited for the blowback.

It didn't take long.

Two days later, Mike showed up at the bait shop.

"That was stupid, what you did up in Westlake," Mike told him.

"You here to straighten me out?"

Mike looked hurt. "The fuck could you ask me that? I'd do them before I took a run at you. We should have our own fucking thing, anyway, not be tied to those limp dicks. Watch, they'll find a way to fuck this Binion thing up."

"What happened, Mike?" Frank asked. "When we left the table, we were supposed to *talk* to Herbie."

"I don't know. I was gone."

"Mouse has something to answer for," Frank said.

"Don't get crazy on me," Mike said. "It's one thing to go insult a boss in his place of business—you get a pass for that because you're Frankie fucking Machine. It's another thing you go looking to square Herbie on a fucking *boss*. Let it go."

"So we just let them get away with it?"

"Hey, Frank," Mike said. "Herbie wasn't exactly Saint Francis of fucking Assisi himself. He did *plenty,* believe me. What we're going to do now is swallow the shit, smile like it was chocolate cake, and get back to business."

Which they did.

As usual, Mike was right.

You have an ex-wife to support, Frank told himself, and a kid who needs orthodonture. You have a man's responsibilities, and you can't go getting yourself killed to get revenge for Herbie Goldstein.

As it turned out, L.A. never took over Vegas, not even a piece of it. Teddy Binion's jewelry collection got cut up and made an appearance on the street for a while, but the Martinis never succeeded in taking over his casino and busting it out. Binion held on until he died of an other-inflicted drug overdose, and his young wife and her young lover took the fall for that.

The only one who prospered from the deal was Mike Pella, who worked the Indian gambling thing and gave it serious legs. It was everything Mike had always wanted, a long-term, integrated scam in which he took from the front, the middle, and the back ends.

He would have been a very wealthy man if he hadn't screwed up.

But we always do, Frank thinks now. That's the trademark of the Mickey Mouse Mafia—we always find a way to screw up. Usually over something stupid. That was certainly the case with Mike, who was on easy street until he lost his temper and beat up a guy in a parking lot.

Before Mike slipped on the banana peel, he was raking in money from Indian gambling and never cut Frank in on a penny. Not that Frank expected it or even wanted it. What he expected was what he got—Mike saying, "I mean, after all, you never really *did* anything with Herbie, right?"

No, Mike, Frank thinks now—*you* did.

The Martini RICO trial has been delayed again, ostensibly because the feds think they have new evidence to link the Martini brothers to Herbie's killing.

But there are two guys left who could connect the Martinis with Herbie's murder, Frank thinks.

Mike Pella.

And me.

Mike's in the wind, and I haven't been indicted.

But Mike thinks I'm cooperating with the feds, and that's why he tried to have me whacked.

Because Mike killed Herbie.

Why didn't I see it? Frank thinks as he rolls south on the 5. It was always Mike who was pushing for Herbie's murder. He knew about the jewels, he knew about the money, and he was going to use the Goldstein windfall to bankroll starting his own family. Mike knew damn well when we went over to Herbie's house that the fat man was already dead.

It was all an act.

Now the feds are back on it, Mike thinks I know the truth and that I'm giving him up. He's cleaning up his tracks, and I'm one of them.

55

Mike Pella comes home from the bar, turns the living room light on, and finds Frank Machianno sitting in the La-Z-Boy with a silenced .22 pointed at Mike's chest.

"Hello, Mike."

Mike doesn't even think about running. This is Frankie Machine we're talking about here. So Mike says, "You want a beer, Frankie?"

"No thanks."

"You mind if I have one?"

"Anything comes out of that fridge but a Budweiser," Frank says, "I'll put two in your head."

"It'll be a Coors, if that's okay," Mike says, walking over to the refrigerator. "*Lite.* Man my age has to watch the carbs. You, too, Frankie, you ain't no kid anymore, either."

He gets his beer, pops the tab off with his thumb, and sits down on the sofa across from Frank. "You look good, though, Frankie. Must be all that fish you eat."

"Why, Mike?"

"Why what?"

"Why did you flip?" Frank asks. "You, of all people."

Mike smiles and takes a drink of his beer.

"I respected you," Frank says. "I looked up to you. You taught me about this thing, about—"

"Things aren't what they used to be," Mike says. "*People* aren't what they used to be. Nobody's loyal to anybody anymore. Things just aren't that way. And you're right—I'm *not* the man I used to be. I'm sixty-five years old, for Chrissakes. I'm tired."

Frank looks at him, and he *is* different. Funny, Frank thinks, how I see him the way he used to be, not like this. His hair is white and getting a little sparse. His neck is thin in his collar, and the skin is wrinkled. So are his hands, wrapped around the beer can. There are lines on his face that never used to be there. Do I look that old? Frank wonders. Am I kidding myself when I look in the mirror?

And look at this place. A used La-Z-Boy, a crappy sofa, a cheap coffee table, a TV set. A Mr. Coffee, a microwave, a refrigerator. And that's it. Nothing made with love or care, nothing that looks lived in, no pictures of loved ones.

An empty place, an empty life.

God, is this my future?

"I don't want to die in the joint, okay?" Mike is saying. "I want to sit down with a beer, fall asleep in my own chair watching a ball game with the Miss July foldout on my lap. I'm tired of all this Mafia crap, and that's what it is, all crap. There's no honor, no loyalty. Never has been. We were fucking fooling ourselves. We're in our sixties now and the better part of our lives is over, so it's about time we grew the fuck up, Frankie. I'm just tired of the whole thing and I don't want no part of it no more. If you're going to shoot me now, fine, shoot me. If not, God bless."

"You killed Herbie," Frank says.

"You got me," Mike says.

"And you were afraid I knew and I'd rat you out on it," Frank says, "and that would queer your immunity deal. So you put a contract out on me. I wasn't going to do that, Mike. I'm not a rat. I'm not you. So if you're worried I'm going to tell the feds—"

Mike laughs. There's no joy in his laughter. No fun. It's bitter, angry, cynical. "Frankie," he says. "Who do I work for now?"

56

Dave Hansen sits at his desk, staring out the window at the buildings of downtown San Diego.

Rain pelts the window like little stones. Occasionally, a gust of wind brings the rain in sheets, striking the glass with a sound like a flock of birds flapping their wings, taking off as if something had startled them.

Most days, you can see the ocean from this window.

And the ridges of Tijuana, across the border.

Today, he can barely see across the street.

It's all just fog and rain.

Tears for Frankie Machine.

57

"Why?" Frank asks.

"Why what?"

"Why do the feds want me dead?"

His head is *screaming*. It's crazy, what Mike's telling me, that the feds told him to put a contract on me. It doesn't make any sense the feds going to Mike, then Mike going to Detroit to get the job done. What's in it for Detroit? What can Mike offer Vince Vena?

"Why ask why?" Mike says. "They didn't tell me *why,* Frank. They just told me *what.* You're right—they made me for Herbie, told me if I did them a favor, I could keep my immunity deal. The favor was you."

"Who?"

"Who what?"

"Who reached out to you?" Franks asks. "Who's running this thing?"

"They'd kill me if I told you that, Frank," Mike says.

Frank gestures with the pistol barrel, like, I'll kill you if you *don't.* But Mike smiles and shakes his head. "That ain't you, Frankie. You don't have it in you. Always your fucking problem."

Mike drains his beer and gets up. "We got us a bitch of a situation here, though, don't we? I don't see any way out of it. You sure you don't want a beer? I could sure as hell use another."

He walks to the kitchen. "Hey, Frankie, you remember summer of '72?"

"Yeah."

"That was a good summer," Mike says as he opens the refrigerator door. He smiles and starts singing:

> *"Some folks are born to wave the flag,*
> *Ooh, they're red, white and blue.*

And when the band plays 'Hail to the Chief,'
Ooh, they point the cannon at you, Lord . . ."

He reaches into the refrigerator, turns back, and points the .38 at Frank.

Frank shoots him in the heart twice.

58

It was suicide.

Mike didn't have the stones to pull the trigger on himself, so he got me to do it, Frank thinks as he leaves the house and gets into the car.

Mike just didn't want to live anymore.

Frank understands.

It's what happens, this life of ours.

Piece by piece, it takes everything away from you.

Your home.

Your work.

Your family.

Your friends.

Your faith.

Your trust.

Your love.

Your life.

But by that time, you don't even want it anymore.

They take him on a downhill curve on Highway 78.

59

Jimmy the Kid waits with what's left of the Wrecking Crew.

Paulie's on injured reserve with his leg wound, but Carlo, Carlo is a gamer, dude. Carlo knows the diff between hurt and injured, and he's going to be there when the whistle blows. Besides, he's got a little payback to deliver.

And payback, as they say, is a bitch.

It was Jimmy who figured it out: Sooner or later, Frankie M. would go to Mike Pella to try to get this straightened out. Pella was his wingman, his boy, his goombah. So it was a simple matter of finding out where the feds had Pella stored, then putting a net around it and waiting.

For Frankie M. to fuck up.

Which he did.

Rode right into the old box canyon.

There are only four roads out of Ramona, and three of them break off the same intersection. So when Frankie M. turns north on the 78, they know they got him. It's the worst-possible route for the man to take, because it winds down the edge of a steep canyon.

A stone cliff on one side of the road, the big drop on the other.

So as Frankie M. goes into the canyon, they put a car behind him. Jimmy's car waits at a turnoff on the other side of the road, about two miles down.

It's like one of them old Westerns, Jimmy thinks.

The dumb-ass cavalry goes riding into the canyon.

Where the Apaches are waiting for them.

Frankie M. is Custer.

And I'm Geronimo.

60

He doesn't see it coming.

That's the thing. Fatigue, heartache, the sheer grind of being on the run combine to make him careless.

Of course they wouldn't hit him at a protected witness's house. That would be giving the game away. They wouldn't hit him close, but wait until he was miles away, then do it.

And make it look like an accident.

So he doesn't see it until it's too late.

The silver Lexus coming up behind him fast, then—

A black Envoy—a big, heavy SUV—roars up, passes the Lexus, and pulls alongside Frank.

Jimmy the Kid's in the Envoy, bopping his head up and down like he's listening to some of that hip-hop crap, then smiles at Frank and jerks his wheel to the right.

The Envoy bumps into Frank's car, sending it toward the edge of the cliff.

Frank manages to correct it, but Jimmy rams him again.

The physics are against him. Something the businessman in Frank knows is that numbers never lie; arithmetic is absolute. A heavier vehicle at greater speed is always going to win the contest. He tries to pull out, letting off the gas so he can cut behind the Envoy, but the Lexus has him boxed in and bangs him forward. Frank's only hope is that a car comes up the other way and forces the Envoy to swerve, but even that wouldn't be any good, because there'd be no place for the Envoy to go and some citizen would get killed.

Which is the only thing I can say for myself, Frank thinks. I never took out anyone who wasn't in the game.

Only players.

He manages to stay on the road for the top part of the sweeping curve, but physics are physics—numbers don't lie—and the bottom half is too much for the little rental car, especially when Jimmy the Kid bashes into it again to make sure.

Frank looks over and sees Jimmy waving bye-bye.

Then he goes over the edge.

61

They say your life flashes in front of you?

Sort of—Frank hears a song.

The Surfaris doing "Wipeout."

"Ha-ha-ha-ha-ha-ha-ha-ha-ha-ha-ha-ha-a . . . wipeout!"

That insane, sarcastic laugh, then the famous drum solo, then the guitar riff, followed by the drum again.

He hears it all the way down.

Wipeout.

Actually, surfers have about a gazillion expressions for going over the edge of a big wave:

Wipeout, certainly.

Off the lip.

Over the falls.

In the washing machine.

Frank's been there before.

Tumbling over and over and over, wondering if it's ever going to stop, if you're ever going to come to the surface, if you can hold your breath long enough to see the sweet sky again.

Only that was *water*—this is earth. And trees, and rocks, and brush, and the horrible sounds of metal being crushed against all of the above— then the sound of a gunshot, which at first Frank thinks is the coup de grâce, but is the gunpowder of the air bag going off. The bag smacks him in the face, then along the sides, and the world is this tumbling pillow, this unfun ride as the car plunges down the side of the canyon, scraping against everything in its way.

It's the scraping that saves his life.

The car scrapes against a tree limb, which slows it down, then against the side of a boulder, then tilts over the edge of a narrow ravine, slides over, and finally comes to a stop against an old post oak.

The guitar riff fades out.

Ha-ha-ha-ha-ha-ha-ha-ha-ha-ha-ha-ha-a . . .

Wipeout.

62

"We should go down there and check," Carlo says.

They have the Envoy and the Lexus pulled off to the side of the road. They can't see the car where it's plunged into the little ravine, but they can see the flames shooting out of it.

"Check on what?" Jimmy the Kid asks. "You can grill hot dogs on him yet?"

The police and fire sirens have already started.

"What we should do," Jimmy says, "is get the fuck out of here."

And they do.

63

Frank crawled out during the last guitar riff.

It hurt like crazy just to unsnap the seat belt, never mind open the door and tumble out, and it's even crazier when he hit the ground. The ribs are at least cracked, if not out-and-out broken, and his left shoulder is a bulge down closer to his elbow than it should be. And he doesn't even want to know what's going on with his right knee.

Doesn't matter.

He has to get away from the car.

He knows he's taking a chance moving at all, that a broken rib might puncture a lung or the internal bleeding might turn into an internal hemorrhage, and then game over, but it beats getting flash-fried when the car goes Fourth of July.

Belly-crawling a good fifty feet away before the explosion, he gets flat to the ground and digs his face into the dirt before it goes off. The concussion is like a blow against his whole body, and he feels his ribs burn like he *is* on fire.

But I'm alive, he thinks.

And I shouldn't be.

He stays flat to the ground for a couple of minutes. For one thing, he needs to catch his breath. For another thing, Jimmy might be coming down for a kill shot. And he knows the firemen and cops will be all over this place, if they're not up there already.

When he catches his breath, he grabs his left shoulder and pops it back into place, biting his arm to suppress his scream. He lies back down and gasps for air.

And it's a good thing it's raining, or the fire might spread faster than Frank can crawl away from it. As it is, the flames are just burning gas and air and not catching on the wet grass or the sodden trees.

Frank starts to crawl away, along the canyon bottom. He figures he needs to get a good quarter of a mile from the accident, and he knows what he's looking for—a place to hole up until dark.

It takes him a half hour to find it—a crevice under a rock on the facing canyon wall. A thick mesquite bush hides the entrance, and the overhanging rock will give him some shelter against the wind and rain. He crawls in. There's just room enough in there for him to pull himself, painfully, into a fetal position.

Looking farther down in the canyon, he can see the firemen spraying the car with a heavy blast. They'll be looking for a body, Frank thinks, and they won't find one. But the cops will track the rented car back to Jerry Sabellico, so that cover is blown.

And his whole survival kit is in the car—his clothes, his weapons, his money.

Everything.

So this is what it comes to, Frank thinks as he tries to work his way into a more comfortable position: shivering in a cave, in pain, everything gone, waiting for night.

64

Jimmy the Kid waits for the hour then turns the local radio news on.

The traffic reporter chirps that both lanes of Highway 78 on the grade just past San Pasqual Road are closed due to a one-car accident.

"A car went through the guardrail and plunged into the canyon," she says. "However, no fatalities have been reported."

"Mother*fucker*" is what Jimmy says.

65

"Your boy Machianno's on quite a tear."

"Yes, sir."

Dave sits across the desk from the regional director. Called on the carpet, as it were.

"First Vena and Palumbo," the RD says. "Now Pella. For Chrissakes, Dave, a witness in the program, gunned down in his own house! How's that going to look?"

"Not good."

"You have a gift for understatement."

Dave doesn't reply, proving he *does* have a gift for understatement.

"Anyway," the RD says. "It looks like Machianno's back at his old career. Find him, Hansen. Find him and stop him."

"Yes, sir."

Dave gets up to leave.

"And Hansen? Machianno killed a federal undercover agent," the RD says. "We don't really want to provide this piece of shit with a lawyer, do we?"

Meaning, Dave thinks as he walks out the door, he's not being ordered to find and stop Frank.

He's being ordered to find him and kill him.

66

It takes him two hours to make it to the top of the canyon.

Aching and sore, Frank picks his way through the brush and rocks in uncertain moonlight and fog. He gets to the top and walks along the edge of the road, throwing himself flat when he sees headlights coming. Each time he goes down, it hurts more and it's harder to get up.

But he has to keep doing it because he knows they'll be looking for him.

67

Jimmy's sitting in the passenger seat with one of those big halogen lights. They'd gone to Costco and bought it when they heard the radio news.

"Shouldn't we get right back there?" Carlo had asked.

"He won't come up till dark," Jimmy had said. "If he's alive at all. Either way, we got plenty of time."

So they'd gone to Costco.

"It's a good thing I brought my card," Jimmy says. Now he shines the light along the side of the road as they cruise slowly up and down the canyon. Tony, Joey, and Jackie are in another car, doing the same thing in the other direction.

It's like *Run Silent, Run Deep,* Jimmy thinks, with the Japanese destroyers steaming back and forth, waiting for the American sub to surface. Because it has to come up—it's running out of oxygen.

Like Frankie M.

"You see anything?" Carlo asks.

"Bigfoot," Jimmy says.

"Where?"

"I was pulling your pud, asshole," Jimmy says.

"Hey, that Bigfoot thing is no joke," Carlo says. "I saw a documentary on the National Geographic Channel. National Geographic don't mess around."

Jimmy the Kid isn't listening. He's thinking it through.

What he's thinking is that Frankie Machine is a cockroach.

You just can't kill this motherfucker.

Yeah, but you got to, so think.

A good hunter thinks like his prey.

So think like Frankie M.

Okay, you're hurt, maybe bad. You ain't moving so fast. You're going to go to cover during daylight and try to move by night. You gotta get out of that fucking canyon, and you ain't going out the other side, because it's too steep, too high, and there ain't nothin' back there anyway.

So you're going to come back up the way you came. You're going to come back up the road because you don't have a car anymore and you're going to have to find transportation somehow.

Okay, but how?

You're fifteen hard miles from the nearest town where you can rent a car. Even if you do, your ID is going to ring bells as a guy who crashed and burned his last rental, but you're Frankie Machine, so you ain't gonna even try that.

So that leaves you two choices: You either hitch a ride or you steal a ride.

Nobody in his right mind is going to pick you up, and you ain't going to stand out in the open on this road with your thumb out anyway, because you know we're looking for you and so are the cops.

So you're going to boost someone's sled.

Cool, but how?

No red lights out here, no stop signs, no gas stations.

So what's left?

What's out here where people are going to stop?

Then it hits him.

"Shit," Jimmy says. "Turn around. Hurry."

"What's up?"

"We're going parking."

68

Danny Carver is about to get bare tit.

Finally.

What he gets for dating a Mormon girl. Other chicks are passing out blow jobs like Skittles, but Shelly will not give it up *at all*. Danny's been at it for three months—taking her to the movies, to the mall, going bowling, playing freaking *miniature golf*—and the most he can get is a quick kiss, no tongue.

He would have dropped her on, like, date two if she weren't so goddamn hot. Blond hair, big blue eyes, and that *rack*. . . .

It took two months just to get her to go parking with him at all, come out here to the roadside parking lot where, in the daytime, the tree-huggers park their cars to go hiking down in the canyon.

But at night, the place is like health class. You got droves of teenagers out here studying sex ed like it's going to be on the SATs, and tonight Shelly is *into* it. Her hand doesn't even come down on his like a castle gate when he starts to unbutton her blouse.

I am in, Danny thinks.

Thank you, God.

I am *in*.

"Oh my *God*," Shelly says.

Oh yeah. You the *man.*

"Oh—my—*God.*"

Her body stiffens and she's looking over his shoulder.

It's her father, Danny thinks.

Six-foot-six Mormon who shoes horses for a living.

Danny's body stiffens.

He looks back over his shoulder.

Bigfoot is in the window.

It's like one of those stories you used to tell on camping trips, about the guy with the hook. Except this guy doesn't have a hook—he has a gun. And he gestures for Danny to roll down the window.

Danny does.

"I'm not going to hurt you," the guy says to Danny, yanking him out of the car. "I just need your vehicle."

All Danny can do is nod as the guy slips past him into the driver's seat.

Frank looks at the girl.

"You can get out now," he says. "And button your blouse, huh?"

Shelly does both.

Frank puts it in reverse and takes off.

69

Jimmy the Kid sees the two teenagers standing out in the parking lot. The boy has a cell phone in his hand.

"We're too late," Jimmy says. "We're too fucking late."

He rolls down the window. "What kind of car?"

"Are you the triple A guys?" Danny asks.

"What kind of car?"

"A '96 Celica," Danny says. "Silver."

Jimmy the Kid roars off.

"We're going to have to call my dad," Shelly says.

70

Frank dumps the Celica off in Point Loma and walks back to Ocean Beach.

If you can call it walking. More like limping, hobbling.

Like some old B-movie monster, Frank thinks, emerging from the swamp. It's a good thing it's pouring like hell and the rain-phobic San Diegans are off the streets, so they can't see this messed-up, bleeding freak lurching along the sidewalks.

They'd call the cops.

And that would be that.

Frank doesn't want to go back to his safe house. It's risky going *back* to anywhere, but he has no place else to go. And he has to go someplace—get out of the elements, clean his wounds, get some rest, figure out his next move.

He unlocks the door of his Narragansett Street pad, not knowing what might be waiting for him in there. The cops? The feds? The Wrecking Crew?

But nobody's in the apartment.

Frank gets out of his wet, bloody clothes and gets into the shower, both to get warm and wash his wounds. The spray stings like needles. He gets out, gently daubs himself dry, and looks at the blood left on the towel. Then he finds the hydrogen peroxide in the medicine cabinet, sits down on the edge of the bathtub, and looks at the deep scrapes on his legs. He takes a deep breath, then pours the peroxide on the wounds.

Sings "*Che gelida manina*" to distract his mind from the pain. It doesn't really work. He examines the wounds, then pours more peroxide into them until he sees the chemical bubble up.

Then he repeats the process on his arms and chest.

He gets up slowly, finds gauze pads and medical tape, and dresses the wounds. It takes him a long time. Hurts to move his right arm anyway, and he's tired—bone-tired. Part of him just wants to lie down and give up. Just lie there until they come and put two in the back of his head.

But you can't do that, he tells himself as he applies the gauze and wraps the tape around it to hold it in place.

You have a daughter who needs you.

So keep your head in the game.

He makes himself a pot of strong black coffee and sits down to think it over.

What the hell was Mike trying to tell you?

That he was working for the feds.

That the feds forced him to set you up.

But why?

Why would they want me dead?

Doesn't make any sense.

Maybe it was just more Mike Pella bull. Like him going to the refrigerator to get the gun, knowing he was about to make his curtain call, and going out singing some old song they used to like back in the day.

Back in the summer of '72.

> *Some folks are born to wave the flag,*
> *Ooh, they're red, white and blue.*
> *And when the band plays "Hail to the Chief,"*
> *Ooh, they point the cannon at you, Lord . . .*

Ooh, they point the cannon at you, Lord, Frank thinks. Keep going, finish it. There's something there.

> *It ain't me, it ain't me, I ain't no senator's son, son.*
> *It ain't me, it ain't me, I ain't no fortunate one, no . . .*

No, Frank thinks.

Not fortunate one.

Fortunate *Son*.

And not the summer of '72.

The summer of '85.

Summer 1985.

71

Dave Hansen is concerned—on multiple levels.

First, Frank promised he wouldn't kill Mike Pella, and then he did. Frank Machianno is a lot of things, and one of them is a man of his word. So it's troublesome.

Second, barely twelve miles away from Pella's body, a car goes over the edge of the canyon, crashes and burns, and yet no victim is found. The driver is traced back to a rental-car company, except no one named Jerry Sabellico holds an Arizona driver's license. There was a Jerry Sabellico, but he died in 1987.

So it has all the markings of a professional cover.

A pro crashes a car twelve miles from a murder site where Frank Machianno is the main "person of interest." You don't have to be Sherlock Holmes, Larry Holmes, or even John Holmes to put that one together.

Third, the crash was no accident. No professional ever speeds away from a hit, ever. And besides, Frank, in particular, does fifty-five miles per hour in order to get the best gas mileage, and drives slower than that in wet conditions.

Four, Frank went to pick up his mad money at a bank in Borrego.

Who knew about the bank? Sherm Simon, and, through him, me. Then Frank goes to see Mike Pella. Who knew about Mike Pella?

Me.

Well, not me *exclusively.*

Us.

So Dave has some mixed feelings when he gets on the buzzer and calls young Troy into his office. They're all working 24/7 on the Machianno file now, and Troy has been at it diligently, helping Dave check DBAs and shell companies to see if they can find any properties Frank might own where he could be hiding.

"What's up?" Troy asks, adjusting his cuff links.

"I have a lead," Dave says. "On Machianno's location."

"Really? Where?"

Dave gives him an address.

72

Summer Lorensen, Frank thinks.

Nineteen eighty-five—the party on Donnie Garth's boat, then the scene at his house. That's what Mike was trying to tell me.

It's all about Fortunate Son.

Frank looks at the clock. It's 3:30 in the morning and there's nothing he can do about it for a couple of hours at least.

The best thing he can do is get a little sleep.

But it's too much effort to get out of the chair, and it hurts too bad to move, so he just leans back and shuts his eyes.

73

Troy drives carefully through the rain, even though there's little traffic on the streets this time of night. But he can barely see in the slashing rain—his front and rear wipers are putting up a brave but losing fight against the buildup of water on the glass.

He drives down through the Lamp, gets out of his car near Island, puts his umbrella up, and walks into a phone booth.

An umbrella to walk three steps, Dave thinks, watching him from a car a block away. With a cell phone clipped to your belt.

Who are you calling, Dave wonders, you don't want a record of?

He doesn't pause to think about it, though. There'll be time to grab the phone records in the morning. He has to get over there before the people on the other end of that phone, whoever they are.

74

Jimmy the Kid Giacamone sets the phone down.

"Let's rock and roll," he says.

Carlo's beginning to think that Jimmy is a real asshole.

75

Jimmy knows he's got to get in and out fast.

A quickie in the sticky.

Wham, bam, thank you, M.

He's in a race with the feds to see who gets there first. No consolation prize for second place, no gift baskets or all-expense-paid weekends at a second-rate resort, thank you for playing, and we hope you had fun.

Winner take all.

Way it should be.

So Jimmy and the Wrecking Crew roll up at the address hard and fast and with bad intent. No more time for subtlety—just go through the door, shoot anything that moves, hope you get The Machine before The Machine gets you.

That's good, Jimmy thinks as the car skids to a stop. I should go in the studio and cut that—"Get The Machine Before The Machine Gets You." Next hip-hop hit out of Motor City.

"Eight Mile" my rosy ass.

He gets out of the car.

The address is a Jack in the Box.

Dave, parked across the street, can make out a crew when he sees one, even in the pouring rain.

76

Dave goes back to his house and works from his study.

It doesn't take too long. The Patriot Act gives him carte blanche access to phone records, and he has the number that Troy dialed within five minutes. It's a cell phone, of course, and that's more complicated.

He still tackling it on his computer when Barbara comes in with a pot of coffee and some oatmeal cookies.

"One of those nights?" she asks.

He nods.

They've been married thirty-five years. She's been through more than one of these nights.

"You look worried," she says.

"I am."

"Taking this one personally?"

"I suppose."

It's one of the things she loves about him, that he cares about his cases. They're not just numbers to him, even after all these years. "Pretty soon," she says. "A few more months and you won't have these nights."

She kisses him on the forehead. "Want me to wait up?"

"I don't even know if I'm going to make it to bed."

"I'll wait," she says. "Just in case."

It takes three more hours to wade through the records—then he tracks it down.

Troy called Donnie Garth.

77

Daylight finds Frank in San Diego.

Counting on the fog and the hour to shield him from view.

And the gun at his hip to protect him from harm.

Frank hobbles down toward Eleventh and Island, where the old men sleep on cardboard on the sidewalk. Limping past the line of the sleeping homeless, he listens to their mumbles and their groans, smelling the body odor of caked night sweats and stale urine, and the stink of rotting skin.

He stops at the door of the Island Tavern and bangs on it. The place is closed, but he knows he'll find the heavy drinkers in there for their eye-openers. After a minute, the door cracks open and a jaundiced eye peeps out.

"Corky there?" Frank asks.

"Who wants to know?"

"Frank Machianno."

Frank hears some muddled conversation; then the door opens and the old man—Frank searches for the guy's name, remembers it's Benny—lets him in and points to the bar.

Detective (retired) "Corky" Corchoran sits on a stool, hunched over the bar, a squat glass of whiskey by one hand, a cigarette in the other.

Frank sits down next to him.

"Long time, Corky."

"Long time."

Back in the day—before the bottle and the bitterness got him—Corky was a damn good cop. On the arm, like a lot of guys, he'd take an envelope to overlook the gambling and the hookers, but Corky was a straight arrow on the serious things, and all the guys knew it.

You beat a woman, you hurt a civilian, you killed someone outside the lines, Corky was after you. And if Corky was after you, he was going to get you.

But that was a long time ago.

"Buy you a drink, Corky?"

"I thought you'd never ask."

Corky was never a big man, but he seems to have shrunk, Frank thinks as he signals Benny to bring another. And his hair is thin and dry, his skin yellowish, drawn tight over the bones in his face.

"I need your help, Corky."

Corky finishes his old drink, then takes Frank's and knocks it back. "What can I do you for?"

"Summer Lorensen."

Corky looks at him blankly and shakes his head.

"Back in '85," Franks prompts him. "You were Homicide then. All those prostitute murders."

" 'No humans involved.' "

" 'No humans involved,' " Frank says. "That's right. Her body was found up on Mount Laguna, in a ditch off the road."

Corky sits there thinking about it for a long time. Just when Frank thinks the old cop has drifted back into the Enchanted Forest, Corky says, "She had rocks in her mouth."

"That's right," Frank says. "It went unsolved, but the department later laid it on the Green River Killer."

Corky pulls a pack of cigarettes from his shirt pocket and lights another. His hands tremble. "Wasn't no Green River Killer. We laid *everything* on that fucking guy. He was a one-man clearance sheet."

"How do you know?" Frank asks. "How do you know it wasn't him?"

Corky shifts into that crystal clarity that winos sometimes get. They don't come often and they don't last long, but he's in one now, and Frank hopes he stays there long enough.

"First," Corky says, "she was beaten to death, not strangled. The Green River Killer strangled his victims. She had trauma marks on her throat, but they were made postmortem. Two, there was no sign of intercourse. He raped his girls. Three, she wasn't killed out there along the road."

"How do you know?"

"No blood smears, Frankie. She'd stopped bleeding a long time ago."

"But she had rocks in her mouth," Frank says.

"So fucking what?" Corky asked. "Her real killer couldn't read a newspaper?"

"So if you knew—"

"The department shut me down," Corky answered. "It came down from on high—'Lay off the Lorensen file. Move on. No humans involved.'"

Corky takes another long pull from his cigarette.

"Beginning of the fucking end for me, Frank," he says. "The top of the slippery slope."

Frank reaches into his wallet, pulls out two one-hundred-dollar bills, and presses them into Corky's hand. It brings back old times.

"Stay out of sight," Frank says. "Don't let anyone know you were talking with me."

Corky stares at him. "You gonna take them on, Frank? Take my advice. Don't do it. You don't want to end up like me."

"You're okay, Corky."

"I won't see another summer, Frankie."

And then he's gone. Eyes sunk back in his head with the thousand-yard stare, and Frank realizes that Corky Corchoran is in a place where he lives alone—somewhere in the past, maybe, somewhere in the future, nowhere in the here and now.

And he's right, Frank thinks—he won't see summer.

And neither, probably, will I.

He pats Corky on the shoulder. "I'll see you."

"Not if I see you first."

Frank turns to leave. He's almost out the door when he hears Corky say, "Hey, Frank!"

Frank turns around.

"We had our day, didn't we?" Corky's smiling.

"Yes, we did."

Corky nods. "Damn right. We had our fucking day."

Frank walks back out into the foggy morning.

All right, think, think. Who else was there that night? Donnie Garth, for one, but that's not going to get you anywhere. There was another girl, the redhead. What was her name? . . .

Alison.

But it was over twenty years ago.

Who would know where she is now?

78

He finds Karen Wilkenson on the polo grounds.

They sit in the valley where Rancho Santa Fe meets Del Mar, the grass unusually green and lush in this wet winter, beautiful now as the early morning mist rises off the flats.

She's in the stables, inspecting her horses.

They're actually ponies, Frank thinks, not horses.

The last time he saw her was in a Price Club parking lot, twenty-one years ago, when a bank vice president was handing her an envelope of cash to provide girls for the party. Karen eventually served two years in some Camp Fed, but she landed on her feet when she married a Rancho Santa Fe Realtor with old San Diego money.

Whores land on their backs when they fall, madams on their feet.

She's still attractive in her late fifties. The face-lift was skillful—her skin looks young and taut, and her eyes still have a shine.

"Ms. Wilkenson?" Frank asks.

She's standing outside a stall, stroking the pony's nose, softly talking to the animal. She doesn't turn around. "It's Mrs. Foster now," she says, "and I no longer do interviews. Good-bye."

"I'm not looking for an interview," Frank says.

"Then what are you looking for?" she asks. "Whatever it is, I'm sure I can't provide it. Good-bye."

"I'm looking for a woman I knew as 'Alison' twenty years ago," Frank says.

"Nostalgia or obsession?" Karen Foster asks, and now she turns around to get a look at Frank.

"Neither," Frank says. "I want to ask her about Summer Lorensen."

Karen says, "You don't *look* like a police officer."

"I'm not."

"Then I don't have to talk to you," she says. "Good-bye."

"Then you don't care who murdered her?"

"I loved that girl like a daughter," Karen says. "I wept for days. As I did for Alison."

"What do you mean?"

"If you are looking for Alison Demers," Karen says, "you will have to go to a cemetery in Virginia. Alison moved back east after Summer's murder. She died in a horseback-riding accident."

"When?"

"A month ago," Karen says. "Who are you? What do you want?"

"I want to find who killed Summer Lorensen."

"The police said that they found that man," she says.

"But we both know better, don't we, Mrs. Foster?" Frank asks.

She glares at him. "I don't know what you're talking about."

"No?"

"No," she says. "And if you persist in harassing me, I'll call some men and have you tossed out of here."

"Don't bother," Frank says. "I'm leaving. And Mrs. Foster?"

"What?"

"When you call Donnie," Frank says, "tell him Frankie Machine says hello."

79

"He's in San Diego."

"That's impossible."

"Tell that to Karen Foster. He was just there."

"Where?"

"Rancho Santa Fe."

"Shit."

"It gets worse. He was asking about Summer Lorensen."

Silence for a few seconds.

"This shit has to stop," Garth says. "You don't shut this down, our end of the deal is off."

"You said you could shut down G-Sting. . . ."

Dave sits in a van outside of Garth's house, tapping into a conversation he's having on the phone.

The other voice is unmistakable.

Teddy Migliore.

Dave goes back to the office. He feels sick to his stomach. Troy talks to Garth. Garth talks to Teddy. Teddy sends Detroit hitters out to whack Frank. Because of something Frank knows about a Summer Lorensen.

Summer Lorensen, Summer Lorensen . . .

There's something there, lurking deep in the back of his head.

But it won't come to him.

He gets on the computer. It only takes a few minutes to get a hit—Summer Lorensen was a prostitute murdered back in the summer of 1985. But what could that have to do with Donnie Garth? Or Frank Machianno, for that matter.

Dave goes back at it, searching for a nexus between Garth and the Lorensen woman.

Nothing comes up.

Then he searches for a connection between Garth and the date of Lorensen's killing. . . .

Bingo.

Hammond Savings and Loan. A boat party with prostitutes had ended up in the conviction of a savings and loan officer named John Saunders for misuse of bank funds. A madam named Karen Wilkenson got a couple of years for pandering. It was all part of the whole savings and loan scandal, and the party had occurred the night before the Lorensen murder.

He types in the name Karen Wilkenson and in a few seconds finds out that she married and is now Karen Foster.

Tell that to Karen Foster. He was just there.

Where?

Rancho Santa Fe.

Shit.

It gets worse. He was asking about Summer Lorensen.

Is it possible? Dave thinks. Donnie Garth killed this girl, somehow Frank knows about it, and then Garth goes to his old mob connections to kill Frank? Offering the shutdown of G-Sting in exchange?

But what makes Donnie Garth think he can shut down a federal operation?

Maybe the reason that a young FBI agent is feeding him information?

Dave looks over his shoulder and doesn't see Troy. He walks down to the men's room and spots the rookie's pressed trousers underneath a stall. He waits until he hears a flush, then sees the trousers come up.

When Troy opens the stall door, Dave Hansen's fist slams him back in. Blood from the kid's broken nose sprays over his white shirt and his French cuffs. Dave grabs him by the throat, turns him over, and pushes his head into the toilet.

"Donnie Garth," Dave says, jerking Troy's head up.

"What—"

Dave forces his head back down and says, "Donnie Garth, you little shit. Is he paying you? How much?"

He lets Troy up again.

The young agent gasps for air.

Then he says, "I'm not working for Garth! I just report to him."

"Who are you working for?" Dave asks.

Troy hesitates.

Dave starts to force his head back down.

Then Troy gives it up.

80

Donnie Garth has the shower blasting. He's standing under the spray, looking out through the glass at the ocean, when suddenly Frankie Machine's standing there with a pistol in his hand.

Garth shuts the water off.

Frank hands him a towel. "Remember me?"

Garth nods.

"Wrap yourself up," Frank says.

Garth wraps the towel around his waist. Frank gestures for him to get out and sit down. Garth takes a chair by the window; Frank sits down across from him.

"I put two people in the dirt for you," Frank says.

Garth nods again.

Frank smiles. "I'm not wearing a wire. *You're* the rat, not me. You know, I always wondered how you got a pass on all that. You get a pass on everything, don't you, Donnie?"

Garth doesn't answer.

"Well," Frank says, "you're not getting a pass on this."

"On what?" Garth asks. He looks small and old, sitting there in the towel, water dripping down his skinny legs into the thick carpet.

"Summer Lorensen," Frank says.

He raises the gun and points it at Garth's chest.

"It wasn't me!"

"Then who was it?"

Garth balks, as if he's trying to decide who he's more afraid of.

"Whoever it is," Frank says, "they're not sitting here about to put one in you, Donnie, and I am. I saw you through the window that night, the little act between Alison and Summer. Then I walked away. What didn't I see?"

"The senator," Garth says, "couldn't . . . perform. It was all set up— the Lorensen girl was *begging* for it, part of the act, but he couldn't get it up. She did everything to him, believe me, but it was a no-go."

"Then what happened?"

"She laughed."

"What?"

"She laughed," Garth says. "I don't think she meant anything by it. I think it was just her, you know, but he got mad. He just went off."

"Go on."

"You were there! You know!"

Because you can't tell one janitor from another, can you, Donnie? Me or Mike, cleaning up your messes for you, what's the difference? Your shit gets cleaned up. You don't have to look at it.

It's clear to him now what happened. They carried her body out to the car and Mike drove her out on that lonely road and dumped her. Had the afterthought to "strangle" her and stuff the rocks in her mouth.

And Fortunate Son walks away clean.

It would have been manslaughter. He would have done what, two or three years, tops? Maybe nothing at all?

But his political career would have been ruined.

We couldn't have that, could we?

Not over some whore.

No humans involved.

And everything stays quiet until Mike starts to take heat over the Goldstein murder, so he starts looking for something to trade. And he's got a big one—except he's not going to put himself in the bull's-eye, so he puts me.

Thanks, Mike.

So Fortunate Son starts to clean up his past, and reaches out to Donnie, who reaches out to Detroit to do it for him.

Because these guys never do their own dirty work.

They have people like *me* to do that.

What did Fortunate Son offer the Combination?

Hell, he's going to be president—what *couldn't* he offer them?

"Did he use you as a go-between?" Frank asks. "Tell me the truth, Donnie."

Garth nods.

His eyes are wide with fear, he's quivering and sweating, and Frank's disgusted that he sees the front of the man's towel stained yellow.

Frank pulls the hammer back.

Hears Garth whimper.

Frank eases the hammer down and lowers the gun.

"Look," Frank says, "they've already tried to kill me and they *did* kill Alison Demers. They're going to clip anyone who knows anything about what happened that night, including you. Or do you still think you're going to get a pass?"

Why shouldn't you? Frank thinks. You always do.

"If I were you," Frank says, "I'd run."

But he knows he won't. The Donnie Garths of the world don't believe that people kill them; they believe that people kill *for* them.

81

Frank calls information and gets the number of the senator's office.

"I'd like to speak to the senator, please."

"May I ask who's calling?"

"Tell him it's a buddy from his Solana Beach days."

"I don't think he's going to be available, sir."

"See, and I think he is," Frank says. "Why don't you tell him it's about Summer, and we'll see who's right."

A minute later, Fortunate Son gets on the phone.

"If you record your calls," Frank says, "I suggest you shut the machine off."

"Who is this?"

"You know who it is," Frank says. "I'll wait."

Fortunate Son comes back on the line a few seconds later. "Okay. Speak."

"You know who this is."

"I have a pretty good guess."

"You have the wrong guy," Frank says. "The wrong chauffeur. I know it's hard to tell the little people apart, but it was Mike Pella in the limo that night, not me. If it had been me, none of this would have happened, because I wouldn't have let you beat a girl to death and get away with it."

"I don't know what you're talking about."

Frank holds the little dictaphone up to the receiver and plays Donnie Garth's narration.

"He's lying," Fortunate Son says.

"Yeah," Frank says. "Look, I don't care. I *should* care that you killed that girl and now you killed that other one, but the point is, I have a life I want to live and a family to take care of. So here's the deal, Senator. I want a million dollars in cash, or I go public with this. I know I can't go to the cops or the feds, because you own them, but I'll go to the media, and then, at the very least, your career is over. Maybe we can't make you for the girl's murder, but we can put you at the scene, and that's all it will take."

"Perhaps we could take the position that—"

"A million dollars, Senator, in cash," Frank repeats, "and I want you to deliver it personally."

"That's not going to happen," Fortunate Son says.

"Which?" Frank asks. "The cash, or you?"

"Me," Fortunate Son says.

"Then send your pimp, Garth," Frank says, and tells him where and when.

A long silence, then: "How do I know I can trust you?"

"I'm a man of my word," Frank says. "Are you?"

"I am."

"Then we have a deal?"

"We do."

Fortunate Son hangs up the phone.

Frank turns off the tape recorder.

He's not a child—he knows they're not coming with any million dollars.

They're coming to kill him.

I could run, Frank thinks. And I could make a good run of it. I could stretch it out for years, maybe. But what kind of life is that? Watching myself slowly become poor Jay Voorhees, until I'm relieved when they finally catch up with me?

No kind of life at all.

So let them come.

Let's get this thing done.

82

"It isn't right!" Jimmy the Kid yells. "*I'll* go. I can take him out."

"He says, despite ample evidence to the contrary," Garth says. "Look, this has been decided."

"By who?"

Garth doesn't say anything.

Which pisses Jimmy off. "Look, I know who we're working for. I know the whole fucking thing, how your senator couldn't get his macaroni al dente, how he killed the girl, how Frankie M. dumped her body. . . ."

"It wasn't Machianno," Garth says. "It was the other one. . . ."

"Pella?"

"Pella."

"Then why the fuck were we trying to clip Frank?" Jimmy asks. "He doesn't know anything."

"He does now," Garth says.

Yeah, Jimmy thinks, because you're a limper dick than your politician buddy and you spilled it all to him. "I can take him."

"It's been decided."

"Nothing has been decided until we talk to my uncle Tony," Jimmy says.

"We've talked to your uncle Tony," Garth says. "He gave the okay. He's already put it into motion."

Jimmy feels like his head is going to blow off. He can't believe what he's hearing. Uncle Tony, Tony freaking Jacks, signing on to a sleazy deal like this?

Uncle Tony is a man. Uncle Tony is old-school.

He digs his cell phone out of his pants pocket and punches in the number. It takes a few rings before the old man comes to the phone. "Uncle Tony, this guy is trying to tell me—"

"Easy, kid," Tony says.

"I can take him, Uncle Tony!"

"You can't, Jimmy!" The voice is harsh, clear, and decisive. "This deal has to be completed successfully. Frankie M. goes; then G-Sting gets shut down."

"Fuck G-Sting!" Jimmy says. "Fuck the Migliores and their clubs. We can live without it."

"Don't be stupid," Tony says. "You think this is just about a bunch of strippers grinding their naked twats on laps? Smarten up. This is just the down payment, nephew. Let the senator cunt make this deal and then he's ours, all the way to the White House. Better than Kennedy, better than Nixon, because we got this son of a bitch by the balls. By the *balls*. Now hang up the phone and do what you got to do."

Jimmy hangs up.

As always, Uncle Tony is right.

But it still sucks, what they're going to do.

83

Jill Machianno balances her ski bag between her hip and the wall as she unlocks the front door of her apartment. She has the door open and is reaching for the ski bag when the tall redheaded woman comes up to her.

"Jill Machianno?"

"Yes?"

"I'm Donna, a friend of your father's."

Jill gives her a stare as cold as the snow she was skiing on. "I know who you are."

"I don't want to frighten you," Donna says, "but your father's had an accident."

"Oh my God. Is he—"

"He's going to be fine," Donna says, "but he's in the hospital."

"Is my mother with him?"

"She's out of town somewhere," Donna says. "Your dad asked me to find you and take you to the hospital. I'm parked across the street."

Jill sets her skis and luggage inside the door, shuts it, and follows Donna to her car.

84

Dave Hansen is at Shores.

Well, at least there's plenty of parking, he thinks as he pulls into the public lot across the street from the little playground.

Donnie Garth is already out there, standing by the vacant lifeguard tower, looking out at the gray sea. He looks vaguely ghostlike in his hooded white slicker. Or, Dave thinks, like a hopelessly out of place Klansman.

Dave gets out of the car and steps over the low wall onto the beach.

"Are you wearing a wire?" Garth asks.

"No, are you?"

"I'm going to have to pat you down."

Dave lifts his arms and lets Garth feel him for a wire. Satisfied, Garth says, "Let's go for a walk."

They head north, toward Scripps Pier.

"This Summer Lorensen nonsense," Garth says, "I don't know what you think you know, but you *don't* know what you're fooling with."

"See, I think I do," Dave says. "That's the problem."

"You're damn right it's a problem." Garth turns to look at him. Rain drips off the edge of the hood onto his nose. "You're a few months away from retirement. Take your pension and go fishing. Visit the grandkids. Forget about all this."

"What if I don't?"

"There are certain people who want you to know," Garth says, "that if you persist with this crusade, you'll leave with nothing. You'll be a security guard on the night shift, if you're not in jail, that is."

"In jail for what?"

"Start with cooperation with a known organized crime figure, Frank Machianno," Garth says. "You've been protecting him. Or how about your collusion in the torture of Harold Henkel? Or assaulting a federal agent. There's plenty, Hansen. More than enough, trust me. And without friends to protect you . . ."

"Oh, you want to be my friend."

"You need to decide who your friends are, Dave," Garth says. "You choose wrong, you end up as a disgraced cop with nothing. Choose right, you can live a happy life. Christ, why would you sacrifice your future for some second-rate hit man, anyway?"

"He's a *first*-rate hit man, Donnie," Dave says. "As you, of all people, should know."

Garth stops and turns around. "I'll walk back by myself. If Frankie Machine contacts you, we expect you to do the right thing. Do you understand?"

Dave looks over the man's shoulder at the waves.

I'd rather be out there, he thinks, in a wave, under a wave. Anything would be better than this.

"Do you understand?" Garth says.

"Yeah."

I understand.

85

Frank sits in the little shack in the hills outside of Escondido. He's known about the place for years—it sits up a dirt road in a canyon above the orange groves. It's a place to hide *mojados*—they live up here away from the *migra* and go down just before dawn to pick the oranges, then return at dusk.

Except there are no *mojados* now.

You don't pick oranges in the winter, in the rain.

Nevertheless, he can smell the tangy scent of the orange trees below.

Makes him nostalgic, sad, that he won't be around to taste the oranges in the spring.

He has one gun and four bullets.

It won't be enough.

They'll be coming with an army—so four bullets, or forty, or four hundred, or four thousand, it won't make any difference, because there's only one of you.

And you can't win this battle.

All those clichés about life—they're all true. If you could cook one more meal, ride one more wave, have a chat with a customer, smile at a friend, hug your lover, hold your child. If you had more time, you'd spend it differently.

If only you had more time.

Stop feeling sorry for yourself, he thinks. After all, you've got it coming. You've done a lot of bad things in this world. You've taken life, and that's the worst thing there is. You can justify it all you want, but when you look back at your life with your eyes open, you know what you were.

All you can do—maybe, *maybe*—is get a small measure of justice for a dead woman.

Take the rocks from her mouth.

Maybe give her daughter a chance for a real future.

The way you'd like someone to give *your* daughter a chance.

Jill.

What's she going to do?

You have to take care of your own daughter.

He calls Sherm.

"Frank, thank God, I thought—"

"Don't thank him yet," Frank says. "Look, I need to know—"

"It was the feds, Frank," Sherm says. "They had me under. It was your buddy Dave Hansen—he had me wired. He passed the info along."

"It doesn't matter now," Frank says. "All that matters is that Jill and Patty are taken care of. If you flipped on me, you flipped on me. I'm sure you had your reasons. It's blood under the bridge—"

"Frank—"

"There are some properties," Frank says. "You know how to dig them out. Something should happen to me, liquidate the assets, make sure Jill's medical school is paid for."

"You can count on it, Frank."

"They have to let me take care of my family," Frank says. "They can do what they want with me, but *they have to let me take care of my family*. That was always the way, back in the old times."

"Patty and Jill will be taken care of," Sherm says. "You have my word."

It's hard to hear the tone of a man's voice over the telephone, especially these tinny cell phones, but Frank is satisfied by what he can hear. It's all he can do anyway, trust The Nickel to do the right thing by the money, even if Sherm did betray him.

If there's a trace of honor left in this thing, they'll let a man go out knowing his family is taken care of.

"Hey, Sherm," Frank says, "you remember that time down in Rosarito? You were wearing that big sombrero?"

"I remember, Frank."

"Those were good times."

"Hell yes, they were."

"Good-bye, Sherm."

"Go with God, my friend."

Frank has set this up so they'll have to come uphill and into the sun. He wants every little edge he can get, even though it won't make any difference in the end. But take, say, Jimmy the Kid out with you, you've done a good thing.

Maybe it'll count in my favor when I answer to the man.

Go with God.

He hears the car before he sees it.

Then the engine noise stops.

Smart, Frank thinks. They're coming in on foot. They'll give the cabin lots of room, work around it, and come in from all sides. He settles in, lays the pistol barrel on the windowsill, and gets ready to put one in the first head that comes into sight.

A head appears, but he doesn't shoot.

Because it's Donna.

86

"They have Jill," she says.

"What?"

"I'm sorry, Frank," she says. "They have Jill."

Frank's barely listening as she tells him the deal. He hears her words, he's taking them in, but all that's really running through his head are the words *They have Jill. They have Jill. They have Jill. They have Jill. They have Jill.*

Your faith.

Your trust.

Your love.

Your life.

Your child.

"Tomorrow morning," she says. "Four a.m. Beneath Ocean Beach Pier. You come unarmed, but with a certain package they want. Do you know what they're talking about, Frank?"

"Yes."

"You give them the package, they'll release Jill to me," Donna says. "You go with *them*, Frank."

He nods. "How long," he asks, "have you been with them?"

"Forever," she says. "Since I was fifteen years old. My father was a drunk. He used to beat me up. It wasn't the worst thing he did. Tony Jacks stopped him; he took me out of there. He saved me, Frank."

When he was done with her, he found her a job and a husband, she tells Frank.

"When Jay left," Donna says, "I was sad, but I wasn't heartbroken. I didn't really love him. I never went back to Tony, but I still *owed* him, Frank. You have to understand that. I kept an eye on things in San Diego for him, that's all."

"You gave them my daughter."

"I didn't know," Donna says, crying now. "I just thought they wanted to talk to her, Frank. I didn't know they were going to do . . . this."

"Tell them I'll be there," Frank says. "With the package. And I'll go with them. If I see Jill, see her safe."

He knows they won't let her go. Knows that they'll kill her. Please God, please let her not be dead already.

Please give me even a small chance to save her.

87

And now he knows that Fortunate Son is behind all this.

Because no wise guy in the world was ever low enough to kidnap someone's daughter.

It would take a politician to do that.

But who do you trust?

Normally, if a family member is kidnapped, you go to the FBI, but you can't do that, because the feds *are* the kidnappers.

Or a wise guy would go to other wise guys to get justice. That's how this whole thing of ours started anyway, wasn't it? *Ma figlia, ma figlia—* my daughter, my daughter. But you can't do that, because the other wise guys all want to kill you.

Go ahead, kill me, but let my daughter go.

But they won't do that, because the wise guys have been corrupted by the politicians.

Lie down with dogs, you get up with fleas.

The irony is, I could have killed Mouse Senior's kid and Billy Jacks' kid—they were both in my sights and I let them walk. But I didn't, because I'm a father, too, and it just isn't done. *It just isn't done.*

So who do you go to? Who do you trust?

You've always been able to trust yourself, but can you trust yourself to gun down the army they're going to bring, and keep Jill safe in the process? Maybe, maybe in your prime you could have done it, but you're twenty summers past your prime. You're old, and you're tired, and you're hurt.

You can't trust yourself to do this.

So where does that leave you?

More important, where does that leave Jill?

The answer is too awful to contemplate.

Face it, Frank says, there is only one chance, and it's not even a very good one.

But it's the only one.

Reluctantly, he sets down his gun and picks up the phone.

88

Dave Hansen remembers a breakfast he had with Frank Machianno at the OBP Café a few years back, some months after the Carly Mack case.

It was after an especially flat session at the Gentlemen's Hour, and Frank was in a rare bad mood. It was something in the paper about a crackdown on organized crime, and Frank just went off on a rant.

"Nike pays twenty-nine cents to a *child* for making a basketball jersey, then turns around and sells it for one hundred and forty dollars," Frank said. "And *I'm* the criminal?

"Wal-Mart sends half the mom-and-pop stores in the country the way of the buffalo while they pay the kids who make *their* cheap crap seven cents an hour. And *I'm* the criminal?

"Two million jobs have gone adios in the past two years, a working man can't afford a down payment on a house anymore, and the IRS mugs us like drunks at an ATM, then sends our money to a defense contractor who closes down a factory, lays off workers, and pays himself a seven-figure bonus. And *I'm* the criminal? *I'm* the guy who should get life without parole?

"You could take the Crips, the Bloods, the Jamaican posses, the Mafia, the Russian mob, and the Mexican cartels, and all of them put together couldn't rake in as much green in a good year as Congress does in a bad afternoon. You could take every gang banger selling crack on every corner in America, and they couldn't generate as much ill-gotten cash as one senator rounding the back nine with a corporate CEO.

"My father told me that you can't beat the house, and he was right. You can't beat the White House, or the House of Representatives. They own the game and the game is *fixed,* and it isn't fixed for *us.*

"Sure, every thirty-eighth blue moon, they'll whack one of their own. Send a human sacrifice to some Club Fed for a couple of years as sop to the masses and an example to the others of what happens to a rich white guy stupid enough to let that fifth ace fall out of his sleeve in full view of the public. But let *me* slip on the cosmic banana peel, and I am going to the maximum hole with the rest of the losers for the rest of my life.

"You know why the government wants to shut down organized crime?

"We're competition.

"That's it. That's what's behind the OC Task Force, your FBI, RICO. RICO? Big government and big business? That is the working *definition* of 'racketeering in conspiracy.' A felony happens every time two suits take a piss together in the Senate men's room.

"So the government wants to beat down organized crime.

"That's hysterical.

"The government *is* organized crime.

"The only difference between them and us is they're *more* organized."

That was Frank's rant on organized crime.

Dave didn't believe it then, but he sure as shit believes it now.

Not that it matters, he thinks. I have to do what I have to do.

I have the rest of my life ahead of me.

The rest of the guys are coming along the beach, but Dave is coming in by boat, from the water.

It seems only fitting.

89

It's cold and dark coming on four in the morning on a winter's day in San Diego.

The famous sunshine doesn't start for a few hours and the real sunny, warm days don't start for a couple of months.

But the storm is over now.

The big swell has blown itself out, and the waves fall gently on the shore.

Frank walks along the beach toward the base of the pier. His body hurts, his chest so tight with anxiety, he can barely breathe.

First he sees the lights of the pier, then the faint glow of a flashlight; then he sees someone walking through the mist toward him.

A young man.

"Frankie Machine?" the man asks.

Frank nods.

"Jimmy Giacamone," the man says, as if he expects Frank to recognize him. Frank just looks at him, so the man adds, "Jimmy 'the Kid' Giacamone."

Frank doesn't respond to it.

Jimmy the Kid says, "I could have taken you, Frankie Machine, I'd a had the chance."

"Where's my daughter?"

"She's coming, don't worry," Jimmy the Kid says. "I gotta pat you down first, Frankie."

Frank raises his arms.

Jimmy pats him down quickly and efficiently and finds the little tape cassette in Frank's jacket pocket. "This is it?"

Frank nods. "Where's my daughter?"

"Just so you know," Jimmy says. "I don't approve of any of this. This thing with your daughter. I'm old-school."

"Where's my daughter?"

"Come on."

Jimmy the Kid grabs him by the right elbow and leads him along the beach. When they get under the pier, he says, "I got it. I got him. He's clean."

A group of men come out of the mist like ghosts, their flashlights in one hand, their guns in another. There are five of them, the whole Wrecking Crew.

And Donnie Garth, except he doesn't have a gun. He holds out his hand and Jimmy the Kid gives him the tape. He pops it into a Dictaphone, listens for a second, and nods.

"Bring her to me," Frank says.

Garth swings his flashlight up and down. An endless minute later, Frank sees Jill walking toward him through the fog, with Donna at her side.

"Daddy."

She looks like she's been crying, but she looks strong.

"It's going to be all right, baby."

"Daddy—"

Frank reaches out and holds her tight. Whispers into her ear. "Go. Be a doctor. Make me proud."

She sobs into his shoulder. "Daddy—"

"Shhhhh, it's all right." He looks up at Garth. "I made copies. They're in safe-deposit boxes all over the world. If anything should happen to my daughter—a robber shoots her, she gets hit by a car, she falls off a horse—there are people who will distribute this tape to every major news network."

Jimmy the Kid looks at Garth.

"Let her go," Garth says.

"Listen—"

"Shut up," Garth says. "I said, 'Let her go.'"

Jimmy hesitates, then nods his head at Donna and says, "Get her the fuck out of here."

Donna starts to take her, but Jill grabs Frank's neck and won't let go. "Daddy, they're going to kill you."

"They're not going to kill me, baby," he whispers. "I'm Frankie Machine."

Donna slips the gun into his hands, then pushes Jill to the ground and falls on top of her. Frank shoots Jimmy the Kid between the eyes, then one of the Wrecking Crew, then another.

Carlo gets a shot away before a bullet blows the back of his head off. The shock knocks Frank to the ground, and he tries to aim at the fourth guy but sees he's going to be too late.

Dave Hansen sees the same thing, haloed by the pier lights. It's a tough shot from a boat, even with a rifle, but he makes it, and puts a round between the guy's shoulder blades.

Frank rolls, swings his gun to the fifth man, and shoots him in the heart.

Garth is running.

Frank gets up to chase him.

They're neither of them young, but Donnie Garth hasn't been through what Frank's been through the past few days, so he starts to pull away.

Frank sees that his legs aren't fast enough, but he knows a bullet will be. He raises his gun to shoot; then a searing pain burns in his chest and his left arm is numb. At first, he thinks it's the bullet, but then he feels his heart crack like a breaking wave and he can't breathe and the pain is awful; he gets off one last shot and has the satisfaction of seeing Donnie Garth drop.

Then Frank stops, grabs his chest, and topples into the sand.

"Daddy!"

Jill's voice is the last thing he hears.

90

Dave Hansen waits until the senator's press conference is almost over.

The senator stands behind the podium, flashing his trademark smile to the reporters, and asks, "Are there any more questions?"

Dave raises his hand.

The senator smiles down at him and nods.

"Do you know your rights?" Dave asks.

The senator looks at quizzically.

"You have the right to remain silent," Dave says, stepping up toward the platform. Two Secret Service guys get in his way, but Dave holds up his FBI badge and pushes through them.

"Anything you say can and will be held against you in a court of law," Dave says as he twists the senator's hands behind his back and cuffs him.

Cameras are going off, and the bright video lights are striking Dave full in the face. He doesn't care. "You have the right to an attorney—"

"This is ridiculous," the senator says. "This is just a political—"

"—and if you cannot afford one," Dave says, smirking, "one will be appointed for you."

"What am I being arrested for?"

"The murder of Summer Lorensen," Dave says.

He starts walking the senator through the crowd, heading toward the waiting car. The media are closing in around them like a crosscurrent in the impact zone. Dave opens the door, pushes the senator's head down, nudges him into the seat, and closes the door again.

He gets into the front passenger seat and tells the intimidated young agent to step on the gas.

Dave's in a hurry.

He's already missed the Gentlemen's Hour.

And he doesn't want to be late for Frank Machianno's funeral.

91

The crowd is immense.

Frank the Bait Guy was *loved* in the community.

There are fishermen here, and surfers, and the Little League kids with their families, and students from the drama club, and soccer kids and soccer moms, and the teenagers who played hoops underneath the baskets that Frank paid for, and the local Vietnamese are out in force.

And men are telling their sons how they caught their first fish on the pier at Frank's annual fishing contest, and old surfers are telling their wives what Frank used to be like back in the days of the long, endless summers. And one Vietnamese guy is telling his kids how Frank stood up for him just a few days ago.

Who isn't here, Dave thinks as he takes a seat in the front row beside Patty and Jill, is the Mickey Mouse Club. The ones that he hasn't already arrested are in the wind, but he's going to pick them up soon, because they aren't that good or that smart.

And Donna isn't here. She's already in protective custody, but Donna is too classy to have come anyway—she wouldn't have wanted to cause any more pain to the grieving daughter and widow.

The flag is draped over Frank's coffin. It was in his will that he wanted a closed casket, so his friends would remember him the way he was in life, not like some wax dummy the morticians made up.

Dave stands as the Marines fire their rifles into the air and the bugler plays taps.

It's long and slow, beautiful and sad under the warm sun of the false early spring day.

That's okay, though, Dave thinks.

Spring was always Frank's season.

The Marines fold up the flag and hand it to Patty, who shakes her head.

They hand it to Jill.

She takes it and smiles a tight smile.

Brave, Dave thinks. Like her old man.

There's one last thing to be done.

It also came straight out of Frank's will.

A second later, the recorded music comes out of the sound system:

> "... *ma quando vien lo sgelo*
> *il primo sole è mio,*
> *il primo bacio dell' aprile è mio!*
> *il primo sole è mio! ..."*

Epilogue

If Hanalei Pier isn't the longest in Hawaii, it certainly is the prettiest, jutting out from a soft, palm-lined beach, with Bali Hai and the green mountains of the Na Pali coast rising in the background.

And early mornings are beautiful.

Soft and warm, year-round, even in the hour before the sun rises.

The hour when the bait guy arrives to get things set up in his little shack at the end of the pier, so that everything will be ready when even the earliest fishermen arrive to try their luck.

They know the bait shack is open, because they can smell it even before they see it—the smell of fresh roasting Kona coffee wafts down the pier and into their noses. If they're regulars, or even if they're nice and polite, Pete the Bait Guy will probably pour them a little cup, and make them listen to a little opera, and tell them a funny little story about how he had to fix the garbage disposal because his *wahini* can't remember not to shove mango peels down *da kine*.

"It's a lot of work being me, *bruddah*," he'll say.

What he won't tell them is about how he had a heart attack on a different beach, and woke up in the ICU, and then in the Witness Protection Program. He won't tell them that, and neither will his friend from the mainland who comes out about every year and surfs with him in the mornings during what is called, even in Kauai, the Gentlemen's Hour.

No, Pete will just smile, share a joke and maybe an odd word from one of his crossword puzzles, and they'll leave the bait shack with everything they need, and smiles on their faces, and a good feeling to start their day.

Everyone loves Pete the Bait Guy.

A NOTE ABOUT THE AUTHOR

Don Winslow is a former private investigator and consultant. He lives in California.

A NOTE ON THE TYPE

The text of this book was set in a typeface called Times New Roman, designed by Stanley Morison (1889–1967) for *The Times* (London) and introduced by that newspaper in 1932.

Among typographers and designers of the twentieth century, Stanley Morison was a strong forming influence—as a typographical adviser to the Monotype Corporation, as a director of two distinguished publishing houses, and as a writer of sensibility, erudition, and keen practical sense.

Composed by Stratford Publishing Services,
Brattleboro, Vermont
Printed and bound by Berryville Graphics,
Berryville, Virginia
Designed by Virginia Tan